WHAT
ONLY
we
KNOW

BOOKS BY CATHERINE HOKIN

The Fortunate Ones

CATHERINE HOKIN

WHAT
ONLY
we
KNOW

GRAND CENTRAL
PUBLISHING

New York   Boston

Grand Central Publishing
Hachette Book Group
1290 Avenue of the Americas, New York, NY 10104
grandcentralpublishing.com
twitter.com/grandcentralpub

First published in 2020 by Bookouture, an imprint of StoryFire Ltd.
First Grand Central Publishing Edition: February 2022

Grand Central Publishing is a division of Hachette Book Group, Inc. The Grand Central Publishing name and logo is a trademark of Hachette Book Group, Inc.

The publisher is not responsible for websites (or their content) that are not owned by the publisher.

Library of Congress Control Number: 2021945913

ISBN: 9781538706404 (paperback)

Printed in the United States of America

LSC-C

Printing 1, 2021

To my family, here and gone

WHAT
ONLY
we
KNOW

July 10, 1971

Salt danced through the breeze, tingling at her lips. Dawn was breaking. Clouds trailed in chiffon streaks across the sky, rose gold and cotton candy pink. The promise of a heat-soaked day to come.

She stepped onto the beach and let her feet find the rhythm of the sharp incline. One step and then another, the shingle crunching, until the ground became softer, the stones giving way to sand and ripples that lapped round her ankles like a kiss.

The sun was coming up, floating over the horizon like an escaped balloon. She moved toward it, slipping through the water as sleek as a ship. Knee-deep, fingers trailing. Chest-deep, feet on tiptoes. The waves whispered at her shoulders, their pull stronger here than at the stony edge. She let them lift her, let her eyelids drop. The seagulls fell silent. There was nothing in her ears but a gurgle as pure as Lottie's giggle.

As she floated, the sea's gentle tempo picked up a deeper swell. The water thickened. It settled in her hair, collected heavy in her cardigan's bell sleeves. She sensed the shore slipping away. Felt sudden cold eddies pricking at her skin, telling her that, if she chose to take it, this was the moment to turn.

She opened her eyes.

Cornflowers bloomed across the sky. Soon, the hotel would rouse itself. There would be discoveries, questions. After that... well, she had little say in what happened after that. All she had was a wish: that he would read what she had written; that he would do what she asked.

The swell grew hungry, sucked up stronger currents. It tugged at her arms, added weights to her fingers, wrapped itself like blankets round her legs.

One has paid for my mistakes; the other will not.

She dropped her head back; let the sky disappear. The world had been out of balance for far too long. It was time, at last, to level the scales.

PART ONE

CHAPTER ONE

Liese

Berlin, September 1936

There wasn't a finger's breadth between them. Paul's eyes were closed, his chin resting on Margarethe's black curls; Margarethe's head was tucked into his chest, her arms draped round his shoulders.

Liese imagined her father choreographing the pose and spinning its caption: *Paul and Margarethe Elfmann—the fashion genius and his beautiful muse.* Two perfectly still figures forming one complete whole.

You're a lucky girl to live with so much love. To have such a perfect family. They all said it—the dreamy-eyed seamstresses coveting Margarethe's velvet-bowed shoes. Sometimes Liese considered puncturing their visions, pointing out how awkward it was to always be cast in the spectator's role. It was easier, in the end, to stay silent.

The seconds dragged; the stillness grew stifling. Liese peeped at her watch: almost three o'clock. She willed the hands to hurry. Finally, the tiny gold pointer clicked into place and, exactly on cue, there it came: a knock on the door that pulled the Elfmanns apart like a knot unraveling. Whatever they whispered to each other was too soft to hear.

Margarethe was the first to untangle, her body reforming into a model's precisely cut lines. She tripped past Liese without looking at her daughter; Liese let her go. Margarethe was never cruel to her daughter or, at least, not intentionally so—she was as perfectly pleasant to Liese when she noticed her as she was to anyone else. Margarethe's life always had, and always would, revolve around herself and, since her marriage, it had also revolved around Paul; the rest of the world hovered somewhere on the edge of her attention. For years, Liese had refused to accept that. She had held fast to the belief that, one day, when she was older, and could join Margarethe on her coffee-drinking and shopping trips, she would finally achieve the close bond with her mother she longed for. But when Margarethe had forgotten her daughter's fifteenth birthday as easily as she had forgotten her fifth, Liese decided it was time to be done with the hope that her mother might change her distant ways. Now, at sixteen, she finally understood Margarethe's narrow limits: a child tidied away in a nursery, grateful for a kiss was one thing; a daughter whose height and curves made a lie of "she can't be a day over thirty" was quite another.

I'll be a better kind of mother when it's my turn. I'll be everything my daughter wants me to be.

Liese watched Margarethe slink away and turned back to her father.

Paul's eyes were wistful, his hand deliberately suspended where his wife had left it, the script of their encounter still running in his head.

Liese waited.

Paul blinked; he sighed; he snapped into action. Countdown. One hour before the salon opened its canopied doors and the 1936 Autumn/Winter collection was deemed a triumph. Or not.

As always, the flurry of preparations before the show had been fraught, the fear of failure tangible, despite the years of success that had gone before. Liese fancied she could see the thoughts tumbling round Paul's head like a deck of cards falling. Would the shapes surprise? Would the colors dazzle? Was Haus Elfmann still ahead of the game? Every season, the same worries and now a new layer added.

Liese studied the names pinned to the spindly chairs. Helena Stahl, the fashion house's Amazonian Head of Publicity, was right: the seats were labeled with some out-of-place and unwelcome faces.

Agnes Gerlach, the self-appointed mouthpiece of the Party-run German Women's Culture Association (an organization Helena dismissed as "beige-clad frumps with no concept of style"), had spent two years begging for an invitation to an Elfmann show. Helena had spent two years delightedly ignoring her. Paul had no more time for Agnes than Helena did: he took her loudly voiced opinions on the "vulgarity" of Germans who insisted on "aping French fashion" personally. Now, however, even the German Fashion Institute was subject to the beck and call of its new Party masters. That meant that, whether Paul liked it or not, the country's fashion houses, who all operated under the GFI umbrella, had to sing to the Party's tune. The *frumps* were in the ascendant, *vulgarity* the charge every salon feared. Agnes had claimed a front-row seat. Paul's sulk had verged on Shakespearean.

Liese scanned the rest of the names while she waited for her father to stop fussing.

Agnes had been placed next to Frau Goebbels. That the Third Reich's First Lady was allotted a VIP spot was nothing unusual, given how many pieces she normally bought. It was her request for a second seat that had caused the problems. This time, Frau Goebbels had her angry little husband in tow. What the Reich's Minister for Propaganda wanted with a fashion show, Liese couldn't imagine. Other than the buyers from the major department stores and the financiers, men rarely attended. Today, however, the stiff cream cards revealed a heavy number of Ober-this and Gruppen-that. Men who, Helena complained, would come in their black uniforms and stop everyone smiling. Liese had never known a show where the guest list was so out of Haus Elfmann's control. And not only the list.

She picked up a program as Paul flicked imaginary dust motes from the candlelit mirrors. The Party had put its stamp on the language the salon could use as strongly as it had dictated who sat in the audience. The new directives, which detailed how German collections could be described, had sent Helena into as much of a fury as the seat allocations. Berlin, not Paris, was now considered the center of the fashion-world—in the Party's eyes, at least. *Hauptmode* was therefore the mandated phrase, not *haute couture*; *schick* not *chic* the stamp of approval. Nobody could fit the clumsy terms comfortably across their tongues, but there they were in the program, exactly as ordered. New faces and new words: small changes, but enough to trip them. Tension trickled through the building like sand through an hourglass.

Paul had finally stopped pacing. He stood in the center of the room, his hands raised. Liese craned forward, her neck prickling, as he clapped three times in quick succession. No matter how many times she played a part in them, the show-day rituals had never lost their magic. With no son to succeed him, Liese was the salon's heir and she had trotted behind him, hanging on his every syllable, since she was eight years old, not caring about anything except impressing him and understanding every strand of the business. On his final clap, the door reopened. Two of the youngest seamstresses scurried in, wrapped in white coveralls like Christmas sugar mice. They paused, one to the left of Paul, one to the right, crystal atomizers wobbling. Liese's nose twitched. A finger click and they were off, releasing the scent from the bottles in precision-timed bursts. The perfume puffed out in a fragrant mist which hung in the air like chiffon. Her father's eyes darted after the girls as they hopped from corner to corner.

Everything danced to the rhythm of the salon's two annual collections. The rites the Haus observed reached their peak on the day each of those was launched. Whether it was the length of the owners' silent embrace, or the number of flowers allotted to a vase, or the order the outfits appeared in, every decision and every moment held weight. And not only did each show have its own carefully calibrated theme, each show carried its own unique scent. The curtain-opener, Paul called it, the palate-tease. There were certain constants: Spring and Summer should be sweet with flowers or citrus-sharp; Autumn and Winter heavy with spices. Beyond that, no one but Paul and the perfumiers knew.

"Do the audience understand it, Papa? How the perfume talks to the clothes?"

"Not like we do."

We. Liese's skin fizzed.

"But if we missed this step out, everything would feel dull and our scene would not set. Why?"

"Because this is theater."

A nod; he was too tightly wound to smile. Besides, how else would she answer? Other children grew up stuffed with fairy tales and nursery rhymes: Liese's magic kingdoms were fashioned in the workrooms and showrooms she had learned to toddle and speak in.

You said the words "satin" and "silk" before Mother and Father. Delightful, but hardly a surprise. Minnie Elfmann, her much-missed grandmother, had woven that anecdote into family lore and never heard the sadness in it that Liese did. Minnie had been Liese's shining light, a vision in feather-trimmed wraps and waist-length pearls; adored and never remote. And never *Grandma.*

"Minnie, my sweet—nothing but Minnie. So much kinder for little mouths."

"And for old faces." Margarethe's stage whispers had always been carefully pitched.

Mother and wife had circled each other since Paul had spotted Margarethe commanding the audience at a Paris salon and whisked her back to Berlin. Any kindness between the two women had been reserved for public use.

"She's as jealous as a cat!"

They both had hissed it.

As Liese grew older and more tuned to the spats, the root of their competition became clear: her father and his constant need to stand center stage. Not that it mattered anymore who had scratched first at who. Minnie had blazed out four years ago, dying before anything as dull as old age could catch her, and left a hole Liese had struggled to climb out of. Now, there was no more Minnie to cover her with kisses, and no one else inclined to. There was no more Grandpa Nathan either, although he was so stern it was hard to miss his presence. Since Minnie's death, he had shriveled away like a hermit into his shuttered mansion, unable to step inside the fashion house that her flair had helped him found. One set of grandparents gone and neither Paul nor Margarethe had any brothers or sisters to offer. As for Margarethe's parents—they were lost somewhere in the rural corners of Alsace on the French–German border, their country ways long cast aside by their elegant daughter.

"So, our clan is a small one—what does it matter? Everyone in Berlin knows who we are."

Another of Paul's pronouncements. As if the public's admiring gaze could make their sprawling mansion in Bergmannkiez any less echoing or empty.

Such a perfect family. Liese wished she could see it, or find it.

She had haunted friends' noisier houses when she could. She had devoured books that described what she longed for. Stories filled with sisters who shared secrets, whose passionate squabbles collapsed into tearfully ecstatic declarations. Whose pretty heads were watched over by mothers with wide hearts and wide laps and spoiled by fathers whose pockets bulged with candy.

Not one of those stories resembled her own life. A mother and father wrapped up in themselves, aware of their daughter only as a part of the business. Uncle Otto, who was the salon's Technical Director and not really an uncle at all. And Michael, Otto's son, who was two years older than her and hovered somewhere between brother, friend, and serious annoyance. As soon as she could toddle, Liese had stuck herself firmly to Michael. She had adored him, he had adored her, and their business-breathing parents had been very grateful for the bond. Michael's hand holding hers had been Liese's anchor on the world; his grin a promise of adventure. They had built dens together, raided the kitchens together, dug up the gardens in search of buried treasure together. The Michael she had grown up with could collapse her into giggles with a look and spin a story out of thin air. His "just imagine if…" had become her childhood's favorite words. At twelve, even at fourteen, Liese would have said that the two of them knew each other inside out and everything was brighter when they shared it between them. Now, his life was outrunning hers, leading him to places she wasn't ready to follow. There were days when loneliness sat on her like a second skin.

"What do you smell?"

Paul was staring at her, frowning; Liese pulled herself back to the present.

"Close your eyes. Remember what we've practiced. Take a deeper breath. Tell me the notes you can sense. Then, put them together and tell me their story."

She did as she was told. She let the chair's padded back, the carpet's plush, the tip-tap of footsteps on the floor above go. She shut her eyes and focused on the perfume's music.

"Cinnamon and cloves." Her nose prickled. "Oranges and gingerbread." Each layer carefully picked out and then, just as carefully, woven back together. "Christmas."

No response. Her answer was too simple.

She pressed her lids tighter. She was good at this. Just as she was good at judging where a pleat should fold, or where a ruffle should gather. And, today of all days, she could not let her father down: her failure would be a bad omen.

She sniffed again, filling her lungs. A thicker note wriggled up through the spice-packed layers. Its smoky heaviness reminded her of the scent that wafted out when church doors opened. A scent she had never smelled in the synagogue Grandpa Nathan herded them all into, when he used to care about such things.

"Incense."

Her father released his breath in a gentle sigh.

Liese let her imagination dive back into the workrooms. She conjured up the muslin-draped costumes and pictured herself walking around them, picking out their details. The deep fur collar on an ankle-length coat; silver thread and crystal beads clustering the shoulders on a narrow bodice; filigreed gold worked in layered patterns. She let her thoughts wander past the dummies and over to the idea books that cluttered the studios: history and art collected in faded photographs and colored plates. Books she had spent hours poring over on quiet afternoons.

Her eyes snapped open. Military frogging, not buttons, to close a jacket, white muffs hanging from jeweled chains like sleeping rabbits.

"It's not any Christmas—it's a Russian one. At the Imperial Court. Girls ice-skating and riding in horse-drawn sledges at midnight. Trips to *The Nutcracker* and candlelit balls."

"You caught it. Well done."

Paul's smile at her cleverness lit up the room.

What was wrong with him? Why must he always be on a mission to spoil everything?

Michael had turned into the after-party's bad fairy, all black looks and muttered curses. Liese watched his fists curl and wished, not for the first time, that the old mischief-loving Michael would come back, not this new version all stamped through with *political understanding*, whatever that might be. It certainly wasn't any fun. He had grown spiky, and self-important, and in need of bursting. Once tonight was over, she would tell him that.

The show had been every bit the triumph everyone was praying for. Even Minister Goebbels had thawed when he saw the military touches. When he declared the collection "a timely homage to the beauties of Prussia," no one was fool enough to correct him. Now, two hours after the last model had stalked through the applause, the champagne was flowing, and the order book was brimming. Haus Elfmann was toasting its future; all Michael could do was scowl.

"How can they fawn like this? Your father's drooling and mine's as bad. They'll both be wearing swastikas next."

And here we go again.

Liese didn't bother to hide her sigh. One sight of a uniform or a Party badge and this newly minted Michael flew into a tirade in a voice more suited to a parade ground. She should have been quicker to run down to the milling reception, not let him catch her off guard on the stairs.

"Can't you let it go for tonight? Yes, there are more Party officials and officers than we expected. But everyone's praising the clothes and being perfectly civil."

Another curse. Thank goodness the stairway's curve meant Paul couldn't hear him.

Liese wasn't a fool, although Michael increasingly behaved as if she were. She knew there was a darker side to the National Socialists than the one currently on display. The Führer's rise to power three years ago had, in her father's words, made Germany "more secure and more hopeful" for businessmen like him. It had also released gangs of brown-shirted thugs onto the streets and plastered the city with posters and placards that were unsettling and not to be dwelled on.

As the regime flexed its muscles, people everywhere, including in hard-to-fluster and Party-skeptical Berlin, were growing nervous. Even the Elfmanns, for all their wealth and status, had not escaped the chill.

Liese, to her increasing irritation, was no longer allowed to walk anywhere without a companion. She had also been pulled out of school long before she was due to leave, with no explanation beyond the excuse of "difficult times." True, that was less of an upset than her curtailed freedom to visit the deer runs in Viktoriapark or the

paper *Der Stürmer*, whose hateful sketches of hook-nosed men drew the eye like a magnet, had disappeared. Berlin felt fresh and hopeful.

As for the stadium, its scale was impossible. "Three hundred and twenty-five acres and seating for a hundred thousand," or so their guide boasted. As they shuffled in, the sun came out and made everything sparkle, from the white-robed choir lined up on the playing field to the huge copper bowl waiting for the torchbearer's flame. Liese couldn't stop grinning, and even hard-to-impress Margarethe declared it was splendid.

Michael had wriggled in beside her, late as usual, causing a disturbance as he pushed through. Liese had considered getting cross with him, until he produced a bag of her favorite chocolate kisses and grinned his Michael grin.

Soon, Liese was giggling so hard as he made up comic characters for the people sitting around them that her stomach muscles hurt from trying to stifle her laughter. She slipped her arm through Michael's.

"I've missed this. You and me, having fun and not fighting."

He turned to her, smiling, but then a ripple ran round the packed terraces and jerked their attention back.

"Michael, what's happening?"

People were nudging each other, pointing.

Michael's face hardened.

The crowd swiveled, craning toward the top of a long sweep of stairs, where a figure stood, silhouetted and tiny.

Liese jumped as a trumpet rang out.

"What on earth!"

She bit her lip as backs in the row in front stiffened. The blast had plunged the stadium into a silence she knew instinctively it would be foolish to shatter.

The trumpet was joined by another and another, until a fanfare trilled. The figure moved down the steps, his entourage following. The arena rose as if it were operated by invisible strings, arms snapping into the air.

Paul slid back to his place and saluted; Margarethe mirrored him. Liese scrambled to her feet a second behind, pulled up by the crowd's movement.

A roar flew through the stands as if everyone had learned a cue, three notes of a chant beating like a drum. Liese caught it up without thinking, her voice blending in with the deep-throated swell.

"What the hell are you doing?"

Michael hadn't moved, despite Otto's frantic prodding. His arm had stayed firmly down.

"Seriously, Liese, what's got into you? Why are you shouting 'Heil Hitler' like one of the Party faithful? Have you gone mad?"

Despite the gap growing between them, he had never spoken to her so harshly before. It brought Liese up with a jolt. She suddenly saw herself through Michael's eyes, standing stiff as a statue, shouting with a passion they both knew she didn't feel. It wasn't a comfortable image. She meant to apologize, but then his lip curled into a sneer and she snapped back instead.

"What's wrong with *you*? It's a politeness, a welcome. It doesn't mean anything."

The roar swept into a storm of clapping as the Führer took his seat; into a whooping cheer as the torchbearer ran into view.

"Besides, everyone was doing it; I was just joining in."

"Oh, that's all right then. If *everyone's doing it*, there's nothing to worry about. It's me who's the fool, not you. And it is a vision all right. The great and the good and their well-behaved wives, our pampered visitors from Europe and even America, all lifting their hands and howling for Hitler. Isn't it marvelous how everyone loves him? Including today—heaven help us—the Jews."

Liese cringed as the man in front turned round and tutted. She knew Michael's patterns too well: he was about to launch into a tirade against the Party straight from his beloved KPD lecture, the one he could repeat word-perfect time after time, as if he'd swallowed a manual.

Liese was not, despite what she had just done, a devotee of Hitler, but it was clear from the profusion of lapel badges and flags surrounding them that plenty of the crowd were. This was no place for Michael to give full rein to his feelings, no matter how honestly held they were. She leaned toward him, her voice lowered to a whisper.

"I don't like it either, truly I don't. But can't we pick over this later, when we're at home?"

She was too late. Michael was off in full spate and not listening.

"The National Socialist Party is the enemy of the working man, and the communist, and the Jew. To participate in, or cooperate with, the Party's orders or their pageantry is an act of betrayal. No one can be allowed to forget that, not ever."

The man in front nudged the man next to him; Liese saw fists starting to curl.

Why must he always be so loud?

She gritted her teeth as the runner lowered his torch and the copper bowl burst into flames. Whatever the truth of Michael's words, all she wanted to do today was enjoy the spectacle, not become it.

"Michael, please, not this again, not here. Fine, I got a bit carried away, but why do you have to be so patronizing? I'm sick of hearing about the communists and how they're going to save the world. And as for the Jews and this reclaimed *religious heritage* you're all het up about, I'm sick of that too. Fine, be a communist if you want; be a Jew if that makes you happy. Don't expect me to be either."

She would have left it there, if he hadn't raised his eyebrow.

"What? Are you going to tell me I'm Jewish again? Saying it doesn't make it real, you know. I don't go to the synagogue; I don't keep Jewish holidays; I don't follow Jewish laws. None of us do, including you, the last time I checked. We're Germans—good Germans, like everyone else here—and that's all we are. Well, except you apparently: you're also a bore."

Michael's answering snarl made her eyes smart.

"Well, forgive me, Princess, for spoiling your day. It's not like the Party are really that bad. And Jewish? You? What a crazy idea. How could the granddaughter of Nathan Elfmann, whose Jewish family fled the pogroms in Hungary, whose father made his fortune in the Jewish rag trade, possibly be Jewish?"

They were attracting more attention than ever—even Paul was looking along the row.

"Michael, for Heaven's sake, lower your voice!"

It was a waste of her breath; he grew louder.

"Seriously, how could I be so dumb? It's not as if anyone could think Elfmann is a Jewish name. Or Wasserman either. Remind me to tell that to the universities I've applied to, who seem less certain of our heritage than you. How great it must be to live in such denial. You'll be telling me next that Jesse Owens is white. Fine, don't be a communist, but don't say you're not Jewish, as if that makes it true."

More heads were turning, none of them friendly.

"Michael, this isn't the place—"

It was like trying to calm a charging elephant with a wagging finger.

"When did you become so accepting, Liese? You used to drive me crazy with your questions—what happened? Don't you care about all the new rules and the curbs on our freedom? Don't you wonder why you can't walk anywhere alone anymore, or go to school?"

"Of course I do, but Father says—" But Michael's hand was up.

"Don't bother, I can guess. He said it's for your own safety, because the Brownshirts might not realize you're a *good German*. Did he also tell you Hitler would bring his hooligan army back into line once the Party was secure? It's horseshit. Hitler's had power for three years—he's as secure as a bank vault. Come on, Liese, you can do better than this. Our glorious new leaders don't care much for Jews and they're getting very skilled at spotting us. Why do they want to do that? Do you want to guess, or shall I tell you? It's so they can remove us. So they can lift us out of our lives."

People in the rows around had started to mutter. Otto, more conscious than Michael of the mood in the surrounding seats, grabbed his son's arm. Michael shook him off. He was so focused on making Liese believe him, she doubted he could see anyone but her.

"What do I have to say to persuade you that danger is coming? You must sense it. Didn't you notice that there were no tramps or drunks on the streets today? All this nonsense about us being 'safer in our beds under our new government.' More horseshit. The streets are empty because the Party's rounding up everyone they don't count as German anymore and dumping them in camps. There's a massive one at Oranienburg, barely an hour from the city. There's rumors of torture there, of killings."

Someone yelled at him to shut up. Liese winced; Michael didn't notice.

"People I know, from the meetings I go to, have disappeared—"

And then his words were lost in the blast of a cannon and a furious squawking as thousands of doves burst into the sky. Liese screamed in fright as the birds' frantic wings shook the air, as their gray bodies merged into a storm cloud.

More faces turned; more complaining.

"What are you doing, making such a show?"

Liese had never seen her father so white.

"It's my fault, Herr Elfmann; forgive me. I upset her."

Liese could see from Michael's stricken face that he was genuinely sorry. He tried to push in between Paul and Liese, but a burly man from the row behind was already on his feet.

"You've upset everyone with your communist filth. And as for this one, screaming like a banshee, and in front of the Führer. It's unpatriotic; it's a disgrace. If you people don't know how to behave, you shouldn't be allowed in."

You people floated off through the stands to be clapped at.

Paul bowed and reached into his pocket. "I must beg your forgiveness: someone has clearly chosen my guests for today rather badly. Their sentiments embarrass me as much as they, quite rightly, upset you. I will make sure they leave immediately. Now, you, sir, you look like a man of good taste. Take my card, please. You must come to my salon tomorrow and choose something pretty for your wife. Will that smooth the day out?"

The wife's beam assured Paul that it would.

Liese stared at her father, waiting for the nod that would signal that this was a charade, a face-saver. There was nothing in his voice but contempt.

"Get out, both of you."

Liese looked to Otto for help, but his expression was studiously blank.

"Don't react. Don't let him see that you're hurt. It's my fault, not yours. And it's about the business, not you." Michael's hand was on her elbow, his mouth at her ear.

Liese shook him off, her eyes bright with tears she wouldn't let him see. He had the sense not to speak again as they crept out of the stadium and back through a city that was no longer beautiful.

*

The whole fortnight of the Games, not just the first day, had been ruined. Paul and Margarethe had carried on with their whirlwind of events and receptions and confined Liese to the house as if she had the plague. Even if she had been allowed out, the gloss had gone: Michael's words had scoured away Berlin's shiny veneer. More importantly, Paul's fury at the potential damage to the salon's reputation had been implacable. If it weren't for her skill with the perfumes, Liese doubted her father would even be speaking to her tonight. Well, he had reopened the door to the only parts of her life that mattered and Michael's moods were not going to close it again.

"Did you ask them, about school and not going out?"

Michael was still growling.

Liese moved toward the stairs and away.

"No, I didn't. I don't care about school, I'm glad to be finished with it."

She shook her head as his eyebrows knitted.

"But I did listen to you, okay? And, despite what you seem to think, I do read the papers. I know there are restrictions—that the Jews can't marry who they want anymore; that they can't vote. I don't like it—of course I don't—the same as I don't like seeing the horrible posters that have reappeared, like you said they would. But, tonight, I don't want to think about any of that. Besides, whatever is happening doesn't mean my father is wrong. It certainly doesn't mean your brand of politics is right. So, can we be done?"

"You haven't listened at all or you wouldn't talk about *the Jews* and *they* as if they were some alien species."

Liese steeled herself for another angry outburst, but all she could hear in his voice was shock.

"I don't understand, Liese, I really don't. Whether you feel part of their heritage or not, you can't deny that your father's family are Jewish, and likely your mother's too, given where they're from. So why do you insist on thinking you're different from everyone else who's been dealt the same label? If you read the papers, you've seen the race charts: the slightest drop of Jewish blood means you're a Jew, no matter how deep you bury it. It means you've no place in the Party's new Germany."

Thinking about the evening later, Liese wished that was the point at which he had stopped. She told herself that, if he had, she would have apologized, smoothed things over; persuaded him to join the celebrations with a smile. He hadn't, so neither did she.

"Liese, come on! Are you really so stupid you can't see that?"

It was *stupid* that had made her hackles flare. That had stopped her admitting that, yes, the charts that the Party had ordered to be published everywhere had frightened her. They would frighten anyone, with their horrible pictures of people who barely looked human and their family trees and diagrams of *Aryan* and *Non-Aryan* grandparents and parents, which were now used to establish degrees of Jewishness. And, of course, she hated the way Jews were written about in the papers, as if they were some other species and not even people. It made her feel sick. On a less important day, she would have admitted that. But this was Haus Elfmann's night: it was not a time for misery. And Michael had called her *stupid* and he had meant it and some lines couldn't be crossed.

Liese whirled on him, spitting out her frustration in a stream she knew as soon as she started owed far more to Paul's thinking than her own.

"Why do you have to speak to me like I'm some kind of idiot? If anyone's *stupid*, it's you. Look at this place. Look at the clients who come here, who spend a fortune here. Look at how much they adore us. Don't you see? We're not the kind of Jews Hitler is bothered with—the academics and the intellectuals, or the criminals. We create jobs; we contribute. The Party knows our value. They would never come after us."

She expected him to stalk away, or snap back. Instead, Michael recoiled as if she had hit him, his face pinched and drawn in a way she had never seen it before.

"I've upset you; I'm sorry. You're right: the way I spoke to you wasn't fair. But I know you, and I don't think you believe this. This is Paul speaking, not you. And I know you're tired of my lectures, that I should choose my moments more carefully. But that's the problem: I can't choose my moments, because time's running out."

Anguish flooded his voice, catching Liese by surprise.

"The world we know is disappearing. Maybe you don't care about school, but I do. And about university. That's all done for me: with my bloodline, with two Jewish parents, there's not one institution left I can go to. If it weren't for Father's job here, and him taking me on, I'd have no place at all to be." He paused as if he was weighing his words. "Do you want to know the truth? What I've never told anyone? I'm scared. I don't like the look of the future, and I'm scared."

He had returned to the Michael Liese recognized, the one she couldn't bear to see in distress.

"I didn't know that. Then I'm sorry too. I hate that we keep fighting. And, if I'm being honest, those horrible diagrams do scare—and disgust—me. And I honestly didn't know university mattered to you so much. I always thought you wanted to work here at the salon, like me. But we'll be all right—maybe the new rules make us Jewish, but no one would think it; no one cares. And it's not like your father merely has a job—he practically runs the place. What is it he always says? 'Haus Elfmann would be bankrupt in a week if I left you children in charge.' You'll follow in his footsteps here; I know you will. You have a great future ahead of you."

Her impression of Otto addressing her parents was so perfect, she thought Michael would laugh. Instead, his face crumpled.

"Michael, *please*. Don't be angry, not tonight. I promise that tomorrow I'll listen as long as you want."

There was a sudden ripple of applause from the floor below. Someone had brought in a gramophone. People were breaking into smaller groups, searching out partners.

"Look: everyone is getting along perfectly. Even Minister Goebbels is smiling. Can't you make an effort, just this once?"

Liese started down the stairs and held out her hand for Michael to follow. He took a step back.

"I am looking, Liese. But I can't see what you see. I don't want to." His voice tightened. "So they're smiling—so what? One day they'll stop. Come with me, to one of my meetings. I could introduce you to people who will help you understand what's really happening."

One of his meetings: he meant the communists. Her father hated them; he said they were the worst threat of all. He would never forgive her if she got mixed up with that and she had no intention of being shut out by her father again.

A record sang out below them, the music slow at first and then the tempo quickening. Liese looked down and caught the eye of André Bardou, the handsome French buyer who had flirted with her today and not with Margarethe. She was sixteen. It was a party. Michael's fears would have to wait.

"This is a reception, Michael, not a rally. I've had an education, thank you. I don't need another."

She turned on her heel and headed for the stairs.

"Fine, stay ignorant." Michael's shout was so loud, one or two faces looked up. "It's probably for the best. Taking a spoiled kid who can't stop thinking like her daddy to a meeting intended for adults would make me the idiot anyway."

She should have known he wouldn't so easily back down. Her palm itched as she swung round.

"You're two years older than me, Michael, not twenty. You can play the big man as much as you like. You're nowhere close to being one yet."

But he'd gone and, even though she'd tried to have the last word, he'd won. Despite all Monsieur Bardou's charming smiles and polished compliments, Michael's parting shot had chipped the night's sparkle completely away.

memory. Mummy making daisy chains in the park on a summer afternoon. Mummy teaching her to make snow angels one long-ago Christmas. Karen could see the two of them perfectly clearly, sitting in the grass and lying in the snow, but it was like looking at a photograph, at something frozen. As if the feelings that went with the actions had already faded.

The clock in the hall struck seven-thirty.

Karen had taken the battery out of the one that had sat for years on her bedside table. It was pink and childish and she hated it. She had wanted to change it for a digital one but Mummy said they were for *big girls*.

Which is what, according to father, I now am.

Karen sat up.

Never mind change it, she could smash it. She could throw it on the floor. Or, better still, throw it through the window and hear the glass shatter. Karen pictured the panes snapping, the shards crashing onto the path. It would make so much noise, the house would surely collapse in the shock of it.

Nothing ever happened inside these walls louder than a door easing shut. Right now, Father was in the kitchen, getting breakfast. Karen could picture him, putting out her cup and bowl, rummaging through the cupboards and the fridge, doling out cereal. Even with all the doors open, she couldn't hear him. He had always padded around the place like a giant gray mouse. *Mummy doesn't like noise, does she?* It had always been phrased as a reminder, never a question. *Especially when she has one of her headaches.*

Mummy's headaches. Their rhythms had ruled the house for as long as Karen could remember. Some days the house was so silent, Karen imagined she could hear the sound of the dust motes floating through the air. She used to wonder if anyone passing by would ever have guessed there were flesh and blood people sitting quietly inside.

Maybe that's why Mummy went to the beach so early, because she was looking for quiet.

No matter how many times Karen tried out that explanation, she could never quite believe it. If her mother wanted some peace, why would she need to go to the beach? They had been staying in Hove; it didn't matter whether it was early or late, or whether you stood in the street or the park, nowhere on earth was as quiet as Hove. Even in summer, the place was as short on life as those ghost towns in the wild-west films her father loved, the ones that had all emptied out in fear of attack. On the first day of their week on the South Coast, Karen had half-expected cowboys to pop up from behind the wedding-cake houses. If only. Hove was dull. Capital D, underlined twice, *dull*, and not by any stretch of the imagination Karen's idea of a holiday place.

It was certainly no place for an eleven-year-old. Karen had decided that the moment they parked the car. The public gardens facing the hotel, which Father insisted were delightful, were ringed with dozing pensioners propped up on the benches like wrinkly babies. The hotel itself, which he kept calling charming, was cluttered and dusty, all drooping dried flowers and finger-marked paint. The prospect of a week there was worse than a maths test.

Karen had crossed the fingers on both of her hands when they arrived in the gloomy reception hall, willing her mother to wrinkle her nose at the fusty smell. To take Father to one side and suggest they switch to somewhere less rotten. To even have one of the silent crying attacks that Karen hated so much but Father couldn't ignore and would do anything to mend. Mummy hadn't done a thing. She had followed Father up the stairs without so much as a glance at the muddy brown drapes shrouding the windows or the orange-swirled carpet stuck to the floor.

Remembering that now, sitting in her perfectly matched pale pink and cream room, Karen realized how odd that lack of any reaction had been.

Mummy had always hated anything ugly. She'd loved pretty fabrics, especially the soft ones, like velvet, or the expensive ones

that were threaded through with silver or gold. Nothing in their neat little house had been allowed to be plain. The curtains were daisy-covered, the cushions striped and spotted. Her mother had been such an expert seamstress, she'd made dresses and skirts for most of the women in the village. Mrs. Hubbard had said she was clever enough to have her own shop. She'd made all Karen's clothes too, although Karen had started wishing she wouldn't. Karen had desperately wanted a pair of blue jeans and a skinny-fit T-shirt with stripes, like Cathy Creggan showed off in. She had asked for those. No, she hadn't, she had *demanded* them.

Another tear dropped. She wished now she had asked nicely and not crumpled up the bib-fronted pinafore Mummy had offered instead. She would gladly have worn a dozen of those hand-sewn dresses if her mother were still here to make them.

Karen blinked hard, wondering if the memories would ever come without the pain. Wondering if she would ever be able to filter the good ones out from the ones she didn't want resurfacing. She needed those good memories: there wasn't anything else left. Not a dress left in her wardrobe or a coat on the hall stand. And there wasn't a photograph. Not that there had ever been many of those.

Mrs. Hubbard's house was stacked with them; every surface groaned under their stiffly posed weight. Karen had spent more of her mother's headache days than she could count in Mrs. Hubbard's front room, happily rearranging the photographs.

There were only two pictures in the Cartright house, both black and white and plainly framed. One of them was of Father's parents, who had died long before Karen was born. She didn't like it: the old man in a drab uniform, awkwardly linking arms with a tightly curled woman, had a rather menacing air. The other one was of her as a baby, lying on a rug and looking cross-eyed. There were no other grandparents on display and there wasn't a single one of her parents, not even a wedding snap. Mrs. Hubbard had generations of those, in increasingly elaborate frames. When Karen had asked Father why, he hadn't answered, his usual strategy.

During the Hove holiday, on their less-than-successful day trip to the far more thrilling town of Brighton, Karen had begged for a photo of the three of them together. She'd got quite upset when Mummy refused, had "made a scene," which was Father's cardinal sin. She had made quite a few scenes that day, wanting some of the fun everyone else was noisily having. Maybe that was why her mother had needed to go alone to the beach.

"Five minutes, Karen! Breakfast is waiting." Father's voice rang up the stairs like a trumpet.

Such a stupid thing to say. Where would it go if she didn't turn up? This bright version of Father was no better than the gruff one; if anything, it was more exhausting. Not that it would last. If Karen were two minutes late to the table, he would be back to rules and regulations, wearing his soldier's uniform even when he wasn't.

He doesn't mean it. He's just doing his best to keep us all running. The voice flew back so clear, Karen looked round for her mother. That was the last thing she'd said when she came to say good-night. The last thing she'd ever said.

Patting her damp face dry with the corner of her skirt, Karen rummaged back through her memories, her daily task since the whole horrible mess had happened, as she tried to push the disjointed images into shape.

She remembered the shock of waking up late and waking up alone. Wondering why her mother wasn't sitting by her bed, strok-ing her hair and whispering that the world was awake and waiting for her. Wondering if that meant today was a bad day, a headache day. And she remembered scrambling into the day-before's clothes; knocking on her parents' door and getting no answer. Thundering down the staircase, wondering if Mummy was sick, or if she was still in trouble from the day before. She remembered crashing into the breakfast room and the white faces turning. Her father

slumped on a sofa as if someone had removed his bones. And the policewoman who took her into a separate room and came back empty-handed when Karen screamed for her father. Who tried in vain to talk over the bellowing "No, I can't come; don't ask me" that was all Karen could hear.

Things blurred after that, although the black dress which itched like sacking jumped out. And the hard lines of a funeral in the army church on the Aldershot base, with soldiers snapping to a salute she had instinctively known her mother would have hated.

There were so many gaps. Long hours she must have spent alone, punctured by a hazy week Mrs. Hubbard filled with ceaseless chatter and uneaten baking. And the day Father took her back to the base—Karen couldn't forget that, although she had tried her best. Father talking about moving away, how life among the other army families might prove easier to manage than staying on in the village. Showing her the shoebox of a house he thought would best replace the cottage where, if she tried hard enough, she still might be able to conjure up her mother. Karen had run away from him and she had screamed. So loudly a white-coated medic came running. That was awful. But Father wasn't. He hadn't shouted the way she had expected. He had held her and tried to calm her and mopped up her tears. That was the bit she needed to hold on to. Not the noise and the fuss and everyone's embarrassment, but Father's gentleness as he carried her to bed and stayed till she slept and answered, without blinking, to *Daddy*.

Karen cradled that memory and then she shoved it aside. What was the point of holding on to it when she wasn't even sure anymore that it had happened? The next day, *Father* was back and moving wasn't mentioned again. Nothing was ever mentioned again.

Father went back to drilling his recruits, or whatever it was he did that seemed to involve long hours away and paperwork that kept him busy into the night. Karen spent her days with Mrs. Hubbard and the parade of grandchildren who trooped in and out and were nice to her "because your mum's dead." When Father was home and not at his desk in the back room, they maneuvered around each other, him hiding behind a book, Karen taking refuge in front of the television. Whatever barrier they could find to kill the slightest threat of conversation.

The bottom stair creaked, breaking the flow of memories.

"I'm coming."

Karen grabbed her creaky new satchel and headed down before Father could come up or call out again, before his voice could tighten. She paused for a moment on the landing, checking her reflection in the hallway mirror. Pale face but no redness. Neat hair, box-fresh blazer. Ordinary.

Miss Larkin, her old junior school teacher, who wore tie-dye tops and mirror-studded skirts, said that ordinary was the same as dull, which was the worst thing to be. Karen didn't agree with that at all. Staring at herself in the mirror, she realized that ordinary sounded perfect, sounded exactly what she wanted. An ordinary girl going to a new school filled with other ordinary girls, who didn't know her. New faces who would believe in the mother Karen wanted to remember. The kind one, the gentle one; the one who was always present. New faces who hadn't watched her mother shy away from the other mums gathered at the school gates. Who hadn't giggled later on when her mother was there like clockwork every morning and every afternoon, reaching out for Karen's hand long after the other children had declared their independence. Who didn't know that Karen's mother had "funny turns." That Karen was the odd one, the unpopular one, the one who never had, so never went to, birthday parties.

Or, better still, new faces who wouldn't ask her anything personal at all. Who would let her forget, for eight glorious hours every day, the impossible, unthinkable fact that her beautiful mother wasn't silent, or absent; she was dead.

CHAPTER THREE

Liese

Berlin, October 1936

"Why is that boy never where he's meant to be?" Otto paced the pavement as the chauffeur hovered.

"The traffic is building, sir. If you want to be on time…"

"Uncle Otto? It's freezing in here. Can I at least close the door?"

"Fine, fine. I'm coming. I'll deal with him later."

Otto scrambled into the back of the Mercedes, cursing as he caught his foot on the running board. The seats were wide, but he still managed to crowd Liese into the corner. Middle age and a comfortable life had curled rolls of fat over his collar and wrapped bracelets round his wrists. *He was a ferocious fighter in the war, completely fearless. Far braver than me*—one cognac too many and Paul became a storyteller.

Watching Otto now, splayed out and puffing against the sand-colored leather, all Liese could see was Lewis Carroll's Walrus, drooling at the oysters.

"Did you remind him what time we were leaving?"

Yes, and he reminded me he had a KPD meeting which was far more important than "the nonsense of fashion" so that was another conversation that made us both cross.

"I couldn't find him. And maybe it's for the best he doesn't come, given the way he's been behaving lately."

Liese kept her tone light, but she was deadly serious. Taking Michael to any of their stockists was a risk: he didn't know when to leave his politics behind.

Otto sighed, but he couldn't argue.

"You two shadowing me was meant to be a simple exercise and all he does is cause chaos. I'm starting to think he's not cut out for this business. Not like you, missy."

Otto tapped on the partition for the driver to start moving and resettled his bulk.

"Perhaps I should be concerned for my job, not Michael's? If you carry on learning the ropes at the pace you're going, Paul will soon have you running the place."

"As if Haus Elfmann could manage without its *Fixer*."

Liese crinkled her nose the way her father did when he used the nickname that had followed the two men out of the mud-soaked trenches where they had met and into the business they now ran side by side. *Whatever we needed—food or wine or a cart when our feet were too broken to walk—Otto the Fixer would produce it faster than a magician.* Now Otto worked his magic on late-running suppliers and overstretched workrooms, and when Paul declared, with more than a touch of theatricality, "All my ideas would come to nothing without him," no one disagreed.

"Besides, you know I don't want to direct the salon. I want to be its chief designer."

Otto's newly recovered smile disappeared again.

"Which, with your talent, I don't doubt you'll be. And Michael was meant to stand in my position at your side, but the way that boy is going...To think I once harbored hopes that you and he wouldn't only be business partners but—"

"Uncle Otto, please!"

Her horror stopped the sentence finishing.

Bubbles of sweat popped out across Otto's pink forehead; Liese refused to meet his eye as he fumbled for his handkerchief. How could he possibly think such a thing, when she and Michael had been brought up so closely they were practically related? Besides, Michael had a girlfriend, a cigarette-smoking redhead he slobbered over like she was carved out of candy. And as for her own fledgling love life...A sudden memory of André Bardou's smiling mouth and stolen kisses at the salon reception, and the secret, so-romantic snatched meetings that had followed, burned her scarlet.

Otto collapsed into a pile of apologies.

"I'm sorry. I've embarrassed you. I won't mention it again. I want to see him settled, and happy, that's all. He's so angry and lost, and every door that closes on him makes his temper worse. I love that boy, I really do, but whatever I say is wrong. And that rabble he's mixed up with: they've turned his head, with their talk of rights and revolutions. His mother always knew best how to reach him. If she were still alive..."

Otto lapsed into a silence Liese had no idea how to fill.

When the car finally glided to a halt in Alexanderplatz, outside a shop whose five sparkling stories dominated the square, Liese jumped out of the car faster than the chauffeur could reach her door. Then she looked up and stopped so suddenly, Otto almost bundled into her. Until a few weeks ago, a sweep of letters across the top story had spelled out the store's name as *Hermann Tietz*. Now, the arch was shrunken, truncated into *Hertie*.

"I can't get used to the new name, no matter how often I see it."

"You shouldn't have to; none of us should." Otto sniffed. "Reducing Germany's oldest department store to this is an abomination. *Hertie* sounds like the lowest kind of cabaret."

Liese stifled a giggle and hurried inside. To her relief, nothing in there had changed. The interior wrapped round her like a favorite dress.

"Fraulein Elfmann, Herr Wasserman."

Herr Bruckner, the store's new Head of Womenswear, stood poised like a conductor at the staircase's turn. His voice carried a snap, which straightened the shop assistants. He clicked his heels and inclined his head; he didn't come down to greet them.

"If we could proceed to my office?"

Liese frowned and caught Otto doing the same, although he hid his discomfort more quickly.

Bruckner was newly in post, but surely he knew how things were done? A tour of the accessories departments, tea in the Palm Court, and then, and only then, into the office to sign the orders they would have discussed along the way. "A gentleman's approach to business" her father called it, based on relationships and civility. Every department store in Berlin ran its affairs the same way.

Above them, Herr Bruckner coughed. "I have other meetings."

"Then we must not delay you."

Otto waved Liese up the stairs, beginning a commentary on October's sudden cold snap as if nothing were out of place.

Bruckner took no notice, leading them to the tucked-away warren of offices behind the sales floors at a pace designed to discourage conversation. They were seated before Liese could unfasten her coat and no one appeared with a tea tray. Otto asked after Bruckner's health and was again ignored.

Liese knew she was there, as always, to observe and not to involve herself in the meeting, but the man's brusqueness was sailing close to an insult. She coughed and fixed on her best smile.

"Goodness, you are in quite a hurry today, Herr Bruckner. Normally, as I'm sure you know, we visit the bag and shoe departments first to discuss the new season's colors and shapes with the salesgirls. I hope we can still make the time to do that?"

Bruckner addressed Otto as if no one had spoken.

"I am surprised to see you, Herr Wasserman. I made it clear in my letter that Hertie will not be buying from Haus Elfmann this year."

"What letter?" Liese swung round to Otto, who also looked through her.

"I received your communication, Herr Bruckner. But, I confess, I could make little sense of it. For one of our most valued customers to not stock our brand? There is surely some mistake? Our prêt-à-porter line has always been an integral part of…"

The pause, the stumble it implied, was short, but it was long enough for Bruckner's face to tighten. For him to register, if he hadn't already done so, that not only was Otto about to say the store's old name, he had also used the French term to describe the ready-to-wear collection, not the German *Konfektion* the new rules demanded.

Otto recovered himself but could not entirely mask the tremor unsettling his voice. "…of Hertie's offering. Your customers expect to find us here, Herr Bruckner. So I felt certain there was still a conversation to be had. I wondered if some adjustment on the price might correct matters?"

Bruckner straightened a pen that was already straight.

"It's always about money with your kind, isn't it?"

Liese withdrew into her seat as Bruckner continued, the echo of the Olympic Stadium's *you people* too strong in *your kind*.

"There was no mistake, Herr Wasserman, not on my part. And, whatever the practice in the past, our customers do *not* expect to find your brand here. They expect to find outfits that are more appropriate. More German."

His contempt tugged at Liese like a toothache. She willed Otto to speak. He sat hunched over as if he was winded, while Bruckner observed him through hooded eyes.

"More German? What do you mean, Herr Bruckner? Dirndl skirts and puff-sleeved blouses?" This time, Liese spoke so sharply, Bruckner was forced to look her way. "Surely not? I know you are new, but can you honestly see the women of Berlin dressing like peasants?"

It was rude. It was also stupid and it played, as Liese realized a moment too late, straight into Bruckner's hands.

"How nastily you use that word. As if modest people who work hard for their country are somehow beneath you. But, given who and what you are, why should your attitude surprise me?"

He reached for a sheaf of papers and began reading from the top one before Liese could think how to defend herself.

"This is the report on your salon's most recent offering. It does not make pleasant reading. *Shamefully tight skirts, naked backs, necklines more suited to a brothel. Garish colors that do not suit German coloring. Designs unfit for decent women.*"

Bruckner put the notes down and folded his hands.

"A *French* collection, in other words. From a house that insults us by claiming to be German. A collection, Fraulein Elfmann, there is no room for here."

Liese was speechless, but fortunately Otto had finally pulled himself together. "Herr Bruckner, Fraulein Elfmann spoke out of turn and with uncalled-for rudeness, but I would ask your indulgence. She is young. She is loyal to her salon and to her family. Not a bad thing, I'm sure you'd agree."

He was gabbling, fawning. Liese couldn't meet his eye.

"As for our last showing—if there are dresses that fit those descriptions, descriptions which, I must say, pain me, please understand these are not the garments you would receive. Our shows always include pieces custom-made for clients whose lives demand a little more, shall we say, *glamour*? If you have specific requirements, then, please, list them. Whatever you want can be done."

"Good."

For the first time since they had entered his office, Bruckner smiled. Liese wished that he hadn't.

"I do have one requirement, Herr Wasserman: get Haus Elfmann endorsed by Adefa. Do that and it is business as usual."

Otto slumped so completely, Liese thought he would slide off his chair.

"You know that's impossible."

"Then we are finished here."

Bruckner rose and walked to the door. Liese stared from one man to the other, caught off guard by the meeting's, and Otto's, collapse.

"Why are you doing this? Goebbels praised the collection. His wife ordered at least a dozen pieces."

Bruckner shrugged as Otto stuttered. "And yet it was Reich Minister Goebbels who wrote this report. What his wife does is no business of mine. I appraised you of our position; you chose to ignore it. And now I have more important matters waiting."

He opened the door, his foot lightly tapping.

Otto clambered up, lumbering like a man twice his age. Liese followed at his heels, with no idea what had happened except that they, and the salon, had been thoroughly insulted.

They sloped back down the busy corridor. No one smiled; no one greeted them. Liese was known to almost everyone they passed and yet no one would look at her.

At the top of the staircase, whose steps now looked steep rather than sweeping, she pulled Otto to a halt.

"I don't understand what that was. Bruckner canceled our contract and said dreadful things, and you let him. You didn't try to persuade him to change his mind. And what is Adefa? Why did you fall apart when he mentioned it?"

Otto gazed out over the bustling counters. "What exactly could I persuade him to change his mind to? That report hardly left me with a negotiating position. And he was right: he had told me his intention; I chose not to believe it. Apparently, there are things even I can't fix. As for Adefa, you know what it is: the regulatory body for the clothing industry. The Party's vehicle for ensuring German fashion is German."

"But that's been set up for ages. It's never been an issue before."

When Otto turned toward her, his face was shapeless.

"You're right: Adefa isn't new, but it has changed. You just can't hear it. The *D* doesn't stand for *Deutsch* anymore but *Deutsch-Arischer*. Aryan. Pure blood. No Jews."

Liese's stomach knotted: his words could have been Michael's.

"But Goebbels came. He smiled the whole time."

Now when she said it, she heard the child's voice.

Otto started down the stairs, shuffling where he once strode. "And then look what he did."

After the store's soft interior, the noise on the pavement came as a shock. Liese stepped too slowly into the bustle and was jostled. Her hat was pulled off by a passing umbrella, her chocolate curls sent tumbling. A group of boys milling on the corner started to point and laugh.

"Get in the car." Otto wrenched the door open.

The gang began waving, whistling and catcalling, aiming blue-tinged comments at Liese simply because she was dark-haired, not blonde.

Otto followed her in, his fists bunched, his face puce. The car accelerated past the shouting. The boys' faces were a blur, but their swastika-emblazoned armbands stood out.

Liese crouched on the seat and tried to focus on the threat to the salon. The Hertie order was one of their biggest, the ready-to-wear collection the business's backbone. If Hertie could cancel so easily, if the other stores followed...

She rounded on Otto, rattling with questions. All she managed to ask was: "What now?"

He didn't reply.

The journey back to Hausvogteiplatz and the salon nestled beneath the square's sunburst-shaped clock passed in a series of images that tied Liese in knots.

While they were inside Hertie, the afternoon had eased into twilight, the street lamps lit and casting a yellow-tinged glow. Normally, their light fell like a blanket, blurring and softening.

Today, the lamps loomed like spotlights, their stare as harsh and unblinking as Herr Bruckner's.

Liese tried not to look at the passing streets, but it was as if Bruckner's cruel dismissal had torn a veil away. Corners suddenly sprouted gangs whose chests puffed with swastikas. Newspaper kiosks bloomed with *Der Stürmer*'s black-bearded monsters. Splashes of paint reshaped themselves into stars etched onto vulnerably thin windows. Her eyes stretched and ached. *Pure Blood, no Jews* whirled round her head like a storm brewing.

"You have to sell!"

Otto was barely inside Paul's office before he began shouting.

"I've warned you for months the day was coming. Well, it's here. If you keep on waiting, I promise you: they'll come in and take it."

Liese tried to follow him inside, but Otto waved her furiously back. She caught the door as he slammed it, keeping it open with her toe, and pressed into the shadows in time to hear her father snort with laughter.

"Dear God, man. Have you joined Michael on the barricades? 'They'll come in and take it'—can you hear yourself?" Glasses clinked; liquid poured. "Here, have a drink. Unless that's the problem and you've already been indulging. Hertie's new chap must be quite a character if this is how he rattles you. What did he do, screw you down on the price? Don't tell me *The Fixer* is slipping."

"He canceled our contract."

Liese waited for a silence, or a shocked exclamation and a torrent of questions. Instead, Paul dismissed Bruckner, and Otto with him, as if he flicked away a fly.

"Don't be ridiculous. We're their biggest-selling supplier. Besides, he doesn't have the authority."

To Otto's credit, he kept his temper.

"Goebbels does. He gave the order to terminate our business. Our collection is apparently too French, designed for whores, not German matrons. And, no, I don't want to hear how charming the Minister was at the show in September. I was there. And I was there today. We're done. They want us out."

"Not this nonsense again. Hitler's vendetta against the Jews."

Liese closed her eyes and willed him not to say it.

"I've told you: you and me, and our families, we're different; we're not the target."

There it was: the same thoughtless line she'd trotted out to Michael, the line she'd been clinging to until today. Liese forced herself to focus on what Otto was saying.

"Different? How can you still go on parroting that? I never thought I'd say this, but you're turning into your father. Is that what you want? To be so buried in the business that you're blind past the end of your nose? He neglected you, and he neglected your mother. He never noticed she was sick until it was too late. Don't raise your hands at me—you know it's true. All the money and the big house and the status he clawed his way up to, and where is he now? Hidden away, eaten up with guilt for the pain Minnie died in. Are you going to go down the same road? So wrapped up in Haus Elfmann and your ego that you forget to look up at the world? That you forget about your wife and your daughter? Liese is already banned from her school. What's coming for her next? What's coming for Margarethe?"

Paul exploded.

Liese heard the roar but not the words. She was too busy trying to work out which of Otto's sentences to grab hold of first. *Banned?* She knew that needed unpicking, but the nonsense that was *guilt* was chiming too loud. Grandpa Nathan wasn't guilty; he was crippled with grief. And what was *neglected*? How could he have neglected Minnie when she was the center of his life? *Not that he'd ever admit it, not in public anyway*—and there it was, clinging to the tail of Liese's recollection: not the words but the little pause

Minnie would leave at the end, which Grandpa never filled. Like he never took her side when the rows broke out, in the way Paul always championed Margarethe.

Inside the office, her father was still shouting.

"You've no right to accuse me of being like him. As if I would ever do anything that endangered my wife!"

And now it was Liese waiting in the gap to hear how much Paul valued her; to hear the lengths he would go to in order to protect his only child.

Nothing came.

He neglected you.

Liese folded her hands to stop them from shaking as Otto's words crashed back. Couldn't the same be said of her father? Paul wasn't as cut off as Grandpa Nathan; Margarethe mattered to him as much as the business, possibly more. But did *she*? If she weren't his heir, would he see her at all?

Liese spread her hands out again, stared at the veins tracing across them. Were blood ties that could prove dangerous, and the bricks of a fashion house, all that bound her to this thing she called family? She was still pushing at that thought as Otto's voice replaced Paul's.

"Then prove it. Take me seriously this time and sell."

His anger had slipped under a weariness that sounded like it pulled from his bones.

"I know how successful we are, how valuable we still seem to be. But that won't last, for all your hoping. This isn't 1933: one day of boycotting Jewish shops and a pile of shattered windows while the Party showed who was boss. This is the start of a purge and it's controlled, it's organized. Go to Hertie and you'll smell it. *Hertie.* How I hate that name. The Tietz brothers were trampled over so fast, they didn't see the takeover coming. What more proof do you want than that? It's like a fire spreading from building to building. Do you know what the driver told me today—and isn't that a warning, that we get our news now from drivers?—Georg Wertheim can't set foot in his own stores: if he tries, he'll be arrested. They swapped the board out under his nose and no one can argue because, according to the new logic, as a Jew he had no right to be there in the first place. That's the new reality, Paul; that's our new world. Jews don't get to be anything anymore, except Jews."

Liese was beginning to understand where Michael got his passion from: if she closed her eyes, it could have been either of them in the office shouting.

"And they're good at this, don't forget that. They know how to turn the truth on its head and make their stories stick."

Suddenly, Otto laughed. The sound was so filled with bitterness, so unlike his usual rich bellow, Liese flinched.

"The truth of how we became the kings of German fashion has all been washed away. It doesn't matter now that clothing was the one trade we were allowed to work in, or that we learned our skills from the bottom up, grubbing a living restitching the dirty rags *good Germans* wouldn't touch. That's not the story anymore. Jews made it to the top because we stole; because we're swindlers and cheats. So now they're going to take it all out of our hands and let *good Germans* prosper. Another year and we'll be gone—from the department stores, the tailoring houses, the fabric suppliers, and the fashion houses. They'll disinherit us properly—make no mistake about that. They'll invent a law to legitimize our destruction. And they won't stop. Not until the German fashion industry is cleaned up and *pure*."

His voice suddenly dropped so low, Liese had to crane to hear it.

"Paul, I'm begging you. If you sell now, we could leave. We could start again somewhere else. Paris or London. Or America: they're crying out there for designers. Wherever you want, I can fix it, like you've always trusted me to do. But sell. If you don't, one morning very soon, that choice will be gone."

Sell.

The word broke through the emotions fighting for space in Liese's head. She so wanted Otto to be wrong, for "we're different" to be right, except Bruckner's contempt had cracked that lie open. But to sell, to leave Berlin, not to be Haus Elfmann anymore. The salon was the one thing that gave them a shape; her role there was the one thing that gave her a future beyond the too-narrow path of marriage and motherhood her social position expected. Liese couldn't remember a day that wasn't governed by the needs of the business; she didn't want to. To sell was unthinkable. To sell was impossible. And yet...To have it all taken. To be designated as one of the twisted creatures in *Der Stürmer*. To be banned from every part of her life. To be reclassified like that was as impossible to imagine as not being Haus Elfmann. Except that it wasn't.

Liese gripped the doorjamb as the world shifted round her. Michael's words swirled back: *there's no such thing as this kind or that.* She closed her eyes as tight as a child wishing for Christmas and willed her father to hear the world changing.

"No."

Paul's answer was too quick, too easy. It pushed Liese through the door and into the office. Neither man noticed her; they were too busy squaring up.

"Things are difficult, I'll grant you that, but I refuse to believe we'll fall victim to this hysterical nonsense. Hitler will calm down; we just need to be loyal and wait out his excesses. You've had a difficult meeting and your nerve has gone, or maybe the strain of Michael's behavior is starting to tell on you. Perhaps you need a holiday."

Paul's patronizing tone had bunched Otto's hands into fists and turned his back rigid. Liese waited for her father to notice his friend's distress and soften. He didn't.

"Haus Elfmann is my life, Otto. I thought it was yours. My father, who you seem to have such little regard for, built this business from a tailor's shop. I am not going to dismantle it and run away because a few store owners are in trouble. Perhaps the

Tietz and Wertheim stores were riddled with irregularities, did you think about that? If so, fine. Let the Party bring in their bureaucrats and their moneymen. Anyone can run a store. What we do is special: we create dreams; we transform lives. That's not a job for uniformed pen-pushers. So tastes are changing? Isn't that the nature of fashion? If they want loose waists and drab colors, we'll make them a line. And we'll carry on with the rest. There will always be women like Frau Goebbels who want life's finer things. I'll talk to her. Get her to talk to him. This will blow over. The Elfmann name is irreplaceable; it is Berlin at its finest. Spook yourself as much as you like: I'm not going to sell."

"Then you're making a mistake."

Liese's voice rang out so loud, both Otto and Paul jumped.

"Liese, I told you to wait outside. This is not your argument."

"I'm what?" Paul moved slowly round the desk, brushing away Otto's flapping hands.

Liese focused on the satin-striped wallpaper rather than her father's narrowed eyes and held her ground. "You're making a mistake, Papa, and you have to listen. Otto is right. Things aren't just difficult; they're falling apart. If we don't do something, as unimaginable as it sounds, we'll lose everything. I was there today, at the store. It was horrible. Bruckner hates us."

"Does he? And that matters to me why?" Paul's voice was like velvet, his eyes like a panther's.

Part of Liese wanted to move away from him; to apologize and be his dutiful little girl again. When she didn't, Paul's voice took on a sneering edge that knotted her stomach.

"Oh, I see where this is going. You think the views of a *shop manager* matter more than mine. You think because a clerk says jump that Paul Elfmann should jump. Are you a communist now? Is that it? Has Michael recruited you for his little gang? Do you want to see everything I've worked for taken away and redistributed to the *masses*?"

"No, of course not!"

Liese gathered herself up, determined not to be silenced.

"I love the salon as much as you do. It's my whole life, as much as it is yours. I don't want to lose it—the thought terrifies me. But you keep saying we're different and I'm not so sure anymore that we are. We're Jews, Papa. Whether you agree with that or not, it's what the Party says we are. We have to face what that means."

You have to face what that means. You have to be my father, do the right thing, and protect us.

She didn't have the language to explain that to him. When he shook his head and sighed, she knew it wouldn't matter if she had.

"To think I had such hopes for you, that I was growing proud of you. Maybe it's time I looked for a successor with a bit of backbone, who won't panic at the first whisper of a problem and let me down."

The first whisper of a problem? Was he truly so deluded?

"When have I ever let you down? Who could have worked harder to learn from you than me? I'm not the one at fault here—"

"Leave it, Liese. I know you mean well, but this doesn't help."

"But I can't stay silent, I can't do nothing. This is my future too..."

But Otto's hand was on her elbow and she was out in the hall before she could find the right argument.

"He wouldn't listen then."

Michael. He must have come into the building while she was fighting her father.

Liese pressed against the door, holding it ajar, and waved him away.

"I don't need another one of your sermons."

Instead of leaving, he slipped in beside her. "What's happened?"

Part of her wanted to chase him away; part of her needed the old Michael. He was, after all, one of the Haus Elfmann family: surely if anyone could understand the shock of this, it was him?

She turned round to face him, so she was sure he was listening. Maybe if she were honest and didn't take up a position, or let him get angry and take up an opposing one, they could find a way through this together.

"It was awful today. At Hertie. They won't deal with us. Their new man treated us like we were worthless. And then, on the way home, it was as if I'd never looked properly at the streets before. I don't think we're different anymore, Michael; I was foolish to ever say it. And I don't think we're safe. Uncle Otto tried to tell Father that and I tried to tell him and, no, he won't listen. I don't know what it is, if it's arrogance or some blind faith in Haus Elfmann's standing. I don't think even your father knows what to do."

She paused, remembering the ease with which Bruckner had insulted them.

"It's going to get worse, isn't it? Father is wrong: no Jew is safe, are they—no matter what they've achieved? No matter how loyal they feel to Germany?"

Michael shook his head.

"Then is Otto right, should we leave?"

"It's one option. Starting up somewhere else. But Paul will have to move fast because that window is closing. Applications to emigrate are getting harder and more complicated and the cost is escalating."

"You said that's one option. What are the others?"

"You could join us and fight back. Or do nothing, like your father wants, and pretend nothing will come."

Liese rubbed her forehead, where a headache was gathering.

"You make it sound like we've got choices, but not one pathway you've offered guarantees that the salon—or we—will be safe. Tell me there's another one that does."

Behind the door, Otto was still pleading for Paul to see sense.

Michael slipped an arm round Liese's shoulders. She already knew he had nothing to say.

CHAPTER FOUR

Karen

Aldershot, August 1976

Frimley base, training cadets 9 a.m.–6 p.m. Mess dinner (Aldershot) 7–10 p.m. Mrs. Hubbard available from 1:30 p.m. if required.

Karen crumpled the note and threw it into the bin. Why did he keep doing this? Writing these ridiculous notes, providing a schedule of his whereabouts, as if she couldn't guess where he was. It was not as if his days varied. It was not as if she cared.

Have a lovely day, Karen darling. I've left you £5: go shopping; treat yourself.

That would be a nice change.

Perhaps she should write back, treat him to her day: bed till whenever; lazing around till it's time to serve chips and get leered at; smoking; playing Thin Lizzy full blast with the windows wide open. That might give him enough insight into her life to leave her alone.

And what was this "Mrs. Hubbard is available"? Why on earth did he think that was news? She was always available, always sticking her nose in. And this idea that Karen still spent her summer holidays with their neighbor: didn't he know that she'd finished with that charade long ago? Sixteen was surely the worst age to be. Still treated like a child. Still two more years before she could go to university and get out.

She turned to where the kitchen table was set and waiting, as it was every morning: the cutlery neatly aligned, the rose-and-ribbon-patterned bowl paired with its matching cup and saucer.

He tries—you could give him credit for that.

Another thing that never changed: when her conscience pricked about her father, it did it in her mother's voice. Karen had stopped wondering why long ago; she preferred to focus her efforts on ignoring it.

She was starving though: last night's lumpy mash and charred sausages hadn't been one of her best culinary efforts. Ignoring the waiting box of Weetabix, Karen jammed two slices of bread into the toaster. He had left orange juice out as well, the chilled jug and matching glass covered by a cloth. She ignored those too and tipped coffee granules into a mug.

Breakfast made to her liking, she stuck a packet of cigarettes in her jeans' pocket and went out into the garden.

It was barely ten o'clock and the air was already too warm. Forty days without rain, a dozen with the mercury climbing over eighty-five degrees; the forecasters unable to promise any change coming. The country was heatwave-obsessed, the spreading drought the only conversation.

Karen blew a series of smoke rings over the lifeless grass. It was so crisp one careless match and it would crackle like a bonfire. *That would be something to fill up the day with.*

If she blew really hard, maybe she could summon up a wind, dance the fire down the lane, red and fat and greedy enough to swallow the school—with any luck, the base.

And then he'd move you somewhere else and you'd lose the last cobwebbed trace of her.

Karen stubbed out her cigarette and fed the ends of her toast to a dusty sparrow, trying to ignore the itch in her eyes. "*Don't cry. It won't bring her back.*" That was good advice apparently—it was certainly all she had ever been given—but sometimes the tears punched like a boxer.

She doesn't deserve them. Karen blinked the garden back into focus. *She left. If she were here, I'd be happy.*

She hated that voice, the one that was definitely all hers, that crept in more and more often and made her feel like a traitor. It was the same voice that pointed out mothers and daughters shopping together, giggling over coffee cups and standing in cinema queues. That made her want to howl for a hug like a four-year-old.

Karen lit another cigarette, put it out, went into the kitchen for more coffee, came back out empty-handed, and didn't know whether to sit or stand or scream. Inside the house, the hall clock struck ten-thirty. How could the day be creeping by so slowly? How could she bear another one that limped along with only her thoughts to fill it?

Karen dropped back into the deckchair and wandered listlessly through her day. She had a waitressing shift at the Wimpy in the precinct, but that didn't start until five. She could go to the pool and swim her mind blank. Except the heat would have already filled up its pools like human soup and the happy families milling there would make her teeth grind. Normally, she would have called Angela, her closest friend and the only one who would put up with this prickly mood, but she was out of contact for at least another week, waltzed off by her parents for a fortnight at the beach they had been too awkward to invite Karen to join.

New school, new faces; new girls who didn't think she was the odd one. A brand-new start and a big circle of friends. That hadn't exactly worked out to plan.

Her first day at secondary school five long years ago flew back so vividly, Karen could almost see her eleven-year-old self outlined in the kitchen doorway. Blazer too big, skirt too long. Hoping so hard that things would get better, it hurt.

*

Army kids. Karen had walked down the lane on that blue September morning picking them out. They were easy to spot. Always in groups, always loud, throwing out their shared impenetrable slang to keep away the unwanted. Even the new year's intake, with uniforms as oversized as Karen's, carried a confidence she couldn't conjure.

As they converged on the school gates, older girls swarmed, sucking up the new members of their tribe. Karen had hovered on the edges of the playground, trying to match names to the few faces she recognized, wishing with every crossed finger they wouldn't recognize her. She knew no one else from her junior school who had got a place at Aldershot County; she had forgotten, however, that there would be girls from the Aldershot army base. Girls she had encountered on her scattered visits there, who found her secluded life in the village, and her too-shy mother, peculiar. Who sniggered at Karen's babyish clothes, as if, at eleven, their flared trousers and checked shirts had made them the height of sophistication.

To her relief, none of them spoke to her as the classes were called into line. For the rest of the morning, Karen scurried where she was told, clutching her timetable with its confusion of teachers and rooms, happy to be a very small part of the herd. By lunchtime, she hadn't got lost, she hadn't stood out. She had found bodies to tag along with; she had swapped names and shared smiles. The day seemed survivable. Then she went into the playground and the nudges began.

The one who swaggered over, her cronies formed up in a block a pace behind, was square-cut and narrow-eyed and far too certain of her standing. She barrelled across the playground, thumping to a stop toe to toe with Karen, swamping them both in the heavy scent of sugared oranges that most of the girls in the school seemed to be doused in. What was it someone had said the perfume was called? Aqua Manda? Whatever the name, breathed in at such close quarters, the smell made Karen's eyes sting.

She wrinkled her nose in an unconscious imitation of her mother; her opponent's eyes narrowed.

"Why did she do it?"

"Who? What?"

Karen's interrogator tapped her finger to her head, much to her pack's delight. "Your mother, stupid. Why did she do herself in?"

Mouths dropped; Karen's new allies shuffled back. No one would meet her eye.

"Come on, slowcoach: speed up and catch me. It was your mother, wasn't it? Who killed herself in the summer? Who was found dumped on the beach down by Brighton like a load of wet washing?"

Nothing made sense, and all of it did. Karen wanted to clamp her hands over her ears and run, but she sensed that would only lead to a chase. Despite her wobbling knees, she stood her ground.

"You don't know what you're talking about. It was an accident."

The girl's throaty cackle turned a teacher's head. "What, she accidentally went swimming with her clothes on? Well that's a different take: she didn't kill herself then; she was just a nutter."

The scream brought the teacher running, but not before Karen had left dripping scarlet tracks across the girl's fleshy face and a bruise already blooming.

She was still kicking when they dragged her to the Headmistress's office. She was still refusing to speak when her father arrived, covered in apologies.

Their hushed conversation circled. *Perhaps it's too soon; she needs more time at home. No, she needs routine and structure. This type of behavior won't happen again.*

It wasn't until Father marched Karen to the car that she finally found her own voice.

"Is it true? Is it true? Did Mummy not drown by accident like you said? Did she kill herself?"

Over and over, until he slammed on the brakes.

"Stop it! I won't have this hysteria. Your mother died, isn't that enough?"

"No! No, it's not. Tell me the truth. Tell me she didn't do it on purpose."

Her father had pushed her grabbing hands away with a force that left her breathless.

"Not when you're like this. Not when you're yelling. You're too old to be so out of control. Why must you be so selfish? Why can't you be quiet? Why can't you be good?"

The same words he'd hurled at her in the street in Brighton, when she'd shouted at him for being dull and old and no fun at all. When her mother had stopped pointing out how prettily the sun shone on the water and started one of her headaches. The day before the world tipped over.

Karen shrank back in her seat.

They had driven the rest of the way home in silence. Karen had gone straight to her room, without making a fuss, without being asked. She had waited for him to come and offer an explanation that would wipe away the dull thud of *she did what that girl said and it was my fault she did it* that filled up her head. He never appeared.

The next morning, Mrs. Hubbard was in the kitchen making breakfast, refusing to be drawn into conversation, pushing her out the door to school.

When Karen stumbled through the gates, a circle widened round her that only Angela had crossed.

"My mother takes pills to stop her crying."

They had built a friendship out of that, a friendship that had gradually drawn others in. The quiet girls, the studious ones. Not the most popular group in the school perhaps, but enough to give Karen a vague sense of belonging.

*

A bee buzzed too close. Karen roused herself. The sun's glare was so bright the garden had vanished.

She blundered back inside, but the house was no cooler. The heat wormed through everything, clinging to the faded curtains, crawling round the carpet's flattened pile. Five years ago, when Father had suggested moving, Karen had screamed herself sick. Now, she couldn't wait to be gone. But not with him. Not anywhere with him.

Karen had picked over every inch of her childhood until it gaped like a wound. No matter how deep she dug into its silences, the conclusion was the same: her mother's death was her fault, she was certain of it. Mother had been gentle. Karen had been noisy and difficult. Not grateful; not perfect. She hadn't been the kind of daughter her mother could properly love, or she would still be alive. Mothers stayed with their children whatever happened—everyone knew that. So Karen hadn't been what her mother had wanted, but she had tried. She had let her mother walk her to school every day, holding her hand although Karen hated looking so childish. She had learned not to complain about the canceled birthday parties and the trips out that the headache days ruined. She had stayed quiet even when the quiet made her want to scream. So it was definitely her fault, but it was Father's fault too. On good days, she could make it Father's fault more.

Karen had loved her mother, her father hadn't. The more Karen pulled at the past, the more convinced she was of that. She remembered bringing home glitter-thick cards and shakily drawn pictures that made her mother smile. She remembered sitting on her mother's knee and not being chased away for "being too big now, Karen," the way her father had reacted when she had tried the same with him. She had kept trying to be what was wanted, even if she had got it all wrong. Her father's efforts hadn't come close.

He had been the one who made Mother cry, trying to drag her to dinners and dances and keeping her up in the kitchen night after night, talking and talking when she was clearly exhausted. He had been the one telling her over and over that she had to "buck up and get better."

Karen hadn't been good enough, but neither had Father. Which Karen considered was hardly surprising. He was cold and stiff and stern. God knows why her mother had married him, or how she had lived with him. Well, Karen couldn't, and Karen wouldn't. Two more years—not so long really—only two and then she would be gone, to a university as far away as she could get.

The heat was closing the walls in. She went to open a window, before she remembered she couldn't. Her mother had painted all the downstairs ones shut. It was such an odd thing to do, but, as Karen suddenly remembered, Father hadn't tried to dissuade her. "Whatever helps, sweetheart; whatever helps." Karen stopped that thought in its tracks: it cast him in a kind light she wasn't in any mood to consider.

Maybe upstairs would be cooler.

The window in her bedroom opened right out. She could set up her easel and work on some sketches to add to her portfolio.

Karen filled a jug with water and ice cubes that immediately began melting and headed up the stairs. Halfway along the landing, she paused. Father must have been in a rush that morning: he had left his bedroom door open. Karen hovered in the doorway. She couldn't remember the last time she'd seen inside. In the days after Mother had died when no one was really watching her perhaps, but certainly not since.

The brightly covered cushions were gone from the armchair; the bed was made with precision corners. The hairbrush on the dressing table was ruled into place. There wasn't a speck of dust, or any sign of a personality: the room could have jumped from a recruiting poster. Its military sparseness filled Karen with gloom.

She was about to turn away when a memory grabbed at her: Mother's jewelry box. It used to sit on the dressing table over by the window. When Karen was little, her mother would let her sort through its trays and emerald-lined drawers. She remembered holding earrings up to her face, twisting her head so the colored chips glittered back from the mirror. Wrapping herself in the necklaces and bracelets and holding up her arms as if she were dancing. Loving all the pretty pieces that her mother never wore.

The heat was dredging up strange thoughts; she couldn't have remembered that right.

Forgetting about her portfolio, Karen crossed to the dressing table and ran her fingers over the red-tinted wood.

Every Christmas and birthday without fail, Father had bought Mother something new. And she wore whatever it was for a day and then away it went, into the box.

Karen sat down on the padded seat, images whirling faster than she could corral them. Father was always so eager when Mother unwrapped the ribbon-tied packages; he always looked so pleased when she smiled. What was it he had said? *Did I get it right this time? Does it make you happy?*

Karen couldn't remember what her mother had answered and why no one had ever mentioned it when the pieces went unworn. Or asked why she had packed them all away and ignored them, even though she must have known it would hurt him. More unanswerable questions.

Where was the box now? Karen stared at the stripped-out room as rage roared through her. What had he done with it? Had he cleared it away like everything else?

Anger was far easier to embrace than confusion, far easier to act on.

She wrenched the top drawer open. There was nothing in it but tidily rolled socks.

Without a care for the mess, she tore through the dresser, tipping out its contents. The drawers tumbled onto the floor, revealing nothing but him. Fueled by a fury she refused to push down, Karen moved on to the wardrobe. Jackets and suits formed up in rows as neat as a regiment. She shoved them aside, dug into the corners. Even if the box were gone, surely there would be one thing he had overlooked, one tiny memento. Still nothing.

Karen stepped back, rumpled and sweating. There was only one place left: the long shelf above the wardrobe's hanging rail.

She grabbed the stool from the dressing table and clambered up, sending hats and scarves spinning. Stretch and stretch and there it was—the jewelry box. Buried at the back, almost out of reach. Karen hooked it out and jumped down.

Throwing herself onto the floor, she opened the inlaid lid. The treasures she remembered were all safely there.

Karen forced herself to slow her breathing and steady her hands, frightened she might break something. She lifted the earring tray out first and ran her fingers over the chains and pendants curled in their compartments below it. Then, as carefully as if she were handling blown eggshells at Easter, Karen lifted the jewelry out piece by piece. She took her time, holding each one up to the light and pressing the metal to her skin, convinced a shiver of perfume still whispered through them.

When she had cradled each one, she laid it on the carpet with its companions, so they formed a circle round her, arranging them by color until there was only one piece left. A heavy oval locket with an E—for her mother's name, Elizabeth—engraved on its lid.

Karen picked it up, but the clasp was caught on the felt lining. As she tugged, a piece of the thin material pulled away at the corner. There was something underneath which looked like the edge of a piece of paper. Expecting a receipt, or a list of the box's contents knowing how Father liked order, Karen teased it out. It was tightly folded, slightly yellowing, and so thin the center tore slightly when she smoothed it out. *Heiratsurkunde* was typed in black script across the top. Karen had no idea what it, or any of the faded words underneath, meant.

She held the flimsy sheet up to the light. There was a signature at the bottom and a date, April 18, 1947, together with a stamp containing what looked like a bear and the inscription *Die Stadt Berlin.* She could also make out what seemed to be addresses. One had vanished down to *Rathaus*, but the other was clearer: *Lindenkirche, Homburger Straße.* And there in the middle, printed in a darker ink that had weathered the years, were two names: *Andrew Cartwright, Corporal, British Royal Military Police; Liese Elfmann, Schneiderin, Haus Herber.*

Karen read them again, but the names didn't change. Had her father been married before he married her mother, and to a German girl? It wasn't impossible that he had been in Germany: his regiment still had troops there, as far as she knew, and, although it was never discussed, Karen knew he had fought in the war. It wasn't hard to picture him stationed in Berlin, or involved in the fighting there. But married to someone else? That was far more of a challenge.

Karen put the paper carefully down and returned to the box. One tug and the rest of the lining gave way.

This time, the document was thicker and blue and she knew exactly what it was. A British passport. Dated 1947—the same as the yellowing paper. It was made out in a neatly printed hand to a Mrs. Liese Cartwright. When Karen fumbled it open, her mother stared back.

"Who is she?"

Karen snapped on the hall light as the front door opened. Her father jumped.

"Why are you still up? It's gone eleven o'clock."

She didn't move from the bottom stair where she had been sitting for what felt like hours. She wasn't certain she could.

"Who is she? I mean, I've seen the picture, so I know she's my mother, but the rest—the name on the passport and this thing— makes no sense." She dangled the onionskin-thin certificate and the passport with the tips of her fingers, keeping them just out of his reach.

"What the hell..." He stepped forward. "Give them to me." The hand he stretched out toward the documents was shaking.

He's afraid. He's acting like he's in charge, but he's afraid.

The knowledge gave her courage, kept her voice steadier than she had thought she would manage.

"Who was she? My mother, I mean. What was her name? It can't be the two here. Liese Elfmann makes no sense and neither does Liese Cartwright. My mother's name was Elizabeth."

And there he was, back again. Chest all puffed up as if he were on parade. Addressing her as if she were one of his rawest cadets.

"Karen, I don't know what nonsense you are imagining, but this is neither the time nor the place. Those things do not concern you; you had no right to take them and I won't tolerate such behavior in my house."

It might have worked if he hadn't been so obviously sweating. If she hadn't heard that pompous tone so often that she was numb to it.

"What are you going to do? Put me on a charge?"

She stood up so that they were more equally balanced and thrust the flimsy paper toward him, although she still kept it just out of reach.

"This thing is German, isn't it? I'm guessing it's a marriage certificate. I've been puzzling over it for hours, wondering if you might have been married before. That seemed the most logical explanation. But how to explain the passport with Mother's picture and this new name on it? Can you help me with that? Is this certificate actually yours and my mother's? Can you explain how that can possibly make sense?" She stopped, gave him a moment to answer, and then whipped it away when he stared blankly back. "Or, you know what, don't bother. I'll take it to the library and find a dictionary. Or, better still, I'll take it to the Head of Languages at school and get her to translate it."

That snapped him back.

"Why do you always go for the most extreme option? Why must you turn everything into a fight?"

He was blustering, turning red; Karen could have picked his next words for him.

"You're hysterical. I won't discuss anything when you're like this."

"That old favorite, what a surprise. But I'm not though, am I? I'm perfectly calm and I'm not letting this go. I know you prefer to hide behind silence, but, this time, that's not happening."

She didn't expect him to rise to the challenge. She thought he'd stay tight-lipped and send her to bed, buy himself some time to find a plausible explanation that he would lay out in precisely clipped tones in the morning. His tumbling words dropped her back down onto the stairs.

"All right, yes, it's a wedding certificate and, yes, it is mine and your mother's. And the reason you don't recognize the name is because your mother wasn't English; she was German. She came from Berlin."

All the fight Karen had been so carefully nurturing drained away.

"That can't be true. That's ridiculous."

She waited; so did he. Now she was the one blustering.

"And, even if by some madness that's right, why didn't I know before now?"

"It never seemed important to tell you."

She stared at the passport photograph while her father stood perfectly still.

"It never seemed important? Really? Are you serious?"

Not a flicker: his shutters had come down.

"This name then, that's on here…Liese…was that hers?"

"Originally, yes.

"But why did she change it?"

His hands were behind his back; his voice had dropped to a monotone.

"When she first came to England, that seemed the best thing to do. Elizabeth was a simpler name to use after the war, a more obviously English one. A German name wouldn't have been a kindness."

Karen stared at the documents she was still clutching, trying to understand how his words could be at once both completely logical and completely unbelievable.

"I don't understand. How could she be German? She never sounded German." And then a memory popped up and took on a new meaning. "She had a lilt in her voice sometimes. I always thought it was so pretty. Are you saying that was an accent? And there were times when she used to stumble on a word, I remember that too, or she would go round in circles until I found her the one she was looking for. I thought it was because she was tired."

"Sometimes it was. Your mother had lost most of her accent by the time you were born. She had learned English as a child and, later, she worked hard at smoothing out her voice."

Karen leaned into the banister as the world began spinning.

"Why did I never question any of that?"

When she looked up, she could see his face had softened. For a moment, she thought he might move toward her, that he might reach for her hand. She thought she might let him hold it if he did. But he stayed where he was.

"You wouldn't have, not then: you were a child; she was your mother. How she sounded to you was, well, how she was."

How can he be so removed? Why can't he see what this is doing to me?

Her anger began rising again. Karen let it come.

"What about in 1947, when the passport is dated? She must have sounded more German then."

This time, her father shifted slightly, although his voice held.

"It was more noticeable, yes. And people weren't always kind. That was why she worked so hard on her voice...and didn't really mix much. I'm not sure what else I can tell you."

He's trying to close me down. He's trying to wriggle away like he always does.

Karen straightened herself. She folded the papers up and wiped her hands on her jeans.

"*She didn't really mix much*. Well, that's true. She didn't have any friends, did she? Why was that? Was it because she was ashamed of where she came from? I've wondered about this before, not that I've ever bothered to ask you. Well, maybe now you can help me. Maybe you can explain why my mother, who was beautiful and gentle and should have been popular, was always alone. Do you fancy giving that a go?"

His hands rammed into his pockets.

Karen's stomach muscles clenched so tight, her voice turned into a growl.

"She came to school with me every day, but she never mixed with the other mothers. When her customers brought their patterns and their alterations, she barely asked them in—she always hurried them away. She said she could tell someone's size by looking, but that wasn't the point, was it? Was she afraid of what people would say, of how they would treat her, even after so many years? Was being German still a sin so long after the war?"

Her father stepped away, his feet shuffling as if one more question would push him back through the door.

"No, that's not it, not exactly. She was shy and she didn't like army life, that's all. She wasn't comfortable around soldiers." He blushed as Karen gaped, something she had never seen him do before. "I'm sorry, I know that sounds strange..."

His voice was shaking. He had his hands out now, as if he finally intended to hold her. Karen pressed herself against the wall and away.

"She didn't like army life or soldiers? Am I being thick here, or isn't that quite a big thing? When you've married one, I mean, and you live next to a base. If she felt like that, why did she marry you? And if you knew that the life she would have to live here would make her unhappy, why did you bring her?"

She left him a pause to reply, but he simply stared at her.

She charged on. "Was it because you made her? Is that why she never talked about her family? Why there's no photos? Because you dragged her here, away from them. I bet they didn't approve; I bet that was it. You were a British soldier bringing her to a country where she couldn't be a German, and to an army town when she hated the army. They can't have wanted that. So was it some weird control thing? I've heard about that, about men who do that. Didn't she love you enough? Did you need her to be on her own, isolated in a strange country, so she'd stay with you? Is that why she ended up killing herself?"

She stopped, panting for breath, her throat raw. The tear-filled *help me* she wanted him to hear impossible to voice, the pain she was in too all-consuming to move past.

Her father was staring at her, not moving, his mouth open and useless. There was such shock on his face, and such sorrow, Karen thought for a moment he might have glimpsed below her anger and seen her need. And then he roared and she knew he hadn't seen her at all.

"Be quiet! Who do you think you are, questioning me like this? What do you think you know about life? All these theories, they're nonsense; they're utterly ridiculous. You're meddling in matters that are nothing to do with you and I won't have it. What your mother was, what our marriage was, is none of your business. This rudeness stops right now, young lady. Right now."

Karen wanted a father; she'd got a parade sergeant. She doubled over, winded, a hand pressed to her mouth to hold back the nausea.

"Oh God, Karen, I didn't mean to sound so harsh. I'm—"

He realized he'd gone too far; on some level, Karen knew that. It didn't matter. He wasn't quick enough to repair the fault. Before he could get any more words out, she ripped the gulf threatening between them wide open.

"It was your fault! She killed herself because of you as much as me—more, from the sounds of it. I hate you. I'll never stop hating you. I wish you had died instead of her!"

She threw herself up the stairs and into her bedroom; gave way to sobs that wracked through the house. If she had paused for a second, if she had turned round, she would have seen her father crying as heartbrokenly as her. But she didn't spare him a glance.

CHAPTER FIVE

Liese

Berlin, July–November 1938

Why was she torturing herself like this? What was the point?

It was July, the summer season was in full swing; in any other year, the book would be bursting with fittings. This year, page after page had stayed blank, the few orders recorded there sitting as awkward as ink blots.

Liese flicked through them, as she had done last night and the night before. A day dress for Frau Posen. An evening gown for Frau Kohlmeier. Three more entries that were equally reticent. No jackets trimmed to match the dresses. No coordinating hats and gloves. No beaded capes or chiffon wraps in a week's worth of colors. A handful of orders, all specifying plain cuts and pared-back trimmings. Haus Elfmann's clientele was not simply shrinking, it was afraid to show off any traces of wealth.

She closed the book and switched off the lamp. The accounts were waiting, but she couldn't bear to look at them. Two years ago, even with the loss of the Hertie account, no one at Haus Elfmann had worried about the salon's financial security. Money was there to be spent; there was always plenty more to replace it. Now, those days felt like a lifetime ago. The banks had withdrawn credit in April; their last backer had swiftly offered his regrets. Liese had slashed the wages bill to the bone, but the red numbers kept rising.

She was exhausted from trying to hold the whole house together. She wasn't, admittedly, balancing the weight alone, not entirely. There were a handful of seamstresses still working. There was still Otto. He did his best to keep the wheels turning, but, with Adefa tightening its grip on the industry, he spent more days on trains, criss-crossing the country grubbing for suppliers, than he did in the salon.

As for Paul... Liese rubbed eyes that ached more than an eighteen-year-old's should. His behavior was erratic. One day he would be close-mouthed and secretive, squirreling away money in padded brown envelopes when he thought she wasn't looking. The next, he would be loud and demanding. He was never listening. He was always "too busy" to consider *what now* or to review empty ledgers. He was maddening and exhausting and no help to anyone.

"I'm best used as an ambassador; you and Otto can manage the shop."

He threw the line out like a compliment or a carefully considered decision, refusing to admit he was as frightened of the future as her, refusing to face it. Liese knew all too well that if Paul stood still for a moment, the way the days forced her to, the silence would stick to him.

The salon was running down, wearing out piece by piece like a tired old watch. There was no more hushed chatter in the public rooms, no more shushed babble backstage. The workrooms were frozen. There were no hissing irons, no clattering scissors, no pulleys creaking muslin-shrouded dresses like clouds across the roof. The curtains in the dressing rooms bloomed dust in their pleats; the gilt mirrors in the showroom sprouted tarnished patches like age spots. Memories were all that made up the salon now, as easily pulled out as pins. The canopied front door opened so little its hinges had stiffened. Their last customers sat at home and summoned, turning Liese into a peddler, hawking her patterns and her ribbons through back doors and garden gates.

"I'm not selling."

Paul's repeated refusal continued to ring through the hallways, not that anyone heard. Not that there was anything left to sell, beyond a building and a tattered idea. For all Paul's bravado, and whether he chose to believe it or not, the Party had still ground the Elfmann business to dust.

So they can remove us. So they can lift us out of our lives…

Michael had been proven right and these days was involved with the resistance deeper than ever. Gone with his comrades far more than around, even though Liese needed him, if only to share her fears. She didn't bother him with that anymore: the demands of *the struggle* always won over the whims of fashion, and how could she blame him for making that choice? Liese lived in the same battered reality as Michael: she woke up most days wondering how dresses could possibly matter.

But I have to keep it all going because what else can I do?

She couldn't imagine what a life without the salon meant. As her father's heir, she had expected to live outside the narrow roles that most women of her social position inhabited. She had certainly never yearned after the purely domestic kind of life that the Nazis proclaimed kept women happy: a home, a husband, children—nothing more. And now, even if she had wanted that, the men she had once mixed with had either disappeared or, with her heritage, wouldn't look twice at her.

There is nothing left but the salon, so the salon must keep going.

She told herself that every day to get herself out of bed, to paper over the truth that the salon no longer mattered, that the world she once inhabited had splintered. That every circle her life had overlapped was slipping away. Clientele; workforce; the fashion community whose origins she had never spared a thought for before the Party changed the rules of ownership and belonging.

As Otto had predicted, Hertie's renaming had been only the start. Business after business had been wrenched out of Jewish hands, or been defamed and ruined. New plaques swarmed across stores and salons. Old owners disappeared as legacies that should have endured down the years were plucked away or left to wither. Faces familiar since childhood had vanished overnight, taking their skills to London or to America, or to anywhere religion wasn't the first question asked.

"We could follow. With our reputation, we wouldn't be starting from scratch. Look how well others have done."

Otto had kept pushing; Liese had kept hoping that Paul would listen, although she no longer bothered adding her voice to the argument. Instead, as fashion house after fashion house closed and reopened, all shiny and *German*, and still no one came for Haus Elfmann, Paul took it as proof that the salon was invincible.

"Down they all go and look at us standing."

Some days, Liese wondered if he was going mad.

The clock on the desk struck ten.

She should go home. She was so tired, more tired than she had ever been through the sleepless nights a show demanded. Sitting now, alone in the dark, Liese could have cried for those days and their nail-biting bustle. They were gone. Autumn/Winter 1937 had been the salon's last showcase, although no one knew it until the day itself dawned.

The excitement and the weeks of work had all run on the same. But, this time, invitations went unanswered and no one requested tickets, not even Agnes Gerlach. Helena Stahl didn't tell anyone that.

"I thought it would be all right. This is Haus Elfmann; nobody ignores us."

A reasonable assumption, if it hadn't been for the Party memos suggesting people should.

The showroom stayed empty. The dresses expecting their debut sat unhatched and unwanted in their muslin cocoons. Paul shouted; Otto wrote letters. Neither was heard.

As Berlin's mood stiffened, the Elfmann clients who could choose where they shopped went to rub shoulders with Nazi wives at Romatzki and at Maggy Rouff—Frau Goebbels' new favorite designer. As for the department stores, the German ones had followed Herr Bruckner's lead and abandoned Haus Elfmann; the international ones were nervous of Hitler's posturing and couldn't be relied on to come.

"You're the last fly in the web. They'll swallow you up too—you wait." Helena's parting shot, delivered when Paul blamed her, nastily, for the show's fiasco. He hadn't listened.

She stretched her stiff neck. She should go home, except the emptiness there would be worse than here. Her parents rushed round their nights as much as their days, flitting through the receptions they could still wrangle invitations to, Margarethe dressed in Paul's designs, as if anyone still cared. There was no one waiting for her, no one to share and soften the day.

Liese stopped that thought as it started to spiral. If she began to feel sorry for herself, she would never leave the chair. If she imagined the next day unfolding exactly like this one, she wouldn't have the strength to step into it.

Not home then, but perhaps the workroom. The seamstresses were struggling with the dress Paul had demanded for Margarethe's upcoming birthday dinner. Its design involved flounced cape sleeves with chiffon cascades which needed delicate work and lengths of material their plundered stores could barely stretch to. Solving the most efficient way to create those would take the concentrated work needed to wear her out and buy a few dreamless hours on the sofa.

Liese rubbed her fingers supple again and was about to get up when the door opened.

She shaded her eyes, expecting a light to snap on. Someone entered, but the room stayed dark. The footsteps weren't Paul's fast click or Otto's shuffle. They were soft, deliberate.

Liese pulled up her feet as a figure headed toward the desk.

Drawers slid open; papers rustled. A hand pushed back an unruly flop of hair.

She switched on the lamp.

"What are you doing?"

Michael stared at her like a rabbit a step away from a fox and jumped, dropping one of the envelopes Liese knew was stuffed full with notes. Envelopes she had so far resisted, despite their temptation.

"Are you stealing? Surely not. You can't need money so badly you'd do that. If something's wrong and you're desperate, why wouldn't you just ask?"

Then he turned more fully toward the light and the money and what Michael was or wasn't doing no longer mattered. His face was striped with blood, his left eye swollen and bruised. He didn't seem to hear her gasp; he didn't waste time on an apology.

"I didn't know if you'd listen. And I'm not taking it for me—it's for the resistance. This money will pay for leaflets and the campaign we need to encourage recruits." His defense gathered speed, bristling him with energy, pushing him onto his toes. "We need to get the word to more people that we're here, that we're fighting back. We need to get the workers out of the factories and marching."

Liese was barely listening: she couldn't take her eyes off the damage to his face. She moved round the desk and reached for his purpling cheek.

"What on earth happened to you?"

He brushed her frightened hand away.

"It's nothing. We ran into a patrol. There was a fight. We got away. If we'd had more men, they wouldn't have chased us in the first place. Which is why we need to pull in more members. It's time to mobilize, Liese: we just need one big push to make people understand what Hitler is doing. How he's feeding his war machine while working men go hungry. How Austria is the start, not the end of his plan. How we have to take action and stop him."

He had snapped to attention like a soldier, his one good eye burning bright as a beacon.

The sight of his cuts and bruises throbbed through her. Liese knew Hitler's annexation of Austria the previous March, and the harsh measures taken there against the communists and the Jews, had lit a flame under Michael. She was hardly surprised that his behavior, that his belief that an uprising was possible, had crystallized. She sympathized—how could she not?—but that didn't mean she had to like the danger his actions exposed him to.

"Forget about all that. Have you seen the state you're in? Won't you let me call a doctor?"

He shook his head. "I'm fine." He grabbed the envelope back from the desktop where it had fallen. "I need to get this where it's needed."

He was wild-eyed, barely looking at her. Liese's stomach flipped as she realized the lengths he was prepared to go to.

"You're going to get yourself killed."

Michael grabbed a second envelope and slammed the drawer shut. The casual way he ignored her fear and helped himself, without any thought for who might take the blame for his stealing, suddenly made her see red.

"Didn't you think someone would notice the money's gone? Weren't you worried who might have been blamed? I don't get it, Michael: some seamstress who's barely clinging on as it is could have lost her job. How does that fit with your love-of-the-worker principles?"

Why didn't you trust me enough to ask for my help? Why won't you let me help you now? was what she wanted to say, but her pride wouldn't let her.

Michael stuffed the money in his jacket.

"Don't be so melodramatic. There's plenty left—too much for anyone to notice what I've taken. And your father can spare it; the struggle needs it far more than he does."

That he was right didn't help. Liese was suddenly so weary of it all, so sick of the stupidity. Paul hiding money while he pretended his business, and his country, was healthy. Michael believing a handful of men and some poorly printed leaflets could slow down a Führer who had rolled over Austria without a hand raised in protest. Her, eighteen and thinking she could stop a crumbling fashion house from collapsing, or that it mattered anymore if it did.

I don't want to do this; I'm done.

The realization caught her by the throat. She didn't believe in the business. Not with the passion she once had, not with a passion like his. How could she?

"Take it."

The speed with which his mouth dropped open would have once made her laugh.

"What am I doing? Why am I trying to pretend that dresses are still important? It's a fashion salon—that's not the same as a family, no matter how much I try to kid myself it is. It's going to fall sooner or later. So take it. Fund your campaign and your recruiting. I hope it works, I really do. And I hope you won't get shot."

She stared at the cuts marking his face and shivered at the prospect of worse.

"Have you thought about that, Michael? About getting wounded or killed and what that would do to Otto? Or about how crushed he'd be if he could see you standing here, clutching your spoils like a common thief, rather than doing the honest thing and asking? When the salon crashes, you'll be all he has. Doesn't that matter to you at all?"

His hands twitched; his face flushed. If he had said *yes of course it does*, she would have emptied the drawers and given him everything.

"No. I can't let it. The cause is what matters. Beating the Nazis is what matters. Family is nothing next to that. And if I can see that, even though I know how much my father cares about me, surely, with the parents you've been saddled with, you can see it too."

He held out his hand. Liese stared at him, reeling from his words, wondering if he was asking for more money.

"Come with me."

"What?"

"Come with me, Liese. You're right: none of this matters. We could use your brains and your courage. I've seen you battling to hold this place together. Think what you could achieve if you put that energy to better use."

"I can't…"

It was an automatic response. But she could. Her parents lived in a fantasy world—that didn't mean she had to stay in there with them, feeding their delusions out of a worn-out sense of duty. She could leave with Michael right now—find a life with more meaning.

His hand was still out. She stepped toward it.

"What would I do, if I came?"

"So much! We need people with an eye for detail, who can think ahead and plan. You would be—"

His excitement was cut short by the front door slamming.

"Who's there? Why can I hear raised voices?" Otto barrelled into the office, dropping his bag as he came. "Don't tell me you two are still finding reasons to squabble? What is it this time?"

Liese jumped back from Michael's outstretched hand, scrabbling for an answer before Michael could mention the money or announce she was planning to leave the salon and join the resistance.

"It's nothing. Michael was lecturing; I didn't want to know. The usual stuff."

Otto wasn't listening; he was staring at his son.

"What happened? Who did this to you? Have you been fighting?"

"Of course I've been fighting. What else am I meant to do?"

Michael was still looking at Liese. "Are you coming?"

She wanted to say yes, she really did. But then she looked at Otto, saw how aged and brittle his face seemed when he looked at his son. Her shoulders slumped.

"I can't."

Michael's curse made Otto wince.

Liese tried to grab his arm as he stormed past.

"You don't understand. They need me; I can't pretend I don't know that. I can't let them down."

He shook her off and ran for the door, kicking it shut behind him with a crash that rattled the walls. Otto was left clutching at air.

"What did he mean? Where were you going?"

"Nowhere. It doesn't matter."

Otto dropped into a chair. He looked old and broken and far too vulnerable to be left.

Liese picked up Paul's brandy and poured him a large measure.

"You're exhausted. Sit quietly; never mind Michael for now. Where were you? You've been gone for ages and it's clearly done you no good. I thought this was meant to be a quick trip, Hamburg and back, but you've been gone nearly two weeks."

Otto drained his glass and held it out for a refill.

"There was nothing to be had in Hamburg, so I went to Munich and Stuttgart, and half a dozen towns in between. All of it hopeless. Everywhere is controlled as tightly as Berlin. Every factory and supplier is plastered with Adefa stickers and has a blacklist of Jewish businesses as broad as my arm. I couldn't secure thread or buttons, never mind fabric. We'll have to cast the net wider, maybe to Poland. That might keep us afloat until the French buyer comes."

The French buyer. André Bardou, firmly holding on to his position as Paris's trendsetter. Paul believed Bardou was still loyal and swore he would come in November with his checkbook open. Once, Liese would have been breathless at the merest hint of his arrival, poring over every detail of their brief, flirtatious meetings. Now, she doubted Otto believed in this lifeline any more than she did.

"You'll kill yourself, and to no purpose. Even if André is still allowed to use us, we don't have the bodies, or the funds, to complete a collection. If he comes at all, he can take the unsold stock from last year. Or not. Other than him, we've virtually nothing: five dresses ordered at most. The fabric we have left can do for them."

The question *what next* hung there unanswerable.

"Let me see."

Exhaustion made Liese clumsy. As she reached for the order book, she dislodged a handful of Reichsmarks which had fallen out of the snatched envelopes.

"Has he been stealing from the salon? Tell me the truth."

His voice sounded so hopeless.

Liese bent to scoop up the notes rather than face him.

"No. Of course not. I gave him some money. I thought he might find a better use for it than me wasting it on stock."

Otto sighed. "I know you're covering for him. He's been taking money from me for months, for this fight he's pledged his life to, I presume. I pretend not to notice. If I tackle him, he'll leave and then what chance do I have to protect him?" His voice broke on a sob. "He's going to end up dead. He's a Jew and a communist, and not quiet about either: what does he think is going to happen to him? We haven't seen anything here yet compared to what's coming; the Party still has its gloves on. That won't last, not now they've had a free run in Austria. Attacks, expulsions, mass arrests, and none of it challenged. They're not taking Jewish businesses there—they're taking Jews."

He was crying freely now, without noticing the tears.

"Why wouldn't your father listen to me? Why wouldn't he leave? I should have gone; I should have taken Michael away when he threw in his lot with the KPD, but how could I abandon your father? The pair of them have torn me in two." His face had caved into shadows and bone.

Liese clutched his hand, but there was nothing she could say to soothe him.

"Michael is going to get killed. If I don't do something, if I don't get him out, my boy won't last the year."

*

How many lies did Paul think André could stomach? Liese twisted her napkin under the table as her father batted the Frenchman's questions away.

"Have times been tough since the Führer moved against Austria? For some perhaps, but not Haus Elfmann. You've heard rumors that say otherwise? Our competitors trying to discredit us—you know how this industry works. The last show? Such a triumph, such a shame that you missed it."

On and on he went, piling up his tall tales until Liese was convinced she would suffocate. Otto had stopped trying to intervene, André had grown steadily quieter; Paul gave no sign that he'd noticed either. He'd been deftly not noticing a thing since they'd stepped out of the November chill and into the warmth of the Hotel Adlon. Liese, however, was raw with discomfort.

All the years her family had patronized the hotel, all the money they'd spent, and yet tonight they were invisible, shuttled into a corner, until André came down to the lobby and rescued them.

Liese had blushed when she saw his frown. Paul had greeted him with overdone delight and swept ahead of André into the restaurant as if he were still king of it. The maître d', who had run the restaurant since Liese had needed a high chair, waved them to a table tucked into the shadows. Paul thanked him effusively for respecting their privacy. He laughed away the long wait between courses and pronounced the empty bread basket a good thing for his waistline. Liese couldn't tell whether his performance was brave or deluded. From his increasingly fixed smile, neither, it seemed, could André.

"Perhaps we should order coffee, balance out the wine?"

Otto motioned to another waiter too busy to notice.

"Let me arrange it. They seem rather stretched."

André rose with a bow for Margarethe and a smile for Liese that shivered with promises. He was so ridiculously handsome, with his dark blonde hair and eyes the blue-green of sea glass. And still as enamored with her as she was with him, or so his whispered asides suggested.

Liese watched him walk away, his stride unhurried, his smile for the waiter generous, and momentarily forgot the embarrassments that had come before. Then Paul opened his mouth and reminded her.

"I told you it would work. A good dinner, a cozy chat. We'll have an order out of him before the brandy arrives."

"This is madness—you do know that?"

Paul put down the fork heaped with the chocolate cake he was trying to tempt Margarethe into eating.

"Excuse me?"

Once the icy stare would have stopped her, but Liese was long past being the good little girl trying to please her father. That had ended two years ago in his office.

"Were you listening to yourself? Haus Elfmann is untroubled? The last show was a hit? What show? André's not the fool you're treating him as. He must know we've not had a collection out in a year, that we're barely able to trade anymore."

She expected fury, or at least indignation. Instead, Paul's lower lip disappeared like a child caught out in a fib.

Liese pushed her dessert plate away, her stomach churning. When would her father start living in the same world as the one she was forced to navigate?

"How did you even persuade him to come to Berlin? What lies did you tell him?"

Paul poured another glass of wine before Otto could move the bottle. His face was as red as the lobster he'd guzzled.

"Don't get high-handed with me, Miss—the salon's still mine; you've not pushed me out yet. And there was no *persuading* because there was no need. We exchanged some letters. He mentioned the illness that kept him out of Germany last winter, and the worries over

Austria that kept him away in the spring. He assumed he'd missed our shows. I don't know what news they get in France about the way things are being done here, so I didn't correct him. No persuasion and no lies. I didn't need them. Unlike you, Monsieur Bardou still respects who I am." He not only looked like a child, he sounded like one.

Margarethe slammed down her glass and glared at her daughter.

"Apologize to your father, young lady. I warned him a little responsibility would go to your head and now here's the proof."

A little responsibility. Liese ignored her. Her father's smile was so smug and self-satisfied it was hard not to slap him.

"What did you think would happen when André came? Even if, by some miracle, he doesn't recognize that the dresses we have left are a year or more out of date, he'll see that the salon's deserted. He'll speak to his other clients. You do know he's going to find out the state we're in?"

Paul swatted her away as easily as he'd dismissed André.

"But he won't. Didn't you hear me lay the groundwork? If anyone says anything negative, we'll call it the jealousy I've already mentioned. As for the salon: we can tell him it's being redone and bring the dresses here. You can retrim them and your mother can model them. He'll place an order and then, when I get word to the Party about the valuable international business we're still doing, they'll beg us to begin showing our collections again. I've thought of it all; I didn't even need Otto!"

He bowed to the table and sat back as if he was expecting applause.

Otto stayed focused on his wine glass. Margarethe broke into coos at Paul's cleverness. Liese couldn't think of a single reply. She didn't know whether to be grateful her father had finally, if uselessly, acknowledged the business was in serious trouble or scream at his unshakable bravado.

"I'm sorry to be the bearer of bad tidings, but I think something's wrong."

André's return was such a welcome distraction it was a moment before Liese registered his words, or his frown.

"There seems to be trouble spreading round the city—a riot, from the sound of it—although that is surely unthinkable. Most of the tables appear to be getting the news."

Otto scrambled to his feet, his first thought clearly the same as Liese's. Not unthinkable: Michael and the protest he'd been promising since the summer.

Liese craned round, expecting to see the restaurant emptying, its well-fed diners running in fear of baton-wielding communists. No one had moved. The waiters still circled; people were laughing. She thought she heard a toast celebrating "a lively and long-needed night."

"It can't be that serious. No one looks concerned."

"Then why is Vogel running over as if he's got wheels strapped under him?"

The maître d' was at the table before Liese could find Otto an answer.

"Monsieur Bardou, forgive me, but your guests need to leave."

"Why?" Liese jumped in before André could speak.

Vogel didn't look at her. "There is a disturbance."

"Then surely we're safer staying here? No one else is moving, so I assume that's what you're encouraging the other diners to do?"

This time, Vogel looked straight at Liese. He didn't offer a smile or a more soothing tone. Echoes of Hertie's prickled her spine.

"That isn't possible. Not in your case. I've asked for your car to be brought round to the garage and would suggest you make your way there at once. Monsieur Bardou, as our guest, this difficulty doesn't involve you. You are welcome to stay here, or retire to the lounge, where coffee is waiting." Vogel bowed and was gone before anyone could work out a response.

André stared from one to the other. "I don't understand. Why would he treat you so rudely?"

"Because we're Jewish."

Liese shrugged as André's eyebrows shot up at the bluntness of her answer. She ignored Margarethe's horrified gasp. There was a strange relief in saying the words and nothing to lose by continuing.

"Whatever is going on outside, Herr Vogel is clearly more concerned about the danger to the hotel from us being here than the risks for us if we leave. Welcome to the new Germany, where the Party hates Jews. Which means anyone who wants to stay in with the Party must also hate Jews." She smiled at him as if they were still flirting. "Didn't you guess we weren't the Adlon's favorite guests? This table is barely in the restaurant. If you hadn't made the reservation, I doubt they would have seated us at all."

André flushed. "Well, yes, of course I noticed the change. I've eaten here with your father and Otto countless times; I could hardly miss it. And there's been some disquieting things reported in Paris about the tightening attitudes here."

He turned to Paul.

"But you've been talking all night as if everything were normal. As if all of the takeovers and the missing faces I've asked about were of no concern. I knew your family is Jewish; I said I was worried. You told me, quite clearly, that the new rules didn't matter because Haus Elfmann was different, too important to interfere with."

Liese burst out laughing and couldn't answer when he asked her why.

Vogel looked over. He gesticulated at the door.

"I'll fetch the coats. Inviting trouble by sitting here won't help."

Otto rose heavily from the table. Paul followed him, his arm round a white-faced and indignant Margarethe.

"Let me at least come with you to the garage. Make sure you get safely away."

Liese realized André was still beside her, his hand outstretched to help her up. She let him guide her through the restaurant, grateful for a shield against stares that felt icy.

"None of it was true then, what your father said?"

"No."

Liese tumbled out a potted account of the business's fortunes as they made their way down a staircase that was far dingier than the lobby's gilded sweep.

"You've been managing the whole thing by yourself? You've always been smart, but you've changed since I last saw you—you've grown much more confident. It suits you."

She glanced up at him. That smile that crinkled his eyes—it melted her every time.

The stairwell was so narrow it was hardly surprising to find him pressed close as they navigated its turns. Despite her brave words, she was shaken by Vogel's complete disinterest in their safety. It was a comfort to find André's hand on her shoulder, his arm round her waist. And when he stopped, when he tilted her chin and kissed her...she thought she knew his kisses by now, but this one was different. The ones before were butterfly whispers that had made her feel giddy. This one encircled her, reached down inside her, demanded another she was more than happy to sink into. His hands were urgent, the wall against her back cold as ice. She could have let the Adlon slide away completely, but then Paul's pleading voice crawled up the stairs and shattered the spell.

"He won't drive us. It's quite ridiculous."

When they reached the basement, both her parents were bristling.

"I keep trying to explain that I can't!" Stefan, their chauffeur, was tight-faced and struggling to stay patient. "The streets are covered in broken glass—the tires would be shredded in minutes. It's not an excuse. I've been out there: it's frightening."

"So what André heard in the restaurant was right: it is a riot?"

André's hand whispered round Liese's back, his fingers falling light as thistledown against her bare skin. She forced herself to concentrate as the driver answered her.

"No. I don't think you'd call it that…" Stefan hesitated. "A riot suggests something unplanned and chaotic. Whatever this is, it's very well organized. Word has it, there's shops smashed and looted all over the city, but it's the Brownshirts and the youth brigades causing the damage, not undisciplined mobs."

"Do the attacks seem random, or specific?"

The cavernous garage almost swallowed Otto's voice.

Stefan's face fell. "I can't be certain; I only saw a handful of streets. But, if what I heard is true, they are very specific. It's only Jewish businesses that have been targeted. Apparently, there's stars and vicious slogans painted everywhere, some of them on windows that haven't been broken yet, as if the paint is a sign of which ones to attack. And there are synagogues on fire all across the city. The one I passed had firemen beside it, but they were hosing the other buildings down, not bothering with the one that was burning."

Margarethe began to shake. Liese instinctively stretched out a calming hand, but Paul was already there.

Stefan continued, quickening his telling as though he wanted it over with.

"It's not just the SA thugs out there on their own; the Security Police are on the streets too. There's rumors of mass arrests, of Jewish houses smashed into and the owners snatched. So, you see, I can't take you home, even if we could find a way round the broken glass. I don't think you'd be safe there."

"We can't stay here."

Paul's voice was even thinner than Otto's. He was right: the garage was freezing and too open to the street to feel safe.

André whispered to Stefan, who reluctantly led him outside. When the two men returned, André was trembling.

"He's right—the streets are dangerous. You can't risk it and there's no point appealing to the hotel again. I have a suite. There is space for all of you in it. If we use the back stairs, no one will bother us."

André rallied. Liese could almost see the mental shake he gave himself.

"This must be a misunderstanding. Yes, there is trouble, but I can't believe it's as targeted as you think. Things looking brighter in the morning is a cliché for a reason."

No one had the energy to argue.

They trooped after him, grateful to have been spared a treacherous journey home. When they reached André's rooms, Liese went straight to the window. It was late, long past midnight, but the sky held the orange tinge of a sunset and its blackness had an uneven texture, like dye that had spilled onto bunched fabric and gathered in patches. She pushed open the pane and tasted smoke in the air, wood-filled and musty. A sudden vision caught at her, of Michael up to his neck in the fighting, and she shivered.

"Close it. Come away."

André had produced glasses and whisky.

Liese held the drink but couldn't swallow it: the oily liquid smelled like the sky.

André smiled round the room as if he were hosting a cocktail party.

"Well, at least you're all safe now and can get a good night's sleep. There's nothing to be done till tomorrow. There's a radio in the corner—why don't I find some music? It might help us all relax."

No one spoke as André fiddled with the dial, flipping backward and forward between stations offering the same bland diet of folk songs or military marches. No one complained when he gave up.

The room split itself into camps. Paul and Margarethe, having already claimed the main bedroom for the night, curled onto the largest sofa and began whispering to each other. Stefan, clearly awkward at sharing such an intimate space with his employers, found a chair in one of the shadowy corners. Otto prowled the room, fussing at the window, sitting down and getting up again until Liese began to feel dizzy.

"Come over here."

André was sitting in an overstuffed armchair he was pretending was big enough for two. Liese hesitated, glancing first at her parents. They were far too wrapped up in each other to notice anything she might be doing.

André patted the seat again; she slid in beside him. He smelled of spices and lime. She let him slip his arm round her, let him nuzzle his lips against her hair.

"Tell me about Paris, André."

He moved her closer into his side until the length of their legs was touching. She smiled and threaded her fingers through his.

"Please, it would be a distraction. Tell me about the music, and the nightclubs, and what the women wear."

André was such a skilled storyteller, Liese completely lost track of time, and place. He had her sipping Martinis under dimmed chandeliers, dancing in rooms thick with perfume and red velvet, running barefoot down the Champs-Élysées hand in hand. When she heard raised voices, she presumed it must be a Parisian *gendarme*.

"Tell me you didn't! Tell me this is some kind of a joke."

Otto was on his feet, looming over Paul, who was slumped on the sofa with his head in his hands.

"What's going on?"

Otto answered Liese's confused question but didn't turn away from Paul.

"I was trying to explain to your father what tonight actually means. That it's an ending. That we have to stop stalling and get out of Berlin. And he agreed."

Liese jumped up, startling André out of the dreamy state he had lulled them both into.

"But that's a good thing, isn't it? So why are you cross?"

"Tell her, Paul."

Her father's voice was so small, Liese had to cross the room to hear him.

"We don't have passports. Not ones we can use. When we were meant to surrender them last month and get the new ones stamped with a J, I didn't do it."

"Why not?"

Paul shrank further into himself. Liese could feel her heart hammering.

"Father, I don't understand. The Nazis were very clear it had to be done. I saw the order. It was on your desk. You must have known."

Paul continued to stare at his hands. "I did. But I thought I could find a way round it. I didn't see why we should be labeled. And then, yesterday, another letter came. If I don't turn them in, I'll be arrested. If I'd been at home when this started—"

Paul broke off as Margarethe cried out.

"Even if I could find a sponsor somewhere in America or Europe to vouch for us, I don't think they'll let me leave the country now, or at least not with the money we'd need…" He tailed off, turned to comfort Margarethe.

His arrogance will ruin us.

"What's wrong, Liese? What has Paul done, or not done? What is this problem with passports?"

Liese didn't know where to begin to explain the humiliations that were becoming a part of their everyday life, that were so alien to the elegant world André inhabited. She was grateful that Otto answered him before she could try.

"We need to leave Germany and start the business again somewhere safer and for that we need paperwork, which Paul now doesn't have."

He turned his attention back to Paul.

"Listen to me. This has made our situation harder, but not impossible—not if we're clever enough. Tomorrow, when things have calmed down, you will go and surrender the passports. You'll tell them it was all a mistake and that you're sorry. That will buy us some time to make plans, to decide where to go.

Not America—that's too complicated. Somewhere closer. I just need to think."

"Well, if you want somewhere close, that's easily done."

André was on his feet, pushing his way into the conversation.

"Paris. You must go to Paris. Isn't that obvious? I've just been telling Liese how wonderful it is, and, if you really think it's time to go, what better place to restart the salon than Paris?"

Otto finally gave André his full attention. "And you'd help with that?"

André beamed at Otto and bowed to Liese. "Of course. I would be charmed to show Liese my city. I would have asked her to visit whether you needed to leave Berlin or not." He caught up Liese's hand and kissed it. "But you knew that anyway."

She didn't. She thought they were simply weaving stories. Then he kissed her hand again and stroked her cheek and perhaps she had known after all.

Otto, at least, was all certainties.

"It's a solution—a good one! We will need fake passports, of course; surrendering the old ones is a ruse and we can't trust that the Nazis will issue new ones. But I can find people to do that, I'm sure."

Liese pulled her hand back from André's caresses. She wanted to embrace Otto's excitement, to see André's declaration as wonderfully romantic, but it all felt too rushed to be real.

"Otto, slow down. How can fake passports be a sensible idea? How often have Mother and Father been photographed, and me as well, at the shows, and goodness knows where else? How many officials know us?" Her spine started to prickle as the reality of Otto's plan hit her. "We'll be recognized—you know we will. And if we're caught with false papers, or you're caught trying to buy them—"

"There'll be a way; just give me a minute."

Liese continued to protest, but Otto wasn't listening and André was trying to pull her back into his arms. She wriggled free, uncomfortable with the rescued-damsel role André seemed to have cast her in. Otto was still talking; he sounded as if he was ticking off a list.

"We have to get out, that's the main thing. This is the crackdown I've been afraid of. The Party have set out their stall now. They'll sweep up the last Jewish businesses; confiscate the money and houses they haven't already seized. Securing a passage outside Europe might not be possible and moving together might be dangerous, but, if we don't go far and we split up, there might be a way. If you aren't with your parents, fewer people might make the connection, and no one will know Michael." His smile was so wide he looked crazed. "Then that's it."

He grabbed André's hand; André jumped.

"You are right: Paris it is. We can make that happen immediately. I'll drive Paul and Margarethe out through Switzerland—crossing the border will be safer that way for them. Michael and Liese can travel by train with you. Liese's French is good, and we can use Ettinger, her grandparents' surname, as a cover. She could be your assistant. And then we'll all meet up in Paris. It's not just a good solution, it's perfect."

"Slow down. Who is Michael?" André's smile had disappeared.

Otto grimaced at the interruption, as if André should know.

"He's my son. He's a couple of years older than Liese. He's a good boy—he'll stay quiet, do what you tell him. You could say he's another buyer, a trainee. There's money in the salon, plenty of it. You can take it and keep it safe until we're all reunited. When are you meant to be leaving?"

André blinked and stepped back. He no longer looked quite as thrilled.

"Next week, on Tuesday. I've other clients to see and plans for the weekend. But, Otto, wait a minute. Liese coming with me is one thing, but I've never met your son. And I didn't realize you meant right away. Why is there such urgency? Liese, help me out here."

She wanted to, but she was waiting for Paul and Margarethe to protest. At the plan's danger; at the separation from their only child. They were folded into each other, not looking at her, barely listening to Otto.

André nudged at her arm.

"Liese, I will happily take you to Paris. But does it have to be like this? In such a rush? Using fake papers like a smuggler, taking a boy I've never met…"

Liese pulled herself away from any hope of Paul and Margarethe thinking beyond themselves and tried to focus on what André was asking, what Otto was demanding. The prospect of Paris, and of André, was certainly enticing, it was something she'd dreamed of in what felt like a different life, but how could she make such a huge decision so quickly? It would be like cutting out a dress without a pattern.

She tried to think clearly.

"Otto, listen to me: this is too fast and too dangerous. Even if you do find the people to do the job and manage to secure the passports, we could get caught at the station buying the tickets. And if Michael gets questioned, do you honestly think he could keep his mouth shut, or pass convincingly as French? There's too many holes in this plan."

"It's my only chance."

Otto was staring at her as if there were no one else in the room.

"I have to get him out—you know that. I should have acted months ago. Using Bardou for cover gets Michael to safety, as well as you. Look at them."

He nodded at Margarethe curled on Paul's lap.

"They'll never make any kind of decision, and they'll never consider you. Do this for me, and for Michael: he'll go if you do. We'll be all back together in no time, I promise. You won't lose your family: you'll help make sure it's safe. Will you help me? Will you do this?"

They'll never consider you. It was true and it stung.

Otto wanted her safe.

She felt André's arm slip back round her shoulders. He cared for her; that was obvious—he had said he had intended to take her to Paris; he must want her safe too. And how could she bear anything happening to Michael if she could stop it?

She nodded; Otto beamed. Her hands were shaking so hard she couldn't steady them.

"It's all right; don't get upset."

She wasn't upset. She was aware how many dangers this decision exposed them to, but André had her fingers cupped in his, patting them as gently as if he held a fluttering bird, and the sensation was too nice to spoil with a rebuttal. She stayed silent.

He dropped his voice so Otto couldn't hear him.

"He's afraid, Liese. I won't pretend to know what's going on with his son, but, if this helps Otto feel better, where's the harm in it? It's plans, nothing more; we won't need to act on them. Tomorrow, you'll see this business outside is all nothing, a band of thugs and a pack of rumors spiraled out of control. You won't have to do anything you don't choose to do. But if you decide to come..." He smiled his soft smile and traced a finger round her wrist. "Then I'll take care of you, I promise."

No one had ever promised her that. Despite her worries about where this road might take them, she wanted to believe that he meant it.

"What are you whispering about? You haven't changed your mind? You'll get them both out?"

Otto's eyes were too bright; his jaw clenched so tight, his neck had set solid.

André nodded.

Otto retired to an armchair, pulled out a notebook and started scribbling.

Outside, the sky's black had dissolved into a sulfurous yellow and clouds had settled over the city, obscuring the streets. Liese felt like a castaway caught on an island. She leaned into André and let his strong arms enfold her.

Silence fell.

Paul and Margarethe got up, went into the bedroom, and closed the door. Otto's head was lolling; Stefan was already fast asleep. Liese imagined the heat from the fires rising, the windows melting. André's grip on her tightened.

"Let me help you forget all of this."

His breath shivered like silk round her neck. There was no mistaking his meaning. Liese shuddered as his lips followed his breath. She slipped round to face him.

"I've never done this before."

If he was thrown by her directness, he didn't show it.

"Do you want to tonight?"

She watched his smile, watched his eyes darken. The models in the salon were perfectly open about sex—most of them had rich boyfriends whose attentions they seemed to adore. "Do it right and do it often and they're all yours, honey" was a sentiment Liese had heard from more than one laughing girl. She would like to have someone who was all hers. She would like that someone to be André.

She smiled back at him. "Yes, I would."

There was another door, with a dressing room behind it. There was a sofa to welcome them.

He led enough; he let her find her own pace enough. Mouths met; bodies connected. Liese stared into eyes that looked only at her, and the riots and the smashed windows and the burning buildings slipped away under one simple thought: *I want this.*

Kristallnacht. Crystal Night. A beautiful name to blanket the orgy of violence the ninth of November had turned into. Liese shivered when she heard how the Party had christened it.

Three days had passed since the night in the Adlon, but the memory of Berlin's shattered streets still broke up her nights. The hours in André's arms had been timeless and far too short. He had been gentle and slow until she had needed him not to be and the only thing she had regretted was the need to stay silent.

When morning came, bringing with it a smoke-smudged sky, André had slipped out before the others were awake. He came back subdued, his hair dark with dust. The news was no more cheerful than it had been the night before, but they couldn't risk hiding in the hotel any longer.

Liese had roused Otto and her parents. There wasn't a moment to pick up the previous evening's discussions. There wasn't a moment for a farewell between her and André beyond a lingering look and a promise that he would call her later that day. The Elfmanns had flown down the corridors behind Otto, to the sound of maids approaching inside the hotel and an ominous silence outside.

The scenes that greeted them when they finally pulled out of the garage were worse than Liese expected, the destruction greater than Stefan had warned them. All the streets from the Unter den Linden to Friedrichstraße were choked with the debris of ruined businesses. The pavements were littered with smashed lamps and display cases and splintered filing cabinets whose contents blew around like snowdrifts. Every window they could see was shattered, the innards of the looted shops and offices spilling out like the entrails of a butchered animal. Road after road was closed, packs of thugs still prowling.

Stefan was forced to ease the car round the edges of the Tiergarten and over the Spree, before taking them in a wide arc that circled the city. The detour he took them on led down through the wide square and elegant shops of the Molkenmarkt. It was as if they followed in the tracks of an invading army. Everywhere was ransacked, the towering Nathan Israel department store ripped open and gutted. Mannequins sprawled out of the gaping windows like crumpled bodies, clothes spilled across the street like dropped washing. Smoke pooled in the air, knitted into gray clouds heady with petrol. The Elfmanns passed the rest of the journey crouched down, without speaking.

Despite the surrounding chaos, Bergmannkiez's tree-lined avenues were quiet and the Elfmann home was intact. The servants, however, were gone. Paul and Margarethe took refuge in the chilly sitting room while Liese ran around, organizing a fire, finding tea and biscuits. Stefan and Otto left again, on foot and in old coats. They stumbled back quicker than Liese expected, gray-faced and shaken. Beyond a mess of graffiti, Haus Elfmann had escaped, but hundreds of Jewish shops and offices were destroyed, dozens of synagogues burned. Rumor had it that every city across Germany could tell the same story. As for the arrests: the numbers the two men had heard whispered were terrifying.

Stefan retreated to his quarters; Paul and Margarethe disappeared into their bedroom. Otto and Liese hunched over the radio, twisting the dial to prize out the scale of the destruction, parceling out the money Otto had recovered from Paul's office into easily hidden bundles. They spent another night huddled on chairs, too sickened to try sleeping.

When morning came round again, Michael appeared, his clothes filthy, his face a patchwork of bruises.

"The Nazis are blaming the Jews. They're saying we started it, that our businesses were burned because we were the ones rioting. It's a bunch of lies. They were waiting for an excuse to ruin us and then some trigger-happy teenager with a Jewish name shot a Nazi diplomat in Paris and gave them just what they wanted. They're going to make us pay for the damage and, when we can't, they'll seize anything still standing."

"Which is why I've come up with a plan to get us out—"

"Otto, hush a minute."

Liese was still crouched by the radio. The bland music had switched to a booming voice and a series of announcements.

"As a result of the recent Jewish-led disturbances, all Jewish firms are confiscated. Jews are banned from public places and subject to a

curfew. There will be no compensation for damaged property. Jews are to pay Germany reparations for the damage they have caused."

"What did I tell you?" There wasn't a trace of satisfaction in Michael's tone.

"They can't do this..." Otto's voice fell away as he realized they just had.

"Then that's it. We have to go. We have to turn my plan into action."

"What plan?"

Liese left Otto explaining to a silent Michael how he intended to lead them all off to France and went to relay the news report from the radio to Paul and Margarethe. They received it as blankly as they had stared out of the car windows.

Unable to face any more revelations, Liese had collapsed into bed and, for the first time since *Kristallnacht*, had fallen into an exhausted sleep that was blessedly empty. When she finally woke and stumbled to the kitchen, it was to find Michael returned and brewing the last of the coffee. There was no sign of Otto.

"He's gone for the passports. Don't look at me like that. He wouldn't let me go with him. He said an old man alone stood less chance of being noticed. He still thinks he's The Fixer and what am I supposed to do with that? Argue? Make him feel old and useless?"

"No. Of course not. You have to trust him—we all do. Did he tell you his plan?"

Michael poured Liese a cup of coffee, sniffed the milk, and grimaced.

"About us taking the train and him driving your parents? Yes. I wish he hadn't. It's not a plan; it's madness. And whether he gets the papers or not, I can't go. I'm needed here. I'll play along with it to keep him happy, but I have to stay. And please don't lecture me about family—I'm not sure I can take it. I can't go; I don't want him to go. And if I hope he doesn't get the passports, where does that leave you?"

Liese drained her cup. She knew that Michael meant every word. She also knew that, if she did leave, she couldn't bear their parting to be on bad terms.

"You can't solve all this, Michael, and you can't stop your father. Where do you think you get your stubbornness from?" To her relief, he finally smiled. "I'm sorry I ever questioned your love for him. I know how important he is to you. And I also know how important your part in the fight against the Nazis is, how much it matters to you to be taking a stand. I wish I'd told you that sooner. And how brave I think you are. If I can see that, Otto certainly can."

She knew better than to notice his blush.

"And as for this plan . . . I don't know whether I believe it will happen, or if I want it any more than you do, but if my parents go, then I have to go too. They're going to need my help to get things back on their feet. Don't worry—I won't try to make you come, although I'll keep up whatever pretense you need so that Otto doesn't panic. You'd have made a lousy Frenchman anyway."

Michael grinned at her as the door opened and Paul stamped in, complaining at the lack of breakfast.

Trying to persuade him and Margarethe to pack, and pack lightly, and listening to their moans about the supplies she and Michael managed to forage drank up most of the day. It was almost four o'clock before Liese glanced at the clock and realized Otto had been gone for hours. Michael had left on some business he refused to discuss and wouldn't return until evening. Her parents had retreated to their well-cushioned sanctuary. She had nothing to do and no one to talk to and she needed to be busy, or she would have to face up to an uncomfortable truth: she hadn't heard a single word from André. The promised call hadn't come. She had hovered in the hall more times than she was prepared to admit in the last few days, her hand fluttering over the receiver, wondering if he had misplaced her number. Each time she had been interrupted. Now she had the house to herself and no more patience for finding excuses.

I'll take care of you, I promise.

Those and all the other words he'd whispered still rang through her head. But so did his hesitation when he realized the speed of the plan, and his reluctance when he heard that plan included Michael.

I need to hear his voice that's all. To run through Tuesday's arrangements and make them seem real.

She went out into the hall and sat down at the telephone table. André had said he was busy over the weekend, but perhaps the Adlon would know his movements and have an idea of when he expected to be back? She might even be able to persuade him to come to the house, to snatch a few hours alone together before everyone else resurfaced. Warmed by that thought, Liese dialed the hotel's number. She listened to the clerk. She put the phone down. She was still sitting there when Michael strode through the door.

"What are you doing? Where's my father?"

She stared at him blankly.

"Liese, where's Otto?"

"I don't know. I don't think he came back. And…"

Michael looked so horrified she couldn't finish the sentence.

"It's been hours, almost the whole day. What on earth is wrong with you?"

He left before she could think of an answer. How could she explain her state to him when she couldn't explain it to herself? She didn't know if she was numb or mortified or furious. At some point since she had put down the telephone, she knew she had been all of those. Numb when she first heard André was gone. Mortified when she had to listen to the reception clerk's amusement as he added her name to the list of women hoping to speak to "our so popular Monsieur," to his surprise that Monsieur had cut short his stay and gone back to Paris "when he does so love staying here." Furious when she realized that André was a coward, that she was a fool.

Otto isn't here.

The reality of Michael's words suddenly cut through her confusion and pushed her to her feet. He had to be wrong. Otto must have come back and not seen her sitting so quietly. He must be in the house somewhere.

By the time Michael came back, his face pale, his eyes red, she had searched every room.

"He's been caught. The Security Police had the counterfeiters under surveillance. They've been sweeping up their customers for days."

Liese thought she was going to be sick. "Where is he?"

Michael was shaking so hard he could barely stand. "As far as I can find out, he's in the detention camp I told you about at Oranienburg. He's rich. He's a Jew. He'll be a target. I have to get him out."

Liese forced him into a chair and kept her hands on his shoulders, as much to steady herself as him.

"But how can you do that? Has anyone even told you officially that he's there?"

"No, but if I file a report to say that he's missing, try to find out more about what happened, the chances are they'll take me in. We work under aliases, but if there's photographs... I've so many names they want, Liese. There's so many lives I could put at risk."

He grabbed her hands and pulled her down into the chair beside him.

"I know what they do, in Alexanderplatz. At the Gestapo headquarters. I know how they get information. I like to think I'm a soldier, but I don't think I would hold out under their interrogation very well."

He started to cry and Liese knew, in the pain she felt watching him, that André's leaving hadn't broken her heart.

Liese took a deep breath, tugged on Michael's arm, and forced him to look at her. "This is The Fixer, remember? We have to trust him not to be helpless."

"What are you saying?"

What I wish I didn't have to.

Liese wiped away a tear. When she spoke, however, her voice was as steady as Michael needed it to be.

"What you already know. That you can't rescue him and not make things worse. I'm so sorry. That Otto is gone, that I have to say this. But he won't thank you, Michael, if you save him and get hurt yourself, or if others are put in danger because of him. He won't thank you at all." She caught him as he slumped forward. "He'll be all right. He's Otto. We have to keep believing that he'll be all right."

She held him until his tears stopped, trying to make herself not care about what she had to say next.

"There's something else…"

Michael barely looked up.

"André Bardou has left Berlin."

"So Father's plan isn't possible."

Michael shook her off and got up again. Liese wanted to tell him that André's leaving was a lot of other things too, but he was prowling the kitchen, his fists all bunched, and she couldn't find a place to start.

"No, I suppose not. We'll just have to wait here for Otto to come back and think of another way."

He stared at her as if he was about to call her stupid again.

"You can't do that. Don't you see the danger you're in? Think about it: once they have Father's name, it won't take long to connect him to the salon, and to Paul. They're still after blood, still smashing up property, seizing whatever homes and fortunes are left. You can't be in this house when they turn the spotlight on Haus Elfmann. And what if this Bardou character told someone Father's plans to get you out before he went?"

"He wouldn't!"

"You don't know that. You clearly didn't expect him to leave. You don't know what they might have offered him, or what he's capable of offering them."

There was nothing Liese could say that didn't turn her into the idiot she knew Michael would call her if he found out the truth. That didn't turn the night she had spent with André into something that shamed her.

She kept her head down, not trusting her face to hold on to that secret, and was grateful for once that Michael plowed on without giving her a moment to speak.

"Never mind being rich and Jewish, which is reason alone to put us all in danger, Father said Paul is under threat because of the un-surrendered passports. If the Security Police think he's about to run, and take any remaining money with him, they'll swoop in a heartbeat. Is there anywhere else you can go? Anywhere people won't know you?"

"In Berlin?" Paul would be horrified at the question. "No. In another place perhaps, but not here. There's money though, plenty of it. Otto brought it from the salon for safekeeping. If you give me a day or two, maybe I could organize a hotel somewhere outside the city, in the countryside. I could ask Stefan to drive us."

"There's no time. They could be on their way by then. Come on, think. There must be somewhere safer than here."

A photograph on the wall caught her eye as Michael paced past it. Minnie in her rose garden countless summers ago.

"Charlottenburg. Grandfather's house. When he died last year, we closed it up, but Father never got round to selling it. The keys must be here somewhere. The grounds are big; the house is secluded. We could go without anyone noticing."

"I doubt that." But Michael sat down and his hands were calmer.

"It could do though, for a few days, until they make the con-nection." He nodded, as much to himself as her. "It's not ideal, but it could buy us time to think up a better plan and, when Father is freed, he would at least have an idea where to come."

He jumped up again. Together, they began pulling food from the cupboards, sweeping the bundled notes into a bag.

"I'll drive you. The fewer people who know where you are, the safer you'll stay, and that includes Stefan. I know he's been with your family for years and you trust him, but no one is immune to what the Party thugs can do. It's not fair to put him in that kind of danger. Tell him to leave—he'll understand. And go and tell Paul and Margarethe we have to be out of here in thirty minutes. And make sure they understand that this move is temporary, that they can't stay in Charlottenburg more than a few days. Will they get it? Will they realize their life in Berlin is finished?"

Liese said yes, but she didn't believe it. Paul and Margarethe had nodded along with Otto's plans at the hotel, but Liese knew they had barely listened there and wouldn't discuss any word of it since.

When she went into their bedroom, the small bags she had begged them to pack were still empty. When she explained that the first stage of the journey was to Charlottenburg, they grew distracted. They pulled out their traveling trunks and began discussing the first dinner party they would hold "to breathe life back into the place." They didn't ask about Otto; Liese wasn't sure if they had even noticed his absence.

Liese stared out of the window as the car crawled through dark streets where buildings still smoldered, trying to ignore Paul and Margarethe's ridiculous chatter. The world had changed beyond repair and yet on her parents went, helpless and spoiled and completely self-centered. They were a burden as heavy round her shoulders as the business had been.

How much longer can I carry their weight?

For the first time in months, she couldn't block out the honest answer.

CHAPTER SIX

Karen

Aldershot and Berlin, March 1978

The breakfast almost stopped her.

Instead of the regulation orange juice and cereal, Andrew had set out coffee and a ketchup-slathered bacon sandwich. Her Tupperware lunch box sat waiting by her plate, as it did every morning, but this time there was a five-pound note, not an apple, sitting on the lid.

Karen put down her bag and took a step into the kitchen.

He's making an effort; you could meet him halfway.

She was tired, more tired than she wanted to admit to her father. The weeks of endless arguments had taken their toll. And she was nervous about her trip—not that she intended to admit that either. She was also hungry and the bacon smelled like heaven.

Andrew was out in the garden, Karen could see him fussing over the birdbath.

Would a goodbye be so difficult? A couple of words and a smile?

She hesitated, her hand hovering over the sandwich. A few months ago, she would have said it was perfectly possible. A few months ago, she could have left the house with a nod, knowing her father had no more interest in delaying her than she had in staying. But now? After almost two years of perfectly crafted non-conversations, Karen had announced that she was joining her German class's annual school trip and unleashed a torrent of protest she couldn't stop.

"Why do you want to go to Germany?"

He wouldn't stop asking, wouldn't leave her alone until she responded.

"Because I'm taking the German exam for extra university points, and the trip will be a chance to practice speaking German outside a classroom."

The clipped answer was all she would give him, no matter how hard he pushed. It should have been enough, especially since he showed no sign that he was prepared to acknowledge what he must know was the truth. *Because I'm looking for answers.* And it was hardly as if he had the right to keep asking. Since that morning eighteen months ago, when she'd found the passport and he'd messed up her life, Karen had been quite clear with him how things were going to be in the future.

"I don't want to talk to you. I won't listen if you talk to me."

She had stormed out as soon as she'd said it and refused to stay in any room her father was in almost ever since.

It had worked: they were, after all, well-practiced at living together apart. All the years of avoiding each other, of not talking to each other, of refusing to find a common language, had set round the house like concrete. Karen had thrown herself into studying, her escape route, and it had paid off. As she approached her final exams, straight As were beckoning and a university place, as her headmistress beamed, wherever she chose. Which would be Manchester, two hundred miles away, not nearby Reading, where so many of her classmates were heading. And she wouldn't be studying English either, followed by a "nice teaching job," as she had once heard Andrew describe his hopes for her. Karen had dreams of her own, dreams that had nothing to do with his narrow view of the world. She was going to be an architect, a great one, and design houses built for sound and light and laughter.

It had been almost bearable, their unconnected existence, and then she had mentioned the school trip and he had come back to life. He was so intent on dissuading her, he followed her into rooms and ignored closed doors. And talked, as always, *at* her.

"Germany maybe—I can see a logic in that. But why Berlin? It's hardly the most sensible choice. The city is completely isolated now inside the East. You'll have to go through goodness knows how many checkpoints and the political situation there really isn't stable. What was Miss Dennison thinking?"

Karen tried ignoring him, but that didn't work, so she reverted to snapping.

"She thinks that we need to understand the country properly and that's impossible without going to Berlin and seeing how the Wall has divided it. Why do you care? Are you really worried some border guard will make trouble because we come from the West, or are you scared I'll start digging up my heritage? That the neighbors will remember I'm not properly English and freak?"

That had shut him up but, for once, she hadn't turned immediately away and she had seen his reaction. He looked so forlorn it threw her.

"You could tell me about my mother's family before I go. If you wanted."

He had opened his mouth, closed it again. The pause stretched out further than Karen could bear.

"Forget it. I thought you wanted to talk, but you just want to lecture. Why does it still matter who comes from where? We've been at peace with Germany for nearly forty years—why can't you remember that? Why can't you accept that the war's long over?"

What was it he'd said?

"You're wrong. You're so wrong. Some things never end. The war's not over and you're caught in its crosshairs just as tightly as me."

It didn't make any sense. And it had scared her. She wouldn't admit that. She had gone back to storming out of rooms every time he brought the trip up. But it had scared her, and the pain in his face when he said it had scared her even more.

He was coming down the garden path—another few steps and he would see her. It wouldn't be a simple goodbye; it would be another fight she didn't have the strength for. As she hesitated, Andrew caught sight of her, raised his hand and started to say something Karen had no interest in hearing. She grabbed the money and the sandwich and ran for the door.

She willed away the Channel crossing. Every stopping point as they wound their way from Calais through Antwerp and Cologne dragged. All Karen wanted was to get to Berlin. She tried her best to be enthusiastic about the journey, if only not to draw attention. She oohed and aahed with the rest of the girls when they were decanted from the coach in picturesque town centers where church spires carved out the skyline and medieval peasants could have wandered unchallenged. She clicked her camera as directed in cobbled squares whose pungent market stalls left Miss Dennison and Miss Grainger—or Denny and Grunger as the girls had long ago christened them—misty-eyed. She swallowed up the facts the teachers stuffed them with, ready to regurgitate them in the endless quizzes they set rather than let the girls loose in the evenings. Anything to make the days pass.

"Barely forty years since those dreadful bombing raids and what a wonderful job they've done. Everything has been so beautifully restored you can barely see the joins."

Denny's favorite line as she huddled her pupils round each day's architectural offering, her voice dropping on *bombing* and lifting on *joins* as if her praise could compensate for the damage.

Karen—"our little architect in waiting"—dutifully admired the stepped gables, the window-studded facades, and the delicate arches. They were beautiful, no one could deny that, but she longed for something that was a little less storybook. For a past she could connect to. Then they arrived at the Helmstadt border crossing point between Germany's East and its West, and all her ideas about the country had to be hastily reassembled.

"No nonsense, girls. No getting off the coach. If the East German soldiers decide to come on board and check your passports individually, be quick when they ask you. They can hold us up for hours here if they have a mind."

Karen peered out of the window, her curiosity piqued by the uncharacteristically shrill edge in Grunger's tone. The physical effects of the Second World War, from what she had seen on the journey, had been tidied away, the devastated cities patched up and made whole again. Germany's battered people, she presumed, must have longed for quiet after the onslaught they had lived through, and then, sixteen years after the war's end, the Soviets had taken the sectors of the country they were given to manage in 1945 and cut them away. Now, there were two Germanys, split by a nine-hundred-mile-long border: the Federal Republic in the West and the Deutsche Demokratische Republik, which contained the still partly West-controlled city of Berlin, in the East. Karen knew that—she had studied that. Seeing its reality, however, was a different thing altogether.

There was nothing storybook about the border. Low windowless huts squatted between the traffic lanes like overweight guard dogs. Red-and-white barriers dissected the road, flagpoles muscled up on either side: stars and stripes and Union Jacks to mark out the West in one direction, the compass-and-hammer-stamped banners of the DDR floating a little higher over the East. There were towers. There were soldiers flinging orders. There were an awful lot of guns.

"They're getting on!"

Whoever squealed was quickly shushed.

The rifles slung across their backs as casually as fishing rods gave the two baggily uniformed boys an older man's swagger. They didn't make eye contact or smile, despite the giggles and blushes that greeted them.

By the time the coach was released, everybody's mood had sharpened. Karen perched on her seat remembering her flippant words to her father: *the war's long over.* She stared out of the window as the no-stops, heavily speed-restricted drive took them past barbed wire and watchtowers. Now she was in East Germany, staring into its blatantly military face, her father's anguished response suddenly took on a new depth.

She wasn't the only one to feel the change. One by one, the girls stopped chatting.

The exhale when the coach reached the checkpoint on the outskirts of Berlin was thick enough to be tangible. That crossing was a far quicker affair, the soldiers jauntily waving them through happily American.

"We've sailed across the socialist sea, girls!" The soldiers' winks had turned Grunger giddy. "And reached the island of Berlin. A little piece of the West clinging on among the Reds."

The coach rattled on; the city unfolded itself in a penned-in muddle that pinned Karen to the window. It was austere rather than pretty—stripped clean of the columns and arches she had expected.

"Don't worry—there are plenty of parks and far lovelier areas than what you see here."

Karen wasn't worried at all; she was fascinated. As they drew closer in, she could see that Berlin had its share of crumbling once-ornate buildings, but these were overshadowed by sleek-sided housing blocks lined up in rows like perfectly polished teeth.

"It's all a bit…clinical." The sniff that followed the sneering comment from the back of the bus echoed round the coach.

Denny smiled across the aisle at Karen. "Take no notice. Your classmates are being classical-loving snobs because they think that's what they're meant to be. This is a city reinventing itself—look with your cleverer eye and enjoy it."

She pointed out an art gallery as she spoke that was all angles and edges and as unlike a home for old masters as Karen could ever imagine. Nothing in Berlin was what she had imagined. It was so different to anywhere she had seen before. Bits of the city were still broken, pocked with old bullet holes and filled with weed-choked bomb sites not filled in since the war. Bits of it were unashamedly modern. Apart from a huge battered belfry flanked by what looked like giant metal honeycombs, there was barely a church spire to be seen. What there was, pulling the eye like a magnet, was the Wall.

It snaked gray and brooding, a round-topped concrete punch twice the height of the people milling past it. It slashed through the city, blocking off streets, cutting across corners, appearing and reappearing as if its map had been drawn by a shaky-handed toddler. Twice, the coach driver took a wrong turning and it jumped out in front of them, dissecting a park, looming over a playground, bricked-up eyeless buildings clinging to its edges like scabs.

Karen was equally mesmerized and daunted by the Wall's blankness, by its hand-in-the-air stop-here brutality.

On the first night, she gazed down from the dormitory window long after her companions had fallen asleep, drawn like a moth to the spotlights which marked out the Wall's grip on the city. Neon blazed on one side; darkness swallowed up the other. Karen followed the outline as far as she could and realized Grunger was right: Berlin, or at least its western side, sat as isolated from the rest of West Germany as an ocean-edged island. Its brightness against the rolled-up-early eastern sector was too much. The lights made the city appear overdone, like it was trying too hard. It looked at once vulnerable and brash.

It looked like the kind of place that wouldn't easily surrender its secrets.

It wasn't until their third and final day that the girls proved themselves fit to be allowed to explore Berlin unsupervised.

By the time that decision was announced, Karen had started to concoct escape plans, convinced she would be trapped forever on the coach shuttling them from one "essential sight" to the next. She had made herself dizzy twisting and turning, trying to read street signs, trying to guess which disappearing corner might lead to the city her mother had known. She couldn't concentrate at the rickety Potsdamer Platz viewing point, although the Wall's death strip and anti-tank traps and the rifle-wielding guards had the other girls excitedly pointing. She tried, but she couldn't share the interest when the scrubby rise between the defenses was revealed as Hitler's buried bunker. The wasteland was too wide, the buildings visible in East Berlin too far away to feel like they had once inhabited the same city. What if part of her mother's story was stuck over there? Karen climbed down from the platform far quicker than the others, feeling the Wall's threat closing in on her, personal and real.

"Go in pairs remember; watch out for each other!"

The girls burst from the coach like a dam exploding, all the teachers' instructions on sticking together and taking care on the subway instantly forgotten.

Karen stuck tight to a group heading toward the Kurfürstendamm until Denny's chirping panic floated away. The shopping street was packed. Crowds weaved round the display cabinets that dotted the pavements and the café tables that were full despite the crisp March air. Karen slowed down, loitering by a theater as if attracted by its posters. Her classmates called out to her to hurry; she called back that she would. Within seconds, they were lost in the blur.

Shoppers swung round her, laden with bags. Waiters flew in and out of wide-windowed cafés five times the size of anything Aldershot could offer. The moment she had been counting down to had finally arrived, but Karen was rooted to the spot, overwhelmed by the size of her task and the pitiful amount of information she had gathered to help her. Giggling through the shopping centers and department stores and trying to sneak into a bar suddenly seemed endlessly attractive.

I need not to be me, the English girl abroad and out of her depth. I need to be somebody smarter.

One of the cafés buzzing with life caught her attention. Karen began to watch the customers flowing in and out. There were plenty of groups and couples, but, unlike in the tea shops at home, there were also women sitting alone, some with books, some simply watching the world pass by; all of them looking perfectly at ease. Spotting a vacant table, Karen shook out her shoulders and dived in.

"Ich möchte einen Kaffee, bitte."

The waiter appeared to understand and an ashtray and matches followed as her confidence increased.

Karen sipped her coffee, lit a cigarette. Nobody knew her; no one was judging. When the waiter returned with the bill, she had her map and the fragmented addresses copied from the wedding certificate spread out ready.

"Konnen Sie mir helfen? Ich versuche Haus Herber zu finden."

He shrugged.

Karen scrabbled round the remains of her German.

"Es ist in Budapest Straße?"

He grinned. "English?"

Karen nodded.

"I don't know Haus Herber, but Budapester Straße is by there."

He pointed toward the belfry that was now drilled into Karen as the Kaiser Wilhelm Gedächtniskirche.

"It's only a few minutes' walk away."

"Danke. And how would I get here?"

Karen passed him the piece of paper with the Lindenkirche's address. He studied it for a moment and then pulled out a pen and drew a black line joining two underground stations.

"That is not so close. Too far to walk. It's not interesting. Houses, nothing special. I can show you better places."

He was very attractive and, from his surprise when Karen got up without taking the bait, not used to being turned down.

She left the café with a spring in her step that lasted almost as long as it took her to walk twice up and down Budapester Straße. There was nothing to see. The shop was long gone; she should have guessed that it would be. And then, as she rubbed at her eyes to stop the pricking tears betraying her, she finally spotted them. Faded letters on a narrow building's lintel, half-hidden by a larger sign, but picking out the name she'd been searching for: *Haus Herber*, the word *Früher* etched above it in slightly smaller script. Karen couldn't remember that exact word, but it was enough like the word *Frühling*, the one for spring, to make *earlier* a reasonable guess.

She pushed open the glass door to a tinkle of bells.

"*Guten Tag. Kann ich Ihnen helfen?*"

Karen hovered on the doorstep, uncertain of anything except that O-level German would be no match for this.

Despite the modern-looking nameplate outside, the interior of Richters Schneiderei was a soft-hued time capsule. Wooden drawers lined one wall, spilling over with pastel spools of lace and curling ribbons. Bolts of cloth stretched along the other two, grouped in a rainbow of patterns and shades. A solid-looking counter marked off with metal numbers ran across the waxed floor like an elongated tape measure. Karen had a sudden image of her mother smoothing fabric across its top, slicing sharp lines with her scissors, and had to swallow a sob.

"*Sprechen Sie Englisch?*"

The woman standing behind the counter moved forward. She was neatly dressed in a dark blue skirt and blouse and far younger than Karen wanted her to be.

"*Ja*. Some. Are you wanting material?"

Karen shook her head. "No. I'm looking for someone. My mother. I think she worked here, when it was Haus Herber. She was a seamstress."

The woman frowned.

Karen groped for the word on the wedding certificate that she had seen echoed on the sign.

"A *Schneiderin*—seamstress? It was a long time ago—1947."

"1947?"

The woman gave a low whistle, which made her look even younger.

"You said your mother, but you are English?"

"Yes, but she was German, from Berlin. Her name was Liese Elfmann."

"1947 is too long for me. But my grandmother perhaps could help. She worked here in the 1940s, before my family eventually took the business over. She is upstairs." The woman stuck out her hand. "Hannah Richter."

The firm handshake made Karen feel steadier.

"Karen Cartwright."

Hannah bustled away, calling for *Oma*. Karen stayed where she was, listening to the footsteps overhead, the murmur of voices. Trying not to hope for the impossible.

When Hannah returned, she brought her older self with her.

"Oma has no English. Tell me again and I will do my best."

Karen spread her story out; Frau Richter watched her intently as Hannah translated it into German. When the old woman answered her granddaughter, she spoke in a stream far too quick for Karen to follow.

"I am sorry. Oma did not know her."

All those words just to say no? Karen tried to keep her smile in place.

"Thank you. For your time. For trying."

She turned to go, nodding to the old lady whose lined face was unreadable. "*Danke. Auf wiedersehen.*"

"No, wait—Oma says she didn't know your mother herself, there were a lot of girls who worked here apparently, and some didn't stay long. But she knew the name you said—Elfmann. She remembers a Haus Elfmann in Berlin before the war. It was a famous...I don't know the word in English; here we say *Modehaus*."

"Fashion house or salon?" Karen could hardly breathe.

"Yes, that sounds right. Salon. Like the French would say it. Oma says it dressed everyone. The father was Paul and there was a daughter, she thinks, called Liese."

Karen could have leaped across the counter and kissed them both.

"That must be her! That must be my mother! Where is the salon now? How do I find it?"

She stopped. Neither woman was smiling.

"What?"

Hannah's English suddenly became rather more stilted.

"It's not possible. Where it was isn't there anymore."

"Do you mean it's like here, it's changed hands? But someone might still remember. Like your grandmother did."

The old lady whispered something too low for Karen to hear.

"No. You don't understand. Hausvogteiplatz, where the old *Modehaüser* were based, is in the East now. Behind the Wall. There's nothing to find, no one to ask."

The answer was half-expected, but it still shook her.

Karen was about to make her excuses and take her misery outside, but Hannah hadn't finished. She glanced at her grandmother, who sniffed.

"And, also..."

The air shifted. Karen felt it like a temperature change.

"The Elfmann family. They were Jewish."

Karen frowned as Hannah started fussing with a length of green fabric heaped on the counter.

"You must know that many Jews lost their businesses during the war? That many didn't survive."

Many?

Karen wasn't sure that was the word she would have chosen to describe the Holocaust, but she didn't know how to say that without causing offense. Hannah still wouldn't meet her eye. Her father had said Liese was German, but he had never mentioned anything about her being Jewish. Unless that was another secret.

Karen kept her voice neutral. "But my mother did survive it. Are you sure the Elfmanns were Jewish?"

The old woman sniffed harder.

Karen glanced at her: the lines on the woman's face had hardened into crevices. The shop's shadowy interior no longer felt charming but choked with a history Karen feared unpicking.

Hannah coughed. "Perhaps she was one of the . . . *Glücklichen.*"

The lucky ones?

Karen still had dozens of questions, but the older woman's arms were folded and Hannah was determinedly busy. Karen nodded a goodbye and ducked out onto the street, retracing her steps back to the Kurfürstendamm.

Its bustle bumped and butted, winding the pavement up into a battleground. Karen spun round, her sense of direction wavering. She knew Hannah had softened her grandmother's words, but Frau Richter's disapproval had still soured the shop. East and West; capitalists and communists; Jews and non-Jews. Berlin was split into too many layers.

Karen leaned against a lamp post pasted with flyers as face after face whirled past. She closed her eyes as the city spun. How many stories was each person hiding?

How many was her mother?

On any other day, Wilmersdorf's sleepy suburban streets would have set Karen's teeth on edge. After the confusion of Richters, she was grateful for their quiet tree-lined familiarity and the luck that had at least left her second destination safe in the West.

From the moment the school trip had been announced, Karen's life had narrowed to a single point: getting to Berlin and unraveling the mystery of her mother. She had set out with a name and two addresses and no clue about anything, as if solving Liese would be as simple as slotting the pieces into a children's jigsaw. She hadn't thought any of it through. She had thought Berlin and her mother's place in it would unroll like a red carpet simply because she wanted them to. She had learned her history well enough to pass exams and never considered war outside her books. She had been intrigued by the Wall's haphazard divisions and barely given a thought to the impact of such a brutal dissection on the city and the people it separated. The arrogance of it made her cheeks smart. That and the wasted opportunity in not talking to her father, demanding that he tell her the truth of her mother's life in Berlin before she came.

Regret stopped her in her tracks, making her long for a telephone booth and his voice. And then she remembered the reality of how things stood between them; how impossible such a conversation would be long-distance when they had failed so completely to have it face-to-face. So now here she was, naïve and clueless; stumbling through a broken city, trying to restitch her family. The irony was almost laughable.

The Lindenkirche appeared before Karen was ready for it.

It was a solid-looking white building with a simple cross on the front and a clock tower peeping from behind a curtain of tall, wide-arching trees. Part of her hoped it would be closed. That, if it was open, it would offer no answers. Then she could go home still nursing her anger, feeding it with another secret her father had kept, another piece of her mother he had stolen. Her mother wasn't Elizabeth, but Liese. She wasn't English, but German. And now she was also apparently Jewish, trailing a history around that Karen sensed carried shadows she had no frame of reference for. She was not, in fact, anyone Karen knew at all.

She crossed the little square, her mind made up to leave and find her classmates, to see how many glasses of schnapps she could drink before anyone noticed. The church door, however, was open.

I'll go in but not stay past a minute. It won't be welcoming. It'll be stuffy and forbidding, like the one on the base.

Karen sloped inside, expecting darkness and air too dense for anything but whispers. Instead, the walls were pale and creamy and the light dancing blue and green through the long narrow windows took her breath away. She sank into a pew and watched the reflections ripple. It was so quiet, she could hear a bird singing in the trees outside.

She was exhausted and hungry and her head was a jumbled mess. She forced herself to focus on the plainly covered altar and tried to picture a bridegroom standing there, holding the hand of a happily smiling bride. When she added her parents' faces to the uniform and white dress, the illusion shattered. Tears she had been swallowing for years began pouring; she no longer had the energy to care.

"Geht es Ihnen gut? Brauchen Sie Hilfe?"

Karen rubbed at her eyes, but the tap wouldn't turn off again.

The voice continued in an English that carried a slightly transatlantic twang.

"Are you needing help?"

"My mother and father were married here."

If the answer struck the man who had sat down in the opposite pew as peculiar, his tone didn't show it.

"And they are dead? Which is why you are crying?"

The handkerchief he handed over blunted some of the directness.

"My mother is."

Karen caught sight of the man's white clerical collar and didn't know if she should admit it was suicide.

"She drowned."

"I am sorry to hear that. You are English?"

She nodded.

"But your parents were German—that is why they were married here?"

"She was, not him; he was a British soldier—he was here in the war."

Karen sneaked a look at the man's face. He had soft brown eyes and a patient smile. Her tongue untied.

"And I didn't know she was from Berlin. And her name wasn't what I thought it was. And now I think she was Jewish, which I didn't know either, but I know that was dangerous here then. And I want to know the truth and no one will help me. And her death wasn't an accident, it was suicide. And I don't know why she did it."

She tumbled to a halt in a fresh wave of tears.

"Come."

The priest got up and held out his hand.

"What is it you English like when everything is falling to pieces?"

Karen sniffed. "Tea?"

"*Genau.* Exactly. We will have tea. And you will tell me all of this slowly and we will see what is to be done."

They had tea and a mound of biscuits, which were sugary and thick with chocolate and stopped Karen's head from aching. She talked without interruption, except when her memories ran too fast for even Father Kristoff's excellent English. When she finished, she sat back, waiting for a stream of sympathy. His response was not what she expected.

"All this pain you carry, does your father also feel it as deeply? No, Karen. Wait a moment before you throw away the question and tell me you do not care. All this blame you pour on him, perhaps he deserves it. But I wonder: can you try something for me? Can you think of your father, for a moment, as someone different to this man you are so angry with? Can you try to imagine how it must have been, in 1947, for a young English soldier marrying a young German girl? Not everyone would smile at that, would you agree?"

The question, if not the task, seemed reasonable enough. And she certainly hadn't thought of the two of them quite in those terms before: Father on the winning side, Mother on the losing. Karen nodded.

"Good. Thank you. But they married, so there must have been a reason to do it. Couldn't we believe it was love?"

She wasn't ready to answer that.

The priest waited a moment but didn't press her.

"You said you think he controlled her. Perhaps, again, you are right. But what if we try this in a different way too? What if he was trying to look after her? What if she wanted the quiet and seclusion you think was too much; what if that was what she needed?"

He spread his hands as Karen began bristling.

"I'm not saying you are wrong, but are you so sure that you are right? All I can be certain of is that too many secrets were kept and that your pain is terrible, and rightly so. But what about his?"

Karen poked at the last crumbs on her plate. This wasn't what she had come here for. Shouldn't a priest provide comfort not difficult questions? She wasn't about to let him judge her life and its wounds so easily.

"Maybe he did love her, but so what? He took her to England, where everyone hated Germans. He made her pretend to be something she wasn't. That's cruel, isn't it? Surely there's no kindness in that?"

Again, the response wrong-footed her.

"What do you know about the war, Karen? Besides that England won."

"I know all about it. I've done it at school."

The day had taught her she knew very little about anything, but she was in no mood to admit it.

Father Kristoff twisted his long fingers.

"You give me the same answer a German girl would give, in the same aggrieved tone. What is it that you have *done*, Karen? Lists of battles? Churchill's speeches? Did you ever do the part that involves people? Do you know what happened in cities like Dresden and Hamburg, in Coventry and London if we are keeping things fair, and here in Berlin?"

"Of course I do. They were bombed."

He looked so disappointed she wished she hadn't been so blunt.

"Bombed. Such an easy word when you haven't lived through it. They were more than that. They were obliterated, wiped out of being. In 1945, when I assume your mother was here, there was barely a building standing—nothing but rubble and dust for miles. The Lindenkirche was one of the few churches not blasted to a ruin. That's probably why they chose this place to be married. People lived in basements; they starved. Women had a terrible time at the hands of the occupying soldiers. The war was hell and, when it was meant to be over, it went on being hell. *Safety* is a different word in a world like that, believe me. If that is what your father could offer, doesn't that make their marrying and going to England a different thing altogether? Couldn't it sound like a rescue?"

She didn't know what to say; how to persuade him that couldn't be right. He was trying to paint the world in shades of gray when it was easier to manage in black and white. Rescue was such a ridiculous fairy-tale word. Father gave orders; he wasn't some soft-hearted knight.

Maybe you could get up today, sweetheart, maybe for a little while? Karen would love it and so would I.

The memory flashed so strong, Karen flinched from it. Her mother in bed, silent and stiff like she could be for days. Father on his knees stroking her hand. "Even if you could make it as far as a chair." Her peeping round the door, terrified Mummy would slip further away. Downstairs again, the bedroom door shut and Father rubbing his face in the kitchen as he pulled together a breakfast they both knew neither of them would eat. And not just once.

Karen could replay that scene on a loop across the years, although she chose not to. Because it hurt.

Because Father should have tried harder and not let Mother keep doing it.

As if he could see her thoughts fighting, Father Kristoff carried on.

"Nothing is ever as straightforward as we think, as our pick-and-choose memories might have it. You also said your mother was Jewish? That makes all of this harder. Have you heard of the Holocaust?"

Was he trying to patronize her as well as shift the ground? They might not have studied that in detail at school, but only a fool wouldn't have heard of it.

Karen frowned. "Yes, of course I have. Six million Jews were killed in the camps. Everyone knows about that."

Father Kristoff's gentle tone didn't falter.

"Yes, they do. That unforgettable number, what we've reduced all those lost lives to. Here in Germany, I'm afraid, worse than anywhere. Even a child can parrot it. It's an easy thing to learn, but it's a harder thing to turn it into bodies and the human cost. Think about it, Karen, consider it properly: all your agony at one death, but who mourns for the millions? There aren't enough people left."

Karen stared out of the window. The day was drawing out, the sky thickening to a deeper blue. A flock of birds had gathered above the trees, swooping up and down in a speckled cloud, ready to roost. They were tiny, sparrows perhaps or starlings, too many to count. She felt her cheeks redden. *Six million.* He was right: she couldn't imagine the scale of it. She couldn't number faces past the few hundred in her school photograph, and half of those were blurry.

She turned back to the priest, mortified.

"Someone said my mother was one of the lucky ones. Do you believe that?"

Father Kristoff shrugged. "Perhaps she was; perhaps her suicide suggests different. We don't know, Karen, what scars are left on those who came through it. We don't discuss such things, although the people who gave the orders and stoked the fires still walk here among us. We don't have the language to even begin. But if Liese Elfmann was the woman you're piecing together, there could be horrors in her past that she couldn't live with, that your father can't tell. Does he deserve punishment for that?"

The right answer was *no*, but she still couldn't dig beneath her pain and find it.

"She left me. He didn't stop her."

The priest took her hand.

"You are carrying a very hard cross. But what about this: what if he did stop her? What if she stayed with you as long as she could?"

Mother in her bed, lying as silent and stiff as Snow White. How many times had Karen feared her mother would simply stop breathing?

The priest held her hand tighter as the room's edges wavered.

"How old was she, when she died? How old were you?"

"It was nearly seven years ago. I was eleven. She was fifty-one."

"She had lived a lot of life before you came. When you are blaming yourself, remember that."

There was the sympathy she had been waiting for; its insight almost undid her.

"How did you know that's what I do?"

The exhaustion that swept over his face was unbearable.

"Because too many of the suffering come here, to the church, to me—looking for answers. And every one of them carries their portion of blame."

"Do you help them?"

"Don't ask me that. I—"

A knock on the door pulled him away. His face rearranged.

"Evening service calls. Will you stay for it?"

Part of her wanted to—she could sense there might be a peace in it, or at least some moments of calm to gather herself back up in. But her watch told the same story as the darkening sky.

"I can't. I'll be in trouble if I'm late."

"Then I have one more piece of advice, if you can bear to hear it."

She nodded. In that moment she could have borne a lot more than one piece.

"When you dig up the past, do it gently. With a care for the living."

The door opened without a knock this time and the priest was swept away by the needs of his parishioners.

Karen slipped out of the back door and headed to the station, shivering in the evening's chill.

The train was busy, full of chatter Karen tuned out. The image of herself watching through the bedroom door, of her father's tenderness as he bent over the bed, had triggered others that flew in as crowded as the birds swarming into the linden trees.

Was it Father keeping her mother up at night, stalking through the kitchen and the living room, talking and talking, or was it her who wouldn't settle? *Come away now, pet. She's not here; she won't answer.* Words that had drifted up the staircase and made no sense, that Karen had pressed down until they were buried and now they nipped at her like nettles. Who was *she* and why wouldn't she answer?

And those awkward Saturday evenings: was her mother crying because she didn't want to go to the dances she got dressed up and ready for, or because she did but the walk to the door was too far? So much of her childhood adjusted around and never questioned.

What if she stayed with you as long as she could?

Father Kristoff had been reclaimed before she could ask what he meant. Before Karen could spill the long-ago-swallowed fear that had resurfaced with his words. That, one day, she would open the bedroom door and the bed would be empty. That the pale figure who could barely find a smile when Karen asked "Do you need anything?" but meant "Do you need anyone?" would have vanished.

Please, my love, eat something. How many times had Father said it?

You get slimmer by the day—tell us your secret! Her dressmaking clients had twittered it on the doorstep as if her mother's tiny frame was a goal to aspire to. Except it wasn't: she was ill. All those days when the face on the pillow was waxen, translucent. When the fingers Karen scrabbled for had no more substance than twigs.

Which is why I was afraid she would vanish and why Father was as frightened as me.

Karen closed her eyes and could have wept for them both.

By the time she got back to the Kurfürstendamm's jumble, her head was splitting.

The street was lit up and swelling with its nighttime traffic, a kaleidoscope of flashing adverts and cinema signs, blaring music and drink-loosened voices. Karen huddled past it all, desperate for sleep and an escape from the collision of emotions the day had let loose. She had lived for years not knowing who her mother was, but she had always thought she knew every inch of her father. Now he was shifting too. This wasn't what she had asked for. She had made a plan; she had carried it out. She had come to Berlin; she had walked in her mother's footsteps. She had found a trace of a flesh-and-blood Liese Elfmann, but every answer only led to another question.

Karen stumbled, her head whirling. She shouldn't have come. She shouldn't have gone to the dressmaker's and let herself be spooked by a malicious old lady. She shouldn't have let the priest open up doors that were doing perfectly well left shut.

She stopped abruptly, swearing back at the man who crashed into her, glad of an excuse to hit out. None of this was fair. If these were her mother's streets, if Liese Elfmann had become whoever she was in this city, why was she still so hard to pin down? No, it was worse than that.

Stepping back from the chaos, Karen studied the passers-by. Some of them looked the right age to have walked here thirty years ago. They might have known Liese; they might have crossed paths with her. And if she asked any one of them what those days had been like, they would throw another shadow on the pile. Karen had come looking for answers and all she had to show for her searching was a far harder question. If this was the city which had shaped her mother, why had she slipped even further away?

Ask him. Ask your father.

The instruction was so loud, Karen started and looked round to see who had spoken. The crowd carried on oblivious.

Ask your father. At least try.

It wasn't her mother's voice. It was her own. The one that she had become so adept at pushing away.

She shook her head, but it kept on coming.

If he's shifting, why don't you?

Karen closed her eyes, took a breath, and let herself listen. These streets had been Liese's, but surely they had been Andrew's too? If even a fraction of what Father Kristoff had suggested was true, didn't she owe her father the chance to tell her? Didn't she owe herself the chance to try to change how they were?

She opened her eyes and stepped back onto the pavement, let herself be swept along with the crowd. There was a part of her that had its roots in this city, in these people, and there was a part of her that was as English as her father. She had come to Berlin to unlock the past and yet he was its key. He always had been. She needed him to be her father, not her enemy. It was time she grew up and told him that.

PART TWO

CHAPTER SEVEN

Liese

Berlin, August 1939

How can it only be nine months since Kristallnacht?

So much had changed it felt like nine years; it felt like ninety. Liese had stopped looking in the mirror months ago. She didn't believe a nineteen-year-old would look back at her; she didn't remember what nineteen meant. She assumed that, a long time ago, she must have imagined being the age she was now. She assumed she had imagined it would bring with it parties and flirtations, kisses and promises. Perhaps even a handful of liaisons, some suitable and some not, before she met the magical "one." If she thought about it now, which she tried her hardest not to do, she also assumed that there were nineteen-year-olds still out there who lived that stardust kind of life. Who had managed to grab more than a fleeting taste of it. Who were able to chalk up the "wrong sort of men" to experience and slip away unscathed. Liese refused to let those girls pop up when they tried, as she refused to allow herself regrets it was pointless to indulge. There were a lot of things Liese's life no longer had, but the days of pining for them were done. Besides, she had the baby: how could parties and flirtations ever compare with that?

Liese kissed her daughter's head and settled her into the drawer she had painstakingly scoured for splinters. The child was perfect. Even Margarethe, who had greeted Liese's pregnancy with all the outrage of a nun and recoiled from *Grandma* as if Minnie were listening, had stroked the tiny cheek and pronounced her "likely at least to be pretty."

She lowered herself onto the fold-out bed as carefully as she could. The midwife had been more efficient than gentle, but she had come, a mercy Liese would be eternally grateful for. The thought of being left to Margarethe's flapping care had horrified her more than the shock of the first contraction. With the city's hospitals closed to Jews, Frau Schenkel's skills were thinly stretched. She had arrived with one eye on her watch, bundled Liese into the apartment's only good bed and the baby out into the world and rolled away with her fee and no more than a dozen words exchanged. Forty-eight hours later and Liese was too much in love to remember anything of the birth but the joy of it.

"I'm going to call her Lottie. You can't say it without grinning."

Liese waited for Michael to compliment the name and its snuffling owner. He continued to stare out of the grime-coated window and took no notice of either. At least he was here. Six months ago, when Liese had finally pieced together her never-ending tiredness and her nausea into something more than shock at the speed with which their lives had collapsed, Michael's anger and disdain had been hard to bear.

"You're pregnant? Are you kidding me? How could you be so careless? Don't you know anything?"

Clearly, she hadn't. Except that she had wanted André and she refused to regret the night they had spent together. How could she? He might have fooled her and betrayed them, but he had left behind a blessing. Gazing now into her daughter's velvety eyes, the burning sky and broken buildings that had led to her coming were as hard to remember as the birth pains.

Liese hadn't expected to fall so helplessly in love with her child. If she had only known how deep and immediate the bond would be, perhaps the pregnancy would have been less of a strain. If she had also known, as she announced the news to her parents in what now seemed the unimaginable comfort of Charlottenburg, how much worse their lives were going to get, she wouldn't have bothered worrying over something as simple as pregnancy at all.

Liese stared round the cramped room which doubled as her bedroom and her workroom and the apartment's only living space and opened onto a second one just as mean. Two rooms and that was it, for three—and now four—of them to live in. The whole apartment could have fitted inside the checkerboard hallway of her grandfather's mansion, and it rang from dawn to dusk with her parents' complaints. Not just about the size, although that was always where the muttering started, but about the peeling walls and the fraying carpets. About the indignities of sharing a bathroom and a kitchen with the occupants of other equally miserable sets of rooms. About the damp which clung to the walls even in the middle of summer, and the smell of decay which wafted through the windows from the refuse left piled up in the courtyard until it rotted.

Nothing had changed since the miserable December day when they had moved into the broken-down tenement that now served as their home. Paul and Margarethe wouldn't make do; they wouldn't make the best of things. They acted as if Liese had swept them out of Charlottenburg and into Cuxhavener Straße on some inexplicable whim. As if she were the one depriving them of soft sheets and rose-scented soaps and all the little luxuries they couldn't live without, that "a good daughter would get if she cared enough."

"Don't they understand that this is partly their fault? That if they cause trouble here, there's nowhere left for you to go?"

Michael had stood in the dank hallway that first afternoon, his hair dripping with snow, every muscle tensed as if he was ready for a fight.

"It's the shock. Leaving Bergmannkiez for Charlottenburg was one thing, but to find themselves having to live somewhere like this?" She had smiled with an optimism she really wanted to feel. "They'll calm down. They'll get used to it. And I can manage."

Liese didn't believe her parents would adjust any more than Michael did, but her stuck-on beam had got him out of the door and back to the underground life his resistance activities meant he was now living. She knew if he had stayed, he would have picked a row with Paul, a row that Paul would be too arrogant to back down from and she would end up engulfed by. All she and Michael had been doing for weeks was fighting and the cause was always the same: her parents' selfish, dangerous behavior. Every time he had appeared in the reopened Charlottenburg house, he had paced the carpets bare. And stretched her patience as thinly.

"Didn't you explain that staying in Charlottenburg was meant to be temporary? Don't they understand that you've already been here too long?"

After the first week, Liese had stopped answering. Her parents couldn't—or, more likely, wouldn't—understand a thing. In the fraught early-morning confusion of their arrival, Liese had begged them to be discreet. It was as much use as pleading with a hungry baby to stop crying. Paul had refused to be "cowed"; Margarethe had applauded his "bravery." That first day, they had thrown open the shutters and strolled in the garden with no thought for who could be watching, and no amount of pleading would keep them indoors. Michael had acted like Liese hadn't noticed their madness or hadn't tried in vain to curb it.

"Can't you control them? They'll be wandering down the streets and waving at the neighbors next. The Nazis have seized the salon. They've seized the Bergmannkiez house. They're hunting for every last bit of Jewish wealth. Even if some snoop doesn't tell tales, it won't take long to track this estate down."

"Why are you telling me? I'm not the one sticking my head in the sand and still imagining I'm the toast of Berlin. But if you think you can get through to them any better, by all means go ahead."

Liese had snapped. Michael had kept on lecturing and not listening. Their closeness on the night of Otto's disappearance had vanished under the weight of old patterns.

"The Nazis are swallowing up Jewish property like sharks at a feeding. If you won't leave the city, at least let me find you somewhere less obvious than this."

If *you* won't.

She would have shouted at that, except there were already too many cross voices competing. Liese might have come to respect Michael's convictions, but that didn't mean she wanted to live with the judgment they trailed. When she had finally lost her temper and yelled that "not everything in the world was black and white—that sometimes it was gray and muddied," he had simply looked blank. Liese had, nevertheless, gone on trying to reason with Paul and Margarethe. She had tried to remind them that this move was only step one; to persuade them to repack their cases and let Michael find them a different city or a countryside bolthole. Every time she mentioned leaving, they stormed through the house like tantruming children.

Michael came less and less; Liese couldn't blame him. She knew his absence wasn't because he didn't care—that it was, in fact, a measure of how much he did. She knew that he was looking for somewhere safer for them all to stay; that she had to trust he would find such a place quickly. She grew steadily better at ignoring her parents, at holding her nerve and holding her tongue. By the second week in December, with the household still undisturbed, she began to believe Paul and Margarethe's foolishness had gone unnoticed. She started opening up the rest of the mansion's rooms, removing the covers from the carved and tapestry-covered furniture in the reception rooms and shaking the dust out from the brocade and silk drapes. She found enough silver candlesticks to soften the burgundy-papered dining room and even, to Margarethe's delight, a cache of crystal jars containing still-fragrant bath salts.

The long-neglected house was starting to feel almost like home. And then came the furious banging.

"Security Police. Open up."

Four men stood arranged on the steps, all in the unmistakeable green uniform. The one at the front, an officer from the flashes on his collar, was holding a clipboard.

"You are?"

"Liese Elfmann."

The officer glanced up from his list. "You are not."

"I don't understand."

This time, his gaze was so direct Liese had to fight not to duck it.

"You are a Jew. You are therefore Liese *Sara* Elfmann. If you had registered as instructed, you would have received your Jewish name and you would answer correctly. Move aside."

He flung the door past her, nodding to the remaining policemen, who marched through on his command.

"The usual inventory: artwork; large pieces of furniture; furs and other good clothing; curtains and floor coverings. Check all floors."

He stepped into the hallway as his subordinates fanned out.

"Has this property and its contents been accounted for?"

Liese couldn't admit a second time that she didn't understand. There was no way she would cower.

"This is my grandfather's house. It isn't mine to account for."

His hand twitched as if he might strike her, but a shriek from upstairs pulled his attention away.

"Liese, what is going on? Who have you let in?"

Paul came storming down the stairs, his silk robe billowing. He paused when he saw the officer, but, to Liese's despair, he didn't make any attempt to moderate his imperious manner.

"Is that ape who frightened my wife one of your goons?"

Liese waited for a fist, or worse, but the policeman merely consulted his clipboard again.

"You are Paul Israel Elfmann?"

That stopped him. Paul sagged against the banister at his new middle name, his mouth flapping. The officer made another note.

"Another one unaware of how Jews are now titled. The order to register was clearly communicated. As was the requirement for you to account for all of your wealth. And yet you have not collected your Jewish papers and there is no record of this property. Or of the business in Hausvogteiplatz, or the house in Arndstraße you previously owned."

Previously thudded through the hall.

"Do you have some difficulty following rules that I am unaware of?"

Paul gaped at him like a child three questions behind in a spelling test.

"I can assure you that none of this has been deliberately done." Liese was amazed how level her voice stayed. "Matters have been overlooked; we are sorry for that. We will, of course, comply with whatever is needed."

The searchlight gaze switched back to her.

"Yes, you will. My men will complete their inventory. You will not interfere. You will vacate this house, to which you no longer have rights, by 5 p.m. tomorrow. Which is a generous time allowance, believe me. If you argue, you will leave now. If anything listed is removed, there will be penalties. If the amount recovered from the estate you have concealed does not meet the debt you owe in reparation for last month's disturbances, additional charges will be levied."

Liese was still stuck at *vacate*.

As he turned to leave, she grabbed at his sleeve.

"But where will we go?"

The blow left her sprawling.

"Wherever your betters decide."

He wiped his hands and stepped over her. He didn't look back.

*

"Cuxhavener Straße 17. Take this. Present it to the building's *Blockwart* by 12 p.m. or he will reallocate the rooms."

"You have been very kind. I hope your bosses appreciate your efforts as much as we do."

Angry Michael had gone; the friend she needed had come back the minute she asked for him.

"Keep smiling. It could be worse. This address is walkable from Charlottenburg. We can make three or four trips to collect your belongings with the time we've got. And it's near the Tiergarten, so maybe there'll be a bit of space and green around it."

He had taken the room authorization and steered Liese away as firmly as he had steered her two hours earlier into the squat building with its endless rows of desks and faceless clerks. Her elbow clutched in Michael's hand was the only part of Liese's body that had felt solid since the Security Police had left the previous day.

It had taken her the best part of the night to track him down, through neighborhoods she would never normally have gone near, but every raised eyebrow and off-color comment that greeted her enquiries had proved worth it. Michael had charmed the flint-faced secretary into believing they were about to be married and "in complete desperation for some privacy." He had cracked the woman's thin lips into a laugh, patting down his pockets and enacting the elaborate pantomime of his papers leaping into the wrong jacket. He had winked and flirted and begged for her mercy and, against all the odds, he had won. Liese had scurried out as the tenant of two rooms, instead of the one room other families were being told to be grateful for.

Not that it mattered. Paul had raged when he was told about the move; Margarethe had sobbed. They had trudged through the snow to their new lodgings like prisoners bound for the scaffold, leaving Michael to balance their overstuffed cases. They had refused to participate in any return trips. Every item Liese salvaged from Charlottenburg was the wrong one. Every item she was forced to leave behind was a treasure. The whole day had been a nightmare;

the only good thing Liese could find in it was her and Michael's repaired friendship. She could even have felt safe from the threat of further police visits, except that, as soon as the Elfmanns had moved in, Michael wanted them moved out again.

"You can't stay—there's something not right going on. Never mind that the Nazis are packing these buildings way over what they were built for, everyone's been cleared from the area except Jews. There's got to be a reason for that, and it won't be a good one."

He was right about the overcrowding. More families had been dumped at the apartment block every day since the Elfmanns arrived, all of them white-faced and bedraggled. Paul and Margarethe shrank from contact with their new neighbors as if danger lurked in the simplest nod. Liese, desperate for news that would explain the world's redrawing, sought their company out. She picked her way round the children playing in the corridors or huddled in the courtyard, in search of their mothers. She was hesitant at first, conscious of how little she knew, uncertain where she fitted. Some of the women she encountered were Jewish to their bones; some were as newly stamped as she was. Some had been rich and were shocked at how low they had fallen; some had been poor and were simply grateful for a roof. Nobody demanded her story or was concerned when she tried but did not know how to tell it. What they shared was more important than what separated them: whoever they once had been, they were all the lowest of the low to the Nazis.

Everyone had a tale of lost homes and lost professions. Everyone who could pull together the fees and a sponsor and a ticket out of Germany was gone. Everyone who was left was afraid and couldn't name what their fear was. There were some who watched each other, who worked out space allocations and muttered. They were carefully ignored.

As the weeks stretched on into a snow-choked New Year and food and fuel stretched too thin, most of the families gravitated together and shared what they could. Liese, exhausted by her parents, gradually began to feel part of a community, and that calmed her. That she was making friends, however, did not calm Michael.

"You're getting too settled. You can't do that; you have to leave. If the rumors are true, there'll be war before the year's end, and that will mean shortages and rationing. God knows how Jews will fare under that. Your money's running out and I can't see your father, or your mother, finding work, unless someone forces them into it. Which could also be coming. You need to be somewhere else, Liese. Prenzlauer Berg or Wedding, where it's easier to slip round unnoticed, especially with the new papers I can get for you all."

On and on. The same tirade every time, until Liese's jaw ached from clamping it. She didn't want to fight him. She knew what was at the root: Michael couldn't rescue Otto from the camp he was still held in, so he had to rescue everyone else. His urgency was easy to understand. His plan made perfect sense, for anyone but her. Michael and his network of KPD-loyal contacts were never still: they swam through the city, shifting location, changing their names as easily as shrugging on new coats. Pulling her self-involved parents into such a transient life was impossible. And then, with her pregnant, it became unthinkable.

When she finally admitted the truth of her condition, Michael's transition from overzealous friend to pompous father had cracked her long-held patience in two.

"I know it's not ideal and André is the worst choice I could have made. Thank you for pointing that out with such eloquence. And I'm grateful for everything you've done, but if you tell me one more time that I can't manage, our friendship is finished. I'm pregnant; I'm not incapable. I ran the business for nearly two years while you swanned round playing the rebel. I looked after everyone then. I can do the same now."

Their row had blown up and spilled out and dragged Paul and Margarethe into the sea of judgment Liese refused to step into. Part of her wanted to walk out then; to let them sink or swim without dragging her down further. But the ties of family, however worn they were, still had enough bite to hold. So she had stayed. She had ignored her parents as they moaned and belittled her. She had taken charge.

The three of them could live at each other's throats, but they couldn't live for long on their dwindling stack of money, or rely on Michael's handouts that came from goodness knows where. Fashion was all she knew, so Liese went back to Hausvogteiplatz, where the freshly Germanized fashion industry still operated, and came back with a job. She never told any of them what that had cost her. How it had ached to walk past Haus Elfmann and find it locked and barred, the windows cracked, the canopy in tatters. How it had stung to stand outside building after building whose names were once a supply-book shorthand and find them whitewashed and rechristened to fit a Germany that no longer had a place for people like her. How deep the humiliation of knocking on doors all along Mohrenstraβe and Kronenstraβe ran, doors that the Elfmann name would once have swung open, and having every one of them slam at the first sight of her papers.

Later, when Liese replayed the day for her parents, she scooped out its humiliations and let Paul believe it was her skills and their reputation that had triumphed. She let him think that the Elfmanns weren't forgotten. She couldn't hit him with the word charity, or admit that, by the time she heard a voice calling, not spitting at, her name, she had no pride left to bargain with.

"Fraulein Elfmann! It is you! What are you doing outside in such dreadful cold?"

The fur-wrapped woman exiting from the coat-maker's, whose receptionist Liese was about to join battle with, was all smiles, as if they had last met in a coffee shop the previous morning.

"And what are you doing back here? We thought you had moved."

Irena Zahl. Liese managed a smile as the name popped back. She had been one of the salon's most extravagant customers, although not one who had stayed a moment past when she should.

Liese had opened her mouth to trot out something meaningless, but the day had scratched open too many scars.

"No, we didn't move. We were chased out, and the house and the salon and everything was taken. We have no money, so I'm looking for a job, but I'm Jewish, so there's not one to be had."

To Frau Zahl's credit, she blushed. Then she came closer and inspected Liese's pinched face and dirt-spattered coat, and she winced.

"A job? But you're not some common seamstress—you're the heir to—"

She had stopped, coughed; pushed the shop door back open again.

"You're someone with skills any business would be lucky to have in their workplace. This showroom and the trade that goes with it belong to my family now. I'm not going to pretend to you that is right. Let me see what can be done."

Liese had begun sewing coat linings and collars that afternoon and had done the same eye-aching work ever since, until her body had grown too bulky to sit at the sewing table.

And as soon as Lottie is weaned, I will have to go back.

Liese stared at the sleeping baby, her heart aching at the thought of leaving her, but there were too many mouths depending on her skills to pretend she had any other choice.

"What are you going to do now?"

Michael had turned away from the darkening window while Liese was fretting at the future and picking over the past. He held up his hands as she frowned.

"Don't jump down my throat. I'm not going to try and tell you what to do or give orders. I wouldn't dare anymore. You've proved yourself stronger than most of the men I know."

His smile was a shadow of the grin that used to turn his face boyish. That had disappeared with the one-line letter announcing Otto's death and giving no reason. Or offering him a body to mourn with.

"All I want is for you to be safe, Liese. Except I don't see how you can be when you're trapped in these streets that are too like a ghetto and worn thin trying to look after what amounts to three babies."

There was too much truth in his words to dismiss them.

Liese could hear her parents moving about on the other side of the wall; she could hear the grumble that would steadily rise to a whine. "We're hungry. What are we eating? Why have we waited long past what was always our dinner time?" The daily complaints that took no account of long hours stitching in poor light or the grind of empty purses, or of giving birth. That cared only for their never-full-enough stomachs and did nothing to fill them. She imagined herself returning to the workroom, leaving Lottie to be watched over by her grandparents; to be neglected. It was as unimaginable as recovering their lost lives.

As the commentary on the lack of cooking smells grew louder, Lottie stirred in her makeshift cradle and began mewing. The soft sound caught at Liese's heart as if a cord still ran between them. Nobody mattered anymore but Lottie. Nobody's needs could come before hers.

"Will you take a letter to Frau Zahl for me?"

She could see Michael wrestling with his previous promise not to direct her.

"Don't worry. I'm not going to keep trying to balance it all. There's a real baby now; it's time for everyone else to get up on their feet."

She nodded to the opening door.

"They can't be my problem to manage anymore. They're going to have to start pulling their weight."

She reached into the makeshift cradle and stroked Lottie's cheek.

"If they want to eat, if they want to live here, they're going to have to stop acting like royalty, rethink their lives, and work."

CHAPTER EIGHT

Liese

Berlin, September 1940–October 1941

"Hush now, sweetheart; don't be afraid."

Liese settled the wriggling baby against her shoulder and wondered who her words were meant to calm. Lottie never cried when the sirens sounded; she barely flinched when the bombs fell. The war's first air-raid alarm had shrieked across the city a year ago, in the early weeks of the little girl's life, and had remained its music. Three long tones, a wail, and a howl. The endlessly repeating pattern rattled Liese's bones; Lottie could chirp it like a song.

"Watch the pretty lights now."

Another unnecessary instruction. Lottie's arms were already out, her fingers curling to catch the red and green flares floating like fireflies past the smudged glass and trace the searchlights' silvery webs. It wasn't the nightly lights or noise that unnerved the little girl, it was silence. When the raids stopped, or in the pauses in between the night's onslaughts, then her eyes grew wide and she started to babble, only settling when Liese cooed and whispered nonsense into her ear. Lottie was a war baby, the whole of her short life shaped by the conflict's sounds and cruelties. If Liese regretted anything about her daughter's coming, it was that.

Two o'clock.

Almost twenty minutes since the last shards of shrapnel had clattered like metallic rain across the windowsill. Perhaps the all-clear would sound in time to snatch at least a semblance of sleep.

Liese lay Lottie on the narrow fold-down bed they shared, starting up a soothing hum as she wrapped the thin blanket round the child's not-plump-enough body.

"The windows and the building have survived another onslaught, so that was lucky."

She began to list the night's blessings as Lottie chafed against the sudden quiet.

"And the ban on Jews using the shelters saved us from a blackout trek, which was even luckier. You know Mummy hates the thought of going underground more than any silly old bomb crashing through the apartment."

The final siren sang out; Lottie's eyelids fell.

Liese eased gently away from the bed and crossed the few paces back to the window. The light show was over; the streets already disappearing back into the dark. Liese shivered as she looked down into the spreading blackness, although the night was warm.

Berlin without its necklace of lights was an oppressive place. Darkness fell on the city, solid and matte. The soft glow of street lamps was a memory. The roads and pavements were marked instead by phosphorescent paint whose spiky daubs reared like fangs. Stripes for curbs, corners, and crossings; zigzags for a flight of steps. Each sign roughly done and patchy, a trap for a too-quick foot.

Nothing in the blackout held the shape it should. Bodies shuffled past each other sexless and hunched, grunting on contact. Busses lumbered along with their windows tinted into slit-thin blue patches. War had turned Berlin subterranean. And suspicious. Even in daylight, nobody spoke in the street unless they had to. Communication had whittled down to nods and eye rolls, to covertly watching and quickly looking away. The Germany preened over by the radio and the headlines and the flag-choked parades wasn't one Liese recognized. That one wore its head up and its shoulders wide. Liese's Berlin was all shadows and tightening spaces.

Three o'clock.

She could hear the bedroom stirring. Another hour and her parents would be up, forced out of bed before they were ready, sitting at the age-scarred table, hoping for breakfast. Facing a far too long walk to the jobs that had swallowed their lives.

I can't find a place in our workshop for them, I'm sorry—no one needs the level of attention Paul Elfmann's presence would bring.

Liese had despaired when she read the first line of Frau Zahl's response to the letter Michael had delivered. The second line, however, had offered the hope of a lifeline: a promise of help to secure her parents positions in a uniform factory happy to pay a pittance to desperate Jews. It was a hard fall for them, but Liese, aching at Lottie's hungry cries, had stood firm against Paul and Margarethe's tears and protests. She had pointed out the rapidly expanding forced-labor laws, which were already sending Jews to grub in quarries and at building sites and roadworks. "To work at jobs you won't survive in." She had insisted, and held food back from them as a promise of what would come unless they listened, until they ran out of arguments.

Threats had pushed the Elfmanns out of the flat and into sparsely filled wage packets. Threats got them through days that left them too drained to bombard Liese with their old litany of complaints.

Exhaustion had aged Paul and Margarethe ten years in the one since the war had started. Lack of light in the factory shed had yellowed their skin and reduced Paul's once bright eyes to peering. Margarethe's inability to sew a straight seam had sent her to the damp potato mountains which passed for a workers' kitchen. Her slim fingers had grown lumpen and knotted and they split any gloves she tried to force over them. Their days were ruled by eight-hour shifts and a five-kilometer walk there and back that soon became a shuffle.

Liese had tried to get bus passes for them, not that they believed her, but none were available for Jews—"with a journey so short, they ought to be grateful." Her stomach dropped every day at the sight of their blank faces and soured with guilt at what she had forced them to do. Then she looked in the empty cupboard and her stomach dropped further. Her parents were broken and Liese felt the weight of her part in that. If their misery meant Lottie cried with hunger for even one moment less, it was, however, a cross she would bear.

Food. The lack of it and the need for it dominated every waking hour. Liese's fan of ration cards were as pretty as a paint chart and as much use at filling empty stomachs. The Party had put a well-regimented system in place to ensure Germany's increasingly stretched resources were best used: blue cards for meat; green for eggs; yellow for fats; orange for bread; and pink for rice and tea and flour and oatmeal. It was a system capable of providing German citizens with a perfectly balanced diet. If only the cards Liese held weren't stamped with a J. If only the shops were open to Jews for longer than the last scrabbling moments before the shutters slammed down for the day. If only the portions allocated to anyone but "honest Germans" would feed anything bigger than a mouse.

Liese had mined every connection like a prospector after gold. Lottie's smile had charmed the childless grocer's wife: if Liese came to the shop early and tickled Lottie into a grin, she could leave a bag that would be filled up with vegetables when she returned later at night. The women whose sewing Liese took in shared a twist of sugar when they could, or a straw-wrapped egg. The women whose children she minded along with Lottie, while they toiled in the factories, did the same. Michael would pop up every week or two clutching a bag of apples, or a knuckle of pork, and no questions asked. She was grateful for all of it, but none of it was guaranteed.

There were days when all Liese could pull together was a handful of turnips and a dry loaf of bread so full of grit she was terrified

Lottie would choke on it. She became a more inventive cook than any of the chefs whose meals she once ate without thinking. She became a gleaner, a collector of rosehips and dandelions and nettles that went into salads and soups that everyone hated and everyone wolfed down.

Whatever she did, it was never enough. Lottie's eyes were a shade too big for her face, her arms and legs not properly covered. When the second word she spoke after *Mama* was *hungry*, Liese sank down and wept.

Four o'clock.

The bedroom door would open soon, the hungry mouths would appear. A hot drink might provide the illusion of a proper breakfast.

Liese collected the box of ersatz coffee that tasted of chicory and smelled burned when it brewed and went to the cramped kitchen. It was so early, at least one of the stove's four flickering burners should be free. The corridor was bitterly cold, the stained oilcloth that covered it stung like ice through Liese's thin shoes and its one lightbulb had blown long ago. There was no milk, not that she would have given that to anyone but Lottie. There was a heel of yesterday's loaf, a scraping of beet-bulked marmalade. That would do for Paul and Margarethe.

Hidden under the bed where Lottie lay sleeping was a muslin-wrapped square inch of cheese, a bag with two apples, and some slivers of meat the black-market man swore was fresh rabbit. That haul would stay hidden until her parents were far away from the flat. It had cost Liese her last pair of earrings and would be gone within minutes. But it would fill Lottie up. It would pink her cheeks and wipe away the pinched hollows for a few hours, for a morning. For long enough to keep going from this day to the next.

*

"Where have they got to, poppet? It's almost curfew time."

Lottie looked up from the bed, where she was putting the rag doll Liese had sewn from scraps through a complicated set of jumps and twirls. She grinned.

"Dinner time?"

Liese scooped her daughter up, trying not to dwell on how easy that task was: two years living on steadily depleting resources had left Lottie with no more substance to her than a pocket full of feathers.

"Mama sad?"

Liese smiled her frown away and tickled Lottie back into laughter. Too much time cooped up, forbidden access to parks or play spaces, or pinned to Liese's side for lack of anyone else to mind her, had made Lottie far more conscious of her mother's moods than any child ought to be.

"Not sad, monkey, hungry like you. Dinner time then. But you'll have to come with me to the kitchen, and you'll have to be good. No getting under people's feet or pinching food that doesn't belong to us. Do you promise?"

"Promise."

The little girl's face was solemn, but Liese knew how fast the child's fingers could flash if she thought no one was looking. She also knew she should tell Lottie that thieving was wrong, that everyone else in the building was just as hungry as they were. But it was her child she heard sobbing in the night when her empty stomach hurt, and her child whose tear-stained hollow cheeks she had to wipe clean every morning, so the guilt came but not the words.

The kitchen was only one turn of the corridor away, but it was a cumbersome operation to get there. Collecting up the food bag and the cooking pot and spoon; balancing that load with Lottie's insistence on helping; making sure everything was locked tight behind her. Liese couldn't leave anything in the communal space for fear of fingers as quick as Lottie's, and she couldn't leave their flat open. By some miracle, or some oversight, the Elfmanns had held on to their two rooms while the rest of the building was carved smaller and smaller. No one had said anything against the Elfmanns yet. That didn't mean that no one—broken by the terrible conditions they were all forced to endure and desperate for some space and dignity for their own family—would.

Her parents' overdue arrival meant Liese was later cooking than usual and the kitchen was empty. The fug of cabbage and turnips from the other residents' meals clung to it like a farmyard. She set to work quickly, dicing carrots and onions and the sparse shreds of meat into water to make a thin soup. She had hoped the meal would last two days. Now the day's harvest was in the pan, she doubted it would stretch between tonight's four waiting bowls.

"Hungry, Mama. Dolly too."

Lottie's eyes were wide, her attention focused on the bubbling pan.

Liese passed her a sliver of carrot with instructions to nibble it slowly and tried not to snap as the little girl swallowed it whole.

Their rations had shrunk to unworkable levels while the pettiness of the restrictions grew. Jews were no longer allowed fish or eggs or fruit, or anything baked beyond sawdust bread. Liese had worked round the rules for as long as she could, then the Party unleashed its newest weapon and defeated her. A yellow star to be worn where it could be seen at all times by all Jews older than six. Overnight, Liese became as visible as a blackout marking. The grocer's wife, with a wary eye for the neighbors, no longer knew her. The black-market men tripled their prices. No one she sewed for had a mouthful to spare.

"Stinky. Stop it."

The pan had caught while she was fretting. Liese whipped it off the stove, ignoring the heat stinging through her hand.

"Back we go, poppet. Help Mummy push the doors."

The flat was still locked, Paul and Margarethe were late enough to make her throat clench. People disappeared now. New families bustled into the block's suddenly vacated spaces; no one said anything about the old. There were rumors about trains leaving the city for unknown destinations, of whole areas emptied. Michael was permanently on edge. Liese had to stop listening when he began ranting, too preoccupied with the day-to-day business of survival to fret over matters outside her control.

When the door finally opened, she was ladling out the meal, scraping the blackened bits into her own bowl.

Another few minutes and we could have had their share.

She managed a greeting and wished she felt guiltier. Then she saw the tears mottling Margarethe's cheeks and her appetite fell away.

"Please God you haven't lost your jobs. Is that why you're so late back? Because you couldn't face me?"

Her voice cracked over their cowering bodies. She could see their distress. She wanted to be kinder, but the thought of managing without even their meager pay lodged a stone in her stomach. Paul opened his mouth, but whatever he was struggling to say wouldn't leave it. Liese's neck prickled.

"Eat up the soup carefully, Lottie. Let it cool."

The child ignored her and continued to work through her portion with her usual efficiency.

Keeping the door ajar, Liese waved her parents into the apartment's one bedroom. It was cramped with three of them inside and noticeably colder than the main room, which held the only working fireplace. Liese could see her breath forming patterns in the air.

"What is it? What's happened?"

Paul held out an envelope. Liese realized Margarethe was holding its twin.

"No. Not these. That can't be."

Every Jew knew what these letters meant: *resettlement.* A word everyone whispered and no one understood.

"Why would you be singled out? Your jobs are important. Soldiers haven't stopped needing uniforms."

"They don't need ones made by Jews. They are letting us all go. They have brought in foreign workers, from Poland and Austria, as skilled at sewing as any of us."

Paul finally sat down on the sagging double bed, settling Margarethe beside him. He unbuttoned her coat and eased off her too-tight gloves as gently as if she were a child.

Liese looked down—the intimacy between them had grown no easier to watch—and opened the letters. They were identical, neatly typed, politely worded. Both carried the heading she knew she would find, *Notice of Resettlement*, and tomorrow's date. Liese didn't know what her parents had been told about when they would leave; she couldn't begin to imagine asking.

"Go to the table. Eat."

They didn't need telling twice.

Liese waited until they were devouring the now-cold soup before unfolding the rest of the envelopes' contents. They were instructions, they covered two sheets, and they were a model of clarity. The exact time the Elfmanns were due to present themselves at the Levetzowstraße collection point was noted at the top of the first page. That was followed by the items they were allowed to take, listed alphabetically, as if anyone still had a detailed list of possessions left to them. Last of all was the number of bags permitted and how these were to be labeled, including the one for cash and jewelry which was to be surrendered on arrival. The second page was an inventory with space to itemize and value every item in the apartment, an amount that would be "set against the cost of your journey, with any discrepancies owing." It was the Kristallnacht reparations system rolled out on an industrial scale.

Liese folded the papers back up, trying to stay calm as she returned to the main room. Lottie had gone back to her doll and wasn't listening to the adults. She sat down at the table and realized she had immediately started picking at its splinters, something she was always telling Lottie not to do.

"Did anyone say when or where you're going?"

"We know it is tomorrow. They were precise about that. As to the place, Litzmannstadt is all we were told. It might be a city in Poland; no one was sure."

Paul's voice was so drained, his shoulders so slumped, Liese wanted to fling her arms round him. As she moved to do it, Margarethe began to cry. Not in the showy, accusatory way Liese was used to, but lifelessly, with fat silent tears that poured like raindrops down an empty building. Paul pulled her up, covered her hair in kisses, and led her back to the bedroom. Liese followed, although neither of them had asked her to.

"Don't, my darling, please."

Paul settled Margarethe on the bed and wrapped his arms round her.

"Perhaps this move will be a happier one. No more slaving. A proper apartment. And we will be together; we got our letters at the same time, so we can be sure of that. What can possibly be so bad if we two are together? What more do we need?"

Margarethe burrowed into him. Paul held her so tight there wasn't a space between their slumped bodies. Neither heard the knock that pulled Liese, blinking, away.

"The notices have gone out to all Jews still working in the clothing factories in Mitte. The news only just got through to us."

Michael hugged her briefly and reached down for Lottie, who had wrapped his legs in a vice-like grip.

"Here you go, Trouble."

He produced a square of chocolate from his pocket that danced Lottie, squealing with delight, back to Dolly and the bed. Liese stayed where she was, in the shelter of his arm. He smelled of clean rain and fresh paint; she could have breathed him in for hours.

"Where are they?"

Liese nodded to the bedroom door. Paul had closed it as soon as she left. She wondered how quickly they had forgotten her.

She was glad when Michael squeezed her hand and pulled her wandering thoughts back.

"I can't do anything to stop this, Liese. I'm sorry. Once the names go on a list, trying to make anyone disappear is too dangerous."

Liese sat back down. The scant drops of soup her parents had been too tired to scavenge had congealed and grown sharp-smelling. Her stomach heaved.

"You've done your best; I'm grateful for it. But you know as well as I do that they could never have disappeared, list or no list. All the moving, the changing names, the attention to detail a life below the radar needs: they don't have the patience, or the capacity. They are helpless; they always have been. Without me, God knows what would have happened to them by now; not that they care what I've sacrificed for them. Not that they care about anything beyond themselves." She tried not to sound bitter but her father's dismissal—*what can possibly be so bad if we two are together? what more do we need?*—stung.

"And now they no longer need you. You can go into hiding and be safe."

Liese stared at Lottie, who had fallen into a chocolate-smeared sleep. She wanted to believe him, but what had really changed?

"I don't know if that's true, Michael, no matter how much you want it to be. How can I hide with her? It's different for you. You can run around Berlin like a shadow. If I were on my own, I'd come with you gladly, but I'm not. You can't take a child into that level of danger. Or, at least, I can't."

He grabbed her hand so tightly, she couldn't twist away.

"*Can't* doesn't work anymore; I shouldn't have let it before. Listen to me. Paul and Margarethe have no choice: they have to do what the letters tell them and go. When they do, the Gestapo will send their squads round. They will empty the apartment and reallocate it. If you're here when the soldiers arrive, they will take you and they will take Lottie. You won't be able to bargain with them. They will have no interest in anything beyond the fact that you are Jewish and taking up a living space they now count as theirs. And if you aren't here, they'll keep looking. You registered; they know you exist."

Liese's head swam at the thought of uniformed or leather-coated thugs anywhere near her daughter. But to run? To slip under the surface and join the "submarine people," as Michael called them, and live like a fugitive? To expose Lottie to God knows what kind of an existence that would entail? It was as unimaginable as jumping into a bottomless pit. There was only one alternative she could think of, although it wasn't one she wanted to choose.

"Maybe I should do what they want and go with my parents? Would it be so bad, Michael, really? To start somewhere else? Surely resettlement anywhere would be better, easier to bear, than trying to manage hand-to-mouth like this?"

His face looked twice as old as his years.

"You say resettlement like they're offering you a villa in the country. You know that's not the case. What's happening tomorrow is a *deportation*; use that word and it sounds far less friendly. The one leaving tomorrow is the third from Berlin in a month. No one has heard from anyone who was sent out on the previous two. The destination they give is always the same, Litzmannstadt, but no one knows exactly where, or what, that is. Except that it's in Poland, where all our reports say the Jews have been corralled into ghettoes, where—"

He stopped.

Liese glanced at the closed bedroom door and knew she didn't want him to continue, and couldn't let him stop.

"Tell me. If you want me to hide out in Berlin and put my daughter in the kind of danger an illegal life would involve, you have to tell me it all. I have to make the best choice."

When he began again, he spoke too quickly for Liese to interrupt.

"There are rumors coming out of the East about massacres. Of trains that leave Germany packed full and arrive empty, and no one knows where the passengers are, except other rumors report thousands of Jews shot and their bodies burned or buried in pits. We're hearing about ghettoes in Poland, in Warsaw and Krakow, which are thick with starvation and disease. Where people are walled off with no medical care, even for the children and the old. Of so-called labor camps where the inmates are worked to death. The Nazis are sending us where no one can follow, or see what they do. They are killing us, Liese. What we suspected was always their plan is happening."

There wasn't a sound from the adjoining room, or from the bed where Lottie lay spreadeagled like a starfish. There wasn't a sound from the streets outside. The world was as silent as if it had stopped turning.

"You can't save them, Liese. You can save her."

It hadn't stopped turning, it was unraveling and Liese couldn't see which thread to follow. If she stayed and the Gestapo came, there would be no second chance. If she ran, chance would be all she had. Whatever she did, her parents were lost. Whatever she did, there was no guarantee she could keep Lottie safe, which was surely her only job. But she could try. And her parents had each other, which, as her father had made clear, was all they had ever wanted.

Lottie stirred in her sleep and pulled her doll closer. She was so small, she looked like she could fold into Liese's pocket. Liese moved to the bed and wrapped her arms round her daughter. Lottie curled round her in return like a vine. Their completeness took Liese's breath away.

"Not tonight."

She shook her head as Michael started to argue.

"They're going into heaven only knows what tomorrow and they're still my parents. I need to be here in the morning—to say my goodbyes. Whatever we've been to each other, whether they need me to do it or not, the family we once called ourselves deserves that much."

"And then you'll come? No more excuses?"

Liese lay against the pillow, cradling her daughter.

She could imagine a life without her parents, although that hurt more than she had words for. It was impossible to imagine a world that didn't spin around Lottie. The love that bound her to her daughter was as strong as iron; it would stand against whatever challenges were coming.

She kissed Lottie's soft hair and nodded at Michael.

"And then I'll come."

CHAPTER NINE

Liese

Berlin, November 1942–September 1943

Live your cover story, lose yourself. Trust no one. Stay alert.

In the year since Paul and Margarethe had been *relocated* and Liese and Lottie had begun living underground, the Nazis' determination to rid Berlin of its Jews had intensified. Their lives were never still. Liese had worn four different names in twelve months and had no doubt that the fifth one was coming. The number of rooms she and Lottie had bounced through had grown too long to count. Michael had led them in and out of basements and attics and cramped carved-up spaces the length of Treptow and Friedrichshain and Prenzlauer Berg since he had pulled Liese from Cuxhavener Straβe, clutching Lottie and weeping. The sight of her parents walking away, hand in hand, bent into each other and not looking back, had broken her more than she could have imagined.

"I can't do it. I can't let them go like this. What if I never see them again?"

She had thrust Lottie into Michael's arms and run down the corridor, screaming at them to stop, deaf to Lottie's frightened cries and Michael's furious shouts.

"You have to stay. You have to. I'll work something out; I'll hide you."

"And what will happen then?"

Paul's face when he turned at her pleading was gray and so aged, Liese would have taken him for a stranger if she had passed him in the street. "They will find us. And you will pay. You and Lottie. We can't live with that."

"It won't happen, it won't!"

When he reached out and stroked her hair, Liese thought her heart would stop.

"We haven't been much use to you." He shook his head as she tried to speak. "It's best I finally face the truth, even if it is too late to mend things. We thought the world would always be ours, you see. And we're not equipped for what it's become. Your mother is my center, Liese; Lottie is yours. Let us go; keep what matters safe."

He turned then, tucked Margarethe's arm into his, and walked away. Liese didn't call out again; Paul didn't look back. When Michael picked her up from the floor where she had fallen, she didn't fight him.

She had no memory of leaving the tenement, or of the first scrambled-into apartment he left them in. None of the places Michael had taken them to since were in areas she knew; most of their dark streets continued to remain a mystery. Every move was made at night and not every apartment was safe to leave, no matter how much Lottie begged for "outsides." Every day dawned so fraught with danger, Liese's nerves were permanently knotted. But at least, as she constantly reminded herself, every day dawned. Even if too many brought with them threats she hadn't known were there to fret over.

"You have to trust no one and you have to stay vigilant. The Nazis aren't our only problem. There are catchers everywhere: turncoat Jews turning us in. They work for the Gestapo, hunting down illegals. Some of them are better at the job than their bosses."

"Why do they do it?"

Michael had shrugged, clearly uncomfortably aware how hollow his answer was.

"Who knows. Money, I suppose. Or freedom to live on the surface unmolested, or to save their own families from the deportation trains. Whatever their reasoning, they deserve a bullet for betraying the rest of us. We've gathered what information we can; one day there'll be a reckoning. Stella Kübler is the worst, but she mostly targets the men dumb enough to fall for her smiles and her flattery. Most of them you can't spot, and that's where the trouble lies. If anyone looks twice at you, or makes an approach and acts like they know you, break eye contact at once and get out of sight."

There were so many rules; all, Michael insisted, equally essential for survival. Liese, determined not to put a foot wrong, memorized every one of them until they ran through her head on an endless loop.

"Stay in if you can. If you must go out, always look smart and spotless, whatever the challenge of finding hot water and soap. Map every street for doorways and alleys that might offer a bolt-hole. Be confident. Belong. Walk head up and shoulders square. Carry a visible copy of the *Völkischer Beobachter*, the Party-loving newspaper. Never run, unless someone is pointing a gun at you and then running will be a waste of time. Never look frightened, or dirty, or out of place. Never look like how they imagine a Jew."

Not that, given the hateful distorted images the Party peddled, any real person ever could. That didn't matter. Posture, clothes, coloring: everything could be used as a weapon; everything had to be rethought.

Liese had ripped the star from her coat and turned her curls from chocolate brown to platinum blonde before she had changed into her first new name. The dye she made Michael bring stank and stung like a swarm of bees had taken root in her scalp. Lottie had taken one look at her brassy new mother and burst into terrified tears.

"She'll get used to it. It's best that I look more like her anyway. Thank goodness Bardou managed to pass on his coloring, or I would have had to put her through the same."

It was Michael who soothed the little girl in the end, who managed to convince her that her new mummy was as pretty as the old. When the child finally fell asleep, he went back out and returned with all the bottles of dye he could find.

"It was a good idea. You won't attract attention like this, and blonde hair makes fake papers far easier to manage. The most useable pictures we get are of *real* German girls."

Liese no longer asked about the ghostly women whose lives she took over. The dead; the bombed-out and the missing; the ones whose identities were stolen from carelessly gaping bags. Nothing mattered, except their name and the town they had come from. She learned that set of rules as quickly as the rest.

"If you are asked for your papers, decide quickly if you actually need to present them. If the police are distracted, or there is a crowd to check through, say that you've newly arrived, that you've not had a moment to register. If you have no choice but to hand them over, say the same thing. You're new here. A seamstress come to work in the factories, still looking for the right accommodation. Tell them you're a widow, that your husband lay down his life for the Fatherland. Blink away a few tears—that usually works. We'll keep changing the documents, so the dates you left wherever you came from don't stretch out so long they make your cover suspicious."

Michael made it all sound matter-of-fact and he swore the fake papers he dealt in were foolproof. He showed Liese the different components so that she could see the care that went into creating them. The blank forms obtained from a network of well-bribed policemen; the carefully shaved-off photographs. How the official stamp was lifted from the old document to the new by rolling across the impression with a hard-boiled egg and transferring it.

As soon as she had her first set, Liese practiced surrendering them, watching her face in the mirror until her reactions seemed normal. The first time she was challenged, she still thought her heart would leap out of her chest; that the documents she held in her rigid hand would scream liar and Jew. In the end, the policeman barely glanced at them, his attention caught instead by Lottie's cheeky beam. Only one guard tried a trick that even Michael hadn't heard of, clutching a bagful of candy and going down on his knees.

"And what's your mama called, pretty one?"

Liese didn't know a man could turn so red until Lottie, her head cocked to one side and her hand plunged into the treasure, answered *Mama* in a world-weary tone.

"But what about in a few months, Michael, when she has more words? Or next year when she will be able to ask him why he wants to know?"

"The war will be done by then. No need to worry."

His stock answer and never one she believed.

Michael had treated Hitler's invasion of Russia in 1941, and Stalin's consequent shift from Germany's ally to its enemy, as if the turnaround was a triumph of communist foreign policy. That "with everyone finally in the right place and standing shoulder-to-shoulder against fascism," the war's end was in sight. Liese could see no sign of that.

Berlin was crippled by shortages, even for those who had held on to their rights. Ration cards were as much use in the fireplace as they were in the shops. The Allied bombing raids were kinder than in other German cities, the targets still primarily Berlin's industrial edges, but the effects were creeping closer, pounding homes to rubble, turning Berlin's citizens into refugees. Twice, Michael had led Lottie and Liese to a safe house only to find its floors reduced to a cellar that was already full.

Everything was rumor. Michael was her only safe connection to the outside. In the few hours Liese had had to consider an underground life before she was plunged into it, she had pictured it peopled with a new kind of family. Communists and Jews, all of them illegals and Party-haters; all working together to keep each other afloat. She had consoled herself with the varied faces she would meet; convinced herself there would be playmates for her too-alone daughter. Now she spoke only when she had to and bribed Lottie not to speak at all. All she had moved into was more isolation.

They were forbidden a radio. They met no one but Michael. Her news came from days-old newspapers and the snippets of gossip he carried with him. Liese had become a master of making games from nothing; Lottie had finally grown used to silence. How well the three-year-old could now whisper broke Liese's heart.

None of the apartments they lived in felt like a home. The furniture was always sparse, the walls and the cupboards always bare. Lottie and Liese's world had shrunk to the size of a suitcase and nothing personal could be included in there. The only thing guaranteed to survive each flight was Dolly; Lottie was immovable without her. Inside was colorless; outside was mostly a memory. If they ventured out, it was rarely before twilight. The families she heard creeping through corridors, or hushing their voices on the other side of thin walls, remained invisible. Michael came alone; he moved them from place to place alone; he never spoke about colleagues or friends.

"We work in cells. Sometimes two, sometimes three. Never more. Someone with writing skills, someone with printing skills, someone with a flair for distribution; that's the ideal. I get lists of safe places, notices of the best times to move you and the others; locations for a document drop. I deal in aliases; I don't ask names. It has to be like that: if they catch me, that's all they catch."

"Don't you get lonely?"

He hadn't understood the question.

"Why would I? I'm too busy. There's always people to move. There's always leaflets to spread round the city. Our system is so streamlined now, even the Nazis would envy it. Our agents have infiltrated the factories, the universities, even the postal system. And you should see how we hide our material. The last lot went out disguised as cake recipes; the batch before that were wrapped in guides about how to work a camera. That one was my idea.

Open them up though and the message is the same: 'Hitler can't win the war; he can only prolong it. You are being robbed of your rights: it's time to stand up for freedom.' Everyone's reading them; there's so many out there, they have to be."

His eyes were as bright as the boy she had found stealing in the salon four years ago. His passion for the struggle and his ideals were undimmed.

Liese envied him. She longed to play a part that would make her feel less of a burden. To be doing something and not simply waiting on the war's end, but, with Lottie so little and so dependent on her, she couldn't find a role.

"It doesn't matter. Keeping Lottie safe is the only thing that counts for now. We need our children, Liese: too many have already been lost. If this is still going on in a year or two, when she's bigger, we'll find you something to help with. Don't worry about that now."

That had been the night when it happened. When the contrast between his life, which burst with purpose, and hers, which felt lost in the shadows, overwhelmed her with a loneliness that choked up her throat. When the urge to be young and carefree pushed aside the constant need to be careful. When Lottie, for once, had fallen asleep so well fed there was no chance of her waking.

Their coming together was unplanned, unexpected; welcome.

A hand to brush away her frustrated tears became a shoulder to cry on. Lips murmuring soothing words drew closer, found a new kind of language. The tempo between them shifted. A first hesitant kiss became an exploration of hands and mouths that dissolved edges. When Michael was the first to draw back, rubbing his eyes, asking, "Are you sure?" Liese took the lead.

"Stop thinking, stop questioning; just be."

For once in Michael's life, he listened.

There should have been awkwardness, the clash of a long-fixed friendship blundering into uncharted territory. There wasn't.

"You feel like coming home."

Michael had whispered that as the sun wriggled through the window's thin covering and Lottie stirred.

Liese had raised herself on one elbow, staring down at him as the sunlight softened his thin features, remembering the last face that had lain next to hers.

"Whatever this is, you won't let me down? I don't want promises and I won't make them, not while we're forced to live like this. But I need to know that, if I need you, you won't let me down."

He pulled her to him, kissed away her doubts as their bodies came back together. Kissed her so deeply at the door when he left that Lottie started laughing.

Liese went through the next few days feeling lighter, less frighteningly alone.

"It was just one night, nothing to make a big fuss of."

Lottie smiled back at her mother and carried on playing.

One night perhaps, but it had surprised them both with its tenderness. And there would be another, if the world would settle long enough to make space. One night that had slipped between her and fear, at least for a little while; that brought with its kisses a sliver of hope.

"He won't be long now, monkey. Another few minutes, that's all."

How many times had she said that in the two years since their hidden life had begun? Too many for Lottie to care. She didn't look up from the bed, where she was feeding Dolly the last breakfast crumbs. The last crumbs of anything, an extravagance that made Liese nervous, despite Michael's sweeping assurances.

"Finish off whatever food is left. I'll bring more for the train and then, when you get to the Spreewald, there'll be so much to eat, Lottie will think every day is her birthday!"

Michael had swung Lottie round and made her laugh and never thought the word *birthday* meant nothing to her.

It had been impossible to start marking the day, so Liese had filed it away instead with all the other missed treats she would one day make up for. Birthday parties, Christmas, ice cream, a pet. The list she carried in her head of everything her daughter's childhood was meant to be, and wasn't, kept growing.

"Be ready by six."

She'd been ready by five, their few possessions packed. Lottie was so used to nighttime flits, she could pull on her dress in the dark. This would be the last change of name, the last change of address, or so Michael had promised. "A safe place to sit out the war" he swore would soon be ending.

So where was he?

"Wait till you see the house we're going to live in. Michael says it's so huge you'll have your own bedroom and there's a garden and an orchard for running around in. And I bet there'll be a cat; all big country houses have a cat."

Gabbling away to stop herself panicking; pouring out another litany of words Lottie didn't know how to react to. Lottie continued feeding her doll without a glance for her mother.

Liese checked her papers for the twentieth time. Lena Edelmann. A name closer to her old one, in case Lottie's rapidly expanding language skills really had remembered anything from before. A new identity playing a widow who had found work as a maid, moving out of Berlin to work on a farm and find her daughter a better life. It made as much sense as any of the others she'd practiced. It would, at least, give her a job and a purpose.

"This will be good for you both, I promise."

Despite what Liese had said that first night, Michael had been full of promises lately. Ever since they had snatched a second and then a third night together; since their connection had deepened enough for her to stop counting. They were more careful now though, neither of them having any desire to add a pregnancy to the tightrope they walked.

"Or not yet."

Michael had blushed when he said that, and grinned like his old self again when he saw Liese's answering smile.

Now, when Liese watched Lottie playing on her own, she imagined her in the middle of a trio of siblings. She conjured the family around the little girl that she had once longed for, and wove brothers and sisters into every story she told. When Michael heard her doing that, he began to pick up the same dream.

"The couple who agreed to take you in are kind-hearted people. They've helped others; they know how to keep you safe. You could make a proper life with them; give Lottie as near as the war will let you to a real childhood. And then, when it's done, I'll come there and I'll get you. We'll come back to Berlin and we'll make a life, the three of us first and then the rest. Maybe we'll find your parents. Whatever happens, we'll start over together, as a family. If that's what you'd like."

Such a shy look when he said that, his face all boyish.

Liese had smiled back at him and realized that, yes, she would like it very much. There was no time for any more declarations, but that felt like enough.

Except today was the first step and he wasn't here. Michael was almost two hours late and he was never late. Punctuality was a code he lived by; that and reliability were the twin pillars of "the struggle's creed."

Liese's stomach churned. Please God he hadn't got caught up in the latest leaflet's distribution, like he used to do in the old days, and had forgotten them, not after all they had been through. They had already been in this apartment too long. Nearly four months. Time enough to be noticed. For the old lady who lived opposite to remark on "how lonely that poor little girl must be." For Liese to be looked at twice by the men clustered smoking outside the block's scruffy door. She hadn't mentioned any of that to Michael. He was watching out for their safety, she knew he was; her appearing nervous would only put him on edge.

Everything was ready—there was nothing left to do and distract her. Lottie was polished and shiny in her smartest dress, although it hung too loosely when it should have been too tight by now. Michael had found them a smarter case than the battered one that had limped beside them from flat to flat. He had also found Liese a hat to cover her grown-out hair. It was a silly pancake of a thing, trimmed with jaunty silk roses more suited to a wedding. It made her plain blue blouse and skirt look shabby, but it would do the trick. The shops had run out of hair dye months ago and Liese, in Lottie's words, was starting to look "stripy."

Eight o'clock.

It would be too late to go if he didn't come soon. The plan, the little she knew of it, was for her and Lottie to catch an early train before the day's checks began in earnest.

"I can't come with you. Even with my brilliantly staged limp, a man my age in civilian clothes draws questions like a magnet. You'll travel with a woman, a country sort who won't attract attention. I'll pass you onto her."

It had annoyed her, that, the implication that she was a parcel who didn't need to know what her label said. It had also annoyed her that he wouldn't give her any details beyond the bare minimum of the town in the Spreewald and a morning train, but the struggle demanded secrecy and the struggle always won. And if it was the struggle that had delayed him this morning, he could forget about her biting her tongue anymore.

"Michael coming."

Liese let go of her breath in a sharp exhale. Lottie's well-trained ears had heard the whisper of footsteps before she had.

"Come here now, sweetheart. We'll have to move quickly if we're going to get to the station on time."

She waited for the customary three raps on the door. Nothing. What was keeping him?

"What did you hear, monkey?"

"Feet banging."

Why would Michael run up the stairs with no care for the noise? Liese took a step back from the door.

"Lottie, I don't think it's Michael. We may have to—"

A door slammed further down the corridor. Another one slammed closer. The unmistakable sound of boots came crashing up the hall.

"Mama's hurting Lottie. Stop it!"

Liese had Lottie's hand held so tight, the tiny fingers had turned purple.

"Quick, get under the bed."

Lottie stared and began sucking her sore hand.

"It's a game, monkey. It will be fun, I promise, but you need to be quick."

Her voice was too shrill, her mouth too stretched. Lottie whimpered and edged away.

"Please, Lottie. Do what I say. I'm going to come under there with you."

"Open up!"

Lottie shot onto the bed like a firecracker exploding and hurled her body across Dolly's.

"Open up!"

There was a knife lying among the bread crumbs on the table. Liese was a finger's stretch away from it when the flimsy lock disintegrated.

A green-uniformed man strode in, wiping his hands. He swallowed her and the room in one sweeping look.

Remember the rules.

Except this wasn't a busy street with places to duck into and Lottie wasn't charming but terrified.

"Papers."

Liese stood as tall and still as she could. "Is something wrong?"

The officer held her gaze for a fraction too long.

"Your neighbors think there is. They think there are all kinds of people hiding out in this building who shouldn't be here. Let's hope you're not one of them." He held out his hand. "Papers."

Liese removed them from her pocket, slowly and deliberately, praying the grainy photograph would withstand his mistake-hunting scrutiny.

"Why is there a suitcase?"

Be polite, not guilty; don't cower.

"I have a new job, as a maid on an estate in the Spreewald. We were about to leave for the station. I am a widow; my husband died fighting for his country."

His expression didn't flicker.

"The address of this estate?"

"Lehde, in the Lübbenau district."

Thank God she had managed to get that much at least.

He was still holding tight to her documents, looking from the photograph to her and back again, like a slowly swooping searchlight.

"Your permit to leave Berlin?"

She handed it over. It felt as flimsy as tissue.

"Mama." Lottie's whimper held the threat of a scream.

"My daughter is afraid; she isn't used to such intrusions. Let me calm her."

She should have been more deferential. The officer's hand whipped out and snaked round her wrist.

"Take off your hat."

"My hair, it isn't as clean as I'd like it…"

He ripped the flimsy straw away, leaving her dark roots and washed-out blonde streaks exposed, and flung it on the floor.

"And another lie. Like your papers are lies. And no doubt this tale about your hero husband. Do you really think we are so easily fooled? What are you? A Jew? What is your name? Do not waste my time with the one printed here." Her torn-up papers followed the hat.

Lottie had started to sob, her breath coming in ragged gasps. *Fight back, keep her safe.*

Liese faced him as squarely as she could.

"I don't know what you mean. My documents are old, perhaps, and a little faded. But they are genuine, I assure you."

"You assure me?" His hand was at her throat before she saw him move. "How clever you think you are with your dyed hair and your stolen name." He squeezed. "Stick to your story if you want. I can kill you as easily here as anywhere else. Then I can kill your daughter." He relaxed his grip a little. "Or perhaps I could kill her first?"

Liese had never seen anything as terrifying as her attacker's slow smile.

"No! Leave her alone. Don't touch her."

He lowered his hand. "Then tell me your name."

"Liese." She paused. "Liese Sara Elfmann."

"So, a Jew. How observant your neighbors are. And the child? Is her father a Jew as well?"

"Her father is a Frenchman."

"So, a whore as well as a liar and a Jew. What a delightful combination."

Outside the open door, the hallway was filling up. Shapes shuffled by, some of them weeping.

"Time for you to join the rest of the scum. Move."

She hesitated; he drew out his gun. She glanced at the table, but the knife was too far away; the gun was too close. Keeping an eye on the soldier, Liese picked up the case and reached out for Lottie.

"Come on now, sweetheart. It's time to go."

But Lottie curled up tighter and wouldn't budge. "No. Don't like him. Want—"

Liese ran and scooped her up before the name spilled, ignoring the child's furious kicking.

"Move. I won't tell you twice. And I will shoot her first."

Liese wrapped Lottie into her coat as the gun barrel swiveled.

"We have to do what he says. There's nothing to be scared of. Hold tight to Dolly."

She followed the pointing gun out of the room into the hall, where the snaking line shuffling down the stairs put an end to Lottie's thrashing. The child shrank into Liese, the rag doll pinned against her chest, her thumb jammed in her mouth. Liese murmured soothing noises into her daughter's hair and wondered which of them she was doing it for.

The pavement they were forced onto was packed, other apartment blocks emptying out with the same rifle-driven speed. Liese scanned the street for a place to run and hide, but every corner and alleyway was blocked.

"Onto the trucks. Men to the left, women and children to the right."

Soldiers were lined up the full length of the pavement, a number of them holding snarling dogs on the end of chains that were so long the animals were within snapping distance of coats and skirts. Lottie squealed at the barking and turned rigid.

"They're just dogs; they won't hurt you."

The beasts' bared teeth made a lie of that.

There was no time to invent a calming story; there was no time to do anything but what they were told. Liese kept Lottie's head pressed into her shoulder as they scrambled onto the truck. When she leaned out to ask for someone to pass up her suitcase, a soldier kicked it away. Liese refused to think about that; she refused to think about anything beyond keeping Lottie quiet and not drawing attention. She found a space and lifted Lottie's chin up to look at her.

"It's an adventure, monkey, that's all, like in the fairy stories I've told you. Do you remember Little Red Riding Hood and Snow White? How brave they had to be at the start, when the wolf and the queen were naughty? And how well it turned out for them both in the end?"

Her voice was too high-pitched; she was talking too fast. She wasn't surprised when someone told her to shut up.

"Where are we going?"

The truck roared away; no one answered. The lorry's tarpaulin had come down with a slam that had turned the vehicle's interior as dark as night and cut the outside away as if a knife had sliced through it. Lottie was sobbing, but not like a child. Her tears were silent things that pooled across Liese's neck like a stain.

"Come on now, sweetheart. Nothing's worth all these tears. I've got you. Nothing bad's going to happen."

Another assurance she couldn't guarantee, with as much substance as every other promise that there would be more food, that there wouldn't be any more running and any more houses that she had wrapped so uselessly round her daughter.

Like every promise Michael showered on me? Liese couldn't think about that; she couldn't think about anything, except staying strong for Lottie.

"Look at me, monkey."

She pressed her nose so close to Lottie's that their hair fell round them like curtains. Promises were all she had to offer, so she would keep on making them.

"This will be done soon and then, when it is, I'll make everything right. We'll go to the big house like Michael said we would and there'll be cake for tea and ice cream and a new dress for Dolly. Does that sound good? Is that something you'd like?"

Lottie gulped and nodded, her eyes closing as Liese rocked her.

I can't do this. I'm only twenty-three; I'm not old enough for this. I can't make this all right. Liese gulped back a sob. An arm eased out in the darkness, and Liese found her own head nestled against a warm motherly shoulder.

She turned into it, for a moment, and let herself, very briefly, cry.

*

Hertie.

Its arches and gleaming windows were unmistakeable, even in the scant minute Liese had to peer at her surroundings as she lifted Lottie from the truck.

Hertie, which meant Alexanderplatz, which meant…

"Line up. Three-wide. Move."

The Alex. The Red Castle. The headquarters of the Berlin Police.

Liese clutched her saucer-eyed daughter and tried not to shiver as the vivid red bricks and squat squared-off tower loomed over them. Maybe Michael would guess where they were and come. Then she remembered the night of Otto's arrest and her advice and knew it was hopeless. Michael would risk his own life for her, she knew that instinctively, but he was bound too tight with the resistance to risk all the rest his capture would mean.

"Round the back. Move."

They were herded, half-running, through a door that was wide and domed and high enough to admit a carriage. Liese lurched as paving stones gave way to slick and greasy cobbles. Lottie's arms clung limpet-tight. There was no chance of an escape, although she kept looking; there were too many guns. Barely a dozen steps and they were across the deserted courtyard and through a second, narrower doorway which led them into a corridor whose heavy wooden paneling ate up the light. Guards streamed in front of the women, slamming open the green metal doors that marched down both sides of the hall.

"Inside. Inside."

They chopped up the column, sending women whirling left and right. The room Liese was pushed into was dark and stank of unwashed bodies.

"Come over here. There's a few inches left."

It was a cell. Liese tried to stay with *room* but couldn't make the word stick even inside her own head. Tiled walls, bodies curled on a plain stone floor; one watery bulb dripping out a thin yellow circle.

Liese followed the calling voice to the furthest corner and slid down into the gap that was offered, making herself into a softness for Lottie. Within minutes, she could feel herself bruising.

"It's not the easiest place to push through when you're balancing a child."

The woman's voice had the texture of gravel.

"Do you have a cup?"

"What? A cup? No. I don't have anything. I had a case but…"

Liese was too worn out to dredge up anything more. As her eyes adjusted to the gloom, the cell's occupants assumed more definite shapes. Women, a scant handful of children. All of them still. If they closed their eyes, they would turn into corpses.

"Don't."

Liese gasped as a hand caught her chin and pulled her round. The woman was younger than her voice suggested, although her face was stretched and haggard.

"You need to stay calm and focus on getting through. Most of us have been here for days, which is why we look so feeble. What day is it?"

"Thursday."

"That's what I thought, although so little changes in here it was hard to be sure. Well, that's good news for you. From what we can make out, the transports from here leave on a Friday. All you've got to survive is one night. That's doable, right?"

Liese managed a nod.

"Good girl."

The woman released her grip and rummaged under her skirt.

"Here. I've got a spare cup. Don't ask me how. They bring us water at midday, usually more at night. And bread, which is always stale, but it's edible. Most of us give a bit of our piece to the children."

Liese shifted Lottie more securely onto her lap. The child's eyes were closed, but her breathing was too quick for her to be sleeping.

The woman snaked out her hand again as Liese tried to look into her daughter's face.

"Let her be. You can't explain this; she doesn't need you to try."

It was advice Liese was more than willing to take.

"You said they'd move us tomorrow. Where do we go?"

The woman eased her back against the icy tiles and groaned.

"A labor camp. Rumors I heard before I was fool enough to end up here suggest the most likely one is Ravensbrück. It's not so far from the city and it's for women and children only, so maybe it won't be too bad." She nodded at Lottie. "You should follow her lead. Close your eyes. Sleep, if you can; save your strength. When they want you to move, they don't wait around."

She didn't speak to Liese again and nor did anyone else.

The crowded cell stayed quiet, the noise never rising above a murmur, even when the meager bread and dusty water came. Liese whispered nursery rhymes to Lottie, trying to wrap the little girl inside the familiar rhythms of *Hoppe, hoppe Reiter* and *Eins, Zwei, Papagei*; the ones Minnie had sung to her long ago. Lottie remained silent or hid behind sleep. Liese dozed in and out of dreams that were as bad as being awake, filled with images of her parents walking away and Michael forgetting her.

When the door crashed open, she—and everyone else—jumped.

"On your feet. If your name is called, answer yes and move into the corridor."

The list ran so quickly, Liese almost missed them when hers and Lottie's names rang out.

"Wet, Mama." Lottie's face crumpled.

"It's not your fault. It doesn't matter."

Liese pulled the child's soaked knickers away and turned her cardigan into a towel. Lottie had recoiled in horror from the communal pail that desperation had made Liese use, and Liese hadn't had the heart to force her.

"There, all good again. When we get where we're going, there'll be new clothes, I'm sure of it."

She wasn't sure of anything. The name Ravensbrück meant nothing. The word *camp* had too many meanings to contemplate. As to why cowed women and huddled children were seen as a threat that needed locking away, she couldn't think of anything that made sense of that.

"Line up. Three-wide. Move."

The same orders as before, but a faster speed demanded from the stumbling prisoners than on the journey in. The column ran double-time back through the corridor and into the courtyard. It was dark, the stars still visible; it was impossible to tell if it was early in the morning or late at night. Trucks waited by the outer door, their engines growling. The women scrambled on, urging the children to move quicker as the guards hurled orders around them.

The journey through the city was too fast to take a bearing. The station platform they landed on was too packed to see a name. The train they were herded onto was so crowded, Lottie was pressed into Liese with barely a space to breathe. Everything moved so quickly, all Liese could do was obey. There were no seats. There were no spaces between the women standing shoulder to shoulder, shrinking away from contact or propping each other up. There were no windows low enough or wide enough to see a chink of the sky. The air hung sour with sweat and the ammonia stink of fear.

Liese braced her feet, braced Lottie against her shoulder. She wriggled up her arm until her watch was visible, counted one hour, then another. The train rumbled and belched out smoke, which seeped into the carriage and covered the women with polka-dot smuts. When the engine finally shuddered to a halt and the doors sprung open, bodies toppled out like bricks.

"Hold tight, monkey. Don't let go of me."

The words didn't need saying. Lottie's fingers bit through Liese's skin.

More trucks were lined up, waiting. The women were ringed by soldiers; any movement away from the crush was impossible. Liese caught glimpses of a cloudless cornflower sky. The fruity scent of pine set her nose twitching.

"Get down. Five-wide. Form up."

Five this time, not three. A new number to shuffle them with.

The women formed into lines, their mouths silently counting along the rows. The guns were too close to risk a mistake.

"Put the children down. Tell them to walk."

Liese was stranded too visibly at the column's edge. She tried to swap places, to wriggle in toward the center and a foot or two of safety. A rifle butt shoved her forward before she could slide in.

"Children down. If I have to repeat that, I shoot."

"You heard what he said, monkey. You have to walk."

"No. Can't. Too tired."

Liese stifled a cry as the rifle cocked.

"Do as you're told. No more arguing."

Fear made her voice harsh.

Lottie's eyes filled with tears. Liese wished that she could swallow the words back. That she could bend down, whisper that she was sorry. Explain that her sounding cross was just part of this strange game they were all playing, but the soldiers were shouting and the column was marching and it was all she could do to keep Lottie upright.

I'll say it later. I'll cuddle the darkness away, as soon as she's safe.

The shouting throttled up again, harsh cries to move, to be quicker, pushing the prisoners down a cobbled road, past a row of balconied houses perched high on a hill and a forest of fir trees that smelled like Christmas. They were marched so fast, Lottie was almost flying, her wrist locked in Liese's hand.

"Eyes forward, mouths shut."

Whips cracked along the lines. Lottie stumbled on, no longer sobbing, although her whole body was shaking. Liese kept pulling and didn't dare look down.

"Stop."

The ground softened, took on the powdery feel of sand. Liese took a breath that tasted as fresh as spring rain, lifted her head, and almost laughed. The setting was picture-postcard perfect, a holiday scene.

A lake stretched out only feet away from where the women had been herded, its placid water a mirror of the morning's blue sky. Linden trees edged the high wall they were standing near and softened the camp's metal gates with velvety green. Liese could see banks of red flowers nodding their way along the neatly laid road that stretched out on the other side.

Hope inched its way back. Liese smiled at the woman shivering next to her. Heads rose across the tightly packed column. The smile passed tentatively on.

Liese loosened her grip on Lottie's wrist, kept her back straight, and bent her knees so she could slip a hand round her daughter's tiny shoulders.

"Lottie, look: it's pretty. There's flowers and a lake you might be able to paddle in."

Other whispers followed hers, spreading out like ripples.

"No talking!"

Not a man's voice anymore—a woman's, sharp and strident.

In the relief of being in a gentler landscape than anyone expected, someone didn't hear, or didn't obey quickly enough. A hand shot out, cracked hard against skin. Another voice screamed; the next slap rang harder.

Guards fanned out and began striding down the rows. Not soldiers but a troop of almost identical blonde women, made thickset and solid by square caps and wide-shouldered black capes. They didn't have guns, but they had whips they sent flying. One sliced through the air a foot away and crashed Lottie into Liese's legs.

"Noses to the front."

The guards began carving the packed crowd ahead of them into slices, forcing their shaking captives in tight columns through the gates. Liese saw a girl stumble; saw another fall under a thick fist as she kneeled down to help. The air grew dark with sobs and slaps and the discordant screeching of "bitches."

Lottie's hand shot back into Liese's and set rigid and clawlike.

Liese ached to scoop her up, to press the white face hard into her shoulder and make a shield against the cruelty unfolding with such malevolent speed.

As they drew nearer the gates, the guards' excitement flared. A whip tore open a cheek a few paces in front; a kick leveled a woman who'd fallen out of line. The slightest movement or whimper, one step's hesitation, and they pounced like jubilant tigers. There was no time to think, no time to do anything other than stay in line and follow the hailstorm of orders.

I'm here; I have you.

Liese poured the words through every inch of her body that was touching her daughter's and squeezed the hand curled inside hers. Lottie didn't respond.

The gates were coming closer now—a dozen or so steps and they would be inside the camp. She could see the women who had already entered marching down the long road between the barrack blocks. There didn't seem to be as much shouting on that side; there certainly seemed to be fewer guards visible. Other women had noticed the change in mood inside the walls. The rows around Liese began to grow calmer, more obedient.

Perhaps it's bad out here because it's so crowded, because we're all so nervous. Maybe things will be easier once we get through.

Liese shuffled forward. Some of the guards had lowered their whips as the women gradually stopped resisting their orders. Liese squeezed Lottie's hand.

Another few steps and then I'll be able to hold you. I'll be able to make all this right.

Her row inched quietly toward the gates. Three more lines in front of them and then they would be inside and safe.

Liese was about to bend her knees and risk another whisper when she felt her arm wrench. Lottie had frozen. What was she doing? There was a guard standing too close for Liese to speak. She pulled on Lottie's hand, but the child pulled sharply back and knocked Liese into the woman behind. A ripple ran along the row.

What is she afraid of?

And then Liese caught it. A scent weaving toward them, raw and meaty and hot. Dogs. Liese groaned. The three guards closest to the gates had dogs running beside them, their leads, like at Alexanderplatz, long and loose enough for the animals to get within pawing distance of the women. The dogs' mouths were open, the scent in the air their foul panting breath. No wonder the prisoners in front of them had entered the camp without a sound: they weren't calm, they were terrified.

"Mama. No. Not walk by them."

A guard turned, her small eyes hunting for the source of the sound.

Liese couldn't risk even the tiniest whisper. She squeezed Lottie's hand instead and tried to pull her forward, praying that speed would smooth the dogs' straining muscles and teeth to a blur. Lottie's legs had taken root. As Liese yanked again, the girl tumbled and the hand clutching her doll shot open.

"Dolly!"

Lottie's cry rose like a bird. She stretched her fingers wide, but the rag doll had already twirled away and landed a pace from where the dogs were pawing. The nearest one pounced, its jaws as wide as if it were grinning. One flick of its bullet nose and the doll went floating back through the air. As it toppled down again, another dog leaped. Dolly's head was caught up in one slavering mouth, her feet caught up in another.

"NO!"

All the silences of the last twenty-four hours, of the last twenty months, gathered themselves into Lottie's scream. Her pain rang around the lakeshore as pure and piercing as a blade.

"Shut her up!"

The guard with eyes as black as ebony chips was coming.

Liese tried.

She threw her hands over Lottie's mouth, but Lottie struggled and bit and thrust them away.

The dogs pulled. The doll burst open in a ragged cloud. Lottie's scream roared like a tempest.

"She's a child. She doesn't understand."

But Liese's plea was no match for the dogs' frantic barking, for the guards' frenzied shouts; for the searching eyes that had found their target.

The hand that grabbed Lottie and tore her away was the size of a man's. Flat and broad and scarred in a zigzag line that ran from its middle finger down to the thickset wrist. It circled Lottie's neck like a collar.

Seconds.

That was all it took. For the snap. For the splash that swallowed the broken body down into the lake. For Liese's world to fall, hopelessly and forever, apart.

PART THREE

CHAPTER TEN

Karen

Aldershot, November 1989

Karen closed the front door, her knees sagging as the night caught up with her.

"Go home—get some rest. He's stable; we don't expect any change for a while."

Home: was that what she should call this place? It was the shorthand her friends still used to describe the houses they grew up in, no matter how many new families and mortgages stood between then and now. Karen studied the hallway's non-descript paint and old-fashioned coat stand, the age-spotted mirror with its fine layer of dust. Nothing had changed in the eleven years since she had lived here.

"Home."

She tried it. It sat no more comfortably with her now than it had then. She knew she should have booked a hotel, taken a moment to think before she jumped into the car, but the thought he might be dying had terrified her. She could do it now, but a day and a night with no sleep beyond what could be snatched in a hospital chair had left her head fuzzy.

It was only a house. Would it be that difficult to manage a few hours inside it? Enough time at least to regroup and maybe take a bath. Karen's skin prickled with the anticipation of hot water and vanilla-thick bubbles. Despite the sharp November wind and the threat of snow hanging in the charcoal sky, the upside-down day clung damp and sticky. The early-morning motorway dash, the overheated ward; the shock of seeing her father so helpless, a gaping hospital gown wiping away the familiarity of his collar-and-tie dignity. A bath then, to straighten her out and settle her nerves.

Karen was on the bottom stair before she remembered that the towels would be cardboard-thin and the soap unperfumed carbolic. Her shoulders reknotted.

"You have to do something; you can't just stand here."

Her voice croaked from a night spent whispering. It still cracked like a gunshot down the hallway, stirring memories like dry leaves as it went. Was that why she'd spoken out loud, to stamp herself on the house's silence? To make the house fit round her for a change? Talking to herself was something she never did, despite living on her own; it was something she had never been remotely tempted to do.

Karen shivered and failed to convince herself the chilly air was to blame.

What is it you English like when everything is falling to pieces? Father Kristoff. She hadn't thought of him for years.

"And it isn't odd that you've remembered him now you've come back here, so don't overthink it."

She threw out the words and followed them, imagining her voice carving out a path like a force field. A form of madness no doubt, but at least one of her own choosing.

The kitchen she eased herself into had the sour edge of too-long-left garbage. Karen opened a window and began rooting through the cupboards. Not tea: seven-thirty in the morning or not, she was past that sort of soothing, and surely she'd been up for so long the rules didn't count. She stretched onto her toes and was rewarded with the bottle of whisky Andrew was never without, whatever his indifference to other home comforts. She poured a generous measure, realized she couldn't remember when she'd last eaten and set about foraging.

The fridge was a forest of Tupperware and carefully parceled-out portions. Karen located cheese and a jar of pickle; slotted bread under the eye-level grill. The kitchen was, as ever, ordered with military precision: the tea towels smartly lined up on their pegs, the floor brush firmly twinned with its dustpan. Not unlike her own neatly kept kitchen, although she doubted Andrew would ever believe that.

"There really is no one at home to take care of him?"

"No, not full-time. I wish there was, but my mother is dead and I'm an only child. Besides, I live in London and he's very happy here; he would never agree to move from Aldershot. And my job is demanding. I have holiday owing, which, of course, I'll use, but then I have to get back to it."

The consultant had shaken his jowls and sighed over modern women's priorities.

Karen wouldn't budge—she couldn't. She struggled to adequately describe her relationship with her father to herself and to the people who cared about her; she certainly wasn't about to expose it to the consultant's insulated ideas.

The nurse had waited until the great man had moved on and then handed over a list of phone numbers.

"Assisted living is your best bet. He'll be here for a few weeks yet; there's time to get things sorted."

Assisted living. Andrew would call it "going into a home" and no doubt hate anywhere she suggested, but what choice did they have?

Karen tried to imagine a world in which she played the doting daughter to her grateful father and poured herself another drink to wash away the guilt. A heart attack and a serious one at that, needing something called stents and a long recuperation: it was the last thing she'd expected. Admittedly, her father was seventy-three, but his military training had kept him fit and he had always seemed, physically at least, far younger than his years.

The sun prodded pale and watery through the window. Karen finished the last of her toasted cheese as the light inched in.

The kitchen wasn't as clean as first appearances suggested. A spider's web looped from the light fitting; rusty stains spattered the cooktop.

Karen turned away: they played such tightly defined roles around each other, he would hate her to suspect his high standards were slipping. Well, she could play the good daughter this far at least. She found a bottle of bleach and steeled her tired body to tackle the cleaning. Then the disinfectant smell flew back hospitals and tubes and translucent waxy skin and she found herself sobbing. The kitchen wobbled, expanding and contracting around her as if she were shrinking.

How could the house still unpeel her like this?

It shouldn't mean a thing anymore. It wasn't as if she had ever been a regular visitor: the nights she had spent under its roof since she left barely made it into double figures. Karen counted back through them, aware that if she revealed their sparseness to anyone else, they would shame her. A couple of miserable Christmases until she found friends with families big enough to absorb her. A handful of trips back in her university days, usually motivated by lack of money. None at all since she'd joined her London-based architects' firm. She wasn't estranged from her father—even in her darkest moments Karen couldn't imagine anything so final—but they had rules. They met now for lunches in neutral places, stiffly edged restaurants in Kensington or Chelsea, where surviving without a spat until the third course classed as a successful visit.

"It wasn't meant to be like that."

She could hear her teenage self sniffing.

"You were supposed to do better. You were going to be kinder and calmer, and start building bridges. Don't you remember? You were going to find your father and let him be the pathway to finding your mother."

It had been a good plan. It had been the plan the whole way back from Berlin, once Karen accepted that the city had left her with bigger questions than she could tackle alone. Father Kristoff had shaken the pieces of her childhood out of their old slots and Karen had traveled back from Germany as determined as a new-minted evangelist not to stuff them back in.

She had failed at the first hurdle.

Her good intentions had proved themselves to be skin-deep. That realization might make her squirm now, but it was the truth. She hadn't tried to mend fences, she had postured. She had carried on doing what she always did: setting her father tests and letting him fail, while she watched in disdain from her precious high ground. Deciding to be hurt when he wasn't at the school gate to greet the coach, or in the house when she tipped her bags all over the sitting room. Conveniently forgetting that she hadn't bothered to let him know the day, never mind the time, she would be returning. Deciding to be disappointed at his lack of interest, even though she had retreated to her bedroom long before he came home, and made no effort to get up before he went out again in the morning.

Karen winced, remembering how she had arranged herself on the sofa the next evening, wearing her best I-forgive-you face.

What had been wrong with her? Why hadn't she run to him when the door opened and surprised him with a hug? Startled them both into the new start they needed? Because she was too proud? Or too angry? Or afraid of what he might tell her, or of what he had failed to? Whatever excuse she had found herself then, or plastered over the past now, it didn't matter: the outcome wouldn't change. Instead of moving toward him, she had waited and he had waited and the moment had crumpled into "so you didn't even bother to miss me then" on one side and a weary headshake on the other. Ten minutes restored to each other's company and they were thrust back into old ways. A few months later, she had left for Manchester and told herself he was glad of it. She had never once asked him if that was true. Now, with Andrew lying in the hospital, all she could feel was the waste of it.

Karen put down the glass and realized, once again, she was crying.

Tell me what you want—at least give me a chance. Stop trying to end us before we get started.

How many boyfriends had hit her with that line? How many times had "I don't mean to do it" died on her lips?

"So you struggle to commit. You haven't met the one you want to get really close to, that's all. When you do, everything will be different."

All her well-meaning friends said it and swept away Karen's "but what if I can't" as if the fear buried in the words couldn't possibly be real.

She had tried. She had let Joe get very close and she hadn't set him tests, at least not ones he didn't know about. She had so wanted it to work, for them to win the whole package, but then she would panic and push him away and fall apart when he pressed her on why. It was Joe who had delivered the worst parting shot of all the ones she had gathered, hurled on a blast of confusion and anger when she shied from cementing two years of shared beds into something more permanent.

"We all have hurt, Karen. You're not a child anymore. You can't keep hiding behind your dead mother."

"And is that what you do?"

The therapist's question Karen could never find the right words to answer. The therapy sessions abandoned, like the pills a doctor offered that remained uncollected, in favor of locking the past firmly away in the past. A strategy that, as far as Karen was concerned, worked. That had got her through the bleak and frightening times when Liese's suicide resurfaced and threatened to engulf her.

I won't be defined by it; I won't be damaged.

Which sounded believable, except here she was, alone, hunched up, and brooding like a passed-over child.

"Enough."

Karen jumped up and put the whisky away before it made her any more maudlin.

The cold in the kitchen was getting under her skin. She needed to take the day back under control, to get back to herself. She headed for the sitting room and the one reasonably reliable fire. Nothing in there had changed any more than it had in the kitchen. The walls still needed a fresh coat of paint. The air still held the dry taste of old newspapers. The mock-coal fire still glowed for too long before the heat broke through.

Karen ran her fingers across the bookcase whose dusty contents hadn't been touched for years and glanced at the drab landscapes spaced out on the walls. The house would have to be sold if her father's new life was going to be paid for. All of it would need boxing up, and no doubt Andrew would demand inventories. He had mentioned bringing home files and papers when he finally retired, so he could stay active, running the regiment's old-boys' association. They would all have to be sorted. More poking through the past, the one thing she had no more desire to do.

Sometimes, in the middle of the night when sleep decided to evade her, Karen wondered why she had stopped, why she had convinced herself her mother's history no longer mattered. Then, the confrontations and the silences and the confusions of long-ago discoveries slammed back and the urge to go delving again disappeared.

What was it someone had said, in the first whirlwind weeks of university, after too much cheap wine had made them think they were grown-up and daring? "How many people really know their parents? How many could honestly bear to?" Karen had latched on to that like a life lesson.

She had worked hard; she had made friends and done well. She had set herself goals and she had achieved them. The degree in architecture she wanted, a starting position in a Manchester practice, a move to London, and the kind of firm whose designs graced magazine covers. Karen had forged a life pointing forward and kept it steadier than she once thought she could. And if sometimes her life was lonely, lacking the one big love her friends all seemed to be finding, there was enough good in it to paper over that. She was happy enough and that was more than a lot of people could say; more than she had once expected. She wasn't about to let returning to this house derail her.

"Which means I can't stay here. I'll book a hotel, get some sleep, and then I'll start on the packing."

That sounded more confident.

She switched on the television, in need of bright-eyed breakfast crews to buoy up her new determination.

"And just because I found something once, that doesn't mean it'll happen again."

Then she glanced at the television and all thoughts of hotels and packing crates vanished.

"As the guards look on in bewildered confusion, the crowds keep on coming."

Karen perched on the arm of the chair as the reporter realized this was his opportunity to make a grab for history and crammed his voice full of meaning.

"The Iron Curtain lifted in East Berlin tonight."

The images unfolding across the screen were hypnotizing, unbelievable. Bodies swarmed like migrating herds out of the Eastern sector's impossibly opened gates; crowds massed on the Western side to welcome them, clutching flowers and over-shaken champagne. Cheering couples danced hand in hand round the Brandenburg Gate. Laughing figures scrambled like ants onto the top of the Wall.

Karen gasped, her throat clenching as she watched the East German guards shouting at the photographers, as she waited for bullets. Instead sparklers, not searchlights, lit up the concrete and the wastelands, and the human tidal wave kept surging.

"After almost thirty years of being firmly barred, the gates between East and West finally stand open."

The reporters carried on as best they could, while denim-clad and fake-leathered hordes surrounded them, clinging to each other, thrusting themselves into the camera as if only by recording the moment they would make its bizarreness real.

"No more Stasi! No more secrets!"

Karen let out her tightly held breath. The journalists sensed danger and swung back to the party, but Karen could still hear the chant. It gathered itself up at the edges of the screen, roaring at the displaced soldiers who shuffled and blinked into shot and suddenly looked frightened.

No more secrets.

The doorbell rang. Karen ignored it. The letter box rattled to a strident "cooee" as the neighbor, Mrs. Hubbard, emerged, drilling for news like a wasp after sugar. Karen didn't hear her. She was lost in the sight of long-separated people crying and hugging. In the possibility of spaces reopening, surrendering their histories.

There's nothing to find; there's no one to ask.

Karen stared at the screen as the house shifted round her. What if that was no longer true?

CHAPTER ELEVEN

Karen

Aldershot, December 1989–March 1990

Karen had never thought of herself as superstitious before, but the Wall's moral, if not yet completely physical, collapse had her clutching at signs. Facing the past suddenly felt like the brave, the in-step-with-the-world thing to be doing.

In the weeks after her father's heart attack, she raced to and from the hospital, torn between watching his slow progress and the far quicker moving news. She was mesmerized by the bulletins, switching between channels, glued to the set as chunks of concrete fell away in haphazard holes and Berlin stepped its way back through them. Instead of searching out a hotel to spend her enforced holiday in, she had decided instead to reclaim the house. To reinhabit its rooms and let her mother back in.

"What if she stayed with you as long as she could?"

Memory after memory surged, and the newly emboldened Karen dived down under them. Every image she could grasp became a stepping stone to the next. She pictured herself as one of the *Mauerspechte*, the "Wall-woodpeckers," with their clinking hammers and pickaxes, who the news reporters obsessed over. Not chipping away at crumbling stone, but peeling back the absences and the stillness; the nighttime ramblings and the tears. Looking closer, listening harder.

"Come away now, pet. She's not here; she won't answer."

How had she missed the sob in her father's voice? Why had she never questioned who *she* was?

As the weight of wasted years pressed more and more sharply, Karen finally did what Father Kristoff had asked her to do and shifted the angles she looked at the past from. It wasn't easy—the events she summoned up had had their narrative set long ago. But she began and, when she did, she discovered that, if she decided Andrew's hand on Liese's shoulder was calming not controlling, she could see the way her mother leaned into it. If she refused to be frightened by the frozen figure in the bed, she remembered the tight embraces and the "I love you; I'm sorry" pressed into her hair that followed the reawakenings.

There were no thunderbolt moments, nothing made any more sense than it had. The stings, however, blunted a little. Karen finally began to see that *mothers stayed with their children whatever happened* could perhaps be less rigid a gospel at twenty-nine than she had believed it to be at eleven.

The need to talk to her father consumed her. She was desperate to lay open her new way of seeing and have him embrace it, embrace her; to spill out the secrets and lighten them both. The nurses, however, too used to frantic sickbed declarations to indulge the ones they could stop, batted her away.

"Whatever that light is in your eye, he's not ready for it. He's had major surgery; he's weak. Let him be."

Even if Karen had dared disobey, she wouldn't have got close enough. Andrew was not the solitary figure she had always assumed: he had as wide a circle of friends as she did. There was always someone by his bed when she arrived at the hospital, reading aloud from a book or the newspaper, chatting quietly, even though he was still mostly unconscious. The visitors were, almost without exception, men, always scrupulously polite to Karen and all of them in thrall to Mrs. Hubbard.

"I've set up a rota of his old colleagues so he's never without a bit of friendly company to keep him going. Clearly you must be terribly busy, you breeze in and out so fast."

The last part was delivered through pursed lips as she copied the nurses and waved Karen's agitation out of the ward.

"Besides, there are more useful things you could be doing with your valuable time. Making a start on clearing the house for one. I have the details of his financial affairs, numbers for bank accounts and the like; I'll pass them over to you this evening. And, as he assumed if this happened you'd be looking for a *facility*, you should know his preferred option is The Mountbank."

Karen slunk away smarting, not confident enough of her standing in Mrs. Hubbard's eyes to mount any form of defense.

When she began tentatively poking at his neatly organized papers, she realized their old neighbor was right: her father had left nothing to chance. Mrs. Hubbard's pointed "why would he, when he couldn't know what you would, or wouldn't, listen to" hardly made sorting through the files any easier.

There were funds arranged to bridge any payment gaps, the details of an estate agent ready for instruction. Everything was laid out as precisely and impersonally as his old holiday notes. Karen knew without searching that there would be no letters brimful of Liese's past tucked away in the binders, no packets of fading photographs waiting to be revealed.

So, what, he was prepared to die without telling me anything?

No matter how hard she tried to block them out, the old hurts kept resurfacing.

In the end, it was a relief to find the envelope.

She had returned to work once it was clear her presence at the hospital was less than necessary, although she phoned for daily updates and raced down the motorway to Aldershot every weekend. Her father gradually showed signs that his recovery was coming;

a buyer appeared for the house; the task of properly dealing with it became too urgent to keep stalling. Karen finally forced herself to begin the packing on a dark Saturday morning, boxing up the ground floor's more neutral spaces before she could face tackling her parents' bedroom and its uncomfortable memories.

The kitchen drawers and the small bureau in the living room yielded nothing unexpected; the hall cabinet contained little beyond telephone directories. She worked methodically, convincing herself her only focus was sorting out the house. As the hours went by, however, the task became the quest she knew it inevitably would be and the past's refusal to cooperate took on the feel of an insult.

The graying rectangle fell into Karen's lap as she shook out one of the last remaining books to be boxed, an unremarkable and faded paperback. Her first response was "thank goodness for that."

The envelope was thin and unsealed, its dried-out flap heavily creased. Karen wiped her hands and wiped them again and discovered she couldn't open it.

It's another dead end flashed through her mind like a neon sign.

It wasn't until her legs cramped, forcing her into a chair, that she steeled herself to slide the envelope's contents out. There were two items tucked inside: a postcard with a street scene picked out in acid-tinged green and yellow, and a photograph in black and white which took her breath away.

She picked up the photograph first. It was the image her imagination had conjured up years ago in the church in Berlin: her parents, impossibly young, on their wedding day. Andrew was in uniform, her mother in a calf-length pale dress and veiled hat. The couple were posed awkwardly outside a grubbier version of the Lindenkirche, with a second man a pace behind. The trio looked like actors in three different plays.

Andrew was joyous—there was no other word for it. He grinned out at the camera as if every birthday-cake wish had rained down on him at once, a wide smile brightening his solid face. Liese, in contrast, was looking down and held her long-stemmed bouquet raised, as if she longed to hide behind it. Her shadowed face and hunched shoulders made her look both bewildered and afraid, as if the simple act of being photographed was overwhelming.

It unnerved Karen to see her mother so uncomfortable, but it wasn't Liese who made her eyes blur. The second man, who was as handsome as her father was plain, was visibly heartbroken. His distress was written in the hand hovering beside Liese's elbow as if he was desperate to clutch it; in the way he couldn't find a smile; in the pleading gaze fixed so hopelessly on the bride. His pain was too intimate to look at.

Her heart racing, Karen turned the photograph over in search of a name. There was nothing, not even a date.

Putting the image reluctantly to one side, she picked up the postcard. On closer inspection, the view wasn't so much of a street as a boulevard. A wide expanse of manicured grass and spotless roads separated two identical rows of pristine buildings which stretched out toward a stately pair of towers. The effect was elegant, deliberately palatial. The tiered-wedding-cake architecture reminded Karen of diagrams of buildings in Moscow she had studied at university.

Unlike the photograph, the back of the card was covered in writing. A title identified the location as Stalinallee. There was a red postage stamp next to that, featuring the hammer and compass she remembered from the border crossing, the wording *Deutsche Demokratische Republik*, and a smeared date stamp that said *1953*. The message crowding the small space was in German, but, apart from the last line whose construction sent Karen upstairs for her old dictionary, its meaning was simple to follow.

Dearest Liese,

I am finally settled; my new home is better than any place I could have dreamed of in the war years, or after. You can

write to me regularly now; whatever you send will find me.
Please let me know you are well; please tell me that we did
the right thing. That he gave you the good life I dreamed
of for you. This silence between us stretches out endlessly.

The handwritten plea was followed by an address picked out in
neater letters: *Stalinallee Block C, 502, Friedrichshain, Berlin, DDR.*

Karen knew at once that the Michael whose name was signed
below the hard-pressed lines was the young man in the photograph.
It was clear from the card's gaps, as much as its words, that he loved
her mother. What she couldn't make sense of was "tell me that we
did the right thing."

She was still puzzling pointlessly at it when the clock struck six
and she realized she'd missed her allotted slot at afternoon visiting.

*I should ring the hospital, check on him; find an excuse before Mrs.
Hubbard comes snooping.*

She made the call, but she didn't put down the card. *1953.*
Karen ran her finger over the stamp and stroked the edge of the
photograph. Thirty-five years. Michael could well be alive, could
be living at the same address. Her father had been in this house
longer than that. Which is all very well, but Aldershot had never
been carved up in the same way as Berlin. What was here thirty-five
years ago was still here. Where was the guarantee of that in Berlin?

Karen spent the rest of the night oblivious to everything but
the possibility of other clues unfolding. She rechecked every book
she had packed and went back through every boxed-up folder,
searching for some scrap that would shed light on the man, on
who he was to her mother. There were no more revelations.
The only thing certain was that this Michael held an important
place in Liese's story. She couldn't ask her father in his present
condition; neither could she afford to ignore what she had found.
All she had was an old address and a sneaking suspicion that

names honoring Stalin might not be in favor anymore. Not very much to go on.

But not a dead end.

"Such a delight to know you've kept up your German. So few do. And a mystery, how exciting! Let me just find my map box and I'm sure we can crack it."

Time hadn't diminished Mrs. Hubbard's busy-bodying, and it hadn't dimmed Miss Dennison's enthusiasm. The moment Karen had appeared, tentatively knocking on the classroom door of her vastly different old school, the teacher had been all squeals and handclapping. Once Karen had produced the postcard and explained she was trying to find out if the address was still valid, Miss Dennison's enthusiasm bubbled over like lava.

"Such a thing to bear witness to, the end of the Wall. I remember it going up. August 1961. I would have been eighteen, a proper little hothead. There wasn't a word of warning, of course. One day it wasn't there, the next it was and, whatever side you woke up on, you were stuck with it. So many people desperate to escape from the East and me and my friends threatening to go and join 'the great revolution.' How crazy we must have sounded. My parents must have been horrified."

Karen stared at her, wrong-footed by the revelation.

"Why on earth did you want to do that?"

Miss Dennison laughed. "If you could see your face. Because we were socialists and young and naïve, and we thought the DDR promised nirvana."

She has such a mischievous twinkle in her eye. Karen had never noticed that before, or how pretty the woman's auburn hair was.

"You were a socialist? That's the last thing I would have taken you for."

"No, I imagine that wouldn't fit the box you all put me in. Don't look awkward; it doesn't bother me. What pupil considers their teachers as people with lives of their own? I never did. We're like parents to our pupils: some kind of *other* that's not quite people. Well, Karen Cartwright, now you're all grown up, let me properly introduce myself: I never was a Miss, I have a husband and two children and, for all its flaws, the DDR still fascinates me."

She hauled a crate full of maps onto the table and began sorting through it.

"Now, close your mouth and let's see what we've got. Here, these two should do it."

She pulled out two maps and spread them out. Both were of Berlin. The larger of the two was yellowing and had a bright red wall rendered across it, so carefully drawn it stood out like 3D. The second had removed West Berlin completely, leaving behind a gaping white space where the sector's streets should have been.

"They're both from the DDR. The one with the red wall on it is from 1961; the other's from a couple of years ago. A colleague brought them back as souvenirs from a conference his less conservative school turned a blind eye to. Look, there it is—*Stalinallee.*"

She pointed to a wide road marked on the East side of the older map.

"Let me see the postcard. Yes, I thought so. This street is famous, or at least it is over there. 'Exemplary homes for exemplary workers' was how it was described to my colleague." She pulled the newer map across. "You were right to think it would be renamed after Stalin died. There: *Karl Marx Allee*—can you see it?"

Karen nodded.

The teacher picked up the postcard.

"Why is tracking this man down so important, Karen? Don't say work—the message on this card is very personal. Is it to do with your mother?"

The question was so unexpected it left Karen groping for a chair, unable to answer.

Mrs. Dennison, a title Karen knew she would take a while to get used to, kept talking.

"We all knew what happened, of course. It was on your records. But your father didn't want anyone discussing it. He was so broken, so desperate for you to make a fresh start. And you were such a spiky little thing, a proper little porcupine. Things would be done differently now, but then..."

"Least said, soonest mended?"

Mrs. Dennison nodded and passed Karen a tissue. Karen wiped her eyes and traced a finger round the blank space on the newer map.

"It's awful now to admit it, but it never dawned on me, when she died, that my father was damaged. He was so, I don't know, stoic. I barely knew him then. I thought I hated him; I certainly acted like I did. And now he's very sick and I'm full of questions, and even if he were well enough for me to ask them, neither of us know how to deal with the other."

She held out her hand for the card and turned it over to look at the signature.

"I don't know why my mother did what she did, and everything I've learned about her since just adds to the mess. So when I found this postcard, it felt like a sign. This Michael matters—I'm sure of it. I think he was in love with her, although I've nothing but a look in a picture and a cryptic message to base that on. He was at her wedding and still worrying about her years later, so I know he must have been an important person in her life. What I don't know is why. So I'm going to write to him, see if he's still there in Berlin. It might come to nothing, but at least I'll have tried. I've spent long enough not doing that."

"Will you tell your father?"

Karen tucked the card into her bag.

"That I'm going to try and track down Michael? No, I don't think so. Afterward, maybe, if there's anything to tell."

She couldn't admit she was afraid that, if she did, Andrew would try his hardest to stop her.

She shouldn't have come. She knew that before the nurse chased her away. She hadn't meant to upset him. Now that she had received an answer from Berlin, all she had wanted to do was share her excitement and show him the letter. How was she supposed to know her father would panic when she produced it? She knew he couldn't talk yet, that his throat was still damaged and swollen from all the tubes they had used. She didn't think he would try so hard to shout, because that was what his twisted face told her he was trying to do, or that his blood pressure would spike so high the crash team would come running. She felt terrible, she really did, but no one would believe her.

"Your father has been seriously ill, he is not yet recovered, and you, despite every warning, have thoroughly upset him."

The Mountbank's warden was clearly struggling to restrain his temper. Karen could barely look at him.

"We had such hopes. He had transitioned well from hospital to here. We were on course to move him from our higher-level care into his own apartment in a month or so; the more independent way of living he quite rightly craves. Well, I'm afraid to say that you could have set his recovery back weeks. We cannot allow this, Miss Cartwright. If your visits are going to upset him so badly, perhaps you should consider curtailing them."

Karen found herself out in the grounds before she could defend herself, still clutching the letter that had caused all the trouble, that Andrew had recoiled from as if it were poisoned as soon as she had told him who it was from.

"What have you done this time?"

Mrs. Hubbard came bowling up between the flower beds like a bad-tempered ram, dragging a thin-haired girl Karen recognized as a taller version of one of the granddaughters who used to torment her when she was young.

"He's in a right state apparently. I had to call Sandra off her lunch break to get me here."

"Why would they send for you?"

Karen had already endured one telling-off—she was in no mood for another. But she stopped bristling and stepped back when Mrs. Hubbard's face contracted.

"Because he's in distress and I'm his 'first-line contact,' as he always likes to call it. As good as next of kin. What? Did you think the person he chose to rely on would be you?"

Before Karen could react, Mrs. Hubbard roared into life like an over-revved car.

"You really haven't a clue. As if he would turn to you after the way you've treated him—neglected him if I'm going to be honest, which it's high time I was. You always were a little madam, looking down your nose. Nothing was ever good enough. You were so cruel to your father, I could have cheerfully slapped you. I had hoped his illness might have brought out a nicer side, but oh no. It's all about you, isn't it? Don't tell me, I can guess: you've been up to your old tricks. Disturbing things, never letting anything lie."

She was red-faced with exertion, a sheen of sweat coating her upper lip despite the stiff February wind. Her granddaughter's narrow gaze shot daggers.

Karen knew she should have kept her dignity and walked away, but the ferocity of this attack, combined with the warden's anger, boiled up her blood.

"How dare you speak to me like this! You're always sticking your nose in, interfering. You always were. In our house all the time, in our business. It wasn't exactly fun for me either after my mother died, stuck alone with him. And I had to go *disturbing things*, as you call it, because no one would tell me anything. Well, here's a thought. Why don't you do something useful for a change and actually tell me something real about my mother, instead of hoarding secrets like he does."

Mrs. Hubbard drew herself up into a square.

"Tell you something *real*? What kind of agony-aunt nonsense is that? Always in your business? Well, thanks be to God that someone was. So you want something *real*? How about this: that I looked after you every time she couldn't, which was a lot. Or how about that I helped run your house as well as my own when your poor father was desperate. That was very *real*—that drove my Bob demented. But what choice did I have, with your poor father trying to look after you, and look after her, and hold down a job, and almost breaking under the weight of it all? It was an impossible task for any man."

She sucked in a breath; Karen jumped into the pause.

"But why did you need to? Why couldn't my mother do it herself?"

"Are you really asking me that? Are you so blind to the past it's wiped out your memory? Because she was sick, you silly girl. Not right in the head. Seeing things, scared of her own shadow, threatening to kill herself so often, Andrew thought he was going mad too with the strain of it. I swear to God he should have left her in Germany and saved us all the bother."

The slap wasn't a hard one, but Mrs. Hubbard screamed as if she'd been slashed with a knife.

Karen stormed away, screeched her car out of the drive, and only slammed to a stop when she realized she had run a red light and nearly caused a collision. Her hands were shaking, not least from the fact that she had just slapped an old lady. She couldn't carry on like this—that much was clear.

There could be horrors in her past that she couldn't live with, that your father can't tell.

Well, someone had better start telling: that she was still scrambling round for the truth was only making things worse.

Karen picked up the letter from the passenger seat where she had flung it and smoothed the thin paper out. After six weeks of waiting, she had convinced herself that her letter, with its guessed-at address and no surname, had no chance of finding a home. Then an answer had arrived, not from Michael, but from his son, Markus Wasserman, replying to Karen's tentative request for information—which she had couched in overly formal German— in perfect English.

It wasn't long and it didn't directly deal with her questions. It expressed his father's deep sorrow that Liese had died. It made no mention of a previous correspondence or any lack of it. It did say that Karen's letter had "disturbed" Michael, that his reaction had made him unwell and had "dismayed" his son, which was why he, Markus, was replying. The tone was clipped, not impolite but not welcoming. Karen had feared a dismissal until she read the last lines.

> *My father has said very little; he is in fact reluctant to say much about your mother at all, but it is clear that she mattered a great deal to him. Her death has affected him deeply. Despite what has clearly been a shock, he does, however, wish to remain in contact with you. By letter or, if you are ever in Berlin, in person. I will leave whatever the next steps will be up to you.*

Karen closed her eyes as rain began to drum against the windscreen.

If you are ever in Berlin. She had been pulling at the phrase since she first read it. Perhaps Michael didn't mean it; perhaps it was a politeness. Perhaps, if he was reluctant to talk, she would get no more from him than from her father. But she refused to believe that or why would Michael want to stay in contact when the letter hinted this son of his wasn't exactly in favor?

She switched the engine back on and rejoined the traffic, maneuvering onto the on-ramp heading to the M3 and London. She was tired of it all. Of being in the wrong; of causing pain and feeling pain; of being no nearer to the mystery that was her mother than she had been twenty years ago. Berlin was opening; Michael was no longer just a face in a photograph. That had to mean something. That must mean her mother was closer.

Karen joined the motorway and accelerated away from the too slow-moving traffic. She was tired, most of all, of waiting to trip over answers.

If you are ever in Berlin.

Karen relaxed her grip on the steering wheel as she suddenly realized what she needed to do. It was hardly the warmest invitation; it was hardly an invitation at all, but she didn't care. Haphazardly probing at the past wasn't going to cut it anymore. It was time to end that. It was time to take control, dive in, and dig.

CHAPTER TWELVE

Karen

Berlin, May 1990

I will await you at the Schillerbrücke crossing point at 14:30 tomorrow. I would prefer an opportunity to discuss your situation before you meet with my father.

Markus Wasserman.

His message had been waiting at the hotel and had chipped at Karen's concentration through a long business dinner with one of the prospective clients her company was courting. Such an irritating choice of words. *Your situation*, as if she was some kind of problem. *I would prefer*, implying she had a voice and then completely ignoring it.

Continuing the pattern of the first contact three months ago, Markus, not Michael, had replied to the two further letters Karen had sent. His communications had been sparse and had all followed the same formula: short, factual, impersonal. He hadn't asked her anything about herself or responded to the details she had offered. He had said little about Michael; he had revealed almost nothing about himself. His only comment about her visit to Berlin was that it was "sooner than anticipated." Karen couldn't decide if he was uninterested, or busy, or simply rude. In the end, she followed his lead: her most recent letter had contained no more than the address of her hotel, her flight details, and her meeting schedule.

A man of mystery. It was the last thing she needed. Even his choice of meeting place was, as the map-scouring receptionist put it, "an unusual one, a bit out of the way." Perhaps he simply didn't like a fuss, and there was certainly plenty of fuss going on in Berlin. The camera-wielding crowds engulfing Checkpoint Charlie had been proof of that.

As her first day in the city continued, so did its contradictions. The meetings her company—who were eager to get a foothold in this rapidly changing Berlin—had arranged for her took her in and out of polished restaurants and shiny offices that sat at odds with the graffiti-covered streets they looked out over. Every conversation started with the Wall's official demolition, which was still a month away, and the opportunities that would bring, but no one could quite define what exactly they were. To Karen, it felt as if the city was rejoining in fits and starts, without any sense of coherence beyond the hope of it. She couldn't escape the impression that this new Berlin didn't yet know what to make of itself.

People passed back and forth through the crossing points in grinning unchallenged groups, but their clothes and hairstyles marked out who was East and who was West and, for all the talk of regeneration, much of the city was still a wasteland.

She paused in the middle of the Schillerbrücke and gazed across the water to the Fernsehturm's ugly-beautiful gray needle. Whatever the city's disjointed mood, it felt right to be back, to have not given up. In another few minutes, she would be at the checkpoint, then, at last, she would be in the East, where the television tower stood. It seemed momentous; a moment needing marking. The one guard on duty waved her through without speaking and barely glanced at her passport.

"You look disappointed. Most people do. Now it's safe to do it, everyone wants to cross with a little more drama."

It was neither the greeting nor the man she expected.

Karen had constructed Markus from his letters and made him rigid and stern, buttoning his suit up tight and pinching his face into disapproving lines. The figure leaning against the parapet could be only a year or two older than she was and was far more at ease with the world than his writing suggested. Her dinner companions the previous night had mocked the clothes worn by the *Ossis*, playing a game in the bar of spot the cheap suit and fake Levis. Markus was dressed in dark brown corduroy trousers worn loose enough to suit his rangy frame and a cream shirt rolled up at the elbows. Add to that his stubbled chin and toffee-colored eyes and Markus Wasserman was textbook handsome. Karen couldn't tell yet if he knew it.

"The last time I was here there was a death strip and rifles. It takes a moment to catch up with the changes."

He smiled. "A good way to put it. Shall we?"

He gestured to a busy road edging a potholed building site and frowned as Karen sniffed.

"It's perfectly safe."

"It's not that. It's the air. It sounds fanciful to say it, but it smells different over here. Harsher, more pungent."

His arm hovered by her elbow the way that, in the photograph, his father's had almost touched her mother's.

"That's because it is. You're smelling dirtier petrol, cheaper cooking oil, disinfectant that's never been introduced to the idea of flowery perfumes. The scent is how you separate communist Berlin from its capitalist twin. That and all the half-finished projects."

He waved a hand at the building works—a vast rectangular train station Karen wasn't sure was coming up or going down.

"This is, or maybe this was, I'm not sure anymore, East Berlin's main station. It was being remodeled on a theatrical scale for visiting Soviet dignitaries. It's a bit of an embarrassment now we're no longer meant to admit how much we loved our long-distance masters."

Karen couldn't tell if he was angry or amused, or giving a performance. Her confusion must have shown.

Markus stopped and gave an odd little half bow.

"I'm sorry. I don't think I've quite got the hang of free speech yet, so sarcasm is easier. Let me start again..."

He began explaining the history of the East's Hauptbahnhof and pointing out the graffiti spreading cartoon-like across the long sections of the Wall that still ran alongside the river, explaining the impact its building, and falling, had made on the area. His spoken English was as clearly formed as his letters had been, with a lilt that reminded Karen of the way her mother had sometimes spoken. He was witty and knowledgeable and excellent company, but she was certain the stream of anecdotes was intended as a barrier. Then they turned a corner and into a square with a high-dancing fountain and whatever Markus was or wasn't saying blended in with the traffic.

"Oh my God. Is this it? Is this Karl Marx Allee? It's incredible—the postcard gave no sense of the scale."

She was standing inside the picture, dwarfed by the boulevard's grandeur.

"How far down does it go?"

"Nearly two kilometers, from Strausberger Platz, where we are standing, to Frankfurter Tor."

When she looked up at Markus, he was grinning.

"You love it, don't you?" He laughed. "Of course—who wouldn't? You said you were an architect; it is why I walked you here. To see your reaction."

Karen wanted to ask if she'd passed the test, but his grin had opened up his face and the charm of it tied her tongue. Feeling suddenly too young for her years, she darted away, found her camera, and began snapping the columned doorways and elaborately carved stonework decorating the high blocks.

Markus indulged her for a while and then ushered her under a yellow sign into a café which had the practical wipe-clean air of a workers' kitchen. They were barely seated before his face changed back into a stranger's mask.

"Why are you really here?"

If I want the truth, I have to tell it.

"Because my mother killed herself when I was eleven and I want to know why."

He recoiled as if she had struck him.

"And, what, you think my father is to blame?"

The idea had never occurred to her.

"No, of course not! But I don't know anything, Markus, beyond the fact of her death and that she was German, which was kept a secret from me, like everything else in her life. I need to find out who she was and why she did it."

Karen paused to gather her thoughts and was grateful he didn't jump in.

"I've been trying to pretend it doesn't matter that she killed herself, but it does. She left me when I was a child and my need for her has never stopped. It felt—it feels—like she abandoned me. That's hard to face up to, to make sense of, but it's left me stuck with my own life. My father and I . . ." She paused. She didn't know this man she was pouring her heart out to; she needed to keep some distance. "He's ill. I may have left things too late with him. I need to move on, so I'm here. Hoping your father might have some of the answers."

She stopped and picked up her cup. The coffee was bland and weak, but sipping it at least slowed her breathing.

To her surprise, given how formal he had been since they met, Markus reached out and took her hand. He barely held it, but she missed his touch the second it was gone.

"I'm so sorry. To suffer a loss like that is terrible. When my mother died, it crippled me for months and that was after a long illness, with time to adjust. I have been distant with you, I know. My letters perhaps haven't seemed very welcoming. This is hard for me, to explain and to understand, so I will try to be as direct as you are. When your letter came, when he learned your mother was dead, my father was broken. That's not a word I ever thought I would use about him. I think, if I am going to be as honest as I'd like, her death hit him worse than my mother's did."

He picked up his own cup. Karen resisted the temptation to offer reassurances. After a moment's looking down, he resumed in the same carefully considered manner.

"Before you meet him, you should understand who my father is, although, and I say this without meaning to offend, that might not be easy for someone who has not come from our kind of system. To the people here, Michael Wasserman is a hero. Everyone knows him—that is how your first oddly addressed letter got through. He fought for the communist resistance during the war against fascism; he has been loyal to the cause ever since. He is a writer and a teacher. He is strong and he is single-minded. His beliefs are so fixed, he's not been, in many ways, the easiest of fathers. But I knew who he was. And then your letter came and it made him weak. He sobbed. It sounds ridiculous, but he became a shadow of himself the moment he read it. That was hard for us both and not something I would want repeated." He stopped.

Karen sensed a protectiveness around Michael that meant she might need to move carefully.

"Is that why you didn't want me to come? You never said it outright, but, yes, I could sense your reluctance."

When he met her eyes, she knew he was a man for whom the truth was the main thing that mattered. There was a challenge in that, but also hope.

"I wasn't pleased that you decided to come here, or so quickly. Your letter made him afraid and that frightened me. I think he has secrets."

His sudden sharp laugh took Karen by surprise.

"That is such a stupid thing to say. Everyone here has secrets. Our wired walls and tapped telephones are what's kept the DDR stuck together for the last forty years. But this with my father is different. This is something more personal than the informing or the blackmail that passed in this country for currency. I said earlier I knew who he was, but that's not strictly true. I know who he is now, what others tell me he is. He never talks about his life before. None of his generation do. I know nothing about his childhood or my grandparents."

His face wears everything he feels.

"My father is the same. Apart from the one picture of his parents I've seen, and that he was always in the army, I know almost as little about him as I do about my mother. I certainly know nothing about his feelings."

Karen stopped. She knew her father's feelings all too well at the moment: he was angry and upset and disappointed in her. He had recovered his voice a week or so after her last visit, but he hadn't wanted to see or speak to her. She had left word with the hospital that she was going to Berlin, that she was going to meet with Markus and, she hoped, Michael. He hadn't responded—not that she expected him to. Since her last disaster of a visit, she had been forced to get the news of his continuing recovery from whichever overworked nurse could spare any time for her calls.

She looked up, conscious she had lost the thread of the conversation. Markus was smiling. It took years off his face.

"Our systems must be more similar than I thought, at least when it comes to parents. I used to get so cross with how closed Father was, how easily he would shut down a conversation he didn't want to be having. My mother always sprang to his defense. She said his silences were normal. That no one who lived through the war wanted to remember either it or the miseries that came after. She said the way he lived, forgetting the past, focusing on what the DDR offered us and what he could offer it, was the right way to be. That was everyone's line, the party propaganda we were all fed. I went along with her for the sake of peace, but now you are here…"

"The past is shifting. And you'd rather it didn't."

He nodded. "Maybe it's the timing of this. Right now, for those of us brought up in the East, the past isn't just shifting, it's breaking down. Everything we were brought up to value is disappearing. There's very little left to count on, except family. And now I find out my father isn't the solid man I thought he was. I don't know if I need that. More importantly, I'm not sure he needs his life questioned and picked over."

The smile vanished; his face suddenly grew stern.

"I won't let you hurt him, Karen. If any of this exploring of yours causes him pain, no matter what you need, I'll stop you."

Karen stared into her cup, where a skin had formed across the cold coffee. The Michael he described, the relationship they had, sounded so familiar it was like listening to her own thoughts about Andrew. She had been right to come; there were answers here. She sensed that from Markus's agitation, from his need to set the rules of engagement.

She nodded as if she agreed, but she didn't say anything. She didn't plan to hurt anyone, but neither did she plan to shy away from asking Michael questions that might prove uncomfortable. If doing one caused the other, she would have to live with it.

For all his charms and his apparent empathy with her situation, how gatekeeper Markus felt could not be her problem.

The building Michael lived in was a time capsule. The hallway was tiled in faded blues and underwater greens, forming a hushed retreat from the outside bustle. Postboxes fashioned like miniature houses marched along one side of the entranceway. The lift creaked behind stout double doors.

"I hope you're feeling fit. The lift looks impressive, but the stairs are always the safest option."

Karen's first impression of Michael's flat as she entered the hallway was that it was spacious, but the interior was visibly aging.

Markus must have seen her frown as he steered her down the corridor toward the living room where he said Michael was waiting.

"He won't decorate. He abides by party directives too strictly. This was the best on offer in 1953, so it's still the best on offer. His pigheadedness used to drive my mother mad."

The once-cream walls were nicotine-tinged. The turquoise units Karen could see as she passed the open kitchen door were scuffed and shabby, and the sparse furnishings in the living room left the flat feeling half-finished. As they entered, Michael rose from a chair by the window. He was tall and smartly dressed and he would have seemed composed except for the tightness round his eyes and mouth.

"You are her image. You could be nobody's daughter but Liese's."

His English was heavily accented and tripped clumsily over his tongue. When Karen thanked him in German, his face relaxed into soft creases.

"Other than Russian, I do not have my son's language skills. That he speaks English so well was his mother's doing. She loved languages—she was fluent herself, and she loved your literature. She never thought Russian and German gave a wide enough view of the world. It was hardly a popular view to hold here, but on that she wouldn't be argued with."

He embraced Markus and led them into a sitting room furnished with books and two sagging green armchairs. A photograph of a smiling woman holding a laughing little boy took center stage on the bookcase.

"You will take some coffee and apple cake? I baked it myself—one of my newer skills."

I was right. He looks in charge of the situation but he's as nervous as me.

Karen tried to sit without hovering, while Michael fussed in the kitchen and Markus fetched a plastic chair and a small table.

"Let me speak to him alone, tell him what you told me about your mother's death. Get that done with."

He left the room. Karen heard a few muffled words, and then a cry and a cup smashing and was glad Markus had taken the details away from her watching.

When Michael returned, his age-softened but still handsome face was twisted, and his tall frame was hunched over. Markus led him to a chair, brought him coffee; sat at his side while he drank it.

"I have explained that you have questions and you have a working knowledge of our language. We have agreed that he will speak in German and I will translate whatever is needed. I have told him we will end this whenever he wishes."

Karen nodded, although Markus's prescriptive manner chafed.

"I am so sorry." Michael's voice was as dry and cracked as a summer river. "That she did such a thing was my fault—her misery was all my doing."

Markus translated as Michael spoke and then reared as he took in what had actually been said.

Karen shot forward, pulling Michael's attention onto her before Markus could instantly close down the conversation.

"How could that be? Markus said she never replied to your postcard. If you weren't in touch, how could you have known what she would do?"

Michael's gaze was so intense, Karen wished he would look away.

"I always knew. After Lottie was lost, I knew one day Liese would follow."

The curtains fluttered against the open window. Karen caught the movement and felt it like the walls trembling.

"Who is Lottie?"

Michael flinched. "You don't know?"

She's not here; she won't answer.

Karen bunched her hands into fists as if she could ward off the answer she knew instinctively was coming.

"Lottie was Liese's first child, my dear. Lottie was your sister."

*

The sky outside the window hadn't switched from its earlier clear blue. The hands on the clock had eaten away little more than an hour. How had a lifetime not passed?

Michael's eyes were closed, his breathing thick. Karen was bone-chilled, her teeth chattering. She didn't know how to be in her own skin. She wanted to howl, for her mother, for her lost little sister, but the tears stuck like ice in her chest.

"I was late to collect her, the unforgiveable sin." His voice was so quiet, Karen could barely hear it. "I was caught up in a raid on the printers where we were meant to collect the next batch of leaflets, pinned down in a crawl space for hours. By the time the soldiers left and I could get to the flat, Liese and Lottie were gone. I am so sorry."

He kept saying it; Karen needed him to stop talking.

"You are in shock. Breathe slowly, deeply. Look at me."

Markus had her shaking hands cupped in one of his, had her chin tilted so she was forced to see him.

"Good girl. Slow down—that's it."

"I am so very sorry."

Why did he keep saying it? Did he want her forgiveness? She didn't know what to say, what to do. She knew none of the blame was Michael's, but she badly needed someone to shout at. Why had she thought uncovering the past would be helpful? How would she ever push the image of her sister's murder, of her mother's anguish, out of her brain?

She stared past Markus to where Michael was curled up, his arms wrapped tight round himself. The way he was looking at her. There was more to the story—she knew it. She could see it in his tear-filled eyes, in his suddenly snapped-shut mouth.

"There's something else, something you're not—"

And then nausea swept her words away. The walls were closing in. She couldn't stay—there were too many horrors in the room.

She jumped up, pushed past Markus, and ran out of the flat with no thought beyond getting away.

"What are you doing?"

Markus pulled her hands away from the lift buttons she was furiously pressing.

"I have to go back to my hotel."

She twisted away from him and ran for the stairs.

"Karen, stop! I understand, I do. But you can't go alone. Never mind that you'll get lost; it's too dangerous. And you will never find a taxi on your own, not on this side. You have had a terrible shock. We all have. I need a drink; so must you. Come on."

He took her arm and steered her to a bar that was as bare as the café. A counter lined with rough stools, a handful of plain wooden tables; fewer bottles on show than she had ever seen in the West. Markus sat her down and fetched a jug of red wine and two glasses half-filled with clear liquid.

"Drink this; it will take the edge off. If you need more, there's plenty."

Karen gulped the vodka, gasping as the rough alcohol rasped over her throat.

"Do you always give so many orders?"

He poured out the wine and passed her a full glass.

"Yes. I'm a doctor. Most days, it's the main part of the job. I thought I'd told you."

"You didn't tell me anything, but don't worry: I'm used to that."

And then the shock sheared away and she burst into tears.

"Good. Get it out."

He moved his chair, pulled her head onto his shoulder.

"Nobody cares. Too many people have cried in here for one more to matter."

He let her sob until she was empty and then found a hand-kerchief.

"Karen, I swear I didn't know about Lottie. If I had, I would have warned you, prepared you. He never breathed a word about it. I can't imagine how it must feel for you to hear that, never mind for him to tell it. So much pain to carry round and so much guilt, for both of them, and now for you. And all the secrecy. It's all right to feel angry, if that's how you feel."

Karen flushed.

"He kept saying he was sorry and I couldn't bear it. I know it's not Michael's fault; I know that he's suffering. He was almost captured himself—what could he have done? How could he have known what would happen? There's nobody to blame but the guard, I know that. But in there, I wanted to hit out at him, I did, and that's awful. And as for my mother's pain, I can't imagine it; I don't want to…"

She took another deep drink.

"The agony of it is unthinkable. To have to witness that; to be so powerless to stop it. What was it Michael said? 'Liese spent the whole of Lottie's little life trying to keep her safe, but in the end she failed.' We know that wasn't her fault, but did she? Did she carry the guilt or, God help her, the blame, her whole life? The damage of that is beyond measuring."

"Perhaps there is your answer. Such an awful thing would explain her suicide."

Karen put down her glass, wanting and not wanting a clear head.

"Maybe. I'd like to believe it's as simple as that. But your father also said he always knew my mother would follow Lottie. If that was true, why did she wait so long to do it?"

Her voice cracked as the question that had haunted the past eighteen years surfaced.

"Lottie was long dead when my mother killed herself, but I was alive. I needed her. How could she do it when she had me to love and look after? Explain that, Markus, with all your medical training. She lost one child and then she chose to leave another. Why would she do it?"

His arm was the only thing keeping her on the chair.

"I can't explain it; I wish I could. I'm not that kind of doctor, although I once wanted to be. It was safer here to deal with broken limbs than broken minds; the authorities were less prescriptive."

He fell silent.

Karen took a deep breath and hoped he would still trust her to do the right thing.

"I have to talk to him again, Markus. I'll apologize for running away so rudely, but I have to speak to him again. My mother carried on. She married my father; she went to England. Lottie's murder is a reason for her death, but it's not the end of her story."

He rubbed his eyes and nodded.

"I think you're right—I do. But not now. Wait until tomorrow. Please. Give him the day to recover and understand you need more from him. After your meetings, after my shift, I'll come for you. Will that be all right?"

It was a question, not a decision taken and delivered. His tone was concerned, not commanding.

Karen managed a smile, managed to look properly at him. There was a kindness in him she could sense ran deep.

"Yes. Yes, I can manage with that."

Markus held her briefly before she climbed into the taxi he had called from the bar. It was barely a hug, but there was a reassurance in its warmth that stayed curled round Karen through the long, sleepless night.

Markus was waiting in the lobby the next afternoon when Karen extricated herself from the day's final appointment, his boxy blue car parked outside. They didn't touch. They didn't speak beyond greetings until they were clear of Checkpoint Charlie.

"He's different today. More recognizable, more in control. More like the father I'm used to, who always works to a plan."

"What does that mean? Is this a warning that he won't tell me everything?"

Markus took so long to answer, Karen wondered if he had heard her.

"Nobody who lived under the DDR tells anyone everything. We've been trained too well. Part of me is wondering now if I am making a huge mistake. If talking to you could have consequences I can't foresee and should avoid."

"You make it sound like I'm a spy!"

Markus managed a smile that was warm enough to relax her.

"I know. I'm not really serious. But this isn't easy. We think before we speak here; we choose language that fits inside party parameters— we are always aware that someone is likely to be listening. The Wall that physically ringed our lives might be down, but I'm not sure that's the one that matters. I don't want to live with those restrictions anymore, so I am trying to shed them, but my father? He will tell you the version of the past he believes that you need, but, no, he won't tell you everything. I'm not sure that he's capable."

Karen could feel her skin tightening.

"He has to. I came to Berlin once before and ended up with more confusion. I can't go away from here again without the answers I want."

"You may have to. My father is stubborn—he sets his mind and it stays there."

Markus shook his head as Karen began to argue. "It's what I said yesterday: you have to try and understand him or you won't get anywhere with him at all."

"Then explain him better to me."

There was a pause and then Markus nodded. "Okay, I'll do what I can. Let's say then that you met him in a different way and tried to talk, like everyone is doing, about Berlin's reunification. He wouldn't engage in a discussion; he would walk away or he would deliver the same lecture on the miseries of capitalism he's been quoting for years. He won't go to the West, even though he's past pensionable age and no one would bother. He still won't call the barrier between the sectors the Wall. Every time he hears it called that, he corrects the name back to the 'Anti-Fascist Protection Rampart,' like a DDR robot. When I was a child, he would make me turn my back on it and pretend there was nothing beyond the concrete but more East Germany. It was ridiculous, but he was unshakable."

Karen laughed at the image of the West-defying little boy—she couldn't help herself—and relaxed even further when Markus joined in.

"Exactly. Stubborn to the point of madness. He lives his life inside strict boundaries and strict beliefs—he always has. Your needs won't push him outside those."

Markus drove into Karl Marx Allee's wider road and stopped the car outside Michael's apartment, his voice and face all seriousness again.

"I'm sorry, Karen, but I would be lying if I promised you a different man."

"What if whatever he tells me isn't enough?" Karen hovered on the pavement, her energy for this next bout already draining. "What if none of it is ever enough?"

Markus could have offered platitudes; Karen knew other men would. Instead, he simply took her hand as he pressed the buzzer.

There was an unexpected comfort in his silence.

CHAPTER THIRTEEN

Liese

Ravensbrück Concentration Camp,
September 1943–May 1945

The guard wiped her hands and walked away as everyone screamed except Liese. She couldn't move. She couldn't cry. She couldn't believe her heart hadn't immediately stopped. She stood in the middle of the screams and the shouts and waited for the end that had to be coming.

"Liese Elfmann. Is that really you?"

The voice cut through the clamor, as clear and crisp and as full of delight as if its owner were hailing her across a dance floor.

"Come here."

Everyone fell back; a pathway opened. When she didn't move, a guard dragged her forward.

"Gently now, especially with those pretty hands."

The man tapping his foot as he waited for her was tall and blond and dressed in a black uniform so exquisitely tailored it looked as if he had stepped from a magazine.

"I was right—I knew it. I'd recognize you anywhere, despite that rather strange hair color you're sporting. But you're frowning: don't you remember me?" He smiled. It made him look colder. "Fritz Suhren? *Commandant* Suhren now, to be accurate. No? No matter. You were rather dazzled by that French buyer the last time we met, or so I recall. Such extravagant hosts the Elfmanns—always the finest foods, the most expensive champagne." He clapped his hands so suddenly, the guard next to him jumped. "And that's why I had my idea, when I saw you there. I could barely believe it was you, to be honest, but the strangest people are turning up here these days. Anyway, this little kingdom you're standing in is all mine, so here is my thought: why don't I return the favor and extend you some hospitality in return for all your family showed me? What do you think?"

Liese couldn't make any sense of his manner or his words. She couldn't speak. She couldn't think about anything, except the guard. About her vicious little eyes and the brick-sized scarred hand that had blotted out Lottie's precious life. Whatever this Suhren was saying was drowned out by the noises she couldn't shake from her head. The scream that ended almost as soon as it began, and the snap, and the splash that had taken her child away. Nothing was as real to her as any of that, so Liese stared at the bright-eyed Commandant in silence and wondered what he wanted with her, and how soon he would stop whatever this nonsense was and kill her.

"She's speechless with her good fortune, how charming! Well, I shall take that as a yes. Off you go, my dear—off you go!"

Suhren turned away before Liese could catch up with him, his attention caught by some other distraction.

"Up the hill. Do as the Commandant says. Move."

Not knowing what else to do, Liese stumbled up the slope toward the row of houses looking down onto the lake, another of the female guards panting behind her.

"Why is he doing this?"

What she really wanted to ask was *Why am I still alive when my daughter is dead?* but the words were beyond her.

"How should I know? The Commandant thinks he knows you; he thinks you have some value. You should be grateful: he probably just saved your life."

And then the pain finally hit, raw and red and wearing Lottie's face.

*

"Still no news. Still looking."

Commandant Suhren had made the same solemn pronouncement at least twice a month, waiting until Liese nodded and smiled in the grateful way he preferred. By February 1945, she must have heard it at least thirty-four times. She had long since stopped believing that the *looking* was true, but on he went with the lying. Liese rarely wondered anymore why he bothered. Presumably, it was all part of the games he loved to play. Or perhaps he still thought she was going to turn her scissors into a weapon and mess up his pretty house.

Doing that had been her first thought, seventeen months ago, when she was marched from the horror that had engulfed her outside the camp gates and up the hill into Suhren's home. He had appeared shortly afterward and looked her up and down as if she were a prize cow.

"Liese Elfmann. What a delight. Finally, I get your undivided attention. I once asked your father for permission to court you, did you know that? He laughed. Can you imagine how much that hurt my feelings? He was happy enough for my family to supply textiles to the great Haus Elfmann, apparently, but to provide a husband for its heir? The idea was 'an outrage.' What a lucky escape I had, when you think about it: what a horror to have been saddled with a filthy little Jew for a wife! The swings of fortune favored me in the end and now look how the tables are turned. Liese Elfmann, my own little seamstress. Oh, we will keep you so busy. Dresses for my wife and her friends; uniforms for me. You'll have a salon's worth of clients again. Isn't that lucky?"

On and on he went, his too-loud voice pouring round her. Then Liese saw the dressmaking scissors he was holding and she snapped back into something like life. She had taken them, cradled them; pressed the steel blades against her skin and imagined her blood pouring.

"I wonder. Do you think about your parents?"

It had been an odd thing to ask. Did he really think she was wondering about anything except her child and how much suffering there had been in those last terror-filled seconds?

She didn't answer; she eventually grew to understand he rarely cared if she did. Suhren was the show; Liese was simply part of the audience.

"Do a good job and I could find them for you. Would having family left alive be a comfort?"

The stupidity of the question had stunned her. Or, more accurately, its cruelty.

Over the next months, at the close quarters Liese had suddenly found herself in, she realized that the Nazis' capacity for cruelty went far deeper than anything she could have imagined long ago in Berlin; that it went beyond the more obvious brutality. She knew Suhren had seen what had happened to Lottie, but he never once acknowledged it, or behaved as if her child's murder mattered. She had wondered, in her first confused days in the house, if Suhren had some sexual motive in plucking her out. If he planned to take what had been refused him before. It wasn't hard to imagine. It quickly became obvious, from the maids' white faces and his wife's watchful narrowed eyes, that he treated his female staff like a buffet. It also became quickly obvious, however, that his distaste for her Jewish heritage would always damp down his desire.

Liese was a trophy Suhren had no interest in touching. The Commandant, and his household, saw her so completely as *other* it was like living inside the sneering posters and the Jew-hating newspapers they all set such store by. They stepped back when she passed them, placing their hands forward like a shield. They discussed her while she moved among them, as if she spoke a different language or had no language at all. As if she had no more ability to possess finer feelings than the cat who scavenged scraps in the kitchen, who no longer turned her head when her latest litter of kittens was tidied away. Not that it mattered; not that anything that happened to her mattered.

"I'm keeping you alive. You're one of the lucky ones!" Another of Suhren's favorite sayings, riddled with pride at the generosity of her "special position" that he presumed she would echo.

Part of Liese knew that she should feel grateful. That every woman thrown into the camp, facing the brutality of those guards every day, would change places with her in a heartbeat. Knowing that, and knowing that she cared nothing for her own life, only filled her with more guilt. His ploy had worked: the promise of finding her deported parents had added to the unreality of everything that was happening and kept the scissors off her wrists for those first sleepwalking few days. Then Liese looked up and saw the lake gleaming below the house where Suhren had put her and realized why she was still living. Lottie was down there; Lottie was waiting.

It was as if a blindfold had been ripped away. *Lottie was waiting.* One day, when all this was over, Liese would go down to the lake and join her child. She would walk out into the water, she would lie down, she would wrap her arms round her baby and never again let her go. Until then, it was a mother's job to keep vigil.

Every night after that revelation, Liese sat at the window of the tiny attic she was locked up in and kept watch from behind its green shutters. Whether the water was still or smooth, rain-filled or iced-over, Liese sang Lottie's favorite songs and told her favorite stories out into the dark, holding tight to the thread that still bound them.

And once she knew her purpose, staying useful started to matter. Liese could see the heavy fortifications round the camp and the bright lights that illuminated it as clear as she could see the lakeshore. As the months passed, she could also see the smoke that rose in thin plumes from behind the long rows of barracks. She could smell the burned tang that even a downpour couldn't rinse from the air, that the rumors whispering through the house had turned into something too monstrous to believe. Being useless at the task Suhren wanted her for, and being sent back into the camp, being trapped inside Ravensbrück, would not bring the lake and getting back to Lottie any nearer.

Liese stopped existing from day to day and taught herself instead a survival-tuned discipline. She kept up her vigil, but she also forced herself into bed. She learned to accept that the nightmares would come. And she learned that she could survive them for long enough to sleep for a few hours every night, so that her eyes didn't close in the day and ruin the fine embroidery that delighted Frau Suhren. She made herself eat the thin soup and stale black bread left out for her when the rest of the household had eaten, so that her fingers could sew a seam without shaking. Liese reduced her world to a workroom and a window. To all she needed to get back to Lottie.

As the months dragged on, rumors reached the house about the worsening conditions in the camp. Whispers about the starvation, the piles of corpses, the breakdown of order, and the guards' increasing cruelty. When 1943 finally ended, it brought no respite. 1944 came in cold and hard and mixed new words into the whispering: *special trucks, selections, gassing*. The charred animal stink in the wind grew stronger. Liese lay in her safe bed and felt her heart shrivel as the guilt gnawed. There were mornings when she pressed the scissors against her skin again and knew how fast it could be over. And then she imagined her daughter, cold and alone, and knew the only way was the water.

Liese stopped listening to anything except her direct orders. She kept her head down during dress fittings and tuned out the chatter. She kept her mouth shut and walked away from gossip. She behaved every day, in the Commandant's words, like "an exemplary prisoner." There were days when she woke and hated herself for waking. It didn't matter.

Because one day this will end. One day I will walk to the lakeshore and I will make all this end.

The same promise repeated like a prayer every day as she worked; as she waited.

*

The months passed unchanging and then April 1945 arrived and brought a morning that started all wrong, that leaped into life far too quickly.

Car engines growled outside on the gravel. Inside, the house shuddered as doors slammed and feet pounded through corridors that shouldn't even be wakening.

Liese was scrambling up, still bleary, when the attic door crashed open.

"Get this uniform on. We have to be dressed and in the kitchen in five minutes."

Hilge, the other prisoner put to work in the Commandant's house, stood in the doorway, a blue-and-white bundle thrust out in front of her. She was a political who considered herself several steps above a Jew. She never spoke to Liese, never looked at her if she could help it. Now, Hilge's proud face was pale and her hands shivered like windblown barley.

"Get a move on; I'm not taking a beating for you."

Liese shook out the striped dress and the jacket with its sewn-on number and two yellow triangles shaped into a star. Their thin fabric was sour with old sweat; the blue-and-white pattern was mottled with dirt and rust-colored patches. She had been given a black dress when she entered the house and had never worn the camp uniform. The thought of putting it on, of what that implied, cramped up her fingers.

"What's happening?"

Hilge drummed her fingers across the door frame.

"You really don't know? Haven't you heard the guns?"

The rumbling disturbing the lake for the last few nights—was that what it had been? Liese had presumed it was the sound of a storm coming; she had watched for the rains that would whip up the water. When they hadn't appeared, she had ignored it.

"I thought it was thunder caught in the mountains."

Hilge's shoulders arched. "Thunder that goes on for days without breaking? Seriously? I swear I don't know how you do it. Cutting yourself off, sewing your stupid dresses and jackets like nothing else matters. You know what, I don't care. The war is done, or as good as, and Germany isn't the winner. And *now* she reacts—there we go. The Russians are almost on top of us. Stop staring at me like a simpleton and get dressed."

Hilge's fists clenched.

Liese shucked off her nightdress and pulled on the striped gown. It was so long the hem hit her ankles and generous enough at the waist and the hips to fit a second wearer. She knew her brain was moving too slowly, that Hilge was in no mood for questions, but she was missing something. Surely if the war was ending, prisoners would be freed?

"Why do we have to dress like this? Frau Suhren won't give these uniforms houseroom. And, anyway, if the fighting is all done, won't they just let us go?"

Hilge threw Liese a grubby white square that matched the one tied round her own head.

"The bitch won't care what we're wearing. She's not here. She's already run with the children. And of course they won't let us go. I'm still a criminal; you're still a Jew—the Nazis still want Germany cleansed of us. All the big houses are emptying; all the prisoners are being sent back to the camp. And I'd rather take my chances there than be shot or, worse, left here alive for the Russians. Come on—get a move on. And cut off your braid."

Liese stopped tying her headscarf. "What? Why?"

"Because if you walk into the camp dangling that, the inmates will know that you're new. They could suspect you've been a collaborator and string you up as a Nazi. I don't care if they do, but I don't want anyone looking twice at me for knowing you."

"Prisoners, down the stairs!"

Hilge grabbed Liese's dressmaking scissors and hacked off her plait in one savage cut, pushing Liese out of the door before she could protest.

Two soldiers were poised in the hallway, rifles raised and ready. They rushed Hilge and Liese out of the house and into a mass of white-faced women already gathered up from the surrounding properties.

"Down the hill. March."

Liese stumbled over the slippery grass, arms out to keep her balance. Spring blossom frosted the trees. The air should have been sweet and apple-scented; it was choked instead with smoke and diesel fumes, and tasted charred and oily. Lorries packed the road running alongside the camp. Prisoners pooled round both sides of the gates; soldiers, not the black-caped guards of Liese's nightmares, herded fast-moving groups in and out.

Liese was swept down the hill and through the gates and steered into a packed parade ground. There was no stopping on the sand this time, no chance to slip away to the water. There was no chance to do anything—she was too busy trying not to scream.

The women like her, who had been sent to the SS houses, were thin and pale, but they were beauties compared to what now surrounded them. The square was filled with emaciated women shivering in ragged dresses or, to Liese's horror, naked and too lost in misery to try and cover the skin stretched tight as a drum over their bodies. Some had shaved stubble-covered heads; others had hair growing back in wild clumps. Everyone was gray; everyone was old.

"Move."

Her group was forced on again.

Liese ran, eyes fixed forward without being told, desperately trying to blank out the stick-bodies moving past her like snapped puppets. Bonfires flared. Scraps of burned paper floated through the air like rotten snowflakes. The red flowers were gone. Some of the barracks were half torn down; judging by the stench, many more were overcrowded.

Orders flew harsh as rocks: "Move, keep left, stay together, stay on your feet, or we shoot." Liese ran, refusing to think, until "halt" brought her column to a tumbling stop.

"In there."

One of the soldiers kicked a door open, while the others herded them into a barracks that was dark and ripe.

"Is everyone in here dying?"

The woman who came in behind Liese pulled off her headscarf and tied it round her nose and mouth as she spoke.

"Everyone in the camp is dying. If you're lucky, you get to do it under your own steam."

The owner of the voice was too thin to claim a discernible age or a gender; only the filthy dress marked her out as a woman.

"Come in—don't be shy. Press yourself close and choose your poison: TB, cholera, dysentery—we've got the whole set."

She climbed off her bunk and tried for a fairground flourish, but the effort was too much and her twig arm sank. The newcomers stayed clustered in the doorway.

"Suit yourself—find a bunk or don't. You'll not likely be here long enough for it to matter at the speed they're running selections."

The prisoner limped toward the disoriented women. Her left leg was badly twisted and wrapped round with scars.

"I'm a rabbit."

She waited, clearly expecting a reaction. Her eyes narrowed when she didn't get one.

"You don't know what I mean, do you? Where have you been hiding? Everyone in Ravensbrück knows about the rabbits—it's the camp's worst-kept secret. You don't know about the experiments?"

She came closer, her hands bunching. An animal stink rose from her blotched and peeling skin. There wasn't a trace of fat to separate her bones from their covering. She looked like one too-quick movement would split her in two. Liese had to fight not to run.

"Of course we know."

Hilge pushed herself to the front of the group, her shoulders squared.

"The Nazis use women here for their medical tests. They broke your legs and cut out your bones. Then they stuck the wounds with splinters and bits of glass and injected them full of bacteria. And you hop until you heal, or what passes for healing, so they call you rabbits. There's a difference between knowing and seeing, that's all."

Liese thought she was going to be sick. The woman didn't move; neither did she do what Liese was hoping she would and tell Hilge she was mad or misinformed.

"So you know about the games they play here, or you're clever enough to know the right answer. That doesn't explain who's been feeding you and where you've come from. Are you brothel women?" Her voice sharpened. "Or those bitches who got pulled out for house workers while the rest of us were left here to rot?"

Liese froze. Hilge didn't falter. "We've been in the Siemens factory, in the plant outside the camp. They fed us because they needed our fingers nimble. Perhaps there was more food there than here."

"*Perhaps?* You think?"

But the woman finally backed off and hobbled away, waving to a corner where the bunks had two inmates crammed in them, not three.

The newcomers edged into the barracks. Liese tried to duck after Hilge but was met with a snarl.

"Don't come after me. I listened to enough gossip to get us past the door in one piece, but you're on your own now."

She disappeared into the forest of bunks, leaving Liese to pick her way through the groaning. Matchstick arms plucked at her; pleading eyes followed her.

I don't want to die like this. She slumped to the ground, knees buckling as the truth hit her. Of course she wanted to die—that was all she had dreamed of since the day Lottie was taken—but she had imagined a quiet death, the water washing her pain away as she walked toward her child. A death with dignity, and in her offering; a penance. Not this brutal shove into sickness or selection.

Death is death—what does it matter? Liese didn't know why but it did.

"Get up."

Liese started as a foot kicked at her.

"Are you deaf? Don't you know anything? The whistles and the yelling means it's roll call. If they come in and find you capable of walking but ignoring their orders, it's a bullet or the ovens."

Liese stared at the furious woman still prodding at her and wondered why she cared.

The woman's heavily accented German switched to a growl. "Not just for you, you stupid bitch. For all of us. Busses have been spotted not far from the gates. White ones, not the green ones they use for gassing. Some countries have finally whipped up the courage to get their people out. I'm not missing the chance of that because you're lost in some dreamworld."

She hauled Liese up, dragged her out of the barracks and back round to the now even busier parade ground. Liese already knew enough not to ask why they hadn't done this first: why the guards had put the women into the barracks only to pull them straight out again. She sensed this was normal, or what passed in the camp for normal. Another way of creating fear and confusion, of stripping away the inmates' humanity, reducing them to creatures without thought, capable only of reaction.

"Are they still killing people, even with the enemy so close?"

The prisoner still holding roughly onto her arm snorted. "Are you serious? That's why they're still killing us."

Liese stared round her and realized all the bodies packing the square were adults.

"The children too?"

"What children? What are you talking about? They're all gone. Shipped out to other camps if they made it past birth, or survived the cold, or the hunger. Why would you think there were children?"

The parade ground was shouted to order before Liese could land on an answer. Numbers began flying through the air thick as the burning paper. Women were pulled into this line and that, some of them forced out of their clothing, some of them not. Liese barely noticed. She had never imagined there could have been a worse fate for Lottie—now she could picture too many.

"That's you. That's the number on your jacket. Move, unless you want the whole line to get shot."

Another snarling voice more tuned to the camp's ways shoved Liese forward into a smaller group carved out from the rest. No one looked anywhere but forward.

Liese waited for the order to strip, which surely meant death. The public humiliation which gave *gassing* and *selection* meaning and explained the thin plumes of smoke. It didn't come.

"Move."

More running, more shouting, more stops and starts. Two women were deposited outside a block with a medical sign, three at another with a pile of wizened turnips outside. And then there was no one but her, standing outside another gray building.

"Get in."

The guard pushed her through a door into a room she thought at first was empty.

"Good—they found you."

She didn't have to look to know it was Suhren.

"No greeting for me? Never mind. Thankfully it's your silence I need, not your less-than-sparkling conversation."

He was sitting behind a desk covered with papers. His uniform was as immaculate as always, each silver flash and button shining. Liese stared at him open-mouthed, wondering what possible need he still had of a dressmaker.

"Lists." He waved a hand across the piles. "Ridiculous amounts of lists that Heaven forbid we don't muddle. All to be checked, the correct orders attached. No matter how close to the end we get, the machinery must keep on turning."

Liese couldn't tell if he was exasperated or amused by the task. She had no clue how it could possibly involve her.

"I've lost most of my men to the front and my women to leading the evacuation marches, but there's still no let-up in the work to be done. This needs someone with a careful eye and nimble fingers and the brains not to discuss it. In other words, you."

He pointed to a table and a stool in the corner.

"Sit there, sleep there. If there is any food left, someone might bring it. You will not leave this building. Something else you might want to thank me for one day, eh? If anyone ever asks? Not such a bad boss when all's said and done."

Liese stared at him, wondering if he was hoping for a favor or some kind of reference. The situation was so absurd she laughed; she couldn't help herself. It was, admittedly, a strangled gasp, she was so long out of practice, but it was still unmistakably mirth.

Suhren rose. She saw the pistol at his hip and wondered if this was finally the moment. He gazed at her; he gazed at the papers filling his desk. He sat down.

"What are you waiting for? Get started."

She lost track of time. The piles of paper for matching never seemed to grow smaller. She lost any desire to laugh when she saw what they were.

More days than not, no food came. There was a bathroom Suhren never went in but offered to her as if it were some kind of palace. Unlike the office, whose brass fittings and woven carpet Suhren insisted Liese keep polished and swept, the fittings in the bathroom were rusted and stained and the thin trickle of water the taps spat out was undrinkably brown. There was no mattress for her to sleep on; no blanket to keep out the cold the thin windows let in.

Suhren arrived each morning not long after dawn. When he left, he locked the airless room behind him. After the first day, Liese stopped looking at the typed sheets of barrack numbers and prisoner numbers and places she had never heard of. She knew what they were; she knew she couldn't stop what was happening. She hoped that the white busses had come and the orders she filled for removals weren't for the green ones. She had no hope that was true. She stopped thinking beyond *one more thing to do and then I will have my ending.*

She could barely see through the grease-smeared windows. At night, she blocked her ears against the cries and the screams, the emptiness that flooded in after the gunfire stopped rattling. She conjured up the lake instead, imagined she could hear the water lapping. Songs and stories, a little sleep; the old pattern. Days and nights spent in silence, her mind far away from the room, frozen in this strange world that was none of her choosing, that went on without ending. And then, one morning, Suhren didn't come.

Liese sat at her table and waited.

The camp was quiet. There were no engines grumbling; there was no shouting. The sun rose high enough to light the room almost to its corners and still the day outside behaved as if it were the dead of night.

Liese got up slowly, ears straining for guns or shouting. There was nothing. Perhaps they had run. Perhaps this was her chance, in this moment between one side going and one side coming. She pushed the door and pushed again and would have wept at her weakness if she had had the luxury of time. Days existing on water and scant mouthfuls of bread had left her arms flimsy. She needed to dig the lock away from the wood. She scoured the room for anything that would make a tool and could only find a fork buried at the back of Suhren's desk. The task seemed ludicrous, a labor better suited to mythical heroes, but the wood was soft and worm-ridden and crumbled like stale cake as she gouged it.

The camp she stepped into when the door finally splintered gave a new meaning to *wasteland*.

She had thought Ravensbrück was brutal when they had shoved her back into it; she had had no idea. It was as if she had wandered into Hell while its demons were sated and napping after an orgy of violence. She felt the stillness like a pause: it was filled with tension, time suspended while the next madness took shape. There were no soldiers visible, or snapping dogs. The bonfires had burned down to drifts of ash. The stinking smoke from the rear of the camp was faint enough to be a memory. The horror in this new underworld didn't shout and stamp, it wriggled. Out of the heaped bodies Liese thought at first glance were kindling piles. Out of the rags that uncurled and crawled as she groped her way past them.

Don't look. Head for the gate—head for the lake and Lottie.

Liese managed barely half a block's length before the whimpers and the corpses and the air's rotting sweetness swamped her. Her knees gave out, and she fell on all fours, retching until she was formed of nothing but empty spaces and bile. She lay curled and spent against a barracks wall, whatever it was she was trying to do forgotten. Not knowing if she was the last person left in the camp still breathing beyond her last gasps; too afraid to go looking.

"What the hell are you doing?"

Vibrations she had not had the strength to notice shook the ground, rolling through her legs and into her spine until her teeth were jumping.

"That noise you're so brilliantly ignoring is the Russian tanks; they're almost at the gates."

An arm caught her round the waist; lifted her off her feet.

"That means soldiers—Russian soldiers. Don't you know what they'll do if they catch you?"

The arm dragged her along. The voice ran on, not waiting for an answer.

"We were out there. When the Germans finally ran, we escaped. What we found in the forests was as bad as in here and drove us back in again. There's women left for dead, so used up by those brutes they've gone mad. Sick women, their own women, women who are barely women anymore. The Russians don't care as long as they can be knocked onto their backs."

The voice kicked a door open and dragged Liese inside a block that smelled of damp and rotten earth.

"You, lying there like that, still so obviously alive. Drawing them onto us like flies to shit with the promise of still-breathing bodies. They'll tear the place apart. We can't risk it."

Liese never saw a face. Hands pushed her through loosened boards into a space hollowed out below the roof. More hands pulled her into a vent so narrow it doubled her over.

"Stay still. Stay quiet. Pray the Russians pass through here quickly. Rumor has it the Americans are the next army behind them—pray for that. They're too fearful of God to treat us like animals."

It took three days for the Russians to sweep out and the Americans to sweep in. Liese and the other women crawled out of the kitchen roof when they heard the accents change over, most of them so weak they couldn't stand. She was bundled into a bed, carried there by horror-stricken boys too young for what they had seen, and put into the care of Red Cross nurses grown too used to it.

"I need to go to the lake."

"Of course you do—who wouldn't want to see something pretty after this."

Smiles and pats and no one listening.

"I can't leave here. Don't make me."

Sedatives and pressing hands and still no one listening.

Then an older man came, with stars on his collar and tired eyes, who waited while she begged to stay. He regarded her so seriously, Liese thought he understood. Until he shook his head like the rest of them.

"This happens; it will pass. You've been a prisoner so long you've grown used to it. You've learned how to survive this and you don't trust the world outside not to be as bad as it was when you came in. You don't need to worry: Hitler is dead; the Nazis are finished. It's safe to go back to your life. Besides, there is disease here and no sanitation—you're in more danger if you stay. We have trains running back to Berlin; we are shipping everyone out. Maybe you'll be lucky and there'll be family waiting."

"You don't understand—my family is here."

She grabbed his arm, but he shook her off.

"Be brave."

There was nothing to be done. She was well enough to work, well enough to leave. Being weak and afraid didn't count: everyone was weak and afraid. Liese was taken to a train that same afternoon and deposited in a carriage packed with women who couldn't stop smiling. Women who were going toward the hope of what they loved, while she was dragged from all that mattered.

She couldn't do it. She wouldn't do it. She wouldn't re-enter some life that wasn't a life. When the train pulled to a stop, she hung back and let the platform empty out. When she finally got off, she stayed in the shadows until the engine regathered its strength to set out again.

She was ready. She chose a place to stand which would catch the moment when the train hit the right speed. She closed her eyes and conjured up Lottie; opened her arms and felt her child tugging.

"Woah there, Miss!"

The shout pulled her back, turned her round.

A man was bounding toward her, a soldier in a brown uniform, bellowing as if he were calling after a shying horse.

"Another step and you'll tumble. You don't want that now."

He spoke German, but his accent was clipped and unfamiliar. His hand was on her shoulder. Liese wriggled, but it was too late: the train was already past her, steaming away.

"What are you doing? What business is this of yours?"

She meant to shout and hit and kick and run down the platform until she caught up with the engine, but he had her arm too firmly held and his eyes were so gentle, she couldn't bring herself to lash out.

"It would be a terrible thing for the driver, what you were trying. Never mind for you."

"I don't care about the driver."

But her body had sagged and they both knew that was a lie.

"I have to do this. You stopping me now won't change my mind. It will just change the timing."

The words came out in a snarl. He didn't step back.

"I'm sorry you feel like that; I really am. I imagine a lot of people feel as bad as you, which doesn't make your pain any less. But there's been a lot of dying already, don't you think? Could we wait a little longer for yours?"

The kindness that filled his eyes and voice was too soft for Liese to fight against.

"I don't deserve this. I deserve that."

She pointed to the tracks and pulled away so fast her head spun and her knees buckled. He caught her as she slipped.

"Maybe you don't. Maybe you do. I'm not the judge here. But I could be a friend. Could we agree on that much?"

I don't need another man in uniform who won't listen to what I need; who won't mind his own damn business.

But her head was whirling and so was the platform and she couldn't find the words she needed to push him away.

CHAPTER FOURTEEN

Karen

Berlin, May 1990

Michael welcomed Karen back into his home as politely as he had done the day before. He made no mention of their previous conversation, so neither did Karen. He poured the coffee that was already waiting, he cut a cake that was clearly freshly baked, and he talked without offering her any pauses.

"Liese told me her story because I pushed her to do it. Her narrative was emotionless and full of gaps, as if it had happened to someone else. I can see in your face you hoped for more, Fraulein Cartwright. So, I promise you, did I. What I have given you is all I have. Her pain was too raw; whatever trust she had left in the world was gone. She wanted to be left alone. It was me who wanted her to stay, who needed her."

Markus had continued to translate for his father as he had done before, watching Karen while he did so. He was waiting, Karen knew, for her to do what Michael apparently hadn't been able to with her mother and push back. Michael had given her so little she barely knew where to start. He had handed her a pencil sketch with no colors, all outlines and nothing filled in.

Liese's sewing skills had taken her out of Ravensbrück; the Nazis' retreat in the face of the Russian army had put her back in. She had returned to Berlin alone, weakened and ill. Andrew had found her at the train station, where he was acting as some kind of army liaison point for refugees and returners. He had taken her to a hospital and Michael had tracked them down there. Two years after that, she and Andrew had married. That was the entirety of what Michael had said, but he knew more—Karen could see it. He was wary, prepared for a challenge, prepared to defend himself.

Markus was right: his father was clever. Well, so was she. He was ready for questions about the end of the war; that didn't mean they were the ones she should ask.

"What was she like, before all this, when she was young? Were you close then?"

His smile came from nowhere and there he was: the young man in the photograph. It was all Karen could do not to gasp.

"Close doesn't seem a big enough word. We had a bond stronger than siblings. Your mother and I grew up together, our fathers were old friends and worked like brothers together in the salon. They had the same plan for us: Liese would have Paul's role as head designer; I would take my father's position on the technical side. And then the Nazis put an end to that. The salon suffered, our families suffered, and so did the relationship between Liese and I. But whether we were in step or couldn't see one thing the same, the Liese I knew was never less than determined. She ran Haus Elfmann almost single-handedly before she was eighteen. She was fiercely protective of Lottie and so determined to be a good mother—the kind she had never had. Her relationship with her parents was a distant, unhappy thing. Liese was adamant her child would have better."

He fell silent. Karen wanted to cry and didn't know who most needed her tears: the little girl who had died before Liese could mother her the way that she wanted, or the little girl Liese had left.

It was a moment before she realized Michael had picked up his story.

"... the girl I found in that hospital in 1945 was changed. She was brittle and angry, with tight walls around her. I guessed something must have happened to Lottie, but I had no idea about the way she had died. How could I? Even with the horrors we were starting to hear about, how could I have imagined something so brutal happening to a little girl?"

He stopped, blinked rapidly; shook himself, and went on. "I suppose I thought Liese was suffering from shock, like so many of the survivors were. You have to understand what a terrible time it was, those first months after the war. People were trying to piece their lives together out of bombed homes and scattered families. Everyone had somebody missing; everyone was searching. Very few found happy endings.

"When Liese got back to Berlin, she must have assumed her parents were dead or, at best, stuck somewhere a long way from Germany. Given the resistance work I was doing, she can't have expected me to have survived. I was the same. I was looking for her but without much hope. I had a whole list of comrades I couldn't trace and not even the right names for most of them. I didn't have much hope of anyone. And then I saw Liese's photograph at the station, with Andrew's name and phone number scribbled underneath it. I have never believed in God, but that felt close to a miracle."

"Was she glad to be alive?"

The question popped into Karen's head and out of her mouth and, perhaps because it was simple enough for her to put it to him directly, its asking took Michael by surprise.

"No. She wasn't."

He stopped, tried to pick up the sentence, and stopped again, his face etched with pain. He closed his eyes and was clearly drifting away.

"Michael…"

"Let him go where he needs to, Karen. Give him a moment." Markus reached over and took her hand. "I know you need answers— let him find them in his own way."

Michael looked as if he had fallen asleep, but his eyelids were fluttering and his fingers were clenched. There was a frailty about him that was suddenly frightening.

Karen knew she had no choice but to wait.

"Did you recognize Suhren when he spoke to you?"

Liese knew what Michael wanted to hear: *Yes, I knew him and he knew me and he saved me because of it.* That implied kindness, a recognition of the dreadful act done to her and a desire to somehow balance it. It was the simpler answer, far easier to explain than: *I didn't remember him at all and his saving me was a whim, a sop to his own monstrous ego.* She couldn't begin to articulate all the twists and turns in that, so she gave Michael the yes that he wanted.

She was exhausted. From Michael's questions, from his apologies, from his neediness, and from Andrew's. They both wanted so much more than she could give. Andrew desperate for her smile; Michael desperate for her story; both of them craving some sign of her affection. All Liese wanted was silence. Nothing felt real; nothing mattered. Trying to put the horror of Lottie's killing into words had almost choked her. But Michael wouldn't stop asking about the camp, or apologizing and begging her forgiveness.

Liese didn't blame him—she really didn't. She had said those exact words, "I don't blame you," and meant them. She couldn't finish the sentence; she couldn't tell him that the only person at fault was her, because whose job was it to protect Lottie if not her mother? She couldn't understand how Michael could still have questions. Why "they broke her neck and threw her into the lake" wasn't enough for him. Why he couldn't understand that everything had ended there, at the gates. It wasn't as if he could bear the truth.

When she had said that, no, she wasn't grateful to Suhren for saving her, that she hated him for it, that all she had wanted to do was die, so how could she be glad he had thrust a life on her, Michael had sobbed. She hadn't had the energy to comfort him.

Part of Liese wanted to help him, for the sake of what they had once been. A bigger part of her was filled up with rage that she was still living and her child was not, and that overshadowed every other emotion. She could feel the anger like a fire, simmering in her stomach, waiting for the spark that would let it spill. She knew that she could reach down and haul that fury-wrapped Liese out, replace this blank version sitting in the bed, holding Michael's hand. It wouldn't take much effort. That Liese would be able to pour out the truth and watch Michael recoil and scrabble for the platitudes he would offer like sticking plasters. She could do that. Except that would only feed the fury and give it a target it didn't deserve, so she had swallowed the words down instead.

She had watched him sob and wished, like she always did, that the ward sister would come and tell him that visiting hours were over. Free her from having to be responsible for anyone's misery but her own. If Michael hadn't been Michael, they would have chased him away, but handsome and whole and charming men were, apparently, a rare commodity in war-broken Berlin. Since the first day he had appeared, the nurses had fluttered round him like giddy butterflies and the rules went forgotten. So Liese had sat in silence, his tears no use to her, and then he had looked up and there it still was, written all over his anguished face: the love she no longer had a heart whole enough to put it in.

"One telling."

He had wiped his sleeve across his face at that and clutched at her hand.

"One telling of all that happened and then we are done. No more questions; no more asking my forgiveness. Do you understand?"

He had nodded.

"What about Andrew? Do I repeat it to him or will you tell him yourself?"

"You do it. Maybe then he'll stop trying to mend me."

Andrew's visits were as exhausting as Michael's. His cheery British *whatever it is, we can fix it* beam, and his determination to play the rescuing knight, was as unbearable as Michael's misery.

"He doesn't mean any harm... It's the guessing, Liese, the trying to imagine what you went through. Tell me the facts and I promise I, at least, won't keep pushing."

The facts. Michael still thought that marshaling those could make sense of the world. His belief in that made the pain on his face too raw to be bearable; Liese had had to look away from him, had focused on a water stain on the ceiling instead. Perhaps if she kept to his beloved facts, she could get through this. If she left everything else out. The agony that had fueled her, that had given her the energy night after night to stay alive and keep watch over the lake's flat waters. The hatred that still flooded her. For the Nazis who decreed that Lottie's life had no value. For the guard who could kill a child without looking. For the Allied soldiers who ripped her away from where Lottie was waiting and pushed her into a world that held nothing worth having.

Michael loved her and wanted her to love him. She couldn't give him that; she was too hollow. He wanted to take her pain. She couldn't give him that either; it was all that was keeping her breathing. But if she swallowed everything she now was down into the silence that filled her, maybe she could give him what he needed to walk away.

Liese pushed herself up against the pillows and gently pushed Michael's hand away. Slowly and deliberately, and without looking at him, she began to lay the facts out.

The minutes ticked past; Michael stayed silent. The waiting stretched at Karen's nerves, but she didn't want to do anything that might stop him finding a way back from whatever memories had caught him. She glanced over at Markus, who smiled a tight smile and nodded. Small gestures, but they lifted her spirits. When Michael finally began speaking again, she had to bite back a "thank God."

"None of us were the same people when the war ended. We had all seen too much, lost too much. And the end of the war wasn't some great healing; it was a mess. Chaos had swallowed Berlin. Andrew stopped your mother disappearing into it. He used his army connections and got her into the Bethel Hospital, rather than being allocated to a displaced persons camp. He told them he was afraid she had TB. She was exhausted and malnourished and had come from a concentration camp, so that seemed believable. He was so protective of her even then: he guarded her bed like a watchdog. But he was pleased when I first turned up—I'm sure of that. Liese had retreated into silence and he was desperate for someone who could fill in the gaps, jolt her into talking. It was… hard when I saw her. She was so tiny against the bedframe. Her hair chopped short, her eyes too big for her face. She had turned young and old, and it broke my heart."

"She must have been pleased to see you?"

Karen regretted the question the moment she asked it.

Michael's voice slipped from the measured tone he was still somehow managing into a jagged stop and start. "No. I don't think I could claim that. She stopped being silent, that's true. She was shocked at first. And then so furious, I thought she would scratch my eyes out. But then it stopped; it all stopped." He paused, his hands fidgeting as if they were fighting the memories. "There wasn't a feeling left in her for me. That's when I knew something terrible had happened. You have to understand that I had seen people reconnect; I'd brought some of them together. I had seen tears and joy, and also plenty of hurt and anger when one person's war seemed easier lived than another's. I could have dealt with any of those. But after that first furious reaction there was nothing. She said the right things: that she forgave me, that she didn't blame me. It was like listening to a machine."

He broke off, Markus following a beat behind, and looked directly at Karen.

"I loved her; I truly loved her. At one point during the war, I was sure she loved me. But then? She didn't feel anything for me at all. Not even the hatred I felt I deserved. I didn't matter to her anymore."

Another piece of the puzzle uncovered, except Karen didn't know what to do with it. Michael and her mother had been in love. She had guessed his feelings from the wedding photograph; she had never considered the love she saw there was returned.

"I'm sorry." The words sounded too easy, inadequate. Karen forced herself to do better. "I can't imagine how hard that must have been for you. But you must have understood, when she told you about Lottie. And she didn't blame you, so you must have hoped things between you would heal over time. Especially when you saw her with my father. She must have been different, more alive, with him."

Markus had been right about the Michael who had greeted her earlier that night. That Michael had taken control of the conversation, delivering what little he said calmly and methodically. Even when her questions had surprised him and pricked at old hurts, his answers had remained considered. Now, he stumbled over his words and wouldn't meet her eye.

"She didn't stop loving me because she had fallen for him, if that's what you think. She was as closed off with Andrew as she was with me. No, that's not quite true: there were feelings there, although they weren't what he wanted. Your father was kind, a true gentleman. Liese saw that. When he sat with her quietly, or read to her, she would smile and grow calmer than I could make her. But so often she was angry with him. There were moments when she bristled with it. She tried to hide it, and I doubt Andrew noticed the way that I did. He cared about her and wanted her to like him. I'm not sure how experienced Andrew was with women, but he'd clearly developed a crush on your mother that didn't have any space in it for flaws. But Liese? She didn't have romantic feelings for him any more than she did for me. I don't think she could."

He poured that out so quickly, Karen had to ask Markus to repeat his translation, to make sure she had properly understood.

"I don't follow. Father was kind and he had helped her, so what reason would she have to be angry with him?"

Michael's fingers locked; Karen could feel him pulling away.

"You are asking about things that were never discussed."

"But you must have had a theory? You must have wondered. Could he have been different when you weren't there? Pushed her too far about her past and Lottie maybe? Did he ever give you any reason to dislike him?"

"No! Not at all! Your father was a very good man. I never believed him capable of treating her or anyone badly. Even later, with the lengths he was forced to go to…"

Michael rubbed his face and shook off whatever it was he was going to say.

"Neither of us knew how deep her misery ran, how broken she was. By the time we realized, it was too late. Or perhaps Andrew guessed and he kept it to himself, thought he could fix things."

Phrases slid in and out of Karen's head. *So protective even then. The lengths he was forced to go to. How broken she was. By the time we realized, it was too late.* They felt like clues, but she had no idea what to go hunting for.

Markus had stopped watching her and was watching his increasingly uncomfortable father. Karen could feel her moment slipping away. Markus looked on the verge of stopping his translation; she had to trust that her German would hold.

"What was Liese like when Father found her at the station?"

Michael shook his head. "He never said, not really. Except that she was weak and wobbling on the platform and didn't seem to know what she was doing."

Then his hands knotted and unknotted. Karen's stomach started to follow.

"If I am honest, I didn't believe him. I think...I think she had been trying to throw herself under a train and Andrew chose not to tell me. He wouldn't have wanted to discuss that, if it had happened. He wasn't a man much given to dwelling on emotions outside his control."

The description of her father was so accurate, Karen couldn't argue with it. The description of her mother about to throw herself under a train was one she wished she had never had to hear.

"Is that a guess, that she was suicidal? Because of Lottie? Or did you know?"

Michael sighed and his words slowed.

"Know is a strong word. How can anyone ever truly know something so intimate? But the deliberately absent way she behaved in the hospital was so unlike her. There was a well of emotion bursting below her flat words, but she wouldn't let any of it out. Except once. When she was talking about the day Lottie died, when Suhren recognized her. She said she hadn't got to do what she wanted and die. She refused to repeat it; she refused to discuss the day again. But I never forgot what I heard."

He stopped as if he was winded. His hands stilled; his body stiffened. It was clear this time he did not intend to go on.

Liese's agony hung between them. Karen's head was hammering. She wanted to leave and never see Michael again, to never hear another word of her mother's terrible story, but there was still a gap, another bit of the jigsaw still out of her reach. Her mouth was as dry as if it were coated with sand, but she couldn't risk asking for water and giving Michael a chance to remove himself from the room.

"My mother wanted to die in the camp, and she wanted to die at the station. And something, including my father, kept getting in the way. Is that why she was angry with him?"

Michael remained silent, his face too tight to read.

"Why is there always something missing? She must have got better. She didn't try to kill herself again then, or not so that you've said. So she can't have stayed like that: angry with him for stopping her, not wanting to live? Please, Michael, that wouldn't make sense. If she had continued like that, surely she would have killed herself sooner, or she wouldn't have married him?"

When Michael answered, all the emotion had leached from his voice. He could have been discussing a stranger.

"What she did or didn't do, and how they were together, is not for me to say."

Karen didn't need Markus to translate that.

"But you know. You were in their wedding photo; you stayed in their lives. You told me that you loved her, that she loved you. My father rescued her and she didn't want him to, that's what you've said. So what happened next? If she grew to love him, you would have said so. You haven't. And yet she stayed alive and she married him and moved to a country she didn't belong in, a country where no German would get an easy ride. Why? What changed?"

Her voice was shrill enough to bring Markus to the arm of her chair. It made no impression on Michael. He had stiffened back into the man with a firm handshake and equally firm boundaries.

"Your mother had suffered a terrible loss. She struggled to get over it. Your father loved your mother and went to great lengths to protect her. Those things I know. As to their marriage and what led up to it, that is not my story to tell."

"Please, Michael, help me understand this."

He brushed her distress away.

"I have told you what I am able to. If you believe there is more, that is between you and your father. You must talk to him."

"Don't you think I've tried? Do you think I'd be here if he would talk back...?"

Michael got to his feet so briskly, Karen lost the thread of her argument.

"This has not been an easy conversation for either of us, but I hope it has helped. If you ever return to Berlin, perhaps we can meet under happier circumstances."

He sounded like he had memorized a script.

Karen gaped at him as he motioned her up and directed her to the door.

"Goodbye, Fraulein Cartwright. Please remember me to your father. It is growing late. It is time I retired for the night. Markus will see you out."

Karen was through the flat and out in the hallway, the front door clicked shut, before she could gather her breath.

"What just happened?"

"He managed you." Markus leaned against the wall and reached into his pocket for his cigarettes. "He's a master at it."

He offered Karen the packet; she took one but couldn't hold her hand steady enough to light it.

"I guessed he would be careful and I was right. He knew exactly how much he was prepared to give and, when you managed to get too close and he realized he'd slipped over his lines, he closed you down."

Karen waited while Markus struck another match and took a deep drag on the cigarette. She was out of practice: the nicotine made her head swirl.

"I didn't imagine it, did I? There were things he said that pointed to something else happening after Lottie's murder. Something that made my mother marry a man who, at one point at least, she didn't seem to like very much."

"No, you didn't imagine it."

Karen dropped the cigarette and ground it furiously into the wooden flooring.

"So what do I do? I leave tomorrow evening. There's nothing here that will open my father up. I'll tell him I know about Lottie and he'll say I've heard everything. But I haven't."

This time, when her voice rose, Markus pulled her into his arms. Her head dropped onto his shoulder; she was almost sure she felt his lips on her hair.

This would be easier. Sleep with Markus and forget all the rest. Go home with a nice memory and move on.

She looked up at him. There was such kindness in his face, and more. If she kissed him, she knew exactly how the night would go…

"I can't." She stepped back, slipped out of his embrace. "I want to, but I can't. I need to go back in there, Markus. I need to try again."

It was a moment before he answered.

"I know. But he won't open up again to you, not tonight."

"Then what do I do?"

"Let me try."

Karen was about to refuse, but he wouldn't let her jump in.

"I'm not taking over; I'm not pushing you away. But maybe, on my own, I can drag something else out of him. Will you trust me?"

Trust. The hardest of feelings, and she didn't need to think before she answered.

She took his arm and went down to the street, let him call her a taxi.

When she got back to the hotel, she crawled into bed exhausted, expecting to lie there picking over every word and every nuance of the night's half-revelations. She closed her eyes, waiting for the lake and Liese's shocked face to slide in, waiting for Lottie's terrified cry. Instead she saw Markus, felt the warmth of his arms like an anchor.

The world steadied itself a little.

She slept without dreaming until morning.

*

"Last night didn't go the way that we hoped then?"

Markus didn't need to answer: his face was as crumpled as his shirt; his eyes were puckered. Karen looped her arm through his and led him into the dining room.

"Get some food into you and then you can tell me."

She fetched warm rolls from the buffet and ordered strong coffee.

"Have you slept at all?"

"I'm not sure."

Markus slathered honey on the bread and devoured it in two bites.

"I think I dozed against the wall in the corridor while I was waiting for him to go to sleep, and then I got home and I was too wound up to try."

He didn't seem to notice he wasn't making sense. Karen waited while the waiter poured their coffee. Markus drank that without noticing either.

"I'm not following you—maybe you need to start at the beginning. What happened when you went back up to the flat?"

"We fought. My father is a stubborn, impossible man and I am an ungrateful son. That was the outcome, although the saying took longer."

Karen pushed her plate away, her appetite gone.

"I'm sorry. Sorting out my family wasn't meant to drive the two of you apart."

Markus sighed. "It didn't. This is nothing that hasn't been said before or won't be said again and it always starts the same way: with something personal that gets knocked down by his political dogma. 'The state has given you a good life, so be glad of it.' 'The state doesn't dig up the past because to do so is indulgent, not productive. Your duty is to respect that.' On and on like a record on repeat. I love him and I admire him, I really do, but the man is a dinosaur. If it were up to him, the DDR would have swallowed up the West, not the other way round. He thinks our lives under the old regime were ordered; I think they were narrowed down to nothing. We love each other deeply, but it's not a gap we can close."

Karen saw the pain on his face and knew, no matter what he said, that she was responsible for part of it. There were as many layers in his life as there were in hers, although she suspected his growing up had been a far more complex thing to navigate.

"You never considered leaving? I don't mean escaping, I mean applying to go to the other side. People did—we saw the reports when it happened."

Markus closed his eyes. For a moment, she thought he was annoyed at the question, then he looked at her with his soft smile and she realized he was simply trying to frame his answer in a way that wouldn't make her feel stupid.

"I imagine those reports made that type of legal crossing over sound easy. It wasn't. It was just as dangerous as crawling through a tunnel or leaping over the Wall. Choices weren't simple here, Karen. Everything had two faces: applying to leave meant rejecting the East, a conscious decision that left your card literally marked. The minute anyone raised a request, the state closed its doors. No university, no decent job, no healthcare; for the one applying and for the rest of their family. And nine times out of ten the application would be rejected. Then, unless you preferred to be sent to prison on some trumped-up and unanswerable charge, the only work available would be what the government you had turned your back on was gracious enough to provide. Working for the state was the end for too many good people: they were turned into spies to keep feeding the system."

"So you felt you had no choice but to stay? Especially given Michael's position?"

"Exactly. If I'd tried to leave, I would have broken Father's heart and ruined his life, never mind mine. My wanting out would equal his failure. So I never really considered it. Being a good son mattered to me more, although he doesn't believe that at the moment."

When she reached out her hand, he hung on to it.

"What happened last night, Markus?"

"I tried to reason with him. To get him to understand that what happened to Liese is still causing damage. That you had a right to know, and he had an obligation to tell. I wasted my breath. He thinks 'this constant talking is a Western disease.' So I lost my temper. Also a waste of breath. Never argue with a man who's spent sixty years soaked in communism. I swear he could win a debate against Death. Anyway, I got nowhere. He asked me to leave and I went."

Karen rolled the crumbs on her plate into a ball and refused to give in to tears.

"You tried. I'm grateful. You've done more for me than you needed to, and I know more than I did when I came. Lottie's death was reason enough for my mother killing herself, whatever else did or didn't happen. People marry for all sorts of reasons. Who knows what really causes anyone to commit suicide. Maybe it's time to accept that I can't find answers that don't want to be found."

"Karen, look at me."

When she did, he brushed away the tears that had escaped her furious blinking.

"That's a brave face, but you don't believe what you're saying and neither do I. Which is why I went back."

He reached into his jacket and took out two folded pieces of paper.

"What are those?"

"Newspaper articles, from my father's clippings file. Michael is a record-keeper."

He grinned as she frowned.

"Not in a bad way—he's no Stasi recruit, although I'm sure they would have loved to have snared him. I told you I didn't know much about his past. Like you with Liese, I've had to piece it together from snippets. I do know that he was captured at the end of the war when the Russians sacked Berlin and he survived that because he was Jewish and because he could speak their language. And then, of course, because he told them he was a communist and had worked for the resistance. He made it through. A lot of his comrades weren't so lucky: they died or stayed missing. What I'd forgotten until you came was that Father kept looking for them, and kept records of anything that might turn into a lead. He was always cutting things out of the newspapers—trial reports and police discoveries. So last night I waited till he was sure to be asleep and then I let myself back in and went through his papers."

Markus held out the yellowing scraps. "What can I say? You've finally turned me into a spy and therefore a good DDR citizen, although I'm not sure I'll be boasting about that anytime soon. Anyway, these were all I could find for the time between your mother's return and her wedding. It's not as much as I hoped. Perhaps he wasn't so systematic with his records then."

Karen smoothed the brittle papers out.

The oldest of the two was dated December 2, 1946. It was short, barely a handful of lines, and reported the disappearance of Commandant Fritz Suhren from his Hamburg cell only days before the Ravensbrück War Crimes trial was due to start. Suhren's name was thickly underlined.

Karen read it through and didn't know what to make of it.

"Do you think Michael was following the trial, or Suhren's escape at least, because of Liese? When he was talking, he kept mentioning protecting her, hinting at the lengths that he and Andrew went to. Do you think they were trying to find Suhren? To bring him to justice?"

Markus waved for more coffee.

"Maybe. That crossed my mind. But it's an odd pairing to go Nazi hunting: a British soldier and a German communist."

Karen waited until the waitress had gone again, her mind whirring.

"Perhaps it's not as unlikely as it sounds? My father was in the Royal Military Police and Michael wasn't short on connections."

The more she looked at the underlined words, the quicker the storyline started building.

"And we know my father liked to play the knight in shining armor where my mother was concerned. Maybe finding Suhren was some kind of offering? Or maybe they hoped Suhren would give evidence at the trial about the soldier who killed Lottie. He must have been there, if what Michael said about him pulling Liese out from the other women right after it happened was true. He would have known who the man was: surely even in that place such a brutal act would have stood out? They could have been hoping to identify the killer and get justice. It actually makes sense when you think about it."

Karen picked up the other cutting, scanning it quickly for a link to Ravensbrück, or the quest she could suddenly see their fathers undertaking. Then she read it again more slowly. The disappointment was the same.

"I don't see what this one has got to do with the other."

The second article, dating from February 1947, was longer—a plea from the Berlin police for help with identifying a body which had been recovered from the River Spree. Karen read the details aloud, hoping Markus might stop her when she reached the connection.

"'The woman's body, which was dislodged from a patch of reeds when the river thawed, was wrapped in sacking and weighed down with a large stone. Preliminary identification has been hampered by what the Berlin Police refer to as "substantial facial injuries." A postmortem is scheduled for next week. It is hoped this will help establish the exact cause of death and furnish some clues to the victim's identity. The victim was well dressed and wearing a wedding ring. Providing useful information in this case may lead to a reward.'"

She stopped and waited, but Markus said nothing.

"I don't get it, I'm sorry. What has this got to do with the Ravensbrück trial or my mother? Unless something had happened—maybe my mother had gone missing? Do you think that might be it: she had disappeared and Michael thought the body was hers?"

She was in danger of crumpling the paper. Markus took the articles back and folded them carefully into an envelope.

"That's possible. Or perhaps, given the trial was coming and all kinds of secrets might have been about to spill out, he thought it was another prisoner from Ravensbrück who had been disposed of, and he wanted to prepare her, or keep her safe. I've no more clue to how these are connected than you. Or even if they are. But whether there's a link or not, I think you should take them back to England. Show them to your father and see where, if anywhere, that leads. In the meantime, I'll do some digging, see if the newspaper the second one came from still exists and has archives. It's not much, but surely it's something new to push Andrew with?"

Karen wasn't convinced, but she put the envelope into her bag.

"What if Michael notices they're missing?"

For the first time since he arrived at the hotel, Markus smiled.

"Then we'll know that they matter."

The dining room had emptied while they were talking; theirs was the last table waiting to be cleared. Karen checked her watch. Ten o'clock. She had hours before her flight. The trip had been exhausting—the demands of new clients and old mysteries had drained her. She felt old, lost in other people's emotions. She glanced over at Markus, at the face which was as kind as it was handsome. His feelings hadn't seemed important to her when she first arrived; that wasn't true anymore. There was a connection between them she knew she hadn't imagined. Something good could come out of this, if she was brave enough to try.

"Would you like to be just Markus and Karen for the day?"

He sat back, watching her carefully. "Explain."

"Two people who've recently met, who find each other... interesting. Who've had enough of the past and not enough of the present."

He grinned. "Who live in the West and have never heard of the East? Who listen to music some people might call decadent? Who spend money without thinking on frivolous things and kiss in the street without caring?"

"If you like."

He jumped up, grabbed her hand.

"I like it, Karen Cartwright. I really, really like it."

This time, when he pulled her into his arms and kissed her, she didn't hesitate.

He looks happy and even better than the nurses said.

There was a croquet match in progress on the lawn behind The Mountbank and Andrew was in the thick of it—laughing at a misplaced shot, bowing in mock deference to a more skillful player.

Perhaps this is who he is when I'm not around: popular, carefree.

It was a sobering thought.

Someone must have spotted her, alerted him. Andrew turned to the edge of the lawn, where Karen was hovering, and put down his mallet. Karen waved and was saddened, but not surprised, when he hesitated and took his time walking over.

"I stayed away because everyone seemed to think that was for the best, but I've been keeping up with your progress. You look even better than I thought you would—you look really well."

She meant it. In the nearly two months since she had seen him, the hollows in his cheeks had plumped out and his face had recaptured its color.

"I know you have. Thank you. And yes, I tire quicker than I would like and I need to take care, but the doctor is happy with my progress. I have my own flat in the complex now—it's very pleasant."

He paused, but not long enough for her to speak.

"I trust your visit to Berlin was what you hoped it would be?"

His eyes were wary, his manner formal. She sensed he would wave her goodbye if she let him.

Karen took a steadying breath: this could not come out rushed and garbled.

"I'm sorry. For everything. For not being kinder. For the things I accused you of. For not being a better daughter."

Andrew took a step back; ran his hand through his hair.

Karen didn't know what else to do but keep going.

"I thought you were trying to control her. I know now you were trying to protect her. I should have trusted you more."

There was a carved wooden bench a few feet away. He sat down heavily on it. To Karen's relief, he left space for her to join him.

"You found Michael then?"

She nodded.

"You know about Lottie?"

When she nodded again, he sank back against the slats and closed his eyes. Karen started to panic.

"Are you all right. Oh no! Is it your heart again?"

"I just need a moment."

Karen was half off the seat to get help when she felt his hand on her arm. He straightened up but didn't move it. Karen sat as still as if a butterfly had found her.

"What else did he tell you?"

"Not much. He said you found Mother at a train station on her way back from the concentration camp. That you took her to the hospital. That you... Michael said you developed a crush on her."

Her father smiled. "That makes us sound like teenagers. I suppose, in a way, we were. Six years of war took our youth away. I was what in 1945—twenty-nine? It sounds old enough to have had plenty of girlfriends, but I hadn't. I certainly had never met anyone as lovely as your mother. And I was a romantic, casting myself as a knight in shining armor. Not that she ever asked me to. I think, if I'm honest, which I was less inclined to be then, she hated that I saw her that way, as someone who needed rescuing. It certainly wasn't how she saw herself. Sometimes, I pushed her too far and her eyes would flare. I liked that sparky side of her."

His cheeks were wet. Karen forced herself not to look at him.

"But she had suffered terribly. She wouldn't tell me much herself, but she had experienced things that went beyond my comprehension. I knew of the camps—we all did by then—but I'd never been in one. And what happened to her daughter..."

He sighed and shook his head in a way that reminded Karen of Michael restructuring himself.

"I should have told you about Lottie, when you were old enough not to be frightened. I'm sorry. At least now you know why she did what she did. You know the whole story."

"But I don't, do I?"

His hand withdrew.

Karen inched forward as cautiously as if she were sliding over newly set ice.

"There are gaps; I can feel them."

"I don't know what Michael's been telling you, but this was all a long time ago. His memories are no doubt hazy."

He had shifted away; she could feel him poised to get up.

"He didn't tell me: that's the point. Michael was really careful. He didn't want to talk about you and her—he said it wasn't his place. But he let one thing slip: he said when he came to the hospital, Mother was angry. Not with him—he said she felt nothing for him—but with you. He wouldn't explain why, or how that changed and how you ended up getting married."

"Because there was nothing to explain."

When Andrew did scramble up, Karen was ready for him.

"Don't, Dad; please."

Her unexpected softness and the use of a term she'd barely even used as an infant pulled him back down faster than her hand.

"I swear I don't want to hurt you. I've done enough of that. If you tell me I've got this wrong, that Mother's suicide was solely because of Lottie and the agony from that she understandably couldn't shake, that she married you for love and there are no more secrets, I'll believe you, I promise."

Karen let her hand drop; stopped talking; gave him the moment to leave. When he didn't take it, when he sat still again, she took the cuttings out of her bag.

"Would you look at these for me? Michael kept them. We—his son, Markus, and I—thought they might be important. He's a good man, Michael's son. He's trying very hard to help all of us through this."

Andrew nodded, although Karen could see he was reluctant. She handed him the piece about Suhren's escape first and waited while he read it.

"We wondered, Markus and I, if you were trying to find Suhren and get justice for Mother."

He passed it back with a shrug and a look Karen could only read as relief.

"I was never that fanciful. Michael may have considered it—he had a network of connections I wasn't privy to—but he never mentioned it to me. Anyway, the French got Suhren in the end, hanged him in 1950. I've no idea about Michael's motives, but this means nothing to me. I avoided the trial and tried to keep any mention of it away from your mother. Revisiting what happened there would have done her no good. I'm sorry but whatever this is, I can't help you with it."

His response was disappointing, but Karen had had enough experience of her father evading her to know when he was telling the truth.

"Fair enough, but what about this one?"

When Andrew read the second article, the change was immediate. There was no relief. His tight edges dissolved as if he could no longer hold himself together. He shoved the cutting back at her as if the words were written in acid.

"Why on earth would he have kept this? Karen, please. I can't..."

Pain furrowed his face. It twisted Karen's stomach to see him so haunted, but the crack she had been searching for had finally appeared and she had no choice except to force it wide open.

"Did you think the body was Mother? Had she read about the trial and run away and you were afraid that someone had hurt her? Were the camp survivors in some kind of danger? Was that why Michael had this?"

"Christ no! It was nothing like that."

He was shivering.

I could make him ill again; I should stop.

She knew that she couldn't.

"Then what was it? Why was some drowned woman important? Was it a friend of Mother's? Someone she was in the camp with? Were you scared what she might do if she found out? Michael said more than once that you were desperate to protect her."

"A friend?" He made a noise that could have been a laugh or a sob. "You're not going to give up, are you? Then yes, I was desperate to protect her; we both were. And yes, it was someone from the camp. Oh, Karen, my darling, you don't get it—how could you? Ravensbrück was a women's camp. All the guards there were female."

Her father, the soldier playing the knight in shining armor; Michael, with Heaven only knows what training behind him.

Karen stared at her father as if she had never seen him before.

"It was the guard, in the river. The one who murdered Lottie. You and Michael killed her."

Andrew raised his head and stared back at his daughter. His face was as white as a corpse.

CHAPTER FIFTEEN

Liese

Berlin, November 1946–April 1947

The shop was quiet.

The frost-laced November wind had pushed the pedestrians back to their firesides, ready for a tucked-in Friday night. Herr and Frau Herber had already left, gone to visit their daughter in the countryside to stock up on the butter and cheese that kept them both round.

Liese was glad of the respite: the shop and its adjoining workroom was a simpler place without them. The Herbers were good, generous people, but they were also gossips and inquisitive, and sometimes the balance tipped too far the wrong way.

She glanced at her watch. Five o'clock and dark as night outside. There was only one more order to prepare, ready for making up on Monday, then she could close and slip away before either of her usual escorts had a chance to appear. She was too tired tonight to be much use as company.

Liese stretched the fabric along the cutting desk and marked off the lengths with tailor's chalk. She could lose herself for hours like this, even when her eyes and shoulders were drooping; that much at least hadn't changed. Even through her time as Suhren's seamstress, the process of assembling the building blocks of a dress had never lost its capacity to absorb and calm her; had never lost its magic. Carving straight lengths of material into intricate pieces, turning them from flat to full so that the finished garment would cling and swing and transform even the thinnest body. It remained magic, *because this is theater.* Although that wasn't strictly true anymore, or at least not in the way her father once meant.

Liese traced the pattern onto the cloth, struggling to picture Paul spinning his spells in Berlin's newly revived but battered and shortage-hampered fashion industry. There was little in it he would recognize, or that she could imagine him wanting to be part of. None of the names who once ruled it had come back from the exile or the hell they'd been sent to. The extravagant dresses Haus Elfmann was once famous for were museum pieces, the shows they put on a myth. Despite the extravagant promises made by morale-boosting magazines, silk and taffeta and crêpe de Chine had become the stuff of dreams, along with unlimited flowers and perfume-thick air and spectacle.

Post-war Berlin was a divided city, hacked into four political sectors in 1945 by the victorious Allied powers and into two sharper, more obvious divisions by money—or, more accurately, the lack of it. The poor, a rapidly growing class, were hungry and cold. They were stuck in queues, surviving from day to day on scraps of food and scraps of coal, with no sense that the war they had lost had ended. The rich, however, who had salted their fortunes carefully away and were bolstered now by the flood of Americans and their dollars into the city, had re-embraced the social whirl. Parties lit up embassies and refurbished hotels; partygoers chased glamour from any fashion house that could get back on its feet and supply it. Competition was cut-throat, customers were fickle; resources were limited and ingenuity prized. The last days of Haus Elfmann, which had demanded a creativity from Liese that the old-style designers would have found horrifying, had proved to be of more value than any lessons in haute couture she had learned.

In the year since she had secured a job at the Herbers' dressmaking shop, Liese had retrained her hands and eyes to learn the language of new materials. Slippery acetates that ran away from the needle; wool mixtures that were too cardboard-stiff to fold and tuck. She had also learned to adapt her designs. Dresses no longer came elaborately sculpted with knife-edge pleats and intricate gathers; there weren't the supplies to create them. Women with new responsibilities and less certainties in their worlds no longer needed morning dresses and afternoon dresses and a week's worth of evening ensembles. Except for the wealthiest, the days of excess had gone. Liese didn't mourn them. The Herbers, however, did and their ambitions far outweighed the little shop that had fallen into their hands when the war had left it ownerless.

It took Liese less than a week to realize that, despite their pretensions, the Herbers were struggling and the shop's existence was threatened. Glad of something to do that filled her days and asked nothing of her but her skills, Liese had risen to the challenge.

She plundered their dwindling fabric stores and spliced together mismatched fabric ends, whipping up skirts and blouses in what some might call patchwork but she described as "rainbow-arc outfits." She encouraged Herr Herber to open up the gloomy store window and filled its space with color. Women tired of gray and bored with narrow skirts that hobbled their knees began to find their way to Budapester Straße. Liese watched as they sighed in front of the mirrors and ran hands down bodies that rationing had turned boyish. She worked offcuts into overskirts nipped in with sashes and bulked out with padding that restored war-starved hips and waists, and used inserts and darts to create blouses stiff with the illusion of volume. Women left the shop feeling like women.

Herr Herber saw the order book fill and began to introduce Liese as *Rumpelstilzchen*, daring clients to bring in any fabric they could salvage for "darling Frau Ettinger, who truly can weave gold out of straw."

"Why does he call you that? Surely he knows your name is Elfmann?"

"No, he doesn't. Why would I use a Jewish name if I don't have to? Germany was beaten, that's not the same as safe."

It was a clever answer to Andrew's confused question, but it wasn't the truth.

Liese wasn't afraid of being Jewish. She wasn't afraid of anything anymore, except memories. She could be Elfmann anywhere else, but not in the dressmaker's. Saying her parents' name there was impossible. Either no one would know it in this business where everyone should, or, worse, it would be recognized. Some well-meaning soul would reveal the unthinkable and fill out that last image Liese held of Paul and Margarethe walking away with a camp name and a too-detailed nightmare. So, at work, she was Ettinger.

Andrew accepted her reason, as she had known that he would: he was too horrified by the whole business of the camps not to. She wished she could so easily stop the rest of his questions. Now that she was no longer in the hospital and seemed more sure of herself, he was desperate to burrow into her history. To know every detail about her family, about her life before, about the dreams she had dreamed there. "So I can get to know you better." As if the Liese then and the Liese now were the same person.

He means well. He cares about you. They both do.

She picked up her scissors as her conscience pricked.

Michael and Andrew: a year and a half out of hospital and she still hadn't shaken the pair of them off. The truth was, she didn't want to. Somewhere along the way, their concern for her had stopped being a burden and she had learned to value them both, despite, or perhaps because of, how different the two men were.

Andrew was the simpler of the two and his company was impossible not to enjoy. He was well read, he had an eye for art that she appreciated, and a way of approaching the world without judgment that carried a genuine warmth. They had fallen into the habit of walking together on the weekends, watching Berlin reshaping, sometimes talking, sometimes not, or sitting in one of the dozens of cinemas that had popped back up, both happy to be lost in other people's stories.

Liese had come to like Andrew very much. She knew he had fallen in love with her; in a different world, it wasn't impossible that she could have fallen in love with him. He was good and kind, and patient. Liese knew that he would do everything in his power to make her happy and he would be very easy to make happy in return. He knew that she was broken, that she had far less to give than he deserved and it didn't matter to him. What was it he had said? "You like me—I know you do. And you trust me. That could be enough, if you let it, to make into a good life. I have love enough for both of us for now; one day, if you let yourself, you might just catch me up."

From anyone else, that would have sounded needy, or weak. Coming from Andrew, somehow it didn't. And that was the problem. He was such an honorable man. He deserved so much more than a woman who couldn't work out why she was still living.

As for Michael... He was in love with her too and that was far harder to ignore. There was such a wealth of history between them, good and bad. Liese had tried to push him away, but he kept coming back. She couldn't pretend anymore that he meant nothing to her. Sometimes she thought she sought out Andrew's company the most because she couldn't trust herself to be alone too long with Michael. He had a way of looking at her that went straight through to her heart, but her heart was still too broken to find room for that.

A wave of exhaustion washed over her, the way it so often did when she tried to puzzle out her future. She put down her scissors and ran her hand over the blue wool she had already cut, noticing as she did so that it was the same deep shade the doctor had worn under his white coat on the day he had discharged her.

"You're well enough to leave us and we need the bed."

It was the last days of Ravensbrück's liberation all over again. She would have argued, if she thought for a moment he would have listened to her any more than the American doctors had then. Or if she had had anything better to say than "I don't want to leave here; I can't deal with the world." Nobody could deal with the world the war had left them with and she was a picture of health compared to most of the wretches the hospital admitted. The doctor knew what had happened to her; there was nothing he could offer to heal that wound but pity. Liese didn't want that from him; she didn't want that from anyone. All pity did was stoke the anger that still crouched in her stomach.

So much rage, constantly churning inside her. Liese stared at the desk, at her scissors and pins neatly waiting and wondered why, when it reared, she didn't glow red or burn everything she touched. Andrew couldn't see it, or chose not to see it, but Michael could. That was the danger with Michael—he saw everything she was. And didn't hide from telling her.

"Maybe the anger is good—maybe it's what keeps you going?"

As if she wanted to keep going.

Then why do you? Why don't you end it like you planned?

Up it popped again: the question she could never quite answer. That always wriggled on into: *It doesn't need to be the lake: there's cars to walk under; there's scissors to cut wrists with—there's a dozen ways.*

It was two years since she had last kept her vigil over the water, joining Lottie her only goal. Two years since she had swayed on the train platform, and yet here she was, still living her life. Something was pushing her to keep on breathing, but try as she might, she couldn't work out what.

When the hospital had discharged her, Michael and Andrew were there, waiting to take over. She wouldn't let them. She had allowed Michael to use his connections and help her find a place to live but had refused to move into his block. She had waved Andrew away when he worried that she was too weak yet to find work. She had hauled herself off to the new tailoring quarter springing up round the Kurfürstendamm and sold her talents to the Herbers with far greater success than she had managed with the wartime businesses who had chased her away. She had carved out a life and she was still inching into it. She still didn't understand why living it mattered.

For Andrew and Michael perhaps?

It was part of the answer, but it couldn't be all of it, no matter how much she valued their affection. No matter that she knew the love they wrapped her in was more than so many people had.

Post-war Berlin was a battered place, its heart pounded by bombs, its streets crammed with the lonely and the desperate. Liese passed them as she walked between her new home in Seydlitstraße and the Budapester Straße shop. Starving children, whose feet were bound in blanket strips whatever the weather, whose faces were sharpened like weasels. Lines of rag-bundled women clearing rubble from Berlin's ravaged buildings, from around the cellars too many still lived in. Women too hungry to manage such physically punishing, pitifully paid work; too hungry not to. With no one left to love or be loved by. Women who would have envied Liese's life as much as the wretches stuck in the camp that Suhren snatched her away from.

Liese knew how lucky she was, but it was hard to feel grateful when she was so filled with guilt.

"Excuse me, are you open?"

She had been so engrossed in picking over her life, she hadn't heard the bell ring. If Herr Herber found that out, his pale face would turn purple.

Liese straightened herself up and smiled at the dark shape letting the cold in.

"Yes, for another half hour."

Never hurry a customer, my dear: there's not enough wealth in the city for us to rest on our laurels.

Frau Herber's lesson chimed louder than the doorbell had.

"And longer, of course, if you need it."

The woman came further in, shaking frosty raindrops all over the floor.

"Perfect. It will be weeks before I am in the city again and I wanted to see about placing an order."

She waved her sodden umbrella at Liese and didn't offer any thanks when Liese took it.

"It's such tremendous luck that I found you. There I was, treating myself to a cake in the sweetest café on the Kurfürstendamm, and in walks a woman in the most darling ruby-red coat. Of course, I had to ask her where she got it and she, naturally, was quite thrilled that I did. And then to find out that the dressmaker who made it is only five minutes away and my dear Henkie so desperate for me to have something special for the winter. Well, this was clearly meant to be."

On and on she went, in a tone her breathy delivery clearly intended to be charming but that hit all the wrong stresses.

Liese was barely listening. She had struggled to listen to a single word since the woman had stepped from the threshold into the shop's buttery light. Her throat was so tight, she couldn't have spoken even if the woman had wanted her to. All she could think was: *How can she look so ordinary?*

The clothes were different. The coat the woman wore was Loden-green and lumpily belted rather than a flowing black cape. Her hat had a feather set at its center, not a swastika pin. But nothing about the heavy figure had changed in three years. The square-chinned face still glowed with health, the cheeks turned as ruddy by the November wind as they had been that long-ago and yet so recent bitter February. The eyes, for all the effort made to widen them with pencil flicks, still sank like currants into the doughy skin. The hair was smartly rolled and not so tightly drawn back, but it was just as brassily blonde as the strands that had once poked out from under the sharply peaked cap. She was a first-class Aryan poster girl, even out of uniform, and every inch of her face and form had been photographed in a moment three years ago and printed on Liese's memory ever since.

Liese couldn't speak, she could barely breathe, but the guard carried on, oblivious.

"And I do so need a new coat, a properly tailored one. I love my babies, I truly do, but..." She patted her middle with a sickeningly coy smile. "Well, they've hardly been kind to my waistline."

"Babies?"

The word splintered as it fell.

The guard swelled with pride. "Twins—two girls, if you can believe it. Such a shock and such a handful. Both Daddy's little darlings, of course. It would be a lot to manage for most people, but my Henkie is such a good provider. He's the mayor of our town and so well respected. Fürstenberg, that's where we live. It's an awfully pretty place, about an hour or so outside the city, although I doubt you will have heard of it."

"The town in the woods, near the lake. I've heard of it."

The guard was too delighted with herself to hear Liese's voice shaking.

"So, to business. How does this work? Do you have a pattern book, some ideas I could look at?"

The notion that Liese could possibly do anything as normal as make this woman a coat was so preposterous, she found herself acting as she would with any other customer. She nodded and waved the woman to a chair placed next to a small table. Gestured to the pile of magazines lying on it as if she were an actress playing a role so well learned it didn't require her brain to take any part in it.

"Such a good selection—how perfect."

That word again, that expectation that the world would fall the exact way she required it. As it had clearly kept on doing for her, and no doubt all the others who had gripped hold of power with their dogs and their whips and walked away when the war was done, as if no part of the horror they presided over was any of their doing.

Liese had seen the reports of the Ravensbrück trial, despite Andrew and Michael's efforts to keep her away from them. The number of arrests was laughable: a handful of faces standing in for a mob.

She moved a step closer, ran through the next set of lines.

"Can I get you a tea or a coffee while you look through the designs?"

The woman opened a magazine and began taking off her gloves.

"Coffee would be delightful, as long as it's the real stuff. And you have sugar."

She doesn't know me. I doubt she's ever seen me.

Liese stood perfectly still, watching the leather unpeel from the skin, watching the white hands emerging. They were too big to be elegant, the right one too scarred to show off.

Scream. Snap. Splash.

Liese didn't move. She hadn't expected to see anything other than that scar to emerge. She carried on quietly watching until the gloves were folded and stowed in the shiny black handbag. Until the woman's attention was fixed on the models and their blank haughty faces.

There was no startling moment when she made a decision. There was no need to work out a plan, or think through what she was doing. Every move that was needed was already known and had been set in motion when the door first opened. Now they unfolded and Liese felt them as much a part of her as her heart's steady beating. There was no voice in her head screaming *stop*. There was no voice in her head except: *this is punishment, pure and simple*. This act Liese now knew was coming was as much a mother's job as her lake-watching vigil had been.

This is what has been keeping me alive.

The realization ran through her like a charge and made the rest simple.

Four paces to the cutting desk, four paces back. All the stored fury turning to fuel now it had finally found its purpose.

"Here you are."

"My, aren't you quick."

It was surprisingly easy. And surprisingly silent.

The blonde head lifted. The black eyes went searching for their sugary treat. If the guard saw what was coming, she didn't have time to react.

One swift move: *scissors up, scissors down.* Glinting blades finding their own path from fleshy lobe to sinewy throat. A red scarf springing into the air, flying out in a curve as if caught by a breeze and then dropping, pooling back round the limp neck.

The body slumped. *Eyes wide, eyes closed.*

All over, in seconds.

"Where are the keys, Liese. Look at me: where are the door keys?"

The shop was in shadow, the window blinds pulled down, although Liese didn't remember drawing them. Time must have ticked on quicker than she thought because Andrew was here, waiting, she assumed, to walk her home, to offer her dinner. He was standing closer than he normally would and his face was so colorless, she wondered if he was ill.

"Why don't you give those to me and then tell me where the keys are. It would be best for everyone if I could lock the door."

That made sense. It was obviously getting late and no one else would come in on such an unpleasant night. And the scissors, which she hadn't realized she was still holding, were slippery and sticky.

She looked down at them. Why were they in such a mess?

"Liese..."

She dropped the blood-soaked blades. Whirled round. The guard was still sitting in the chair. Her coat had stiffened and smelled metallic, and a stain had spread out like an ink blot under her chair.

"What have I done?"

Liese remembered the door opening, the woman coming in as vividly as if it had just happened. And that terrible moment of recognition. And that voice talking, going on and on. The rest was a blur, a series of snapshots; some she desperately wanted to stay out of focus.

"Babies. Oh, dear God, she had babies."

Once she let the images spool back, they wouldn't stop coming.

"I've killed her and she had babies. Unless, please God, she's not dead?"

Liese ran to the body, grabbed its wrist, and began scrabbling for a pulse.

"Is it possible she's not dead?"

"No. No, it's not."

Andrew pulled her away from the cold skin she was clutching.

"Look at the blood, Liese. No one could survive that."

He was right. There was so much of it, on her as well as on the body. Liese sank onto her heels and stared at her scarlet-stained hands. The need to explain, to somehow make it right, overwhelmed her.

"It was the guard. The one who killed Lottie. She walked in like a customer, wanting a coat. She didn't know me at all. I didn't think. I just did it. I've longed to do it. Dear God, I've longed for it all this time. I just didn't know." She rubbed at her hands, but the blood wouldn't shift. "And now it's done, and we have to call the police."

Andrew pulled her back to her feet with a roughness she didn't know he was capable of. "Are you crazy? We can't call them. Look at her: you can hardly say this was self-defense."

"Why would I want to?"

"Because they'll hang you! And don't you dare tell me that's what you want. Don't you dare. Where are the keys?"

"What?"

His grip was so tight, she could feel her arms bruising.

"Where are the *keys*, Liese? For the front door?"

"Let go of me and I'll get them."

He released her. She ran and grabbed them from the hook, gave them to Andrew, and turned back to the telephone. He pulled her away before she could lift the receiver.

"Leave that. As soon as the door's locked, we need to clean this place up, and you."

"No. I told you: we need to call the police. This is a crime, a terrible crime."

Andrew's eyes were so dark it was frightening.

"And I've told you already, we're not going to do that. Go and wash your hands while I tackle the floor."

He pushed her through the velvet curtain into the kitchen and grabbed a cloth and soap flakes.

"Hurry up. And then fetch me some sturdy cloth and some string."

He was too wound up to argue with. Liese scrubbed her hands until they were raw and then collected a pile of old potato sacks and a bundle of twine. When she came back into the shop, ready to stand up to him again, she was thankful to see he had come to his senses and was speaking on the telephone.

"I'll tell them who she was. I'll explain what she did. Surely they'll understand."

He slammed down the receiver when he saw Liese reappear and took the sacking she was holding out to him.

"Thank you for making that call. I'm glad you could see there's no choice."

Liese reached for his hand but he shrugged her away.

"There's always a choice. I wasn't calling the police, I was calling Michael. He has a van and we need it."

Not Michael—not standing witness to this.

Confessing her crime to the police suddenly seemed far less important than not having to confess it to Michael.

"Andrew, no. Don't bring him into this, I'm begging you!"

His face changed; his voice switched from fury to what sounded like fear.

"Don't do this, Liese. Don't make yourself into some kind of sacrifice. I can't live with that. Michael won't be able to live with that. Please, please, if you have any care for me at all, just do what I say."

He looked so broken, so desperate. Whatever force had been pushing Liese on since she picked up the scissors drained away. She moved through the next moments doing only what he asked. Helping him roll the body onto the sack, helping him pile the cleaning cloths on the guard's chest. But when the doorbell rang, she wouldn't let Andrew answer it and she gave Michael barely a second to take the scene in. She needed to face him and face her actions before Andrew told a more edited story.

"It's the guard who murdered Lottie. I cut her throat."

Michael stared at her. He opened his arms. All she wanted to do was fall into them, but Andrew grabbed him instead.

"And if we don't sort this out, she's going to give herself up to the police and she's going to hang. So help me. Are you listening, Michael? Help me, or she's lost."

"Michael, no! Don't listen to him; listen to me."

But Michael turned away from her and spoke only to Andrew.

"I need something heavy. I need to destroy her face and make sure that nobody recognizes her."

He scanned the shop and picked up a sewing machine.

Liese darted forward. "That's wrong! That won't work!"

She was about to explain, but both men rounded on her.

"Don't look if you can't stand it but let us do what we must."

She was exhausted, her limbs trembling. Faced with Andrew and Michael, not listening to her, so united and so determined to do what *they* clearly thought was in her best interests, it was easier to give in, to convince herself she could still somehow make this right later. She stood back. She made herself watch, and not argue.

"We need to take her to the river."

Their voices were so low, she wasn't sure which of them spoke—not that it mattered. Michael and Andrew were focused only on each other and the tightly bound package now balanced between them.

"You don't understand—"

"You need to come with us. You can't stay here alone."

Neither of them were listening to her. It was clear they still thought she would call the police. They bundled the body and Liese into the van, intent only on where they were going.

"At least tell me where we're going."

"There's a point across from Schloβ Charlottenburg where the river quickens. The current should take the body down from there to the Havel and out to wider waters. It's better to let the river move her than us."

Once Michael answered her, without turning round, neither man spoke to her or each other again, except when Andrew told Michael to slow down or risk being stopped by an army patrol. Once the American military jeep passed by, Berlinerstraβe stayed empty. There was no traffic to slow them on the Schloβbrücke or in the maze of broken streets that bordered the river. Liese knew there was no point in speaking, that their actions had taken on their own momentum in the same way that hers had. When they drew close to the tightly packed treeline, Michael pulled the van in.

"It should be quiet enough here, as long as we move quickly. Anyone hanging round this place will be too drunk to know what they've seen, or be believed if they try to describe it."

He jumped out, followed by Andrew. They wrestled the body out of the back and told Liese to wait. She couldn't—the light on the water spun too strong a pull. She followed them as they stumbled over the muddy ground, both men struggling to stay upright. It had rained for most of November and the river was full, branches caught in it and tumbling.

She won't lie as peacefully as Lottie.

"On my count, and on three."

Michael's whisper swelled in the silence.

The bundle rolled toward the water. There wasn't an arc this time; it was more of a plunge. And there wasn't a quicksilver splash but a crash as the water opened. A greedy roar that ran through Liese's bones and ripped away the silence that had been forced on her in the salon.

"This is all wrong. Why wouldn't you listen to me?"

She stopped and sucked in a breath that came out in a scream.

"How can I have been so stupid? All I had to do was lock the door and keep you away. This was my fight, not yours, and now you're messed up in it."

Michael and Andrew broke into a run and caught her between them as her legs slipped from under her.

"It doesn't matter. No one will find her. Look at the river: it will take her for miles, toss her to bits." She pulled and pushed against them, but they wouldn't let go.

"No it won't. She won't lie peacefully—how can she? This won't end it. Don't you see? I've killed her and this won't end it. She had babies. Children of her own—two little girls. One more than what she took from me. She'll be found. She'll be identified. And you'll pay a price that was only ever mine."

She was long past a whisper. Her voice bounced round the trees like a trumpet calling.

"Liese, take a breath. I destroyed her face. You know I did. No one will know her."

Michael's arm tightened round her shoulders as if his words were reassuring.

"No. That's what I was trying to tell you. You got it all wrong. It wasn't her face that mattered. It was her hand. The scar on her hand. That's how they'll know her and track her to Lottie, and to me."

Michael's arm fell away.

"And now you two are in danger. Because of me. What I've done makes me as evil as her. It makes me worse."

She spun round and began stumbling her desperate way toward the water. Michael lunched forward to grab her. Liese felt his hand catch at her sleeve, but she tugged too hard for him to hold her and left him floundering in the mud.

"Andrew, for the love of God stop her!"

"Let me go! You have to let me go. You have to let me make it right!"

She was quick, but Andrew was quicker. When he caught her, his grip was so tight she couldn't pull free.

"Make it right? Are you crazy? How does you ending up in the water make any of this right?"

He pinned her arms so tight she couldn't struggle.

"I won't let you, Liese. I won't. I can't have done all this to watch you die. Neither can Michael."

Her strength fell away. She wanted to run and yet she wanted his arms. No—she wanted Michael's arms.

"Come back to the van. Please. Let us find a way through this."

It was easier to follow than fight. She climbed in beside Andrew, her teeth chattering. She couldn't look at Michael, who was gripping the steering wheel so tight his hands looked like claws.

"What have I done?" she couldn't stop asking on the dark journey home, although both of them begged her to. "What have I done?"

"You did what you had to and now we must live with it."

It was Michael who answered. This time his voice was as broken as hers.

*Ich erkläre hierbei, daß ich, Andrew James Cartwright,
geboren am 13. März 1916 in London, gewillt bin Liese
Wilhelmine Elfmann, geboren am 15. Juni 1920 in Berlin,
zu heiraten.*

Liese read the typed note through to the end while Andrew sat
quietly beside her.

"It's a declaration of intent to marry. British soldiers wishing to
marry German citizens are required to make them."

"I know what it is. It's not the words I don't understand."

Her voice shook. She couldn't stop it shaking. Or her hands.
Herr Herber had sent her home on Monday and again on Tuesday,
fearful she was starting a fever. If she told him about the dizzy
spells, about the hallucinations, about the square shape that kept
flickering into the shop and fading out as she turned, he would
be convinced of it. If she broke down like she wanted and told
him what she had done, how many would she drag behind her
to the gallows?

"It's an insurance policy."

Liese struggled to surface from the shop floor's horrors. Andrew's
voice had changed into Michael's. Increasingly, she found she
couldn't tell one man apart from the other.

"In case the body is found. Which it won't be. But if it is, this
keeps us safe."

She picked up the neatly lined sheet of cream-colored paper.
It was signed by Andrew, witnessed by Michael; officially stamped.
It looked weighty, like it already carried their vows. She was still
missing something.

"I'm sorry, but I don't understand. How does getting married
keep me safe? If she's found and identified, if she's somehow linked
to me, a change of name won't matter."

So many *ifs*. And so many promises.

It will all go to plan, don't worry. The connection between you and her is too thin to see. Go back to work at once on Monday morning, no matter how impossible that sounds. Act normally and this will pass. You are not alone in this.

Michael making his claims as confidently as Andrew. Both of them convinced she believed their keep-the-future-safe wishes would work. Didn't they understand that she had taken a life? That crimes as dreadful as that left deep stains and had to be punished? She forced herself to stop shivering and to focus on understanding this latest twist in their plan.

"You said that, even if the worst happened and the husband was traced, he must know his wife was a Nazi and he wouldn't want that coming out. If that's true, surely he won't want to stir up publicity. So what's changed?"

Andrew slipped the certificate out of her hands and smoothed it back out.

"Nothing, except that we've had more time to think. The Ravens-brück trial has put the spotlight on the crimes that were done in the camp. Yes, the husband would be a fool to come forward and make a fuss over her death. But others could hold grudges and might recognize old photos of her if any were published. And Suhren called out your name at the camp, Liese; he linked you to Lottie's killing even if that wasn't his intention. That may have registered with someone."

She could see the logic, but it didn't answer her question about where the idea of marriage had come from. She stared from one face to the other and, for the first time since the guard's killing, the two men separated out.

"I don't understand. Why marriage? And why you?"

Why not the right one?

It hung in the air even though she hadn't said it.

Andrew looked away.

It was Michael who answered her question, although he sounded like he was reading instructions.

"If you marry Andrew, he can take you to England. If it falls out like Andrew said it might, you wouldn't be safe in Germany."

"England?"

The idea was so ridiculous, she couldn't find a question to fit it.

Michael sat back and let Andrew step in. He tried a smile, but his face was as exhausted as Michael's.

"It's the safest place. You killed a mother, Liese. You told us: she had two babies of her own. If you're caught, you will hang. We would face prison at the very least, but you would definitely hang. I know that you don't care much for living, but the thing is, we can't live with your death. At the state's hands or your own. If that makes us selfish, so be it."

It was the first time Andrew had directly acknowledged how deep her pain ran, or what it could lead to. Liese couldn't meet his eyes.

"I'm sorry…"

She didn't know how to finish the sentence. She was sorry for killing a woman with two children. She was sorry for all the unhappiness that would inevitably follow her actions. She was sorry she had put Michael and Andrew in danger. She wasn't sorry the woman was dead. She didn't know how to put any of that into words. Andrew, as always, spared her the effort.

"Don't worry. We're simply making plans to deal with whatever eventuality arises, that's all."

Plans, nothing more; we won't need to act on them.

Liese forced herself to look properly at Andrew. He was so solid. His words might echo Bardou's, but the two men shared nothing else. She could lean on him, on his quiet confidence, and know that, unlike everyone else, whether they meant to or not, he'd never let her down. That held such comfort in it. But she couldn't love him, not in the way he deserved, which meant she couldn't marry him. She thought that her silence every time he had spoken about the future had told him that. She had never wanted to hurt him.

And yet perhaps by letting him keep hope alive, I already have.

"Andrew, please. You know how much you mean to me, but this? I can't—"

Andrew shook his head. "There's no need to say what doesn't need to be said."

He picked up the marriage declaration and put it in his pocket.

"It's insurance, something to make us all feel safer. It won't be required."

Until, as Liese knew it inevitably would be, it was.

"Two visitors, Fraulein Ettinger? It's a good thing the snow has kept our customers away this morning or I would have to scold you."

Liese didn't need to leave the kitchen when Frau Herber's tight voice called her, or see the men's pale faces, to know that the body had been found.

She fetched her coat. The three of them walked without speaking to a quiet café on the Kurfürstendamm.

Michael waited until they were seated and their coffee was poured before he broke the news.

"They pulled her out yesterday, at Lindenufer, just below Spandau, where the Spree meets the Havel. One of my contacts at the police bureau there told me the news this morning. We still have a number of female comrades missing; he thought it might be one of them. It's unusual, even in Berlin, to find a woman whose clothes suggest she is of good standing murdered. It will make the papers tomorrow."

Liese stirred her coffee round and round, waiting for Andrew to speak. She presumed they would have divided the story between them.

"The body got caught in a reed bed and came up with the January thaw."

Andrew kept his eye on the waitress wandering between the half-empty tables as he spoke.

"It was simple bad luck. Another mile down the river and we would have been clear."

Simple bad luck: it felt more like a judgment.

"All this time, she was so close. Barely ten miles away."

Liese caught the glance that ran between the two men, saw them steel themselves in case she collapsed. She felt instead strangely calm, relieved in fact that the waiting was over. Eight weeks and one day. Fifty-seven mornings, fifty-six nights. So much willpower harnessed to move herself through them. She could feel her head lolling. She knew that tonight, as crazy as it sounded, she would sleep.

"They will trace her back to me, won't they? In the end?"

Michael looked away; Andrew nodded.

"It's not certain, but I think the odds against it have shrunk. There's been so much reported at the trial about the guards' cruelty; about the brutality they used so easily against the prisoners. There's a lot of anger at how many of those women got away. Even in a place as dreadful as Ravensbrück, Lottie's murder must have stood out. And you said there was a noticeable scar on the guard's hand. She will be identified from it. However her husband tries to downplay what she was, someone will remember her; someone will step forward."

Michael slammed his cup down and swore as coffee splashed across the table.

"They should give you a medal."

The waitress looked up but clearly thought better of coming over.

Liese reached out and slipped her hand round his. His fingers were stiff and cold. When he spoke, his voice choked and turned him back to the boy she used to tease in the salon.

"It should have been us, Liese. Marrying, building a future. Giving Lottie brothers and sisters, the way that we planned. All of this, every cruel twist of this, is my fault."

He was wrong, but the time for arguing over it had long passed.

She squeezed his hand as hard as she could. She couldn't stay and risk the danger that would put him in. She couldn't watch him suffer anymore; she knew he would never leave her or stop trying to protect her, not unless she forced his hand. So, despite the pain she knew it would cost, she had to make him go.

"If they come for me, they'll find you two. What you did will come out. I cannot bear to see either of you punished. That is all that has kept me going. That is what has stopped me doing anything else that would bring attention, from the police, from a coroner." She held on as Michael flinched. "I don't care that much about me anymore—you know that. But I can't let anything happen to either of you."

"Then choose me."

She heard Andrew's strangled gasp but she couldn't think about that; she couldn't be distracted or let Andrew's voice in. She focused instead on Michael's face. The distress in his eyes took her breath away, but she forced herself to stay steady.

"I'm good at hiding, Liese—you know that. Or maybe we don't need to hide. We could go to Russia with the connections I have, start again there. I can keep you safe. I love you. I can look after you, I promise."

I promise. The two words that were all Liese needed to push him safely away.

She kept hold of his hand and she lied, for all three of them.

"I don't love you, Michael. I can't. There are too many broken promises already between us. There are too many shadows."

It worked. Michael got up and stormed away; Liese let him. She stayed upright; she stayed dry-eyed—she couldn't allow herself to feel. She took what comfort she could in the knowledge that this would keep Michael away from prison and the shadow of a noose; it would keep him safe and free to start a new life.

She slipped her shaking hands under the table and turned to Andrew. He was watching her, his body so still it was as if he had frozen. If he understood the truth of what had just happened, of the sacrifice she had just made, he gave no sign.

"How long will the arrangements for the wedding and our leaving take?"

"A month at the outside. It will need a minimum of two weeks to organize your travel permit and passport. We have the permissions in place, which speeds everything up. I'm due to leave Germany shortly; I can request that moves up quicker. And I've found a church for the wedding that's suitable. If that's all right? I can change it, if that was presumptuous."

He suddenly sounded as hesitant as a schoolboy.

Liese dug deep and found him a smile. "I'm sure it will be fine. Put it all in motion. There's no sense in delaying. I'll hand in my notice tomorrow. I'll be ready."

The relief in his sigh almost unfroze her. That and the brightness in his eyes he hid by busying himself with the bill. He was happy. He was too sensitive to the danger that still threatened—and to her—to show it, but Andrew was happy.

Liese waited while he fussed with the change and the correct amount for the tip and forced herself to breathe, calmly and slowly. She wouldn't insult him by faltering.

The risks these men had taken. She hadn't asked them to; she hadn't wanted them to. All she had wanted was for them to let her finish her story the way that she chose.

And you could have made sure of that; you could have pushed them away, but you didn't.

She had clung to them, because she needed them and, in very different ways, she had cared for them. Now she had to pay that debt along with the rest.

They got up from the table; Andrew helped her on with her coat.

He's doing this out of love. Because he is happy and he has hope.

Liese slipped her hand into his and chose to be glad at that.

She focused on the goodness that was Andrew and clung to that choice as hard as she could through the whirlwind weeks of preparations that followed.

When nothing about the body appeared in the press beyond the fact of its discovery, she turned the choice into a promise, into a charm. She wrapped herself up in its hope like a cloak and hid behind it. From Michael's misery at the sparsely attended wedding she had told him not to attend but he couldn't keep away from. Through the shock of a windblown crossing across a sea far grayer than any lake. Through lonely days in a hostile village where her accent was enough to make backs turn.

Andrew is happy. I choose to be glad at that. Andrew deserves that, so my choice is enough.

A promise, a charm, a spell. After a year in England she had worn the words thin, but she kept on repeating them, praying that, one day, every last bit of them might turn out to be true.

CHAPTER SIXTEEN

Karen

Aldershot, May 1990

He didn't look at her. He made a space between them on the bench so they wouldn't touch. He spoke steadily, with a speed which didn't offer pauses into which questions could leap. The economy and efficiency of her father's telling was as marked as Michael's.

"The guard came into the dressmaker's shop where your mother was working. She didn't know Liese; Liese killed her. It wasn't planned. Michael and I disposed of the body, but not well enough. It was found and identified. We didn't think Germany was a safe place for Liese to be after that, so I married her and brought her to England. The burden of it all, in the end, was too much."

When he finished, his voice finally broke into what they both knew was a sob. He turned it into a cough and wouldn't meet Karen's eye.

"Believe me, I never wanted to tell you. I didn't even want to tell you about Lottie. But this? It wasn't who your mother was. It really wasn't who she was."

The sparse recounting had taken no time. The croquet game was still in full swing behind them on the lawn. The sun didn't appear to have moved through the sky. Nothing in the day's summery mood had altered the way that it should. There were no lowering clouds, no shadows extending creeping fingers over the grass; the temperature hadn't dropped from the gentle warmth it had held when Andrew started.

And yet my father just told me that my mother was a murderer.

No theory that she and Markus could have imagined would ever have come close to this. The need for the solidity of his arms overwhelmed her, rushing back jumbled memories of Berlin. First of Markus and then, hard behind them, an older one. A time capsule of a shop and a sour-faced old woman.

"I was there. At the dressmaker's shop. It's called Richters now. I found it when I went to Berlin in 1978 with the school. I stood in the place where it happened."

He didn't react; he looked too drained to react to anything. He looked like he wanted to run.

"Why did she kill her?"

It was the most inadequate question. Karen wasn't even sure why she asked it or what answer there could be except "Lottie." But she had to say something: if she didn't, if her father—who was poised on the edge of the bench—walked away, this revelation would disappear into the silence they were so practiced at living in. So she opened her mouth and said the first thing that came into it. As it had done with Michael, her simple directness worked on Andrew like a key.

"Revenge." Andrew sat back enough to suggest he might stay and uncurled his clenched hands. "That's what she told me at first and I believed her. It seemed obvious enough. Then later, when she..." He paused. "This isn't easy for me. It's not a conversation I ever wanted to have with you. Or with her. For a long time the whole...event...wasn't discussed. I couldn't bear it; I didn't think your mother could stand it. Then, when the weight of it became too much for her and she started to talk...there were more layers. She talked about the guard's death like she had been carrying out a punishment. A 'mother's job' she called it. But that made it sound deliberate, thought out, and I'm not sure it was. All I *am* sure of is that what she did that day didn't bring her any peace. If anything, it added to her suffering."

The scale of that clawed at Karen's skin. "You said you were the one who found her, with the body?"

He nodded.

"I went to walk her home. One of us, me or Michael, often did, especially on a weekend. I think I was planning to suggest going to the cinema—it was something we both liked to do. She was just standing there, blood everywhere." He coughed, swallowed hard. "It was me who brought Michael into it. I couldn't have managed it all on my own."

Karen had thought fixing more detail onto Andrew's, and Michael's, part in the story would make it more real. It didn't. She still couldn't grasp the events he had described. Her quiet and gentle mother, who had never raised her hand, clutching a murder weapon. The father she knew, the military policeman who lived his life by discipline, and Michael, the controlled man she had met in Berlin, hiding a murder, dumping a corpse. Two men who lived their lives by strict rules, a woman who she would have said wouldn't have hurt a fly; all of them acting so out of character. And then Karen remembered the only truth that must have mattered to Andrew and Michael, the agony that Liese had suffered with Lottie's death, and knew that, as impossible as it all sounded, it also sounded horribly true.

Andrew was shifting again, looking over to the lawn as if he was hoping for a rescue. Karen wanted to let him go. She wanted to let it all go. She wanted to curl up in a ball and hide and never talk about any of this again. She gripped the bench to stop herself rocking and pushed on.

"How did you feel? About covering it up?"

He turned to her, his exhausted expression transformed to astonishment. "How did I feel? I have no idea. I didn't think about it, not in the moment. I cared about her; Michael cared about her.

She needed our help. What should we have done instead? Contacted the authorities? Watched them take away a good woman to hang?"

"No! Of course not."

His voice softened as hers rose. "We all paid for it, Karen. All three of us. No one walked away from that night unmarked. But at least she walked away. What we did in the shop, what I did in bringing your mother here, was the right thing to do. The only thing to do."

She heard it then, the tremor in his voice which rang with uncertainty.

Didn't she love you enough? She'd hurled that at him years ago, without any other thought except the hurt she could cause. Watching his spent face now, Karen realized her father had spent his whole marriage haunted by the same question.

"I'm sorry—so very sorry, Karen—for having to tell you this. And for all the other things I should have said and never found the courage."

The apology took her by surprise. How long had she waited to hear that? Now, Karen wished she had played her part better and not fought him, that "I'm sorry" had never been needed on either part. She wished she knew him well enough to wrap her arms round him. She settled instead for honesty.

"Don't, please. There's just as much fault with me as with you. You were trying to protect me, like you tried to protect her. I was too angry, too wrapped up in myself, to see it."

This time he didn't turn his back when his eyes filled.

"Thank you for saying that, but the blame isn't equal and I won't let you go on thinking it is. I'm your father. I'm meant to take care of you, but I got the doing of it so wrong. Your mother died and then I kept her away from you. She wanted me to tell you about your sister. She told me to do it; she knew you needed to hear it. I didn't know how. I thought you were too young when she died. Then you weren't, but I was a coward and I kept missing the moment to be brave. I failed her and I failed you. That has been as hard to live with as her dying."

It was the longest, most personal speech she had ever heard from him. But before Karen could acknowledge that, Andrew shook his head as if to clear out the memories and got up. Karen felt the newly closing gap between them lurch open again and panicked.

"Please don't leave it like this, with more holes. What do you mean she told you? How? When? Why did it matter to her, that I knew what had happened? Don't you see? I don't know her and I so need to know her."

The words came out in a cry of pain she couldn't stop.

"That's the worst of this. Ever since she died, she's kept shifting. Everything I learn drives her further away. And I know there were good things, but they've got lost under the bad. I need my mother back, Dad. I really need her back."

It was Andrew who took the leap they both were yearning for. He reached out a hand and pulled her into as close to a hug as the two of them knew how to do.

"I know you do. I'm not leaving anything unturned, not this time. Come with me, Karen. I'm going to do what I should have done years ago. I'm going to help you to find your mother."

His flat was brighter and more personal than Karen had imagined it would be. She wandered the rooms, glad of a distraction. The walls were washed in lemon yellow; cheerfully checked curtains framed the windows. There were daisy-printed cushions on the sofa in the living room that Karen knew her mother would have liked.

"You've put out photographs."

Three elegant silver frames decorated the main bookcase. Her mother's passport photograph and Karen's baby shot had been remounted and reframed and flanked a larger print of Karen, looking awkward in her graduation gown.

"It wasn't a kindness to have photos around when your mother was alive and then, well, I hadn't learned the habit. Mrs. Hubbard suggested that a new home deserved new ways."

"What do you mean, it wasn't a kindness?"

Andrew adjusted Liese's picture before he answered.

"Simply that. Liese was frightened by images of herself, and displaying my family only reminded her that all trace of hers was gone."

There were so many questions Karen was burning to ask, but this new confiding felt too fragile to rush at and overload. She waited while he busied himself with the inevitable tea and a home-made fruit cake he was quietly proud of. The similarities between him and Michael kept growing stronger. Karen was beginning to sense why they had both loved Liese; why their lives had ended up tangled together.

"Mother never found her parents then?"

"There was nothing to find, except their names on the lists of the dead. The deportation they were on was sent straight to Auschwitz; they were murdered almost at once. She never stopped blaming herself for that."

More guilt bleeding into the jigsaw that was her mother. The depths of it were devastating, unacceptable.

"Why would she do that? Shoulder so much blame? Markus said she would have carried Lottie's death the same way, despite the fact there was nothing she could have done. That broke my heart, even though I knew he was right."

Her father glanced up and smiled. "This Markus sounds like someone you listen to."

Karen nodded. "He is."

She could see he was interested, but this wasn't the time.

"But I don't understand how Mother could blame herself over what happened to her parents? She couldn't have stopped them being deported."

"I know. There was nothing she could have done. Like she could do nothing for Lottie. I hate that she felt the weight of all that misplaced guilt, just as you do, but I could never ease the burden. In the last years of her life, Liese became convinced a lot of things were true that couldn't possibly have been. That she had sent her parents to their death because it was her idea that they went out to work was one. That she had done something shameful in the camp she couldn't, or wouldn't, explain but had to pay for was another. That the renewed interest in tracking down Nazis in the sixties meant she would be discovered and hunted and would be called to account for the guard's killing or something she did in Ravensbrück. I don't know. None of what she was afraid of made a great deal of sense and me saying that, as I did over and over, made no difference to how deeply she felt it."

The fear of photographs. Her mother's averted face at her wedding, the upset on the pier at Brighton. Did it all stem from the same twisted feelings of guilt and the fear of discovery? How had Liese continued as long as she had if that's what her life was?

Karen picked the sultanas out of her cake and lined them up like cherry stones.

"Was that what the nighttime ramblings were about?"

Andrew nodded. Karen couldn't begin to imagine the strain he had lived under, that he had hidden from her for years, that she had unwittingly added to.

"I remember how she was. The headaches that sent her to bed for days, the bursts of energy when she never seemed to sleep. You in the kitchen trying to calm her. And how overprotective she was. With me, with that weirdness over the windows. Surely she can't have been like that from the start? Did she worsen? Did she get help?"

Her father took so long to answer, Karen wondered if he still suspected that an attack or a harsh judgment was coming. When he did speak, he was slow and painstakingly deliberate.

"She was often…removed. She always had odd ideas she wouldn't explain. She grew less certain what was the past and what was the present as the years went on. She loved jewelry, but she would only look at what I bought her inside the house and never wore it outside in case anyone thought we were wealthy. That was some throwback, I imagine, to the way her Jewish family was treated, but she wouldn't say when I asked her. And she always had one foot walking with Lottie."

The way he said that sprung tears to Karen's eyes, but she waved him on when he tried to stop and comfort her.

"I knew, when I found her at the station, that she didn't want to live. So did Michael. But something kept her going and we never had the courage to ask her what. We couldn't live with her death, you see. We thought if we refused to accept it would happen, it wouldn't. Perhaps it really was some hope of revenge that got her through the days, although I doubt that she knew that. And then, after she killed the guard, she kept herself alive for us, for me. She never said it, but I knew that, by helping her, Michael and I had become another debt she felt she owed payment on. I always knew that I had borrowed her; that her scars would catch up with us one day. Our marriage…Perhaps it wasn't the great love story I was so desperate to turn us into, but there was love on my side and real affection, maybe even love, on hers, I promise you that. It was a proper marriage because she wanted that too…"

He stumbled and reddened and couldn't meet Karen's eye.

Karen's heart went out to him as he tried to battle through this unaccustomed openness. She was starting to understand what the dignity she had dismissed as coldness had cost him.

"It's all right, Dad. There's things that should stay private."

He nodded and managed to recover his composure. "I never thought there would be a child, not after so many years. And then you came. And you were wanted." His face suddenly lightened so much he looked a dozen years younger. "That first night I held you was a miracle."

"And Mother?"

Karen didn't want to ask. When he replied, she could hear the answer she dreaded curled in the spaces.

"She loved you. When the nurse put you in her arms after you were born, she laughed with delight. I'd never heard her properly laugh before. It was beautiful."

He stopped.

"But?"

Andrew's voice was so quiet, Karen had to lean in.

"She got sad. The baby blues they called it, nothing to worry about, meant to last only a few days. Except it didn't. She had good spells and bad spells; the bad ones got longer."

"So her death wasn't because of Lottie, or because of the guard's killing. It was because of me?"

And there it was: the question she had long ached to have answered finally out. Not mixed with blame and hurled out of spite, or loaded with anger, but simply and heartbreakingly put. It cost so much to ask it and, although the pause was agony, she was grateful her father took time to consider his answer.

"No, Karen: it wasn't. You've lived too long carrying a fault that was never yours. Perhaps, yes, your birth was a catalyst for what came, but so was the war and my saving her and marrying her and bringing her here and a dozen other things I doubt even she could name. Your mother was badly damaged by her life. She was ill. But she loved you with every bit of her that could and that's the truth."

He got up and left the room before she could gather her thoughts up to speak. When he came back, he was carrying a cloth-covered blue book.

"She was brave, Karen. All the battles she fought and yet she kept on going longer than most people I know would have managed, soldiers among them. Nobody talked about depression in the fifties and sixties. You pulled yourself up and got on with it. That was the language I had, that most doctors had. Or they gave you pills. She hated them; she wouldn't take them properly. When she did, they stopped her functioning and made her paranoid. When she didn't, it was like she had to live all her lives in one day. It was exhausting, for both of us. I never knew which Liese I was coming home to, or which one you had seen."

"Which is why Mrs. Hubbard stepped in."

Karen remembered the slap and squirmed. If her father knew, which he surely must, he had the heart not to mention it.

"I know she interferes, but she was—and is—a lifesaver. But this isn't about her."

He held out the book. "I found this when your mother died. I'm not sure what to call it: a journal perhaps, or a scrapbook. She must have started keeping it not long after you were born. One of the doctors might have suggested it, to try and marshal her fears, or it was her own doing for the same end. I don't know. I don't imagine she intended either of us ever to see it, but it helped me. Eventually. I think it might do the same for you."

Karen opened the flimsy cover and began turning the pages. There were cuttings pasted into it, thickly speckled with annotations and longer pieces of writing in both English and German.

Her father stopped her as she flicked through to the end.

"You need to take time with it, follow it in order. My dictionary is on the bookcase if some of the German is harder than you can follow. I've been brushing up my skills."

"Why didn't I find her book when you were in the hospital and I cleared out the house?"

She knew the answer before he supplied it.

"You gave it to Mrs. Hubbard for safekeeping."

"I had to. It wasn't something for stumbling over. And you would have got it, whatever happened to me. I'd written a letter to go with it, if my treatment didn't work."

He got back to his feet.

"Sit with it now, as long as you need. I'll be in the garden when you're done. I want you to come to me when you are. It doesn't make easy reading. But you'll find her in there, Karen. And I hope you'll find the forgiveness you need. For yourself, for me, if you want that. For her."

She heard the scrape of the kitchen table and the whistle of the kettle long before she was finished. The light had faded outside, drawing Andrew in. He didn't disturb her. Reading the scrapbook had taken a number of stops and starts: the entries were muddled and without any thread of time or narrative to link them. It took Karen an age to find a pathway and decipher a voice she could follow.

All the stuck-in clippings appeared to date from the early to late sixties. Their subject matter would have seemed wildly at odds with each other without Andrew's brief description of Liese's obsessions. They veered between highly prescriptive advice on all aspects of motherhood and childcare, and a whole series of articles reflecting the upsurge in the early 1960s in the demand to bring Nazi war criminals to justice. Every article was accompanied by scribbled thoughts and questions—about what made a good mother; about what made someone a murderer. As with the more personal, undated, and untitled handwritten sections, their tone became more desperate as Karen worked her way through them.

There was a pattern to the fears but no discernible order in the way the pieces were put together. Sometimes articles were stuck on top of each other in a jumble of crying babies and new medications, as if her mother was overwhelmed by competing anxieties. Sometimes there was a grouping which suggested one obsession had dominated. Newspaper reports from the 1963–1965 Auschwitz Trials ran over half a dozen pages. The details of the charges presented, and the defenses offered, were thickly underlined; the same questions about where the guilt lay scribbled over and over.

Karen found the longer entries, the ones where Liese had laid her soul bare, the hardest to read. They ran round and round in endless circles and were filled with a restless spirit that made her weep while she read them. Karen tried, but she couldn't get through them all. The anguish in the loops Liese clearly couldn't break out of was unbearable. The ever-present shadow of failure. The inability to trust herself as a mother, so caught up in the lessons of the past that a loudly crying child still meant danger. The knowing and not knowing she was safe, the inability to see soldiers as anything but a threat. It was little wonder she had always dreaded going to the base. That her mother could separate Andrew from the pack, Karen realized, said a lot about her father's kindness and the strength of their marriage.

To Karen's relief, not every page was so bleak. Every so often there was the trace of a lighter day. When her mother recorded personal milestones and celebrated them.

> *My clever baby walked today. My precious girl smiled and lifted her arms when she saw me.*

> *She has so many words, every day a host of new ones—they tumble from her. She is the cleverest little thing.*

> *How will I ever be able to tell her off? She is such a little monkey, into everything she shouldn't be, and then she looks up at me with that grin and my heart melts.*

Her mother had captured these moments in a rounder script and surrounded her delight with garlands of beautifully drawn roses. Karen began hunting these entries out, combing through the pages for glimpses of herself and of happiness.

Her father's carefully phrased guidance proved right. The scrapbook was soaked in pain and hard to read. It was clear that her mother believed, although she could not, or would not, coherently explain it, that her actions had knocked the world off-kilter. That she was a danger to her daughter. That the crime she had committed, and the ones she judged herself guilty of, came with a price attached; that one day the universe would demand payment. There was paranoia and terror imprinted on every page. It was a side of her mother Karen knew was there but had never wanted to see, no matter how much closer it brought the real Liese.

It also wasn't the whole story. Karen found another woman inside the writings. One with a quick mind and a full heart. With a determination to understand what had created the horrors she had been plunged helplessly into, horrors that had rewritten the happy life she had expected to live. Her mother was plagued with demons but she was also, as her father had said and Karen had felt since she first heard Lottie's story, determined and brave.

Have I found forgiveness?

Karen stared out of the window at the dark edges of a lawn which was as immaculate as the one at her childhood home. She knew her father, who was still waiting quietly in the kitchen until she was ready for him, hoped the answer to that would be an easy "yes." The truth was, however, more complex.

For her mother battling on in the face of such suffering, what else could it be but forgiveness? Karen was flooded with it. Except it wasn't unreserved. If Karen was honest, and in the face of the day's revelations there was nothing else to be, a tiny, illogical voice still wished that she, the second-chance daughter, had been enough to alter the ending Lottie's death had set in motion.

That wasn't a voice, Karen knew, that she would ever entirely silence, but she had made herself a number of promises as she read through the book. That she wouldn't blame her mother anymore for leaving her; that she would learn to accept that her mother's last chapter was written long before she was born. That, too, she would try to forgive herself for not being good enough, and try to wipe those words from her future. She sensed there was a role for Markus in that, a role she wanted him to play.

There was forgiveness then, for herself and her mother. As for her father: the answer wasn't no and it wasn't quite yes.

Karen would never doubt his love for her mother again, or for her. She knew everything he had done was born out of the desire to protect them both. But the tiny voice ran through this new acceptance too. Wishing that he had taken charge and been more honest, that he had done what he said her mother wanted: told her the truth and saved them both all the added hurt. His failure there would take time to fade to a scar she no longer needed to pick at. Not quite forgiveness then, but not punishment; not anymore.

As to the second question her father had hoped she would answer, *Have I found my mother?*, the answer to that was no less layered. She had and she hadn't. There was enough in the scrapbook for Karen to add flesh to the bones of the facts, but there were still gaps, still shadows. Liese's life could be uncovered, but its depths and nuances could only ever be truly understood by the woman who had lived it. That was the scrapbook's real story: for all Karen searched and all she found out, the life her mother had lived would always keep her a finger's stretch out of reach.

As Karen watched the sky move through blue to purple, she realized that knowledge was enough. To move forward. To turn the last page of the book to what her first skimming, and her father's gentle warning, had told her was waiting there.

It was a letter. She assumed he must have pasted it in. It was in her mother's handwriting, but it wasn't scrawled like the journal entries. Its intentions weren't lost in a sea of jumbled questions. It was carefully, elegantly written in pale blue ink, on faintly lined paper headed with a stylized picture of The Hove Beach Hotel. It was addressed to her father and signed by her mother and it was dated Friday, July 10, 1971.

PART FOUR

CHAPTER SEVENTEEN

Liese

Hove, England, July 1971

Eins, zwei, Papagei,
drei, vier, Offizier
fünf, sechs, alte Hex
Sieben, acht, Kaffee gemacht.

Liese snapped awake as sharply as if an alarm were ringing. She couldn't tell if the voice dancing through her dream had been her own or Minnie's, but it was loud enough to turn the silly song into a shout.

Andrew was snoring gently, the bedclothes on his side arranged as tidily round him as when he had first climbed in. He had always been a deep sleeper, sinking down within moments of picking up his book. "Not even a page managed last night" was his usual morning greeting.

With the nursery rhyme, whose bouncing rhythms had enchanted her as a little girl and then done the same for Lottie, still chiming through her head, Liese inched away from his warmth and fumbled on the bedside table for her watch.

Four o'clock.

That strange not-quite-sleeping, not-quite-waking hour that sat on the bridge between the night and the day. An hour Liese had watched tick by far too often.

She shifted uncomfortably, her bare arms grating against the rough nylon sheets. The dream had gone—she never could catch them once she woke. Lottie had been in it though; Liese was sure of that. Playing somewhere just out of reach, like an actor calling out their lines offstage.

Andrew hadn't completely closed the thin curtains before he got into bed. Perhaps that was what had really wakened her. There was a sliver of moonlight shining into the bedroom, turning the scuffed writing table and chair into something rather grander. Liese seemed to remember that the curtains had got caught up the night before when he tried to draw them, the cheap fixtures they hung from straining his already brittle mood. It was hard to be sure; yesterday was a bit of a blur. Brighton's gaudy brightness had brought on a headache she knew had bitterly disappointed Karen.

Images of tantrums Karen was too old to throw niggled at her sleepy memory. Demands for money and rides and ridiculous amounts of candy. Andrew had grown angry; Karen had grown angrier. Liese had retreated. She increasingly found that the best strategy when the two of them, who were as strong-willed and stubborn as each other, although neither could see it, started butting heads. She had been doing that more and more lately, leaving father and daughter to sort out and settle their differences. Pretending she didn't know why.

The scratchy sheets were impossible to stay in now that she was awake.

Liese got up and went to the window, meaning to ease the threadbare fabric across. Her dressing gown was on the back of the door—putting that on might offer a barrier between her skin and the bed. She began tugging at the curtains, caught sight of the view, and stopped, mesmerized. The moon hung as low and heavy as a cat full of kittens, so close to the horizon a nudge would sink it. Above it, the sky's black had whittled to navy at its edges, like a pool of ink spreading. Liese stood on her tiptoes, craning over the square and the gardens, hoping for a glimpse of the sea. Imagining the water wriggling free of the moon's tugging and stretching itself out ready to welcome the sun.

It will be today.

The thought leaped like a splash. Liese quivered, waiting for the second voice to come. The one that shook its head and wondered. It didn't.

"Then it will be today."

The relief sank her into the thinly padded chair set under the window. Liese closed her eyes and let the decision settle round her, felt it fitting as warm and snug as a well-washed robe. The steps she had to take next had always been there, waiting. Now she was ready, she knew they would reveal themselves.

She got up and dressed quietly in the clothes she had hung over the back of the chair the night before. A simple belted sundress, a long-sleeved cardigan, flat open-toed sandals. Nothing showy. Choosing her clothes the day before she intended to wear them was such an unusual thing for her to do even Andrew had noticed. Liese couldn't remember how she had answered when he had pointed it out. Out of habit, she brushed her hair and rubbed cold cream into her face and hands. She didn't bother today with mascara or lipstick.

She checked her watch again and then slipped it off and laid it next to her wedding ring on the bedside table.

Four-thirty.

Almost three hours before Andrew's alarm clock would jolt him awake. There was time to do things properly, just as she had always intended she would. Time to make sure no doubts or questions lingered.

Liese began to move quicker: now the decision was made there was nothing to be gained by delaying.

She fetched a pen from her handbag, creeping like a mouse round the room as she did so, although Andrew's deep breathing told her there was no need. There was a small stack of writing paper and envelopes piled at the back of the rickety table. Liese sat down and smoothed out the one sheet she would need. The letter did not have to be long—there was no explanation she could offer Andrew that he didn't already know—but it had to be written. For Karen's sake. To make things as right as she could.

My dear Andrew,

She paused. That was something she had rarely called him, although she knew how much he loved to hear it. That or any other endearment. Another regret to add to the list she hoped this last act would atone for. And the next line, that seemed to come so easily now, was one she wished she could have tried out in person. Was it too much to hope that reading the words would make up for her silence?

You have been a good husband and a kinder one than I deserved. I want you to know that. And I want Karen to know she has always been the best of us—the best of me. I want you to tell her that. Before you give in to the grief I know my leaving will cause you, I want you to tell Karen how much I loved her, that this is none of her doing. That some part of me will always stay with her. Will you do that for me? Will you promise?

I cannot stay any longer. It is as simple as that. And I want to go at my choosing, on a good day when the world is clear and I know what year I am living in; whose voices are real. That feels very much like today. I know you have been waiting for this. I know you have dreaded it. I hope you can understand and forgive me.

Tell Karen about Lottie. That will be hard—you won't want to do it, but it matters. I can't give you the words; you must choose them, but you must tell her the truth. That she had a sister who was murdered, that so much went wrong because of that act. If you don't, she will think me leaving is her fault. I can't bear that; I can't throw that shadow over her. Don't wait, Andrew; don't think she needs to be older. You have done so much for me already and I have never thanked you for any of it, but please: do this.

You should also know, if you don't already, that this is no more your fault than Karen's. And that I have loved you. Try to believe that; try not to keep doubting it. I know it should have been said a long time ago. And believe also that this thing that I am doing is a kindness. A repaying of the debts that weigh on us all.

Liese put the pen down. She was tired. If she carried on with this thinking and writing, she would be too tired to do what had to come next.

Hold Karen for me. Tell her that you love her. Tell her that every day.

There was nothing more to be said.

She signed her name quickly and put the letter in an envelope, which she laid on her empty pillow. She stopped, stared down at the face that had been part of her life for so long. Andrew was still snoring; still, on some level, content. Liese reached out to touch his shoulder and stopped. If he woke and saw her standing there, he would guess and he would stop her. There had been too much of that.

The hallway outside their room was deserted, the hotel sleeping and silent.

Liese tugged her cardigan round her, her shoulders suddenly cold. Karen's door was next to theirs, only a few paces away. Liese hovered, uncertain for the first time since the decision had come to her. Karen was still so young; Andrew was not the most effusive of men. What if this was wrong? What if it caused Karen more harm, not the good she intended? Perhaps if she slipped inside, took a moment to look, to drop a kiss on that beloved face, she would know. The impulse became an ache, propelled her fingers toward the door handle. And then Liese paused.

The slightest sound and she will wake up and the choice will not be mine anymore.

Karen was as light a sleeper as her mother, something Liese had only realized a few months ago when she caught sight of her daughter's white face pressed against the banisters long after she should have been asleep. When Liese realized that the child had been watching as Andrew tried to calm the chaos of another nightmare-driven night, a night when she had gone hunting for Lottie and then thought she was the one being hunted. Liese had no idea how many other episodes Karen had witnessed. From the frozen way the child sat, rather than rushing down the stairs demanding to know what was wrong, she guessed this one was a long way past the first. Liese had wanted to warn Andrew that Karen had been there. She had wanted to talk to Karen, to offer some explanation that would soothe the wide eyes that followed her all the next morning. She hadn't done either. She had retreated back into the safety of silence and not looked up when other nights spooled out as messy.

And now she is as attuned to my moods as Lottie once was.

She took a step away.

This is your last chance; don't be a coward.

Liese eased the door open. Karen was sleeping on her back, her arms flung out. A memory flew back of Lottie spread out like a starfish, and she had to cram her fist into her mouth.

A few paces there, a few paces back. You can do it.

She crossed the floor as quick as she could, before her knees or her tears betrayed her. Karen stirred slightly, smiled at something in her dreams. Liese leaned forward, brushed her lips across Karen's soft hair, and then she fled from the room before the urge to scoop her daughter up became stronger than the urge to protect her.

I am no good to her. I hold her back; I keep the world too far from her.

She crept down the stairs, refusing to allow herself to turn round.

Twins—two girls. She reached the ground floor, her mind stuck on two children who would never remember their mother. On the memory of Paul and Margarethe walking away, swept up to an unimaginable death from the jobs that she had forced them out into. Stuck on the women whose numbers she had stapled to lists and sent to the same fate. On a guard who was an animal but whose children were innocent. The balance sheet wasn't done with her yet. The price paid this time for her carelessness could not be Karen.

I have to trust to Andrew now.

She had to believe Andrew would protect his daughter with the same fierce strength he had always shown for her. She had to believe Karen would one day understand that she would live a happier life without a mother too scared to let her embrace it. Without a mother whose sins spread out like a stain and ruined the lives of those she was meant to protect. Liese loved Karen; she loved her as much as she had ever loved Lottie. Liese had been terrified all the way through her pregnancy that she wouldn't have any love to give, that she would look at her baby and see only shadows. And then she had held Karen and felt such a deep connection, she had been astonished at the purity and newness of it. She hated that pain was coming for her daughter. That was terrible, but Karen was young and Liese had to believe that her pain would pass.

I can't turn back. I can't tear up the letter and pretend I can stay and things will be better.

Only a truly heartless mother would do that.

The bolt on the front door was heavy but easier to open than others she had fought. Liese stepped out into the fresh green embrace of a slowly waking day. The sky's dark was diluting, black swapped out for a deep blue that was already spotting with pink. The trees in the gardens that ran between the wedding-cake houses were softening, losing their nighttime jagged edges. There was no one around. It was too early for anything but birdsong.

It is today.

The refrain carried Liese through the short walk across the dew-soaked grass and down to the shingle. The sea spread out before her smooth as French Navy satin, frilled with cream lace where it trickled over the shore.

If this is wrong, if it won't pay the price, the water won't want me.

She knew that it would.

Salt danced through the breeze, tingling at her lips. Dawn was breaking. Liese breathed in the morning and stepped onto the beach.

CHAPTER EIGHTEEN

Karen

Berlin, October 1990

No one who looked at Andrew Cartwright could fail to see the soldier he had once been, even at seventy-four. Despite being tired from the early-morning start and, Karen suspected, nervous about the journey to come, his back was straight, his shoulders were square, and his walk still carried a snap in it. He had dressed for the occasion—his first time flying—in a tweed suit and overcoat that attracted admiring glances as he walked through Heathrow. Within five minutes, his bearing and impeccable manners had so impressed the British Airways check-in staff, he had bagged the upgrade to First Class that Karen had never once been offered. She was proud to be seen with him and told him so, taking a quiet delight in his awkward blush.

"Do you want anything for the flight? A newspaper or a magazine?"

"My book will do me fine, but thank you."

A formality had crept back between them since May's revelations, although their meetings nowadays were consciously more regular and their conversations always couched in considerate tones.

Liese's last letter, and Andrew's subsequent account of how he had fallen apart on the day of her death, had dredged up old memories and knocked Karen more off balance than she could at first admit.

No, I can't come; don't ask me.

His furious response to Karen's plea on the day of Liese's death, that he come to her and help her make sense of their loss, had resurfaced. She had forgotten how his shout had echoed round the hotel, or, rather, she had worked hard not to remember it. He had recounted his memories of that day the same night he had given Karen the scrapbook, pouring them out honestly and surrounded by apologies. How he had gone to identify Liese's body and then found himself alone on the beach, weeping so hard no one would come near him. How he had come back to the hotel, horrified by his behavior and desperate to make up for it. How he had given in too easily when he was told Karen was sleeping and best left. Karen had gone away feeling sorry for her father but sorrier still for the little girl whose wounds she was afraid she would never completely shake. She had woken almost every morning in the following weeks replaying the shock of his failure to be the father she needed. The father that Liese had asked him to be.

"Did you tell him that?"

"No. I gave him the book back and said I was tired and needed to think. I haven't mentioned it, or anything else, since."

"I understand why, Karen." Markus had been as direct in his responses as ever. "You must have been drained from the reading and the memories. But I thought you were done with old patterns. Won't more silences just drag you both back to where you were when you started out on this quest?"

The telephone conversation with Markus had been snatched and brief, and Karen had hit him with so much information, she had wondered part of the way through if she sounded a little mad. By the time she was done, the cost of the call had flown to an unsustainable level. She had gabbled it to a close and left Markus with barely enough time to offer her anything more than those few words of advice beyond "I'm here" and "I care." When she eventually let it, his advice had sunk in. Now she was glad she had followed it.

Liese watched her father letting the First-Class Lounge staff fuss round him. Explaining her feelings of anger and abandonment had been harder than she wanted, although easier than it would have been six months earlier. She had planned what she wanted to say so that it wasn't loaded with blame. So she could lay out carefully the mistrust that had grown up around what she had seen as her father's lies, and how that had hardened over the years. So she could make him see how the pain that mistrust caused had made her want to hit out; how it still cut deeper than she wanted.

She had managed to deliver her speech calmly; her father had listened with scrupulous care. He had accepted everything and apologized, allowing her to do the same. They had agreed that there was hurt inflicted on both sides, that neither of them had any desire to go forward in the same conflict-fueled way. They had agreed to make a proper effort to be in each other's lives. Andrew now called once a week and asked interested questions about her work. Karen visited him at least every other weekend. They were careful with each other, but they were inching forward, discovering that they were more alike than past resentments had let them see. Lately they had brought Liese into their conversations, offering memories of her good days to each other like new friends tentatively exchanging gifts. More recently still, Karen had let him ask the occasional question about Markus.

Markus. In a few hours, she would be back in the same city as him. She had been longing for that for the past five months and now the thought of seeing him made Karen's hands clammy. Andrew was occupied, caught up in some animated discussion about cricket Karen had no interest in. She helped herself to another cup of coffee and took Markus's latest letter out of her bag.

It wasn't easy to speak, with his work shifts and the cost of calls, so letters had remained their main line of communication. Markus hadn't got much better at writing them. His preference was still for facts, for straightforward exchanges of information that he promised to "fill in when I see you." His reactions on paper were far more muted than in person, and he rarely mentioned the presumably difficult conversations he must have had with his father. Sometimes Karen read through the brief pages wondering what this relationship she hoped was developing between the two of them actually was. If it had been merely a sidebar to her mother's story. And then a line would appear in the middle of a tightly written message. A sudden tumble of words that suggested what was going through his head might not be so different at all to the dreams that kept flourishing in hers.

I wish I was with you, to hold you. I hope it's not wrong to think you want that too.

You were brave and you found her. A lot of people would have run from what you uncovered, or never dug in the first place. You are really quite something, Karen Cartwright.

And her favorite, from the letter she was holding, which made her grin every time that she read it.

Promise me you will phone me when you arrive in Berlin, the first minute you can. I'm counting the days like a schoolboy.

"You're daydreaming, Karen. They're calling our flight. It's a busy one apparently, packed with journalists flying out to cover tomorrow's reunification ceremony. I've been asked twice if I'm some kind of writer. It must be the suit."

Her father's eyes were twinkling; he looked ten years younger.

Karen grinned. "I should take a photo of you and send it to Mrs. Hubbard. Prove to her that my 'crazy ideas' haven't put you into a box like she predicted."

He laughed and offered her his arm. "Just be grateful you weren't there when I told her I was going with you to Berlin.

She was incensed. It was like watching a rather square volcano explode." He grinned so broadly Karen stopped in her tracks and stared at him.

"You're not, I mean...*with* Mrs. Hubbard...are you?"

His shout of laughter turned heads. "No. I can assure you, I am not. But..."

"What?"

"If there was someone else, would you mind?"

Karen stared at this man who kept revealing new depths every time she thought that she knew him.

"Was? Or *is*?"

He blushed. "Is. It's early days. But if it develops, I'd like you to meet her."

"Of course."

Karen handed over their boarding passes and tried not to grin too widely. She was about to ask more when her father shook his head.

"Okay. I won't pry, I promise. Not yet anyway."

A stewardess handed them both glasses of champagne; Karen noticed Andrew's hand was shaking when he reached for it.

"Are you nervous about the flight? Tell me you're not feeling ill."

He turned away and looked out of the window before he answered.

"No. It's neither of those. If you must know, I'm a little on edge at the thought of meeting Michael again."

Karen's shoulders relaxed. "That's understandable. It has been a long time, almost fifty years. That still surprises me, you know, how young you all were when it happened. I suppose it won't be easy digging it all up again."

His face when he turned to her was so bleak Karen flinched.

"No, Karen, it won't be easy—not easy at all. You're learning not to blame me for Liese dying. What if Michael has only just begun?"

*

"It's me. I'm here."

"At last! I haven't been able to concentrate all day, waiting for you to call."

And there it was, the joyful reaction she had hoped for.

"Father is exhausted from the journey and his first sight of Berlin after so many years. He's gone to bed."

There was a pause and then a laugh that gurgled from the telephone wire to her toes. Karen could hardly concentrate on what he was saying for picturing his brown eyes.

"So what are you proposing, Karen Cartwright, to do with your night?"

To spend it with you. To be Markus and Karen again.

It was all that she wanted. Given the warmth in his voice and his delight when he answered her call, she wasn't sure why she couldn't quite say it. The hours they had spent on her last trip, wandering through Berlin on holiday from their lives, had been perfect, more romantic than any date deliberately planned to be that way.

She must have paused too long. His voice suddenly dropped and grew serious.

"Are you still there? I want to see you, Karen, tonight. Just you; away from everything that is coming. Can I do that?"

Give him the room number—don't waste any more time.

That, too, was what she wanted, but saying it into a telephone seemed too quick a step. She needed to see his face, that was all. To put the two of them back into place.

"We passed a bar on the way here. On the corner of Kluckstraße and Lützowufer, near the canal. I could meet you there? I could head there now and wait for you."

He arrived so fast, he must have broken every speed limit. The bar was little more than a cellar, as dark and sparsely populated as the one they had gone into in the East. When Markus saw the two shots of vodka and the jug of red wine Karen had ordered, he grinned.

"No crying tonight, I promise."

He clicked his glass to the one she raised.

"I don't care if you do. With everything you've learned, you've got good reason."

He didn't take his eyes off her as they drank.

"Do you want to talk about your mother, or her letter? We've covered so little of it and nothing of what you feel."

Karen shook her head. He was still watching her. She had to take the plunge. If his page was different to hers, she wanted to know. Before tomorrow, when her father met him and wondered. Before she risked her heart any more than she had.

"Not tonight. I don't want this to be about anything but us tonight, Markus. If there is an us."

She had poured the wine out, but neither of them had touched it.

If he tells me I've made a mistake and his concern for me is nothing more than friendship, I'm going back on the next plane and Markus can manage the rest on his own.

The silence continued a fraction too long for her shivering nerves and then Markus got up and held out his hand.

"There will always be an us."

She didn't mean to do it, but his face was so serious and his tone so dramatic, she couldn't help herself. She burst out laughing, and fell in love when he joined in.

"This is your fault—it's the effect you have on me. That sounded so good in my head and now I've turned into some cliché of a brooding Hollywood hero."

He pulled her up. She was in his arms, kissing him. They were outside, kissing each other in the street like teenagers until the cold reminded them that there was a hotel room waiting.

"There will be an us now, I swear it."

This time, he said it as they fell onto the bed, breath quickening, clothes already half lost. Karen didn't laugh. She held his face close to hers and repeated the same promise. And then he kissed her through to her soul and there was no going back at all.

When she woke after the few hours of sleep they had finally succumbed to and he was still lying there, she wanted to cheer. Then she glanced at her watch and she panicked.

"You have to go. Before my father comes and catches you. I'm serious—it's gone seven. He'll be up and ready for breakfast, and I'm too old to get raised eyebrows for this."

She had to throw the duvet over him he laughed so loud.

"Seriously, Markus, this is not how I want the two of you to meet. My father is nervous about this afternoon. No, it's more than that: he's afraid—he used that actual word—about seeing Michael again." She stopped. Part of her wanted to find softer words, but this was Markus, a man who believed life should be open and direct, and he wouldn't thank her for trying. "He thinks your father might blame him for my mother's death."

Markus looked up from tying his shoes.

"I can't guarantee that he won't. He hasn't said much since you told us it would be both of you coming, although him holding his thoughts tight is hardly a surprise. And he's on edge too, although he blames the fuss over reunification. To be honest, I don't quite know how to handle their meeting. If it goes wrong, then the rest of the plan falls apart. I thought I should tell them what I found out about the guard as soon as the greetings are over. What do you think?"

Karen nodded. "That could work. I haven't shared any of it with Father yet."

"Okay, good. If we treat them like they are still both in this together, maybe they'll act that way. Who knows, Father might see parallels between him and Andrew finally reuniting and Germany's political situation and decide to deliver a lecture not a judgment.

Your father's on his own if he does." Markus reached for his jacket. "And he has agreed to come here rather than meet at his flat, to the 'dreaded West,' as he called it, which hopefully he won't do so loudly today and ruin the party. That could be a sign of good intent."

Karen's eyes widened. "How did you persuade him to break a lifetime of principles and do that?"

"I told him Andrew was much feebler than him and would struggle to travel...What?"

He ducked as Karen aimed a pillow at him.

"It worked. For a communist, Father is very competitive. To be honest, I thought it would be easier to manage him if he was off home ground. There is a condition though."

Markus's voice lost its laughing tone. Karen waited.

"There is a ceremony later today, before tonight's big celebration, to mark the passing of the DDR. I doubt anyone beyond the faithful will notice it's happening, but Father wants to go and I said I'd go with him. It would mean a lot if you would come too."

Karen passed him the wallet he was looking for, wondering how such a simple request could make him look so awkward but not sure how to ask.

"The thing is, I've told him about you and me, about how I feel. He's uncertain. A 'decadent woman from the West' isn't what he imagined for me. Not that he called you that, but I've no doubt that, on some level, he thinks it. And then there's the connection with Liese and all that stirs up. I just think, if you were there today, at something that's so important to him and who he is, well, he'd set a lot of store by it."

He tailed off, looking younger and more adrift than she'd ever seen him.

Karen smiled and startled herself by suddenly feeling tearful. "Then of course. How could I miss it?"

"Thank you. That makes me happy. I've hopes it will do the same with him."

Markus wrote down the details and kissed her and was halfway out of the door before he turned back and grinned. "I should have told you first, how I felt. Not my father. Is that what you're thinking?"

Karen laughed. "I'm not thinking anything except you don't need to tell me. I already knew."

She blew him a kiss and waved him away before her father came knocking. She knew it would be a while before she had enough composure to go down to breakfast.

I already knew.

It was the truth, and now there was a new truth to consider: that the words "I love you" didn't matter—what mattered was what she had seen in Markus's eyes and felt in his kiss. She'd spent years treating the *I love you* she had always demanded to hear as the Holy Grail, putting more faith in what she heard than in anything else. All the relationships that had crashed down because of her desperation. All the relationships that had failed because, once the words were said or, worse, forced out, she no longer cared. And now here she was, in love and loved and finally listening; feeling the hurts starting to heal.

"You have missed your turning—this is Hausvogteiplatz. Go back one corner and turn at Markgrafenstraße. Gendarmenmarkt is only a short distance away from there."

The man waved his arm in the direction from which Karen had just come and walked away. She stared after him, unable to move, everything he had said after Hausvogteiplatz fallen into a blur. The dark interior of Richters Schneiderei and her seventeen-year-old self standing on the threshold so hopeful and so naïve flew back more vivid than the bright October day she was currently standing in. Hausvogteiplatz: Haus Elfmann had stood here.

Karen whirled round, convinced if she moved quickly enough a signboard or a set of ghost letters would reveal themselves over the lintel of one of the narrow buildings. When that didn't work, she had a wild impulse to run from door to door, knocking and shouting out the Elfmann name and demanding that someone, somewhere, must remember—must be able to point her to the place where the salon had stood.

Karen was at the first corner, hand poised when she remembered Frau Richter's pleated mouth and folded arms and the shadows that clung to the old woman's disapproving sniff. She sank down instead on one of a group of iron benches surrounding a fountain in the center of the small square.

She didn't want to do this frantic searching anymore. It was foolish to try, doomed to end in failure and that hollow feeling in the pit of her stomach that she didn't want to make room for anymore. It was fifty years since Haus Elfmann had towered over Berlin's fashion industry. That was another lifetime; in this part of the city, it was another country. She needed her energy for the future now, not the past.

Ignoring the pigeons who had immediately come flocking, Karen gazed up at the highest point she could see: a sunburst clock, picked out in faded red and gold on a rooftop still bearing the traces of what once must have been delicate carvings.

My mother must have known that clock in its grander days. She must have sat in the square and listened to the fountain play and watched the light and the clouds dance across the clock's golden hands.

Karen tried to picture the Liese who once would have sat where she sat now. Fifteen or sixteen years old, the daughter of a wealthy fashion house, a young girl filled with dreams. She breathed in slowly, filling her nose and mouth with the woody scent of the bronze and cream chrysanthemums planted round the fountain and imagined her mother chattering here to her friends. She listened to the water splash, watched a group of sparrows taking a dust bath, and imagined Liese and Michael trading secrets and squabbling, inhabiting the up and down but always so entwined relationship he had described. Although she knew that it couldn't be true, given Berlin's history of war and division, the little square felt untouched, unchangeable.

She didn't need a sign; she didn't need proof. The salon had been here, Liese had been here, happy and hopeful. Karen closed her eyes and let herself feel and knew that was enough.

She walked slowly back down Mohrenstraße, turning where she had been told, taking time to study the narrow buildings with their elegantly arched windows that lined this part of the street. The pavements were far quieter here than the eager bustle she had left behind at the Tiergarten and Potsdamer Platz. Karen was glad of it. With no one else around, she could step back in time and find Liese, walking a pace in front, lolling a pace behind, running about and real. She could see the whip of her mother's skirt as she dodged round a corner; hear her laughter chasing through the birdsong.

By the time Karen stepped onto the wide marble-like paving stones that covered the Gendarmenmarkt's large sweep of a square, she felt lighter than she had done in months.

"Are you all right? You're a little later than I thought you'd come; you didn't get lost, did you?"

There were so few people gathered there, Markus had spotted her almost at once.

Karen shook her head and hugged Liese closer. "Where is everyone?"

She could see a huddle of figures grouped round the bottom of a flight of steps which marched up to a classically colonnaded building. Other than that, the vast space, with what looked like a pair of identical churches placed one at each end, was deserted.

"I thought this was a ceremony. I imagined it would be busier, more on the scale of what's planned for tonight."

"No. Tonight is about something starting, a joining together that people want to bear witness to and be part of. What you see here is the opposite."

Markus took her hand and led her toward the steps.

"This is the diehards of the East coming to mourn. Everyone else has already turned their faces to the West."

His tone was measured, but there was a tightness in his face Karen hadn't seen there before. She wanted to ask him how he felt, what this goodbye meant to him, but he was already steering her toward Michael, who was fixed in position at the side of the building. He was watching them come, standing ramrod-straight and dressed in a black overcoat with a cluster of medal ribbons above the breast pocket. There were a handful of other spectators arranged round him. None of them looked younger than forty. The flight of steps he was standing next to was wider than she had first realized—there was space along them for a hundred people or more to stand without feeling crowded. There were only four figures there, uniformed men in officers' peaked caps, who clustered at the bottom looking oddly small and out of place. There was no one waiting to join them, none of the foreign dignitaries or Heads of State Karen knew had flocked to Berlin to witness the reunification ceremony planned for midnight at the Brandenburg Gate.

"Thank you. For attending this."

Karen shook the hand Michael stiffly held out.

"Andrew raised no objections to Markus taking you away?"

"No, of course not. We visited the Reichstag this morning and the Gate before it got busy. He was glad to go back to the hotel and—"

The rest of her too-quick response was lost as a band marched into the square and came to a halt beneath the flagpole, where the DDR's hammer-and-compass-adorned flag was still flying. The tune they struck up took Karen's breath away, its melody was so haunting.

"'*Auferstanden aus Ruinen*'—'Rising from the Ruins.' It is the DDR's national anthem. This is the last time I imagine that we will hear it played."

Michael's voice choked and fell silent. Markus took his hand and held it while the music swelled. Karen watched the two men standing as one as the ceremony began, joined by a love and respect that overran their differences, and had to rub her eyes.

Everyone around them was staring ahead and mouthing the anthem's words. No one was actually singing.

The two ranks of soldiers who had followed the band stood stiffly to attention behind a standard-bearer. Some saluted; some kept their arms down and looked awkward; some blinked away tears. As the music stopped and silence fell, one of the officers hunched on the steps walked stiffly forward and gave a short, muted speech in which the words "comradeship" and "loyalty" featured heavily. No one clapped when he finished. The standard-bearer marched his gaudily fringed banner away, its head pointing down. The red and black and gold flag was pulled from its pole in one smooth movement and folded inside out so its colors no longer showed. The band launched into "*Das Deutschlandlied*," the tune that would now represent the whole of Germany. No one clapped to that either. When it was done, the band and the soldiers marched away and the spectators melted silently after them. Less than ten minutes had passed and a country that had stood and birthed generations who had known nothing else but the DDR for forty years was gone. It was one of the saddest things Karen had ever seen.

"This must seem very foolish to you. My need to say farewell to a regime most people will be delighted is over."

Michael was staring away into the distance, his face set in hard lines.

Karen wasn't sure how to answer. "You don't need to apologize..."

He turned on her so fast, she jumped.

"I am not apologizing. Why would I? I am proud of what this country was. I came out of the war with nothing: no family, no home. Nothing but my beliefs in a fairer society, and the DDR nurtured those and nurtured me. I wasn't on the outside here: the tolerant, equal way of life I wanted for the future was what everyone wanted. We had ideals; we cared for each other. We weren't easily bought by trifles the way the West was. Why should I regret being a part of something so pure?"

He sounded so angry, but it was grief; Karen could feel it pouring from him. Her German was strong enough now to understand what Michael said, but she waved Markus back in case her nerve, or her words, failed her. If she had any chance of winning Michael's respect, she had to stand up to him and speak from the heart.

"You shouldn't. And you have misunderstood me. I was actually thinking that this ceremony didn't feel like enough. This is an ending, a funeral, I suppose. Surely it deserved more marking than this lonely spectacle, whatever your view of the DDR's politics. More than something that felt, I don't know, embarrassed?"

Michael's face softened. He finally smiled. Not for the first time that day, Karen felt the prick of tears.

"It seems I owe you a different apology. It appears I have misjudged you." He paused while the soldiers exited the square. "An embarrassment. That, I am sad to say, is a well-chosen word. That is what the DDR will be in this newly united world. It will pass into history as a relic, a museum piece only remembered as real while its old men and women are still standing."

"Except for the damage done to so many lives in its name." Markus was also watching the last soldier go. "Those will be raked over and last, no doubt, far longer than the country ever did."

The two men stared at each other. Karen knew there was a question Markus needed to ask but couldn't quite get to. She slipped her hand in his.

"Do you think that would be a bad thing? That the sins are remembered?"

She was relieved for his son when Michael answered.

"No, Karen, I don't. I think there are men who must be held to account for what following our ideals too rigidly led to. And I think there are people in great need of answers. Who deserve every assistance to find them. No matter what you might think of me after our last meeting, or since you learned what your father and I did, you have taught me the value of that."

He crooked his elbow and held it out to her. "And now this part of the past has been laid to rest, shall we make a start on our own?"

Karen hesitated before taking his arm. "My father is afraid that you blame him for Liese's suicide."

Michael nodded as they began to make their way across the square. "Maybe, until I see his face and hear his side of the story, that is true."

The drive to Karen and Andrew's hotel was a subdued one, each of them lost in their own concerns about the forthcoming reunion.

Karen had hoped to have a few moments alone with her father to explain what Michael had just witnessed and how saddened it had left him, but Andrew was already waiting in the sofa-stuffed lounge. He was dressed in his tweed suit and had a pot of tea on one side of him and a newspaper folded to the crossword on the other. He had never looked more impossibly English.

The introductions and reintroductions were awkward. Hands knocked into each other; stilted greetings became overlaid and muddled as Karen and Markus rushed in to soften them. Although Karen knew he had been practicing and he was clearer than she expected, Andrew's German was hesitant from lack of use. Michael refused to understand it as well as he could and made a show of turning to Markus, until Markus threw up his hands and refused to translate what did not need translating. Andrew ordered tea for everyone; Michael insisted on coffee. Karen was beginning to despair of finding any safe or common ground, and then they sat down and the men's similarities almost overwhelmed her.

It wasn't just their appearances, but their manner that meshed. Both were tall, broad-shouldered, and strong-featured, and gray hair and age's sharpening and softening had rendered them more of a match than they were in the wedding photograph. Their voices, too, were an echo of each other, the tone in each deep and thoughtful and better tuned to serious conversation than light-hearted amusement. And they both caught the same look in their eye when Liese was mentioned: warm and wistful and sad.

"You never kept in touch?"

As Karen intended, the question cut through the start of a potentially awkward silence and took both men by surprise.

"No." It was her father who answered. "We never had any understanding that we would. Beyond one letter to say that we had safely arrived in England, I don't think I ever considered it."

He paused. Karen watched him choosing his words, picking his way through a language he hadn't spoken properly in years but was determined not to be defeated by.

"With hindsight, I would say that was deliberate, wouldn't you, Michael? Neither of us wanting to play any more part in the other's life than we already had."

Michael nodded. "With you, yes. I did, however, write to Liese, although not as regularly as I would have liked. It wasn't easy, especially when Western intransigence forced Russia to blockade Berlin in 1948 and cut it off from the rest of the world. But once that was lifted, I did my best to stay in touch. Did she show you my letters, or tell you about them?"

Andrew shook his head. Michael sighed. It sounded as if he was letting go of a long-held hope.

"Then it is as I feared: my letters meant nothing to her. She never wrote back to any of them. I convinced myself at first that, because I moved around so much in the first years after you left, her replies didn't reach me. Then there was no answer to the card

I sent in 1953 with a permanent address and I couldn't fool myself any longer that she cared. I stopped writing after that."

Andrew refilled his cup. "I may have had a hand in her silence. I encouraged her to leave her life in Germany behind. I didn't necessarily include you in that but—"

"You're not sorry if that's how she took it."

Andrew shrugged. "It's not as if remembering did her any good, so, no, I'm not sorry at all."

Karen watched with increasing unease as the two men circled each other. They were both so stubborn; both so determined to prove that they had cared for Liese the best. She didn't want the meeting to fall apart before she outlined her plan for the rest of the trip, but she had a nasty feeling that's where it was heading. She glanced over at Markus, who nodded and interrupted in time to stop Michael from snapping back.

"It might not have been your influence, Mr. Cartwright, that stopped her writing. It could have been guilt, or fear."

Michael's tightly contained anger shifted from Andrew to his son. "What are you talking about?"

Markus turned to his father, speaking slowly enough so that Andrew could keep up, waiting if Karen needed to help him, and continued as if he hadn't registered Michael's sharpening tone.

"Karen has told me about the problems Liese was having in the last years of her life. We haven't had time to discuss those yet, but I understand a fear of being caught runs through the scrapbook she kept, as well as guilt for a number of things she saw herself as responsible for. Some of her 'crimes' make more sense than others, but the events surrounding the guard's death were chief among them. Perhaps she felt she had left you in too much danger. You were, after all, the one on the ground if anything came to light. Perhaps staying in contact was simply too much for her."

"Markus might be right."

To Karen's relief, her father's voice had lost its combative edge. He rubbed his eyes and coughed, and his tone grew softer.

"She missed you, Michael. If she got your letters, they would have meant a good deal to her. She used to mention you sometimes, after Karen was born, and wonder if you were all right. It occurred to me then that I should try to find you, but I didn't know how. I knew nothing about the postcard until Karen uncovered it. Liese could easily have forgotten she had it."

He stopped suddenly and then sat up straighter. "I'm sorry, Michael. I owed you more. The truth is, I was afraid. That one day, despite what she decided when the body was found, that she would leave me and choose you. I was afraid of that my whole marriage."

He slumped back as he finished, as if the confession had winded him.

Michael stumbled as he started to speak. Karen gripped Markus's hand to stop him trying to find Michael's words for him. When he recovered himself, Michael's voice was as soft as Andrew's.

"You are so wrong. She wouldn't have. She never could have. You heard her say it: when Liese looked at me, all she saw was Lottie's shadow. It hurt beyond words to hear that, but I had no doubt she meant it. She chose you, and that was the right thing. The only chance of happiness, the only chance of safety Liese had lay in marrying you."

Andrew was already shaking his head.

Karen repeated Michael's words in English in case Andrew hadn't fully followed them but it was clear that wasn't the problem: he understood what Michael had said, but he wouldn't accept it. Karen couldn't bear to see them both trapped in a loop of guilt and denial. She turned to Markus. "Tell them what you know."

He jumped straight in on her cue with the facts. "There was an investigation into the murder."

His directness snapped Andrew and Michael out of the fog that was circling them exactly as Karen had hoped. Their heads shot up as if they were pulled by the same string. Markus turned to his father.

"The original article that you kept about the body being recovered was from the *Berliner Morgenpost*. I went to their offices and had a dig in their archives. There were more reports filed than the one you kept. You never saw any of them?"

"No."

It was clear from the shock on Michael's face that he was telling the truth.

"Once Liese left, I threw myself into my work. I was writing then, and I was more and more in the Russian sector of Berlin, more immersed in the doctrines that eventually split the East off from the West in 1949. A newspaper like that would have quickly slipped off my radar. And the papers I did read wouldn't have mentioned the death of a Nazi, unless there was a specific link to Russia or the communist struggle." He shrugged. "I have lived my life in a narrow world, Markus. I am too old to apologize for it."

"I don't need you to. All that matters is that you both know the truth now."

"They identified the guard then? I assume it was from the scar on her hand?"

Her father sounded so tired; Karen slipped her fingers through his and squeezed them.

Markus nodded. "Yes. From what I could gather, it took almost six weeks in the end to get the postmortem done and marry up the body with the missing persons' report. Her name was Hilda Grieff; she was thirty-four. She had lived her whole life in Fürstenberg. There was nothing special about her, except where she chose to work and half the town, if the paper is to be believed, found employment in the camp the same as her. At first, her husband raised the roof and demanded her killer be found and brought to justice. Then he went quiet and that's when the *Morgenpost* got interested. It didn't take them long to discover she had been a guard, especially as the

Ravensbrück trial was still ongoing. They managed to unearth a picture of her in her uniform. It jogged memories. Someone remembered Lottie."

"Then the thing we were most afraid of happened."

Karen wasn't sure which man said it.

Markus corrected himself quickly. "Yes, but it wasn't as clear-cut as I made it sound. Someone remembered a child being murdered by the lake, but no one remembered the name and the dates were hazy. But the paper ran the story packed full of outrage, and if Liese had been in Berlin and seen it..."

"She might have panicked and confessed."

Michael was poised on the edge of his seat, staring at Andrew. "We did the right thing getting her away—you realize this proves it? Whatever the outcome, our—no, your instincts were correct."

Karen and Markus sat back as Andrew nodded.

"Thank God. Thank God. I was never sure. I was always worried it was only my own interests I was serving."

The mood between the two men shifted. Michael reached out his hand; Andrew grasped it. They sat in silence, heads down, hands clasped, as still as if they were carved from stone.

When Markus continued talking, his voice was thick. "After that disclosure, the investigation into Grieff's killing seems to have faded away. The last report I could find simply said there were no leads. I doubt anyone had the appetite for it: justice had, after all, been served and against the right person. The trail ended there."

"Thank you."

They loosened their hands and separated back out into Andrew and Michael.

Markus nodded to Karen, who struggled to steady her voice. "So now you know. You helped her as much as you could. You saved her, and yourselves, which I imagine is what Liese intended. That's what I want to hold on to, not where it led. It's what we all need to hold on to. And so we thought, Markus and I, that perhaps it was time for Liese and Lottie's story to have an ending, for us at least. We thought, if it's something you both feel up to, that we would like to visit the camp."

She left a pause for them to voice their objections, but neither man took it.

"The site is in quite a state apparently and the Russian authorities who took it over after Germany's partition are reluctant to let anyone in. They're afraid of attracting fascist sympathizers, I suppose, for want of a better word, and they still have soldiers based there. But Markus, well, he used your name, Michael, and managed to get permission for us to have some degree of access. And he's found a woman, an ex-inmate, who will meet us there and act as our guide. We could all go together, the day after tomorrow, and say our goodbyes. If you thought that might be helpful."

She trailed away. Michael and Andrew were so silent she couldn't read their reaction.

"It is a good plan, Karen; a kind and thoughtful one. I can see why my son is so taken with you." Michael smiled as she blushed. "It would help me and, I imagine, you?"

He turned to Andrew, who nodded and took Karen's hand again. "Good."

Michael sat up, clapped his hands, and changed back into the Michael Karen knew.

"And now it is time for you two to go."

"What do you mean?"

The abrupt change of tone from thanks to dismissal wrong-footed Markus. Karen, who was slightly giddy with relief at how well, in the end, the reunion had gone, struggled not to laugh at his indignant frown. Michael completely ignored it.

"This has been a day of revelations that need digesting. Right now, Andrew and I have years to catch up on and conversations which require only us. Berlin is celebrating; you should be out there with it, grabbing hold of your future."

"But what about you? How will you get home?"

It was Andrew's turn to adopt Michael's dismissive tone.

"What, don't you think a soldier and a resistance fighter can organize their way round dinner and transport? Or a night of fireworks and a party, if that's what we decide?"

He grinned as Markus blustered.

"Go on, do as Michael says, the pair of you. Let he and I be as young or old together tonight as we choose."

Karen pulled Markus up. "They're done with us. And they seem to be understanding each other just fine now. We should run before they change their minds and make us listen to them reminiscing."

She blew kisses at their smiling fathers and dragged Markus out of the hotel before he could argue. Michael was right: it was time to grab hold of the future she knew was there waiting.

It was dark outside, the cold air already thick with the dry sulfur-edged smoke of the fireworks blooming in pinks and blues and greens across the black velvet sky. Crowds had begun streaming across the river, making their way to the Brandenburg Gate, although there were still hours to go before the Liberty Bell would toll and Berlin would be pronounced whole again. Karen and Markus were immediately swallowed by a laughing group. People were draped in the black, red, and gold flag that now represented all of them, some of them, Karen noticed, wearing theirs like a cape, their heads sticking through where the DDR symbol had once been.

The contrast between the scene unfolding on what, for the next few hours at least, was still the West and the ceremony Karen had witnessed in the East was so pronounced she shivered and pressed close into Markus's side.

"Do you think reunification will be as good as everyone hopes?"

"No. It will be better, and it will be worse, but it is here and I'm young enough to be glad of it." He grinned down at her. "The Wall has come down and opened doors I never expected to walk through. I could move to the West side, study psychology in the way I always wanted to; collect on a dream or two."

Opening doors and collecting on dreams; it was her turn.

"I could come here too. My firm is opening an office in Berlin. They'd like me to head it."

He stopped, his grin so wide his eyes disappeared into crinkles, and swept her into his arms. Karen laughed as her feet left the floor.

"Are you ready for this?"

His answer was almost lost to the whooping crowd and the music blaring in competition from the windows around them. Almost, but not quite.

"For all of it, Karen Cartwright. For all of it."

CHAPTER NINETEEN

Karen

Ravensbrück Concentration Camp, October 1990

The drive from Berlin to Fürstenberg took almost two hours. Michael provided a running commentary on the mechanics of the DDR for most of it.

The crumbling, increasingly potholed roads Markus kept cursing were intended for military and agricultural use not "idle day-trippers" and therefore could not be held to "Markus's ill-informed notions of higher Western standards." The great swathes of farmland, which were ten times the size of anything Karen had ever encountered in England, were "collectives" and "models of production the West could learn from." Nobody really listened; everybody humored him.

As they grew nearer their destination, however, and the bleak machinery-dotted landscape gave way to thick woodlands wound through with rivers and lakes, even Michael grew silent. The canopy of trees which danced above them in sun-soaked shades of green and gold was too lovely to be comfortable, given the horrors it had sheltered.

"That must be the town. We could stop here for coffee and a break if anyone needs it." Karen pointed to a narrow spire poking out from the forest and a line of sloping red tile and moss-covered roofs.

As more wood-framed buildings popped up between the trees, she had to stop herself from saying how sleepy and charming and storybook pretty it was. Andrew's "it should look more ashamed" better summed up everyone's feelings.

No one wanted to linger. Late-morning hunger pangs were forgotten. They drove on in silence, exiting the town along a cobbled road that rattled through the car's flimsy chassis and into their bones. There was no signpost for Ravensbrück anywhere along the route, although Karen kept twisting about trying to find one. In the end, Markus had to beg her to sit still.

"This is the right way, past the railway station. Ilse said we just keep driving, that you stumble on the camp rather than see it. To put it like she did, 'the Nazis preferred secrecy and that suited the town.'"

Ilse Neumann, the woman who had survived three years in the camp. Markus hadn't stopped talking about her since a colleague had heard about the proposed Ravensbrück trip and arranged a meeting. "Formidable" was the main word he had used. Karen had pictured a fierce, warrior-looking woman, with more than a touch of the Amazon about her. The one waiting as they parked the car opposite the high wall and the firmly closed gates was small and wiry and wearing tweeds not unlike Andrew's. When she walked over to introduce herself, Karen couldn't help but notice Ilse had a pronounced limp.

"Which one of you is Michael Wasserman?"

Ilse's gaze swept over Michael and Andrew as if she were inspecting a cohort of rather disappointing troops. Both men straightened.

Michael stepped forward as if he was about to salute. Ilse didn't waste time letting him speak.

"Good. Well, it's your name that got you all in here, so you'd best come with me and calm down the Russian."

She nodded briefly to the others and crossed back to the gates, beckoning Michael to follow her. From where she was standing, Karen could see the fringes of the lake. She turned away, refused to follow her desperate impulse to run to it. They had all promised each other that they would go there together, that it would be the last thing they would do here. Karen knew if she thought about her mother standing by the water, about the guard stepping forward and seizing Lottie, her knees would buckle. She focused instead on the gates where Ilse was deep in conversation with a soldier who looked like he should have still been in school.

Whatever was said worked. Hands were clasped, backs were slapped, and the gates were opened. The soldier gestured the rest of the party over to join Ilse and Michael and drifted away. Karen crossed the road quickly, Markus and her father trotting behind, and followed Ilse inside, avoiding the broken tree stumps and roots crawling round the outer wall's edges. The sight that met her as they passed through the heavy metal gates was nothing like she expected and brought her to an abrupt halt. The space they were standing in was sprawling and desolate, half of it covered in cracked concrete, half of it overgrown in a tangle of weeds.

"I thought there would be buildings, the same as I've seen in pictures of the other camps. Lots of prison blocks laid out like army barracks."

Ilse shook her head. "There was once. When I was put in here, there were dozens of them fanned out along both sides of a wide road, bordered, for some reason that no one ever understood, with beds full of red flowers. But the Russians turned the site into a tank base in the 1950s and smashed everything down. Where we're standing now was once the parade ground, where they did roll calls and their never-ending selections. Where most of us started and finished if you like."

My mother was Jewish, which makes me Jewish too.

The realization had never hit Karen before, but now she couldn't escape it. What Ilse was describing could have happened to her. But for a trick of time it could be her standing in this frozen square, waiting to find out if her death would be quick or drawn out. Karen blinked at the realization of how real it all was, of how the lives that had ended, and endured, here mattered and deserved to be told. Behind her, one of the men sniffed and turned it into a cough. Her own eyes were so dry they were stinging.

"How many women were brought in here?"

Ilse began leading them further inside, pointing out where the main barrack blocks had been as they went.

"In total over the whole war? I'm not sure anyone knows that number for certain. I've heard a hundred thousand mentioned, but since the Soviets took charge, no one has really investigated and there's been no records released that I know of. All I know is that the number who survived is far lower than the number who came in. And that we came from all over Europe—France, Germany, Poland, Russia, even a handful from England. So many different languages. Add in the Romanies and all the different dialects and this place was a veritable Tower of Babel."

"Who was in here? Was it mostly Jews?"

Ilse shrugged. "There were some. More at the start, or so I was told, but the guards rinsed them out pretty quickly. We were all sorts: Jews, communists, gypsies, lesbians, prostitutes, Russian female soldiers. Every *flavor of affront to womanhood* you could find. I suppose that the only thing we had in common, apart from being women, was that the Nazis considered us deviants and surplus to requirements in their new vision of Germany. And we got caught."

Ilse smiled; there was no humor in it. She gestured to a pile of broken masonry covered in weeds.

"This is where the ovens were. I came in as a communist. If they'd known I was also a Jew, I'd have been straight in here."

Karen couldn't think of a single reasonable response. When her father spoke up, she was glad to hear another voice, although his wavered as thin as the sparse grass dotting the concrete.

"Would my wife have suffered? As far as we know, she was only in this place for a couple of weeks, at the end of the war. We know about the selections and the gas chambers; there's been rumors about medical experiments. So I'm wondering if she would have suffered here? As much as the women like you did, who were forced to cope with it longer." He glanced down at Ilse's crooked leg. "Who were cruelly treated."

There was a silence. Karen desperately wanted Ilse to answer with a simple *no* and knew that she wouldn't.

"I don't know how to answer that, how do you think I can measure it? Does a week leave fewer scars than a month, than a year? Is a short exposure to horror worse than a long one you somehow adjust to? This place was Hell. There is no other word for it. No one walks through Hell and comes away without burns. We suffered, all of us. But you know that, or you wouldn't be here, looking for the parts of your wife you never quite knew."

There was a pause. Ilse looked away from them.

"Some suffered and died here. Some were set free. I doubt there is anyone who escaped, who still escapes, the suffering."

"What do you mean?"

Ilse turned round and finally looked Karen full in the face rather than flinging her comments back at the group.

"Some of the pain is easier to spot. With your mother, perhaps, you can trace it in the choice that she made. For others, the pain is more silent, but it's still there. No one talks, you see. No one remembers. There is a memorial here, at the lake. It is beautiful. But it is a Russian memorial, for their women, for communist martyrs. A very specific thing. The rest of us are forgotten. Scattered, voiceless, unheard. Most of us can't even find each other. We live with our nightmares and we live with the shame of what this place did to us, what it brought us down to. It is as I said: whoever we have become, we live lives still shadowed by what happened to us here."

Karen expected to hear pain in Ilse's voice; the weariness in it was worse.

"What do you want? What, if anything, could help you?"

For the first time since they had arrived, Ilse's tough manner let in a degree of warmth as she answered Karen's halting question.

"No one has ever asked me that." She bent down and picked up a piece of the rubble. "We were brought together by a place. Now we need different places. To find our stories in. To be remembered in."

Karen nodded, her mind whirling with thoughts it was impossible to voice.

No one had any more questions after that.

Andrew and Michael, Karen could see, were worn out. Markus was hovering around them, taking elbows when they reached rough ground, whispering words of encouragement when the old men faltered. Ilse led them back out of the camp and onto the lakeshore to where the Russian memorial stood. It was, as she had said, heartbreakingly beautiful. A bone-thin woman stood on a plinth, her head held up toward the heavens, cradling the broken body of a second woman, who was visibly nearer to death, in her arms.

Ilse offered to tell them the statue's story; no one wanted it—they all had their own version.

As Ilse stepped back, the four of them formed into a line looking out over the lake and its long-buried secrets. No one spoke; there was no longer any need.

One by one, they kissed the two white roses they had each carried from the car. One for Liese; one for Lottie.

One by one, they threw the flowers out over the calm water.

There was no splash. There was no spray.

Each rose landed gently on the surface, as perfect in their beauty as the love that they carried.

EPILOGUE

Berlin, September 2001

We need places. To find our stories in. To be remembered in.

Karen watched the sun play across the sleek silver walls of Berlin's newly completed Jewish Museum.

This is one. More are coming.

"It's really big. Did you build the whole thing?"

Karen realized Lottie was tugging at her hand and switched her attention off the museum and onto her daughter.

"No, monkey. I was a small part of a very big team. Come on— let's go inside. There's something special Daddy and I want to show you, before the museum opens to everyone else tomorrow and gets really busy."

She smiled at Markus, who swept the little girl into his arms and followed Karen's lead through the huge entrance hall and down to the lower floors and the main exhibition galleries.

"There we are."

She didn't need to point it out. Lottie had already wriggled out of her father's arms and flown straight to the display case whose contents shone like a beacon even though the main lights weren't yet on. By the time Karen and Markus caught up with her, Lottie's nose and hands were pressed against the glass.

"Isn't it beautiful?"

Lottie nodded but she didn't turn round.

The dress that had mesmerized the little girl was cut from gold lamé and flowed like liquid over the mannequin. It had a fluted train and was clasped round the middle by a rhinestone belt with a butterfly-shaped buckle. The most eye-catching part of the design, however, was the sleeves. They were a confection of swirls and pleats, each one wrapped in a wreath of material so intricately twisted it coiled round the fabric like a vine. It was the kind of dress Karen knew visitors would imagine springing into life once their backs were turned.

"Do you see the card, Lottie? This dress was made by Haus Elfmann, the fashion house Grandma Liese's parents owned, the one that she grew up in. Remember I told you about that, and how clever your grandma was with a needle? Opa Michael always says sleeves were her specialty. This dress could be one of hers."

Lottie smiled at the mention of her grandfather. She adored both Opa England and Opa Michael as she called them, and they had shed years, and the last traces of their old resentments, with the little girl's birth.

"Why is that in there?"

Lottie pointed to a porcelain doll propped in the corner of the case, dressed in a miniature version of the gold gown.

"That's the really special bit. The museum staff let me put it in there. It's for the other Lottie—the one you were named for."

Lottie patted the glass as if she were stroking the doll's blonde hair. "Your big sister who went to heaven?"

Karen nodded. "The doll and the dress are here because her story, and Grandma's, is one of the stories that this museum was built to remember."

Lottie turned to her mother, her eyes bright as diamonds in the dimmed hall. She wrinkled her nose in such a perfect imitation of Liese, Karen's heart fluttered. Depending on her daughter's mood, Karen could see traces of all of them in her heart-shaped face: Andrew and Liese; Michael and Markus; herself. More and more, however, as Lottie grew, Karen could see the strongly defined and separate character the seven-year-old was already becoming.

"Do you think I could be like her?"

Karen frowned.

"Like Grandma Liese? Do you think I could make dresses as beautiful as that when I'm big?"

Karen reached for her daughter at the same time as Markus's arms encircled her; she couldn't trust herself to speak. All the pain that had marked the past had finally been laid to rest; now it was time to look back and find the good, to feel her family stretching forward and stretching back, part of the same whole. To know that her Lottie would have the childhood Liese had dreamed of for both her girls: filled not with secrets and silences, but light and laughter and a safe place in the world. All the things Karen could give her child because—in this newly woven family that united all the strands that had been her mother and father's lives, and the countries that had shaped them—she had finally found them for herself.

Karen leaned back into Markus's arms and held her daughter tight, knowing that her mother and her sister were there, inside their embrace. Knowing that the past was finally at one with the present, no longer a burden but a part of them all, to be treasured and carried. Into a future founded on hope.

A LETTER FROM CATHERINE

Hello,

Firstly, and most importantly, a huge thanks for reading *What Only We Know*. I hope you enjoyed reading it as much as I enjoyed writing it.

If you want to keep up to date with my latest releases, just sign up at the following link. I can promise that your email address will never be shared and you can unsubscribe at any time.

catherinehokin.com

I have been fascinated by the Wall for as long as I can remember. I was born the same year it went up. Like Karen, I took German at school for extra university points, visited Germany at seventeen, and stood at the Helmstadt crossing point, mesmerized by the guns and the dogs and the way the border had sliced a community in half. And I vividly remember watching the Berlin Wall topple in 1989 and the crowds streaming through, barely able to breathe as I waited for the guards to open fire.

I am lucky enough to be able to spend a lot of time in Berlin and walk its streets, putting my characters into place. If you have an opportunity to go to the city, the open-air Berlin Wall Museum at Bernauer Straße is somewhere I would urge you to visit—go through the gate into the graveyard the Wall sliced in half and you will really feel how brutal the dissection was. A visit to Ravensbrück will take you a little further from the center, but it is also one you should make if you can: the juxtaposition of the camp's site and the beautiful countryside it sits in is a sobering one. And please go to Karl Marx Allee and walk its length—trust me, your jaw will drop the way Karen's did.

As you have probably guessed, my characters are very real to me, so thank you for spending your time with them—I hope you have found it worthwhile. If you have a moment, and if you enjoyed the book, a review would be much appreciated. I'd dearly love to hear what you thought, and reviews always help us writers to get our stories out to more people.

I hope too that you will let me share my next novel with you when it's ready—I have a new set of characters waiting to meet you...

It's always fabulous to hear from my readers—please feel free to get in touch directly on my Facebook page, or through Twitter, Goodreads, or my website.

Thank you again for your time,
Catherine Hokin

 @cathokin

www.catherinehokin.com

Cathokin

Acknowledgments

As every historical fiction writer does, I immerse myself in the timeframe I am writing about. I watch films, listen to music, and read a huge number of books while writing my novels. There are some I could not have written *What Only We Know* without and I would like to single them out for a mention: *If This is a Woman* by Sarah Helm, a comprehensive and brilliantly written account of life inside Ravensbrück; *The Last Jews in Berlin* by Leonard Gross; *Berlin at War* by Roger Moorhouse; *Nazi Chic* by Irene Guenther, which is the definitive fashion history for this era; *The Wall Jumper* by Peter Schneider and *After the Wall* by Jana Hensel for life in the DDR; *A Tale of Love and Darkness* by Amos Oz, one of the best accounts I have ever read about the impact of a mother's suicide on a child.

I owe thanks to many people. Tina Betts and Kathryn Taussig, my wonderful agent and editor, for their insight, patience, and hard work—this book has, again, been a great collaborative experience. To the whole team at Bookouture who got behind it, especially Kim Nash for her energy and passion. To Claire and Daniel, my trusted beta readers, for their never-failing love and support and excellent way of phrasing a critical kick when it's needed, and to the wider writing community I'm lucky to be part of who cheer on every success. And, lastly but never least, to my husband, Robert, who I couldn't do a step of this without. Much love to you all as always.

Reading Group Guide

Discussion Questions

1. How does the title *What Only We Know* prepare the reader for the story?
2. The novel is constructed around a dual timeline. Are both story lines equally engaging? Were you more invested in one than the other?
3. Was Karen's anger with her father after she found the passport and the wedding certificate justified?
4. Should, or could, Liese have done more to make her parents face reality?
5. Could Michael have done more to keep Liese and Lottie safe? Could Liese?
6. Was Liese justified in killing the guard? Should the men have helped her conceal what she had done?
7. Liese loved Michael, but she married Andrew. Was this a fair thing to do? Was it ever more than a marriage of convenience?
8. Was Liese a good mother to both her daughters?
9. Liese's end is a tragic one. Do you think she saw it that way?
10. Does the novel have a satisfying end?

Author Q&A

Q. Where did the inspiration for *What Only We Know* come from?

A. There were two key strands involved. I have been fascinated with the physical division of Germany since I was sixteen years old and visited the country on a school exchange. I have a photograph of myself standing at the Helmstadt crossing point but I don't need that to remember the details. I had never seen anything like the guards holding machine guns, or the dog runs, or the scar the border fortifications had dug across the countryside. Or heard stories like the one our guide told us about the family and friends who were less than a mile away on the other side of the split town but whom she hadn't seen in almost twenty years. The second strand was the issue of survivor guilt. When I was a child, my grandfather lived with us. As a very young man he had served in World War I and survived all four years of it, including some of its most horrific battles. All his friends, however, died. Those years were a small fraction of the ones he had lived, but they never left him and I never forgot that.

Q. Did you discover anything unexpected during the research?

A. My research process is a detailed one and always uncovers a lot of surprising and, given the subject matter, often very sad nuggets. The experiences of the "rabbit women," which was the nickname given to those who were experimented on in Ravensbrück, is well chronicled, and their strength and courage is incredible. What

I didn't know about was the ceremonies held in Berlin to mark the passing of the DDR, one of which I describe in the novel. I was able to watch a video of this and there is such a strange air of furtive sadness about it, particularly when viewed in the light of the huge celebrations for reunification held hardly any distance away at the Berlin Wall. I have friends who were born in Eastern Europe and they have very fond memories of their childhoods that can be at odds with the way we focus on the more repressive elements of those societies. Many people have described reunification as a swallowing up and obliteration of the DDR and that is an interesting perspective.

Q. Are any of your characters based (however loosely) on anyone you know?

A. I get asked this so much and it is such a dangerous question! All writers are magpies, picking up character traits from everyone we know, and I also use far more of myself than I will ever disclose. Perhaps the best answer is the quote on a mug my daughter bought me: "Please do not annoy the writer. She may put you in a book and kill you." She bought me it after my husband suffered that exact fate…

Q. Which character was the hardest for you to write?

A. Liese was the most challenging, both because of what she endured and how she chose to "atone" for it. Bleak things happened to her, but I did not want hers to be a bleak life and I hope readers can recognize that there are moments of real happiness in it. Suicide is also a very difficult subject to write about, but I felt that this was the right choice for her—and it was a choice she made at a point where she was very clear about her reasons—and one that throws up such a mix of emotions, both for those who go down that path and those who are left. There is a lot of sadness in Liese, but there is also a lot of love and it was important to me to balance the two.

Q. A World War II novel means writing about horrific situations. When you were plotting the book, did you discard any ideas because they felt too dark?

A. I discarded a great deal of what I read and know about the period, particularly when it comes to the camps. They are places I do not want to linger in and I find it distasteful as a reader when fiction writers delve too much into the worst details. The writing maxim "go in late and leave early" seems to be a very fitting one here. I have also made a conscious decision not to dwell on what happened to the women in Berlin after the Russian army arrived in 1945. I want to make my readers think, and I hope they go away and look things up if I have stimulated their interest, which is why I always cite my favorite source books, but I'm not in the business of turning stomachs.

Q. You've written four World War II novels. How do you find the motivation to revisit such a bleak time in modern history?

A. It was a bleak and fear-filled time, but wartime is also a period— at least for writers—filled with hope and courage and one in which everything people think about themselves is tested. Would we be the brave ones who stand up to hatred? Would we have the courage to resist, to say no, to put ourselves, quite literally, in the firing line? I am more interested in small stories than massive political events, and the stories from World War II, as it passes out of living memory, are still coming to light. I find it fascinating that we are still learning what people were, and were not, capable of then. This is why I keep going back there, to find the personal narratives that are caught up in the sweep of history.

Q. What were some of the challenges with writing a dual timeline?

A. To keep both story lines equally as important and equally as involving, with similar levels of tension and pace. The more modern story line cannot simply be there as a device to tell the events of the earlier timeline; it has to be a complete narrative in its own right. The two strands must also be linked so that readers never feel they have completely stepped away from one character as they read about the other. In *What Only We Know*, Liese has lost a child and Karen has lost a mother: They are both linked through the trauma of the holes that have been left in their lives and they are both badly at odds with their worlds because of that. Perhaps the hardest challenge, however, is deciding whose story to start with, because that is where the novel then takes its structure from. I started in the contemporary timeline but I started with Liese because, to me, everything flows from her.

The Challenge of Remembering

I have spent much of the last few years researching concentration camps, in particular Sachsenhausen, which is featured in my novel *The Fortunate Ones*, and Ravensbrück, where part of this novel, *What Only We Know*, is set. With every visit, and everything I write, the question I have tried to hold uppermost in my mind is: How do we remember these places in a way that respects the terrible suffering that happened in them?

Writing anything about the Holocaust demands accuracy and tact. Both the conditions and practices in, and the geographical placement of the camps, varied enormously and what is true of one is often wildly inaccurate for another. The two camps I have come to know in detail do, however, share commonalities that have shaped how they are now presented and remembered by the world.

First, both were built in close proximity to Berlin: Sachsenhausen adjoins the small town of Oranienburg, about an hour's train ride from the city; Ravensbrück is forty-five minutes farther on in the same direction. Neither camp is isolated. Officers lived in the mansions around Sachsenhausen and a large SS housing estate bordered the camp—local girls married the men who served there and families lived within earshot of the camp's brickworks and "shooting gallery" where so many of the prisoners were executed. Ravensbrück nestles in the shadow of the picturesque town of Fürstenburg, with its cobbled roads, church spire peeping over the tree tops, and peaceful lake. Inmates arrived in both places via the local train station and were openly marched past the homes of local residents. It is fair to say that, socially and economically, the two camps were part of the fabric of the area they stood in.

Following the end of the war and the division of Germany into East Germany (the DDR) and West Germany in 1949, they were both also situated in the DDR, a geographical rewriting which has had profound implications for how the memory of what happened in them was shaped for future generations.

The preservation of former concentration camps did not simply happen. Given the state of Europe in 1945, it required deliberate decision-making on the part of governmental bodies and private agencies, as did the placing of memorial plaques and statues. The first memorial was established at the Majdanek extermination camp on the outskirts of Lublin in Poland, when the Soviet Army liberated it in July 1944. Three years later, the Polish parliament proclaimed that Auschwitz would be "forever preserved as a memorial to the martyrdom of the Polish nation and other peoples."

What would be preserved, and how it would be memorialized, also required deliberate decision-making, and these decisions were made within very different postwar political systems and sensibilities. In Israel, for example, the Holocaust is seen as part of a continuum of antisemitic persecution; in Japan it is always presented with a link to the nuclear apocalypse at Hiroshima. German memorials built before the reunification of the country in 1990, as reflected at Sachsenhausen and Ravensbrück, followed a pattern Sybil Milton describes in the excellent anthology about politics and remembrance, *In Fitting Memory*:

"In Eastern Europe the memorials were usually seen as forms of symbolic politics under the direction and financial patronage of the central government. In Western Europe the memorials were usually left to private and local initiative and thus developed in an ad hoc and piecemeal fashion."

This political slant is very evident at both of these camps. Sachsenhausen has two monuments to the dead, both of which were placed in 1961. The smaller of the two is a traditional pieta-style depiction of two inmates carrying a gaunt corpse. The larger, which is almost five meters tall and dominates the camp, is a tower topped with eighteen red triangle-shaped badges—to commemorate the nationalities of the political (not Jewish) prisoners held there. There is a statue at its base, entitled *Liberation*, which depicts an idealized Russian soldier with his arm round two strong inmates. Sachsenhausen was a site of great suffering for the Russian soldiers held there, but the many critics of the tower's central position and its subject matter argue that it marginalizes the Jewish experience.

Like Sachsenhausen, Ravensbrück is also, in many ways, defined by the socialist regime that took initial control of it. The chief monument there, *Tragende* (*Bearing*), shows a strong woman carrying a far weaker one. According to Sarah Helm—whose *If This Is a Woman* is the definitive history of Ravensbrück—the statue was inspired by Olga Benário Prestes, a German communist militant who was imprisoned at Ravensbrück and gassed at Bernberg and subsequently became a heroine in the DDR. That she was also Jewish, and that she was murdered because she was Jewish and not for her politics, does not appear in the official history.

The often very difficult conversations about how we remember the places of the Holocaust are ongoing things, particularly in countries that were occupied by the Nazis. France, for example, built a memorial at Natzweiler-Struthof—the only concentration camp built by the Germans on French soil—in 1964. A museum at the internment camp at Les Milles, a site that was run by the French and therefore raises thorny questions about collaboration, wasn't opened until 2012. In 2018—after repeated public references to the concentration camps sited there as "Polish camps"—a law came into effect in Poland that threatens up to three years imprisonment to anyone who "publicly and untruthfully assigns responsibility or co-responsibility to the Polish Nation or the Polish State for Nazi crimes."

In many of the places I visited, including Sachsenhausen, the question of why these memorials exist remains under constant scrutiny—particularly as the sites increasingly become part of the tourist trail. The historian Gunther Morsch, a previous director of the Sachsenhausen memorial, has been vocal in interviews about the need to reexamine our approach to these sites, particularly in a political climate that is seeing a rise in populism and the far right.

"We want to keep honoring the victims. And most exhibitions are about their fate. But it has become clear that the emphasis must be shifted to the perpetrators' motives and the structures that enabled these crimes to be committed [because] more and more visitors are rightly asking, 'How could such a thing happen?' and 'Is it possible today?'"

Unfortunately, in the interview this was taken from, he had to answer the second question with "yes."

If I can add anything, other than that we should keep talking about what the phrase "to remember" means as well as doing it, it is this: If you are able to visit either of the two camps I have written about, don't take a tour—they'll whisk you through and serve up a potted history. Take the train, walk the short walks, read the vast amount of literature available to you there, and stand still. You'll need the space that gives you to feel and to think. The people who suffered there deserve no less of us.